FRONTLINE WARRIOR

A soldier makes his own luck on the battlefield. The danger lies in flying blind against an enemy who seems to know his every move before the moves are made. He wants to know more about the man, acquire a stronger feeling for his enemy. Then it's blood and thunder all the way.

Bolan's thunder, and the blood of Tien to grease the war machine.

"Mack Bolan stabs right through the heart of the frustration and the hopelessness the average person feels about crime running rampant in the streets."

—*Dallas Times Herald*

Accolades for America's greatest hero Mack Bolan

DON PENDLETON's
MACK BOLAN

FLESH AND BLOOD

A GOLD EAGLE BOOK FROM
WORLDWIDE.

TORONTO • NEW YORK • LONDON • PARIS
AMSTERDAM • STOCKHOLM • HAMBURG
ATHENS • MILAN • TOKYO • SYDNEY

First edition October 1988

ISBN 0-373-61413-6

Special thanks and acknowledgment to
Mike Newton for his contribution to this work.

The family is the test of freedom; because the family is the only thing that the free man makes for himself and by himself.

—G. K. Chesterton,
"Dramatic Unities"

We can't always choose our families, but we choose our causes, and decide when it's time to shed our blood on the behalf of others. In the end, that choice, that exercise of options, makes us free.

—Mack Bolan

To the men and women of the FBI's Violent
Criminal
Apprehension Program—VICAP.
Good hunting.

"I don't care *what* you think," the customs supervisor growled. "I like to eyeball anything from Bangkok, just on general principle."

"But jeez, a *coffin*?"

"Hey, life's hard, okay? Don't get your gonads in an uproar." As he spoke, the supervisor shot a sidelong glance at the woman in black. "They don't get ticked about these things the way your Anglos do. They're used to it."

The younger customs man was green—it was the first day of his second full week on the job at L.A. International—and he made a practice of deferring to experience, especially when it came embodied in the form of his direct superior. But prying into coffins was an aspect of his occupation that had never come to mind.

"I don't know, sir. She's crying."

"No, she's sniffling. There's a difference. Wait until you bag some rich bitch from the Valley, tryin' to sneak a diamond bracelet past you like it was a collar for her dog. *That*'s crying."

"Still—"

"For all we know, this babe could be the Asian Oscarwinner for performance as a weeping widow. You follow?"

"I don't know...."

"We're checking out the stiff, Barrett. That's it."

"Yes, sir."

The supervisor wore a well-rehearsed expression of concern as he approached the grieving widow. Eighteen years in customs had deprived him, to a large degree, of any true respect for human privacy or feelings. Members of the public were the enemy, intent on smuggling their curios and souvenirs, their liquor and their jewelry, their cash and drugs, for personal advantage and outrageous profit. Every one he bagged stood in for ten or twenty who were bound to get away, no matter how you tried to read their faces and their attitudes. He knew that tears came cheap.

"I'm sorry, ma'am," he said, not feeling sorry in the least, "we'll have to take a look inside."

"I understand."

They could have X-rayed box and stiff together, but it would have taken extra time to move the coffin, waiting for the porters, not to mention all the extra paperwork that went along with use of the equipment. Add it up, and you were looking at an easy hour's overtime, and all for what? The X rays might not show anything when you were done...but that was not the same as saying there was nothing to be seen.

In eighteen years, the supervisor had been schooled in what to look for under any given circumstances: screws or bolts with bright new scratches on their heads, and little shreds of wood or metal sticking out where screws had been removed and carelessly replaced; the lining of a suit—or coffin—stitched with thread a half shade off the color of the other stitching, indicating that the lining had been opened, and, perhaps, stuffed full of contraband; the nervous, shifting eyes and perspiration on the upper lip, which sometimes gave away the novice smuggler.

The woman's papers were in order. A certificate of death confirmed that the cause of the deceased's unfortunate condition hadn't been infectious, or the proximate result of any crime. Two passports, one of them mere excess baggage now, indicated that the dead man and his wife were naturalized Americans of Asian birth. The export tags from Bangkok, and a letter—certified—from a mortician in Anaheim, expressed the intent to carry out a proper funeral.

The supervisor liked it when the paperwork was in order, but the fact had never put him off his guard. It simply made his job that much more interesting, and it tacked on several counts of perjury for all those affidavits when he finally found the hidden stash and hauled it out for all to see.

The coffin wasn't locked—who ever heard of corpses trying to get out?—but there were several sturdy clamps to be unfastened, and he gave Barrett the pleasure. Let the new boy scratch up his knuckles on this one; it would make his pleasure that much keener if they found some kind of contraband inside the box.

Barrett was finished, and the coffin gave a little sigh—its vapor seal releasing—as they raised the lid. Some years before, a coffin from Auckland had been opened to reveal a cache of automatic weapons, lying in the place of the deceased, but now a whiff of formalin and wax forewarned the supervisor that they wouldn't find an arsenal inside *this* box.

From all appearances, the dead man had been middle-aged, but who the hell could say, with Orientals? He was older than the woman, that was obvious, and in a flash the supervisor tried to picture them together. Youth and creeping age; abundance and infirmity. He shook his head and frowned. It took all kinds.

The presence of a corpse inside the casket didn't satisfy the supervisor's curiosity. He checked the hardware on the box and scanned the lining for a telltale interruption of the stitching, without result. The padding seemed to have no lumps or bulges—not unless they were concealed beneath the body—and he was considering a pat-down of the dear departed's pockets, when he realized that it was nearly lunchtime. Screw it, dead was dead, and he could always bag the next one, after he had put away a chili dog with extra onions.

"Everything appears to be in order, ma'am. We're sorry for the inconvenience."

"There is no need to apologize. I understand you have a job to do."

The supervisor kept his plastic smile in place, but silently, he cursed the condescending bitch. What would she ever understand about his job? His life? She was a foreign transplant, looking for the gravy train, and from her garb, the ornate fittings on the casket, he would guess that she had found it. Rather, her old man had found it, made his bundle while Americans went scrabbling for two-bit jobs, and now he had the decency to die and leave his widow with a nest egg, to begin her life anew.

He sealed the casket personally, brushing aside Barrett's helpful hands. The simple part was opening a box, but closing one could be a bitch unless you knew what you were doing, and he didn't plan to waste his time while some green rookie fumbled with the latches.

When he had it, when the porters had been called to bear the box away, the supervisor let himself relax. Another quarter hour to his chili dog, and he could almost taste it. The Asian widow was forgotten as he took his place on line, behind Barrett, to judge the new man's style. He scanned the waiting line of homeward-bound tourists, and smiled at recognition of a nervous rich bitch from the Valley.

Things were looking up.

A HEARSE from Orangewood Mortuary had been standing by, the liveried driver and attendant waiting to receive their cargo. They were in no hurry, perfectly content to wait in the event of some delay. Their passenger—or one of them, at any rate—had all eternity ahead of him, and he wasn't in a position to complain.

The drive from LAX to Anaheim took nearly an hour and a quarter, decent time for twenty miles of travel on the most congested highways in the world. The driver kept his eyes on traffic, paying no attention to the widow, who was riding shotgun. Matters of security were left to the "attendant," who crouched on a jump seat in back with the stiff. The L.A. freeways were a crazy house on wheels, where lunatics would shoot your butt off for an illegal lane change, but the driver took advantage of the human tendency to give a hearse wide berth. He cruised through Hawthorne and Gardena, Compton, Bellflower and Norwalk, as if he owned the suburbs, bogging down in sluggish traffic only when he got to Buena Park. It didn't matter whether you were dead or not; nobody got past Disneyland without at least a minimal delay.

The driver thought about conversing with the widow, but he let it slide. She might report him, claim that he was pumping her for information, and he didn't need that kind of grief. It was a damn sight easier to hold his tongue and concentrate on weaving in and out of traffic. The rig was like a shark that had its belly full; the little fishies all around it knew they were safe, for now, but it reminded them of pain and dying, all the same. The driver felt a surge of power, knew it was illusory and loved it nonetheless.

The Orangewood Mortuary was an old, established firm with roots in the community and clients populating boneyards from Los Angeles to Irvine, Fullerton to Rancho Palos Verdes. Still, the dying business wasn't what it used to be, and family ownership had passed, in recent months, to other, more creative hands. The current management was future-oriented, and they paid a decent wage, which kept the driver satisfied, cooperative and quiet. Why should he care what became of certain clients, just as long as paydays kept on rolling around? It didn't cost him anything to make the trip from LAX in silence; on the other hand, it paid him very well.

At Orangewood, he backed the hearse in to a kind of loading dock and killed the engine, scurrying around to let the widow out, escorting her inside before returning to assist with the transfer of the box. A pair of undertaker's helpers had arrived by that time, to assist in carrying the client, but the box and occupant were heavy, even so. Inside the mortuary proper, the driver was happy to surrender his position, lay his burden down and seek the clean, fresh air again. He hadn't been in the embalming room thus far, and had no wish to check it out. All things considered, he was not inclined to ask himself precisely why a stiff embalmed in Bangkok should be taken for another dose at this end of the journey. It wasn't his business.

While willing hands conveyed the casket to its final destination, there was business to be settled with the grieving widow. She had managed to compose herself in transit, and was able to produce a smile when the proprietor appeared to offer his condolences and thank her for her patronage. She knew the envelope he handed to her would contain five thousand dollars and a one-way, first-class airline ticket back to Bangkok, where her payoff from the mission would allow her to relax in style. She could be rich in Thailand, with five thousand dollars. For a while, at least. Until she had the opportunity to make another run.

She didn't give another thought to her lamented loved one, now divested of his casket and his suit, which would be sold and burned, respectively. In fact, he was a total stranger to the "widow"; she had never seen his face, in life or death, and didn't care to see it now. She knew what had become of him and did her best to push the mental image from her mind. Five thousand dollars helped in that regard, as well.

If the idiots at customs had removed her "husband" from his coffin, torn the box apart, they would have come up empty and embarrassed, with potential lawsuits on their hands. They might have thought to search the clothing, rifle through the pockets, but again, the end results would have left them looking like the fools they were. If either of them had remarked on the condition of the corpse itself, the

Y incision sealed with ragged stitches by a Bangkok coroner, she would have told them that an autopsy was mandatory in such cases, where a foreign citizen in seeming perfect health collapsed and died from no apparent cause. In the pursuit of microbes, it had been expedient to gut her darling like a fish, examining his entrails for a clue to cause of death. Would either of them care to lift the cheap toupee that covered scalp wounds, and discover how the cranium had been removed?

It would have taken courage and authority beyond the supervisor's to demand a new evisceration of the corpse, and so the heroin had passed unnoticed, plastic kilo bags jammed tight inside the dead man's hollow abdomen, another tucked inside his empty skull. The death certificate had marked his weight at something just above two hundred pounds, and if the dear departed had somehow, against all odds, picked up an ounce or two in transit, who would be the wiser? It was deadweight, anyway.

She didn't know, or care to know, what happened to the China White once it had been retrieved at Orangewood. Swift cremation of the corpse would clean up any odds and ends of evidence, while runners bore their precious cargo off to cutting rooms and distribution points. The lady didn't deal in drugs, and didn't wish to know the details. She was paid to travel, and to weep on cue, like any other mourner in the sideshow of the funeral trade.

But once, just once, she would have liked to see a fraction of the money that her late, lamented "husband" earned for faceless men in...what? A week? A day? She thought that a fraction of the proceeds could have set her up for life in Bangkok, fixed things so that she would never have to work again.

And as the thought took form, she banished it at once. Such thoughts could lead to trouble, even death, and she wasn't prepared to join the nameless lump of flesh who had accompanied her from Thailand. When she made the run again, as she undoubtedly would do, the lady planned to fly first class. She had no interest in the cargo bay's decor.

Far better to be safe and silent, with the warm night spinning out ahead of her, a web of diamond-studded darkness. She could lose herself among the shadows for a while, and in the morning she would find new strength to face the light of day.

Her silent partner on the flight from Bangkok would be ashes in an hour.

CHAPTER ONE

The day had started well enough for Lok Tranh. His Costa Mesa grocery store occupied a choice location at the intersection of two streets that formed the heart of the Vietnamese community, and Asian wives were early shoppers. He had taken in several hundred dollars already, and it wasn't yet ten o'clock; if the trade kept up throughout the afternoon, he would take home another tidy profit from his labors.

Smiling to himself as he went on about the task of stocking shelves, Lok Tranh reflected that Orange County was, indeed, the land of golden opportunity. In Saigon, he had done a decent business, but the cloud of war had shadowed every day of his existence, bringing grim reminders of disaster in the offing. When the worst had happened, in the form of rank capitulation to the jackals from Hanoi, Tranh had been fortunate enough to slip away, his family's departure lost in the confusion that had gripped a once-great city. Lost, as well, were most of their belongings, articles he had worked a lifetime to accumulate, but foresight had permitted him to squirrel away some money, and they weren't altogether destitute.

They had been better off, all things considered, than the vast majority of refugees who fled from Vietnam before the juggernaut of "people's revolution." There had been delays, deceptions, squalid living quarters to endure on their journey to America, and on arrival, they had found themselves cast in the role of strangers, interlopers in a country they were ill-prepared to understand.

Of course, there were similarities between Saigon and the United States. The southern capital of a divided Vietnam had borne the imprint of an occupying army—in its bars and dens of prostitution, in its gambling halls and fast-food restaurants, in street slang spoken by the children of a wasted generation, in the neon signs that touted Coca-Cola, Shell, the Bank of America. Surviving in Saigon had been a dress rehearsal for Tranh's final move to the United States, but it hadn't prepared him for the hard realities of prejudice, discrimination, borderline poverty.

The journey had consumed three-quarters of his savings, and establishing a new career in the United States was an expensive proposition. His salvation had been other refugees, Orange County's staunch Vietnamese community, which spared no effort in the protection of its own. A former Saigon banker had provided Tranh with the low-interest loans he needed for the acquisition of a home, the grocery store that would eventually make his fortune in America. When times were lean, during the first few years, his neighbors in the Asian ghetto were supportive, satisfied to know their charity would be repaid, or passed along to other needy souls, when Tranh was able to support himself and his family. In five years' time, he'd become affluent enough to sponsor other refugees from Vietnam in the United States, and he'd been happy to oblige. Lok Tranh had never shirked a duty in his life.

If there was any cloud on his horizon, any blight upon his days, it was personified in the endemic violence of the street gangs. Worst among them were the Thunder Dragons, vicious youths who exacted tribute from the local shops and waged war against their weaker rivals in a bid for total dominance. They would not shrink from murder, if it served their purposes, and they were said to number better than a hundred, their ranks swelled daily with recruits from local schools.

There had been gangs in Saigon, but they specialized in petty theft and ran from the police like naughty boys afraid of whippings from their fathers. They were urchins of the street, most of them orphaned and made homeless by the war, surviving on their wits and living hand to mouth. At worst, they were a nuisance, children to be pitied when the anger over thefts of fruit and vegetables had faded.

Nothing had prepared him for the Thunder Dragons, with their stylish jackets and their arrogant defiance of authority, the knives and pistols they brandished freely in the face of any opposition. The police and sheriff's deputies made efforts to control the gangs, but in the meetings they held to pacify the Asian merchants, law-enforcement spokesmen grudgingly admitted there was little they could do to guarantee the sanctity of shop and home. Without a list of adult witnesses, no single member of a gang could be convicted of the smallest misdemeanor, and for juveniles the "punishment" prescribed was usually probation, or a brief vacation at the county's "honor farm." If any member of the Thunder Dragons, through the grace of God, should be imprisoned for a felony, the other ninety-nine were still on hand to punish prosecution witnesses and make their lives a daily living hell.

The first time he had suffered broken windows at his grocery, Tranh had talked to the police. That night, his windows had been shattered once again, and on the evening after. Several hundred dollars out of pocket, he had prudently withdrawn the charges, and his troubles had evaporated...for a time. Within the week, a spokesman for the Thunder Dragons had appeared at Lok Tranh's shop to praise his common sense and civic consciousness. A wise man, he was told, could see the writing on the wall and realize that Asian problems couldn't be resolved by white American police. If Tranh, an honored and respected businessman, was suffering from vandalism, members of his own community would lend a hand to ease his suffering. The Thunder Dragons would be more than happy to protect his fine establishment from further harm, and it would cost him next to nothing.

"Next to nothing," in the long run, was computed at an average of five percent of the storekeeper's gross earnings for the week. Collections were on Friday mornings, and an average week found Tranh depositing a hundred dollars, more or less, in the hands of his protectors. It wasn't a princely sum, but over seven years he estimated that the Dragons had secured nearly seven thousand dollars for their "services." The money could have gone toward home improvements, college educations for his growing children, sponsorship of other refugees from Vietnam. By stealing from his till, the Thunder Dragons had been robbing others, as well.

This morning, Tranh decided, it would stop. When the collector for the Dragons came, he wouldn't pay, and if they broke his windows, he would give their names to the police. His bold example would encourage other businessmen to stand their ground, and when the Dragons saw their former victims forging a united front, they would retreat. He hoped.

Tranh glanced up, smiling at the jangling bell that heralded a customer... and felt his stomach twist into an aching knot. A slender, long-haired boy, called Gecko by his brother Dragons, lounged against the checkout counter, near the entrance, waiting for Lok Tranh to pay his weekly tribute. Gecko was the usual collector for the neighborhood, a sneering lizard who, for all of his affected menace, was less threatening than many of his comrades.

This time, however, Gecko hadn't come alone. He was accompanied by a second, larger boy, whom Tranh had never seen before, his squarish face and chunky torso seemingly constructed out of cinder blocks, all cunningly disguised as flesh and bone. He radiated power, of the brute variety, and there was emptiness behind his eyes as he regarded Lok Tranh with vague disinterest.

"Honorable Tranh, you keep us waiting." Gecko's smile was like a thin slit in a melon: cold, inanimate.

"You keep us waiting," his companion echoed, stumbling on the words.

"You know why we are here."

Tranh swallowed hard. "I cannot pay you."

"Cannot?"

"Will not."

"Ah." It was the first time Tranh had seen what he supposed to be genuine emotion in Gecko's face. Anticipation, tinged with pleasure. "You are insubordinate, old man."

"Get out!"

"And rude. I think you need a lesson in the art of courtesy."

Tranh bolted for the produce aisle, where he would find the knife he used for trimming stalks, but he had covered less than twenty feet when Gecko's hulking friend reached out and snared him by the collar, spinning him around and hurling him against the checkout counter with explosive force. His lungs were emptied by the impact, motes of dusty color dancing on the inside of his eyelids, and he scarcely felt the boots that jarred his spine, his ribs, his kidneys. Tranh was suffocating, once removed from common pain, and he believed that he was dying when the rain of blows abruptly ceased.

Expending all the energy he had, Tranh cracked open his eyelids, saw Gecko rifling his cash drawer, stuffing currency and coins into his pockets.

"Stupid move, old man," the lizard told him as he stepped across the shopkeeper's prostrate body, heading for the door. "From five percent, you just kicked in your daily take on Fridays for the next three months. Consider it a lesson. Next time you get rude, the Thunder Dragons may not be so generous.''

They left him, Gecko's friend delivering a final kick that loosened Tranh's bowels, and he fought back the bitter tears of shame as he began to crawl across the floor, a broken man bereft of dignity.

He wouldn't call police; of that much he was certain. The gruff detectives couldn't help him, couldn't offer him protection, relocation, if he testified against the Thunder Dragons in the white man's court of law.

A single hope remained, and he would have to seek it from Lao Fan.

NOL KWON HAD NEVER LIKED the antiseptic smell of hospitals. It lingered in his nostrils, turned his stomach, calling up the childhood memories of doctors' offices that seemed to have a great deal more in common with the Inquisition than with places of healing. He remembered ether, dripping on a paper mask held tight against his face, the sickly feeling as he lost control, the pain that racked his body as the anesthetic grudgingly released its hold. The doctors of his youth, in Vietnam, had been a clumsy and uneducated lot, but he had seen them often, suffered through the applications of their art, and he had pledged that he would never place himself in healing hands again.

The hospitals in Anaheim, of course, were very different, but their medical aromas were the same, and Nol Kwon felt his apprehension mounting as he moved along a pristine hallway, toward the nurses' station. Ancient memories were nagging at him, but he pushed them back and concentrated on his newest dread, all other thoughts forgotten in an instant.

There had been an accident, the nurse had explained to him on the telephone, and then a police officer had come on the line, his tone officious, brusque, as he inquired if Nol Kwon had a daughter by the name of Sumi. There had been an incident at her school, a gang of boys who made themselves a nuisance, and Sumi had been injured. Could he come to the hospital at once?

He could, and as he reached the nurses' station, Kwon was suddenly aware of uniforms, approaching from his left. He hesitated, waited for the officers to join him, listened to their bland condolences without a word. When it was time for him to speak, he asked specific, pointed questions, flinching as the answers were returned in kind.

The "incident" was gang rape, by a group of six or seven boys, and Sumi had been beaten viciously when she attempted to defend herself. Her nose and jaw were broken, as were several of her ribs, three fingers on her right hand, two more on her left. Kwon had a fleeting thought of the piano music Sumi loved, and bit his tongue until he tasted salty blood, the pain relieving him of any need to weep before these strangers.

She had suffered internal injuries, but her condition had stabilized, a nurse explained en route to Sumi's room. She was sedated at the moment, and he shouldn't try to wake her. Incidentally there were some pressing questions on the subject of insurance, if he had a moment . . . ?

An officer suggested that the paperwork could wait, and Nol Kwon bore the nurse's sour glance as he had borne the other burdens of his life, in silence. He would answer any questions from the policemen once he'd seen his daughter, verified that she was still alive, whatever else she might have lost.

The semiprivate room was sunny, walls done up in light pastels, vibrant with artificial cheer. Kwon was relieved to find the second bed vacant; he would be alone with Sumi for the moment, will her to survive, before he left to do what must be done.

The gentle face that was the center of his world was battered, misshapen, a rubber tube extruding from the flattened nose. He knew Sumi was asleep, but with her bright eyes swollen shut, she might have been awake and he wouldn't have known the difference.

He dared not think about what lay beneath the tented sheet, what marks her slender body might display. At fourteen years of age, she was—had been—a virgin, still in love with music, animals, the world at large, a wide-eyed novice to the mysteries of boys and sex. Kwon wondered what her eyes would see when she could open them again, and this time, all alone with his enduring pain, he wept.

His wife, Jiajun, had sought to join him when he left the house, but he had forced her to remain at home, asserting his prerogative as husband and the master of his family. Whatever might confront him at the hospital, Nol Kwon would face it first, alone, and thereby shield his wife and his other children from the brunt of tragedy. With Sumi before him, scarcely recognizable, he knew that his decision was a wise one. He could never have controlled Jiajun if she had seen the savaged face of her firstborn; it would have been beyond his strength to silence her and thus save face.

He couldn't bring himself to touch his daughter, to stroke the bandaged hands that lay atop the coverlet. Internal injuries, the nurse had said. Nol Kwon had little doubt about her meaning, and the rage within him suddenly felt hot enough to make a smoking cinder of his heart.

The policemen were waiting for him outside the room. Did he know a gang of street punks called the Thunder Dragons? Had they ever threatened Sumi? Bothered her in any way? Had she been friendly with a member of the gang, perhaps, or any of their rivals? Did she always take the same route home from summer school?

Kwon answered the questions as best he could, surprising the police with his apparent stoicism in the face of such an outrage. When they left him, he supposed they would share a joke or two about inscrutable Vietnamese, but he was past all caring. There was nothing they could do for him or for Sumi, and Nol Kwon summarily dismissed them from his thoughts.

Suppose the animals who had despoiled his daughter were arrested? Would the "justice" found in courts satisfy his burning need for vengeance? Would the Dragons even come to trial? And if he offered up his daughter as a living sacrifice, to testify against her rapists, would she live to see another birthday? Could the men in blue serge uniforms provide a guarantee that Kwon and his family wouldn't be murdered in their beds?

He knew the answers, even as the questions racketed around inside his skull. Whatever justice he obtained, he would be forced to seek out for himself . . . but it might not be absolutely necessary for him to pursue his cause alone.

Perhaps, if he was fortunate, he might find justice with Lao Fan.

"THE GOLD! Be quick about it!"

Trembling, Eungwon Ng abandoned his position at the register and moved along the wall in the direction of a door marked Private. On his heels, the tall boy prodded him with a revolver, urging him to hurry, and the jeweler concentrated on survival, closing off his ears to the excited sounds of others cleaning out his display cases, dumping rings, necklaces and bracelets into shopping bags.

Inside his private office, Ng moved briskly to the safe, which occupied a corner near his desk. He muffed the combination on his first attempt and drew a warning crack across the skull that drove a lightning bolt of pain between his eyes.

"No more delays!"

He knew the boys might kill him if he offered any resistance, and the gold could always be replaced. He was insured for theft, and with creative paperwork, he just might turn a small profit on the deal, provided he was still alive to file a claim. Survival was the first imperative. He focused on the combination lock and willed his trembling hand to get it right.

So far, it was a simple robbery. The three boys had been wearing ski masks when they barged into his shop, two of them armed with knives, the leader hauling out a nickel-plated .38. They didn't wear the customary jackets of a fighting gang, but if he'd been forced to make a judgment on the basis of their voices, Eungwon Ng would have been reasonably certain that the leader was a member of the Thunder Dragons, known among his worthless friends as Moon. Ng couldn't have produced the necessary proof to build a case in court, but it would never come to that.

He had the combination now, and the door was opening. Ng allowed himself a small sigh of relief. They wouldn't kill him; there was no purpose to it, and the Thunder Dragons had a reputation of regarding murder as a business proposition. If the victim of a robbery couldn't identify his adversaries, if he offered no resistance, it would be a waste of time to take his life.

The leader set his weapon on the safe and shot a warning glance at the jeweler as he produced a shopping bag from underneath his jacket. Ng stepped back and pressed his spine against the wall, refusing to be baited. He would no more try to seize the gun than he would throw himself before a speeding train. In either case, his efforts would be fruitless, and the end result would be the same. While he survived, there was a chance that he could take his insurance agent for a ride—an altered invoice should be adequate to do the trick—and there was still a chance for long-term justice. If he lived.

The coins and ingots disappeared in seconds flat, and his assailant casually retrieved the pistol, smiling through his mask as he stood up to face the jeweler.

"You've been most cooperative," the bandit said, and Ng would have bet his life that it was Moon. "My compliments."

He didn't understand precisely what was happening as Moon took aim and fired. The gunshot was a thunderclap inside his tiny office, and the fist that struck his knee was sheathed in chain mail, bristling with spikes. His wounded leg collapsed beneath him, and the floor rushed up to meet his face with stunning force.

Rough hands were tugging at his sport coat, rolling Eungwon Ng onto his back. He saw lips moving through a long slit in the gunman's ski mask, but the voice he heard was blurred as if with distance, indistinct behind the roaring in his ears.

"Remember, when you see the cops," Moon said, "it could have been your life. It still *could* be. You understand, old man?"

His moan was mercifully accepted as an answer, and the mask swam out of range, the ceiling and its single, inexpensive fixture coming into focus. In a moment, he would try to reach the telephone, but first he needed time to overcome the pain. He needed time to let the boys evacuate his shop and fade into the noontime traffic.

He was still alive, in spite of sticky blood that he could see pooling on the floor around his mangled knee. In spite of numbing pain, the fear that he might never walk again without a limp, he had survived. And there might still be justice.

In the morning, when he woke with nurses at his side and found that nightmares sometimes lingered into waking hours, he would call Lao Fan.

"HE'S LATE."

"Don't sweat it. He'll be here."

Despite his studied pose of relaxation, So Hoo Minh was getting nervous. He would never understand why the accountant always made their meetings public, when the Thunder Dragons could have gone to his place just as easily. *He's scared of us,* Minh thought, and smiled, although he knew it wasn't true. If anything, the older man was probably ashamed to have them in his office, let alone his home. It rankled, but there was no arguing with the accountant or his people. Not if Minh desired to stay in business. Not if he had any wish to keep on breathing.

As the warlord of the Thunder Dragons, So Hoo Minh was used to being treated with respect, sometimes with awe. He wore the reputation of a fearless killer like a badge of honor, but he also knew that there were times when it was rash to throw his weight around. If he offended the accountant, it wouldn't be long before the Dragons found their buyers going elsewhere, throwing trade to their competitors—perhaps the Bamboo Warriors or the Flowers of Death. They would be stripped of their protection contracts, and if they resisted, might discover that their rivals had a newfound sponsor. One with cash, troops and guns to spare.

Minh lit a cigarette and crossed his legs, his free hand resting on a fat valise, which filled the seat beside him. In the middle distance, kids were playing in the surf and chasing one another on the sand; behind him, traffic rumbled in a steady stream on Ocean Avenue. Minh liked the beach, in principle, but also felt exposed there, out of place. He would be happy when his business was completed and he could retreat to safer, more familiar ground.

This would be a special meeting. In addition to the usual payoff from protection, he had gold and jewelry to sell. With any luck at all, they might get twenty-five cents on the dollar for the haul, and Minh was adding up his share, imagining the party he could throw, when Rabbit, his companion, dug an elbow in his ribs.

"He's here."

The car wasn't a limousine, but it would do until one came along. Minh flicked his cigarette into the sand and lifted the valise. He couldn't see the driver or the passenger through the tinted windows, but he knew the drill by heart and slipped into the back seat without an invitation. Rabbit, on the bench alone, pretended not to notice, but one hand was tucked inside his jacket, the fingers wrapped around a stainless-steel Colt Commander. Three more Dragons, armed with shotguns, sat in a Camaro with its engine running, half a block downrange.

He smiled at the accountant. "How's it going?"

"Busy. Always busy." Charcoal eyes behind the horn-rimmed glasses fixed on Minh with frank disinterest. "Let's get on with it."

"Sure thing." He sprang the latch on the valise, extracting bills that had been bundled into thousand-dollar lots. "Eleven grand this week. Not bad."

"Is business off?"

The tacit criticism stung, but Minh contrived to keep his smile in place. "It's seasonal. Some of the shops claim revenues are down. You want me to apply more pressure?"

The accountant thought about it, frowned. "I'll let you know," he said at last. "What else?"

Minh pushed the bag across the seat and let the older man examine it himself. "Gold ingots, leaf and coins," he beamed. "Plus bracelets, necklaces and rings."

"I'll go a dime."

Minh lost his smile and tried, without complete success, to get it back. "A dime? It should be worth a quarter, easy."

"Guess again. I can't move any of the jewelry as it is. The stones will have to be removed, the gold melted down to lose the markings." Minh imagined something like a spark of anger in the accountant's eyes. "It was a foolish thing to shoot the jeweler."

"Yeah, I know." Minh felt the color rising in his cheeks. "I'm taking care of it."

"Selective violence is a powerful inducement toward cooperation. Random violence breeds contempt and chaos. You would do well to remember that in future."

"Yes."

"A dime or nothing."

"As you say."

The older man produced a wad of crisp new hundred-dollar bills. "The jeweler has reported losses of three hundred thousand dollars to his insurance company. Allowing thirty-three percent for fraudulent inflation of his claim, deducting medical expenses that my client feels obliged to pay for charitable reasons, I make your share fifteen thousand. Fair enough?"

"Of course."

He might have trouble with the others, when they saw how short the take had fallen, but he dared not raise a beef with the accountant. If any of the Dragons muttered loud and long enough, he would refer them to their brother, Moon, whose psycho act had cost them all five thousand dollars. Brooding to himself, the warlord wondered how Moon might like to eat the severed fingers of his gun hand, one joint at a time.

Minh pocketed the fifteen thousand, made a show of thanking the accountant, hesitating on the curb before he closed the door. "Same place next week?"

"I'll let you know."

The tank slid into traffic, disappeared, and Minh allowed his plastic smile to slip away, replaced at once by something like a snarl. "Let's go!" he snapped at Rabbit, stalking off toward the Camaro while his gunner hustled to catch up.

"Hey, how'd it go?"

"We got a dime."

"A *dime*?"

"You heard me."

"Yeah, but shit, a dime? That's less than thirty thousand."

"Try fifteen."

"Fif*teen*?"

He turned on Rabbit. "Are you fucking deaf or what?"

"I heard you, man. I'm just surprised, that's all. What happened to the difference?"

"Moon happened."

"Shit."

"He'll think shit, when I'm finished with him."

"Trigger-happy bastard. Are you going to whack him?"

"I haven't made my mind up yet." Minh smiled. His anger buoyed him. It had a focus now, and he could use it to his own advantage. He grinned at Rabbit, as cold as death, and said, "Right now, I'm leaning toward a manicure."

CHAPTER TWO

The restaurant enjoyed a reputation for expense and quality, the former guaranteed by its address, the latter seen to by a European chef who, it was said, had served the British royal family before he pulled up stakes and emigrated to America. This afternoon, Ngo Van Tien was less concerned with the cuisine than with the restaurant's location. Theoretically it stood on neutral ground; in fact, the neighborhood was totally surrounded by the territory of his enemies.

Competitors, he thought, amending the assessment. There had been no real hostilities as yet, and if he played his hand correctly in the scheduled meeting, war might be avoided for a time. As a committed realist, he knew the clash couldn't be totally averted, but he thought it could be postponed, and every day his own position strengthened, shifting the advantage further toward his side.

The dapper Asian checked his watch and said, "Too early. Drive around the block."

"Yes, sir."

The sleek Mercedes limo made a lazy circuit of the neighborhood, Tien and his companion studying the shop fronts, the expensive vehicles that filled the parking lots. Tien didn't expect an ambush here, but it wasn't beyond the realm of possibility. He scanned the streets and rooftops, seeking traces of gunmen, finding none. This time, it seemed, his adversaries were content to talk.

Beside him, Anh Diem Giap seemed apprehensive, ill at ease. He had opposed the meeting, warned Tien against potential treachery, and when his master demonstrated an intention to proceed, he had insisted on accompanying Tien to guarantee his personal security. It was a role Anh Giap had managed to perfect, with years of practice, from the war-torn streets of Saigon to the avenues of Orange County and Los Angeles, where different—but no less deadly—perils lay in wait. In Ngo Tien's defense, Anh Giap had killed no fewer than a dozen men, dispatching them with pistols, knives and his large bare hands. Giap would have sacrificed his life on Tien's behalf without a second thought, a token of their friendship, which extended over thirty years.

Anh Giap and Ngo Tien had been young men in their twenties when they met in 1955. The occupying French had only recently departed Indochina; the partition of an ancient country into the component parts of Laos, Cambodia and a divided Vietnam was under way. Great powers argued in Geneva, sketching boundary lines on maps, debating the advantages and risks of free elections. In the slums of Saigon, Giap and Tien were more concerned with personal survival, bent on gaining wealth, security and respect by any means available. If that meant offering "protection" to the local merchants, hiring thugs to do their dirty work or dealing with the Burmese warlords of the Kuomingtang, so be it. Life was hard, the streets were unforgiving and a ruthless man could build himself an empire with investments of determination, sweat and blood.

In time, Tien and Giap became known throughout Saigon as men of influence and power. Ngo Tien had grown into a diplomat of sorts, a statesman of the streets, adept at winning hearts and minds, procuring concessions from his enemies. When reason failed, the matter was referred to Giap and his enforcers, men who valued action over words and never failed to get results by one means or another. Partners in a new growth industry, Tien and Giap had forged close ties with the Diem and Thieu regimes, including various Americans among their chosen friends and allies. Gambling clubs and prostitution were the mainstays of their early operation, and they gladly funnelled cash into the secret coffers of conservative administrators, fully conscious of the economic dangers posed by Communist ascension, willing to accept immunity from prosecution in return for their unfailing patriotic fervor. Escalation of the war in 1965 had brought new troops to Vietnam and opened up new markets for narcotics: soldiers anxious to forget their sorrows, and civilians eager to experience the East in all its many aspects. When a faction of the CIA had come in search of information, trading cargo space for heroin aboard its U.S. Air flights home to San Francisco, Tien and Giap had found a new horizon for their empire. Fresh investments in America had helped to blunt the shock of Saigon's fall, and property in Southern California was waiting for the two respected businessmen when they took their final leave of Vietnam.

The new land had new challenges in store for arrivals, but a tight community of refugees was growing by the day in Orange County, merchants for the most part, with a sprinkling of peasants who had lost everything before the Hanoi juggernaut. Uneasy with the white man's justice, they had turned as one to trusted leaders who had served their interests in Saigon. As paragons of the community, Tien and Giap were happy to oblige with charitable contributions, sage advice, support for recent immigrants. Their source of income was a matter of no consequence to those they served, who were pleased to serve them in return.

The major stumbling block for Tien and Giap, thus far, had been the old-line Mafia, with its established contacts in the courts and law enforcement, prostitution rings and distribution networks for narcotics, contraband, pornography. The ruling capo of Los Angeles, Don Girolamo Carlotti, was himself the son of immigrants, but he'd man-

aged to acquire a native's prejudice in areas where new arrivals might affect his pocketbook. Thus far, Orange
County had been lost to the Italians by default, without a
major confrontation or a loss of troops on either side. But
Tien's expansion into Hollywood and L.A. proper, cou-
pled with his move to form a loose alliance with some others like himself—in San Francisco, Dallas and New York—
had shifted Don Carlotti toward a stubborn hard line of resistance, threatening reprisals if the Asian syndicate was not
content with what it had.

The sit-down had been Tien's suggestion, and Carlotti
had surprised him by agreeing after only fleeting hesitation. They could speak as men, explain their different points
of view and possibly avert a shooting war that would prove
costly to both sides. Anh Giap had feared some treachery,
but Tien was willing to accept a reasonable compromise…as long as both hands of his enemy remained in view.

His driver found a parking space and killed the engine,
stepping back to hold the door for Tien and Giap. He would
remain outside, and if they didn't reappear or send a predetermined message in an hour's time, he was instructed to
depart immediately, spread the alarm that would initiate
retaliation on a massive scale. If Don Carlotti had a trap in
mind, he was about to learn that treachery could be expensive.

Subtle lighting, air-conditioning and fragrant odors from
the kitchen greeted Tien and Giap as heavy double doors
swung shut behind them, cutting off the glare of California
sunshine. A maître d' in formal evening wear was waiting to
receive them, smiling in the knowledge that his tip this afternoon would almost certainly be larger than their waiter's
starting salary. He led them to a private dining room, where
two men waited at a table set for four.

Tien didn't recognize the men who rose to greet him, but
he smiled and shook their hands: a young man, tan and

muscular, in tailored clothes; his middle-aged companion rumpled, scowling underneath a crop of salt-and-pepper hair.

"Vincenzo Moro," the younger man said by way of introduction, "and our *consigliere*, Toto Esposito." At the mention of his name, the older man put on a smile that had all the warmth of an unsutured surgical incision.

"We had hoped to speak with Don Carlotti."

"Yeah, I know. My uncle sends you his apologies, but he was called away on urgent business. I'm his underboss, and Toto knows the Family business inside out. Don Girolamo hoped you would consent to speak with us."

The insult was undoubtedly deliberate, and Ngo Tien could feel Giap glaring at him, silently entreating him to rise and leave the table, tossing down the gauntlet for their adversaries. In another situation, Tien might have surrendered to the rising anger he felt inside, but there was too much on the table for a rash response to sweep it all away.

"I see no reason why we should not speak as men."

"All right, that's great." A waiter had arrived with menus, and Vincenzo Moro raised a cautionary hand. "If you'll allow me a suggestion, Mr. Tien, this chef turns out the best veal in the city. It's a treat you won't forget."

"Of course, the veal."

Anh Giap insisted on examining the menu for himself and ordered steak to spite their host. A porter brought their choice of wine, and Tien pronounced it excellent, his partner offering a grunt of acquiescence as he drained his glass.

"A toast," the younger mafioso said, his glass upraised, "to the success of our negotiations."

Glasses clinked around the table, and they drank the toast, with Giap and Esposito trading looks of undisguised hostility. If left alone, they might have sought a quicker, more direct solution to the present competition, but Tien preferred to make his gains without unnecessary loss of life, if possible.

"Your business has been doing well, I understand."

Tien allowed himself to mirror Moro's smile. "It has been adequate. We hope for better days."

"It never hurts to dream."

"And Don Carlotti's trade? I trust that he has not been suffering."

"We all get by. There's lots of competition in the marketplace, these days."

"Indeed. If I may speak with frankness..."

Moro took the hint at once. "We're clean, no sweat. My uncle owns an interest in this place. It gets swept out for bugs as regular as clockwork."

"Excellent." Tien replaced his smile with a more thoughtful, introspective face. "It is my understanding that Colombian cocaine has weakened your position in the market. As well, blacks and the Hispanics have made inroads on your family's gambling concessions in the neighborhoods of Watts and East Los Angeles."

"We've had some setbacks," Moro told him, shifting in his chair and reaching for his wineglass. "Nothing we can't handle, given time."

"Your uncle has been most concerned, I think, about incursions in the sale of heroin."

"We're always interested in smack," the mafioso said. "Don Girolamo helped to pioneer this territory, back when Deej was still the man to see, from San Diego to L.A. He opened up the border routes to Mexico when I was still a kid in knee pants."

"But the so-called Mexican Connection has been proved unreliable, I think," Tien countered. "The pipeline has been infiltrated by American narcotics agents, and the product, when available, is certainly inferior to China White."

"So far, no argument."

"The quality and relative availability of Chinese number four, compared to your Mexican brown, has eroded your sales in Orange County, as well as Los Angeles."

"I'd say we still have a pretty good lock on L.A.," Moro answered.

"I was no doubt mistaken," Tien purred. "My reports, as imperfect and vague as they are, indicate that your share of the heroin market in greater Los Angeles has been reduced, in the past eighteen months, to a margin of forty percent."

"I'd advise against betting those odds."

"I was never a gambler, in spite of my dabbling in small games of chance."

"You've got high stakes in this one."

"Indeed. But I think that the game, played correctly, can benefit everyone, to an extent."

"No big winners?"

"Perhaps no great losers."

"I'm listening."

"Your problem—and by all means stop me if I am mistaken—your problem is centered on dwindling supplies. While the DEA dries up your Mexican sources, you find that the markets of Asia are closed, for the most part."

"We've got our connections," the Mafia underboss answered defensively.

"Yes. You have Chang in Macao, and Tuan Shih in Hong Kong. They are known to me." Tien was delighted with Moro's reaction, although he betrayed no emotion himself. "You have found their supply to be smaller and slow in arriving, I think, for the past several months."

"You a Gypsy, or what?"

"I am simply a businessman, charting supply and demand. In a business like ours, you will find that continued supplies are essential to long-term success."

"We've had dry spells before, with the French and the Turks. They blow over in time."

"Time is money, I think you Americans say. While you wait for the rain, other farmers may harvest their crops and grow fat on the proceeds."

"A dead man can't put on much weight."

"Theoretically speaking, no man is immortal," Tien replied, "but my purpose today is to settle our differences, not to increase them and touch off a long, costly war."

"So, let's settle. You've spelled my problems. Let's hear the solution."

"Détente. Coexistence. Survival. The market is broad and expanding each day. There is room, I believe, for two merchants to prosper and grow."

"Just like that?"

"If your uncle has no strong objections."

"I think you're forgetting a couple of things here, like balance of trade, and that problem you mentioned with steady supplies."

"We are willing to listen, if Don Girolamo has any suggestions for sharing the market without acrimonious conflict. That done, I believe you will find your supply problem vanished, a thing of the past."

"Sounds like blackmail to me," Esposito cut in.

"Sounds like business," the younger Italian responded. "I'll see what my uncle thinks. Really, that's all I can say."

"It is all I could hope for."

The waiter arrived with their food, and the four men confined their attention to excellent meat for the next several moments, Tien quick to offer his praise for the veal. Giap allowed that his steak wasn't bad, and the rivals began to relax, making small talk about their respective endeavors, the problems they had encountered with lawmen and poachers, the brash independents who seemed to spring up overnight.

"I remember a time," Moro said, "when you couldn't do squat in this part of the state without running it past the padrone for his blessing. The junk and the women, the gambling, forget it. I'm talking an absolute lock. Second-story jobs, skin flicks, the chicken trade, hot cars—the Don took his cut off the top, and the grunts kissed his hand for the privilege of forking it over. These days, you've got niggers and wetbacks and gooks—no offense—but you've got all these guys up the ass, and they're running around like they've been here forever. Like none of the credit for starting it all should belong to the Family. You know what I'm saying?"

Tien was accustomed to prejudice, and if the truth was known, he and Giap shared the capo's contempt for blacks and Latinos who dwelt on the underworld's fringes like jackals, surviving by theft from the kills made by lions.

"I understand perfectly."

"Yeah, you know, I kind of thought you would. I could tell from the first time I saw you, you weren't like a lot of these guys. There's no talking to some of them. All they know is a hit in the head."

"The Colombians?"

"Ay." Moro rolled his eyes heavenward, raising his palms. "Give me strength. They're like crazy men. All they can think of is stealing our money and cutting our throats if we try to talk sense, man to man. You'll be seeing some changes there. I guarantee it."

"I wish you good fortune."

"Wish those guys good fortune, if you want to be wishing for someone. When Don Girolamo comes down on their asses, they'll need all the help they can get."

"At such a time, your family may have need of friends."

"My uncle's got no beef with that, as long as friendship doesn't cost him too much, out of pocket."

"Certainly. I understand completely."

"These supplies that you were mentioning...can they be guaranteed?"

"We have not lost a shipment in the past two years."

"That must be some security you've got there."

"Planning, with a willingness to spend the necessary sums in certain quarters, to assure cooperation from officials."

"Greedy bastards. Everybody's got his hand out."

"Everyone needs bread."

"They don't need mine."

"I choose to think of it as an investment in the future. Money, after all, is nothing more than a contrived and artificial medium of exchange."

"I'll tell you what else money is, my friend: it's *power*. Show me someone without money in this town, I'll show you raw meat, waiting for the dogs."

Tien spread his hands. "All the more reason, then, for our respective families to seek a fair accommodation, rather than expending fortunes on a pointless contest for the streets. As allies, we can share the profits of a growing industry and minimize our losses, crushing any minor opposition with concerted force."

"I like the way you talk. You're educated. I could see that right away. You've got a sense of style."

"You flatter me. I am a humble businessman, who wishes nothing but to prosper in an atmosphere of peace and harmony."

"Yeah, right. I'll tell you something, here: I feel that way myself. I got a hunch my uncle's going to feel that way when I spell out your proposition."

"I am gratified to hear it."

"Course, there's still a lot of details need to be ironed out. The territories, import costs, whatever. I don't think we need to cover all of that this afternoon."

"With all respect, Don Girolamo may desire to join our future conversations."

"You can bet on that, damn straight. I think it's safe to say he wouldn't miss it for the world."

The waiter cleared their plates away, and Ngo Tien declined the offer of liqueur or coffee. "We have many business trifles yet to deal with," he explained.

"I get you."

"All my best to Don Carlotti. I regret that we have still not met in person, and I trust his pressing business was successfully concluded."

"Pressing business? Oh, yeah, that. It's just the usual, you know?"

"Indeed."

"I'll give him your regards, and we'll be getting back to you."

"I shall look forward to our second meeting, Mr. Moro, Mr. Esposito."

The *consigliere* flashed a grimace that was probably his most endearing smile, a flicker that surrendered swiftly to his normal frown. The beaming maître d' led Tien and Giap back through the restaurant, where tables had begun to fill with stylish men and women, sporting perfect tans and blond hair in abundance.

In the car, Tien let himself relax. Their hour still had three full minutes left. "What did you think?" he asked Anh Giap, when they were moving.

"You already know my feelings. I do not trust the Italians."

"Nor do I. But then, I do not fully trust our contacts in Macao and Hong Kong, either. Trust is not an absolute necessity, when doing business at arm's length."

"Carlotti has insulted us."

"It was an old man's way of saving face. Next time, he will be there."

"I am not sure that there should be a next time."

"Oh?"

"They mean to use our contacts in the Golden Triangle, and then dispose of us as soon as possible."

"Of course."

"But if you know this—"

"Did you think that I had visions of an everlasting partnership with Don Carlotti?"

"Sometimes, Ngo, I do not know *what* you think."

It was a compliment, from one who sometimes knew Tien better than he knew himself. "The Mafia has certain useful elements, which we can turn to our advantage over time. Carlotti's contacts in the courts and city government, for instance. He will introduce us to his pet officials as a sign of faith in our agreement."

"And if he does not?"

"He will. In time, his people can be made to realize the Mafia is dying. Politicians are survivors. They will choose the winning side."

"And when we have them?"

"Then, Carlotti and his Family will be superfluous. Dead wood. What happens to dead wood, my friend?"

Giap smiled. "If I recall correctly, it is normally cut up and burned."

"So, there you have it. Ashes, in due course. But *only* in due course, my brother. Do I have your word?"

"Of course." Giap sounded hurt. "When have I ever stood against you?"

"Never in my life. You are a faithful friend and partner."

"I will confess, you had me worried for a moment."

"Calm yourself. We have already lost one homeland, sacrificed through treachery. I do not plan to lose another."

"To the fire, then, in its time."

Tien lifted an imaginary wineglass. "To the fire."

CHAPTER THREE

The waiting always made Lao Fan uneasy. He was vulnerable, open to attack while he remained in one location, and the public nature of the meeting place provided him with nothing in the way of reassurance. He had seen men murdered on the city streets at rush hour, their killers disappearing in the crowd and lost forever. Modern city dwellers wouldn't get involved at any cost, wouldn't risk life and limb to help a stranger, when they could as easily walk past, leaving someone else to play Good Samaritan.

The Long Beach pier was safe enough, presumably. A few yards distant, tourists strolled the decks and passageways of the *Queen Mary*, dry-docked for the entertainment of a generation that had never gone to sea. The fishermen were out in force, lines dangling and tangling across the rail, good-natured arguments erupting briefly, drowned in frosty beer. A steady stream of passersby showed every color of the human rainbow, each one of them apparently oblivious to Lao Fan's presence.

He had bargained for a rendezvous outside Orange County, although Long Beach barely qualified, and in the last analysis, Lao Fan supposed that it made little difference. Ngo Tien was spreading out his wings, these days, to cast a shadow on Los Angeles and Hollywood. He might have watchers anywhere, and there were still the Thunder Dragons to contend with, roving jackals who had recently outgrown their turf, expanding into territory held by other gangs, their arsenal supplied by elders in the Asian syndicate. The Thunder Dragons knew his face, and it might not go well if a member of the gang should spot him now.

Lao Fan still cherished fleeting hopes that Tien might not be conscious of his mission. That the gang lord knew his name and recognized him as an enemy, the wiry Montagnard had no doubt whatsoever. Lao Fan's had been the voice that cautioned merchants that their payments of "protection" to the Thunder Dragons served, in fact, to help support Tien and his sadistic aide, Anh Giap. Lao Fan had warned them of Tien's participation in narcotics distribution, prostitution and pornography, illegal gambling, the rumors of a new alliance with Italian gangsters in the offing. He hadn't been secretive, hadn't attempted to conceal himself or change his number when the phone calls started. But neither had he been a major threat.

Until today.

Lao Fan had learned to hate the human parasites like Tien in Vietnam. While he and his Hmong compatriots had sacrificed their lives, their futures, in an effort to defeat the Communists, another sort of enemy was living, fat and happy, in Saigon. The underworld had prospered in a war economy, black market sales of medicine and food expanding into traffic in narcotics, women—even children—if the price was right. A serviceman away from home might seek a rousing game of chance, companionship, the simple pleasures of a drug-induced oblivion. If there was profit to be made, the modern warlords sniffed it out and sank their grasping, greedy hands up to the elbows in a hundred filthy trades. Corruption of police and politicians was an open secret in Saigon, a propaganda boon to Reds and revolutionaries who despised the Thieu regime. Lao Fan thought little of the criminals, as he spared little thought for worms and roaches in his daily life, until he learned that some of them were trading with the Vietcong, supplying arms and medicine to terrorists and traitors. Looking deeper, he had seen the web of violence and coercion the jackals spun around their own, extorting tribute from the merchant class, professionals, the military. Small arms and explosives, smuggled out of ARVN bases, had been turned around, employed to kill Americans and South Vietnamese. Lao Fan's own brother had been killed by an American grenade while dining in a sidewalk restaurant, and countless other allies had been slain or wounded, thanks in part to the unbridled treachery of "honored businessmen."

Lao Fan had hoped that Saigon's fall, if nothing else, would purge the gangs, their leaders carted off to prison or appointments with a firing squad. In fact, while several ranking mobsters had been jailed or executed by the new regime, most had possessed the foresight to abandon Vietnam while hostile troops were driving south. Their fortunes were already safe in foreign banks, and as respected "patriots" they had been welcomed to America with open arms, the indiscretions of their past concealed with the collusion of their allies in the State Department and the CIA. As refugee communities sprang up around the country, populated by the rabble of a wasted land and greeted by the natives with reactions ranging from hostility to mere indifference, Vietnamese survivors looked within themselves for comfort, continuity, support. Too often, they achieved stability by falling back upon the counsel of the same men who had dominated them in Saigon, and the gang lords quickly recognized the New World as a land of golden opportunity.

Lao Fan, for his part, had refused to grant the Communists an easy victory. When the Americans withdrew their ground troops, the Hmong had countered by increasing their resistance, dealing with the Vietcong in language the terrorists could understand. Lao Fan and his compatriots continued fighting after Saigon's fall until the rigors of attrition left them hopelessly outgunned, outnumbered by the enemy. Evacuation, in itself, had been a slice of living hell, a ragtag fleet of refugees adrift without sufficient food or water, lacking proper sanitation or medical attention, shunned at every port of call. America had finally, grudgingly, accepted the survivors, but Lao wasn't content to settle, build himself a carbon copy of his ruined life. He was a warrior with a mission: someday, somehow, he would carry home the struggle and redeem his people from their latter-day oppressors.

In the meantime, though, there was a living to be earned, and he had found employment at a restaurant in Santa Ana. The proprietor had been a kindly, older man who treated his employees with respect and paid them well. Lao had worked in the kitchen for a week before a member of the Thunder Dragons had appeared one evening to collect the owner's regular "insurance" payment. It had galled the Montagnard to see his white-haired friend and benefactor groveling before a boy of tender years, but he was wise enough to rein in his anger, avoiding a public scene that might result in later damage to the restaurant or danger to the owner's family.

Another week slipped past, and when the bagman made his next appearance, the proprietor had handed over something less than usual, explaining that his business had been off for several days. The boy had smiled and slapped the old man's face, still grinning as he waited for him to respond. Humiliated, the proprietor had taken it, and three more blows, with tears of outrage streaming down his cheeks. Lao Fan had turned away and clenched his fists so tightly that his fingernails drew blood. He dared not move against the Thunder Dragons as a member of the staff, when any action he attempted might rebound against his friends...but, still, he knew there must be something he could do.

The next week, on collection day, he called in sick and spent the afternoon at home, preparing for an evening's adventure. Shortly after dusk, he walked the seven blocks from his apartment to the restaurant, picked out his blind and settled in to wait for the arrival of his prey. The Dragons' cocky bagman was on time, as always, and Lao Fan had let him pass, allowed him to collect his money, waiting while the weasel took time out for some suggestive comments to the waitresses before he left. The wiry Montagnard was waiting, ski mask covering his face, as his quarry passed the alley's mouth a second time. In an instant he'd made the collar, taking his assailant by complete surprise and dragging him into the darkness of the alley.

He would have to give the weasel credit; there had been a certain reckless courage in his style as one hand slid beneath his jacket, coming out with ebony nunchaku fighting sticks. But courage never took the place of skill in martial arts, and as the punk began to twirl his 'chuks, it was immediately obvious that he had seen too many kung fu movies. Lao Fan had feinted to the left, gone low, inside a sloppy overhand that barely grazed his shoulder, hammering with fists and knees until the punk lay crumpled at his feet. He'd been tempted to apply the 'chuks and let the bastard drag himself back home on broken legs, but he had dropped them in a garbage can instead. The money he extracted from the boy's pockets totaled more than seven thousand dollars.

The restaurant's proprietor had gaped in shock, when Lao Fan placed the money on his desk next evening. Embarrassment had vied with fear and struck a compromise, the old man finally agreeing to accept the cash, with firm insistence that he not be told where it had come from. Two nights later, when the restaurant was razed by gasoline bombs after closing, that and all his other cash on hand went up in flames.

Lao Fan had seen the bombing as an act of war, but he wasn't prepared to face the Thunder Dragons by himself. A crude surveillance of the neighborhood had verified that every shop of any consequence was paying tribute to the gang, and interviews with several merchants had convinced Lao Fan that they would be of no assistance in his fight. He had gone on to speak with every one in turn, regardless, briefing them on his intention to defeat the Thunder Dragons, urging them to stand beside him if they dared, encouraging them to report the hoodlums, testify if necessary, anything to break their hold on the community.

Along the way, he heard the same refrain a hundred times: police were useless, never on the scene while vandals, thieves or rapists did their work, unable to protect a witness while the courts delayed, postponed and stalled. A blind man, selling papers, told Lao Fan of his attempt to testify against the Dragons who had robbed his newsstand twice within a single month. He had been blinded by a gunshot wound that left him in the hospital and close to death for seven weeks; police, meanwhile, were powerless to win indictments, since a blind man cannot pick his suspects from a lineup. Time and time again, new versions of the same old story were repeated to him, in the strictest confidence, as victims bared their scars and vowed to help him—if, and when, the state could guarantee protection for themselves, their families.

Alone, Lao Fan had made the rounds of law-enforcement agencies. The sheriff's office had been understanding, even sympathetic, but the cases he described were technically outside of county jurisdiction, and he was referred to the police. Those officers, in turn, had pledged to rid the neighborhood of Thunder Dragons overnight, if only they could get their hands on witnesses who weren't afraid to testify. Protection? Certainly, but he would have to understand that they were working on a budget, understaffed and underpaid, without sufficient troops to handle everything at once. Perhaps, if witnesses would volunteer for self-imposed protective custody...

Disgusted with the runaround, Lao Fan had taken up surveillance of the Thunder Dragons on his own. He followed bagmen, not to rob them, but to trace their movements, listing drops and "clients" in a notebook that he carried everywhere. Within a month, he had observed four drug transactions, dozens of extortion payoffs, and he knew the address of the gang's main headquarters in Anaheim. He knew some thirty members of the gang by name, had photographs of each, and he was working on a file of home addresses, to facilitate arrests when his material was handed to police.

Along the way, Lao Fan had been first curious, and then concerned, about the weekly meetings held between the warlord of the Thunder Dragons, So Hoo Minh, and a distinguished-looking older man who rode in a Lincoln Continental, dressed in fine, expensive taste and glowered through his horn-rims like a stern professor on examination day. Lao Fan had memorized the Lincoln's license number, traced it through the ruse of posing as a witness to a recent traffic accident, and learned that it belonged to an accountant, one Nguyen Kao, with offices in Buena Park. Discreet inquiries had revealed that Kao worked on a retainer for a single client, Ngo Van Tien, whose interests included produce, entertainment, transportation and investments in a host of other fields. From gossip in the Asian neighborhoods, he had been able to complete a picture of those "other interests"—from narcotics, child pornography and prostitution, on through gambling, extortion, wholesale theft of merchandise for bootleg distribution through a string of "bargain" outlets, county-wide. Anh Giap was the enforcer for the operation, and Tien's connection with the Thunder Dragons seemed to be twofold: he licensed their extortion racket, skimming profits off the top, and fenced any merchandise the reckless youth acquired through burglaries and strong-arm robberies. While publicly deploring gangland violence, Tien was reaping handsome profits from the Dragons every day, and he had feelers out to some of their competitors, as well.

With names and dates and photographs, Lao had returned to the police department. A detective who resembled Groucho Marx had spent an hour listening to Lao Fan, studying his evidence, and finally suggested that "the Feds" might be more helpful to his case, all things considered. Pressed for explanations, he had muttered something vague about potential jurisdictional disputes and cases that were "too damn big" for a department that had felt the budget crunch already.

Seething, Lao Fan had gone to see the Feds. He tried the FBI first, visiting the Bureau's office in Los Angeles, where he was well received until he asked what might be done to stop Tien's systematic rape of the community. The smiling agent had responded with a lecture on the limits of the FBI's authority, its prior arrangements with assorted other agencies in law enforcement. Local crimes, the sort described in Lao Fan's notes, depicted in his photographs, were clearly matters for municipal police. If those investigators happened to discover evidence of federal violations, why, the Bureau would be pleased to act on a request for interagency assistance. Why, then, had police referred him to the FBI? Sometimes there was a mix-up; maybe they had *really* been referring him to DEA.

At Drug Enforcement headquarters, Lao Fan's reception was entirely different: cool, reserved, without a bare suggestion that cooperation might be possible. The DEA administrator who allowed him thirty minutes on a Wednesday afternoon was taciturn and unsmiling as he listened to Lao's story, scanned his notes and pushed the photographs around his desktop with a pencil, like a man afraid of leaving fingerprints. The agency appreciated any help from citizens, and someone would be checking out Lao

Fan's complaint, in time. Was Ngo Tien familiar to the DEA? Was anybody working on his case? The stone-faced bureaucrat was not at liberty to say. Perhaps, if Lao Fan would consult the FBI...

Disheartened, he had gone to Immigration, on the off chance that Tien or some of his subordinates might still be aliens, subject to deportation as undesirables. The officers were courteous but firm, refusing to discuss the case of any individual where laws involving privacy might leave them open to a civil suit. Lao Fan had left them with a list of names and copies of his notes, in any case, a hedge against the possibility that someone, someday, might decide that Ngo Tien was worthy of investigation. Customs officers were no more helpful; they had pricked their ears and squinted through their spectacles at the mention of narcotics, but without a firm description of the smugglers, a hard line on their point of entry, there was nothing to be done. Lao Fan would understand, of course.

He understood, all right. He knew that he had wasted weeks, collecting evidence for agencies that refused to act, each citing regulations that were carved in stone. They all commiserated with him, shared his anger at the crimes that had been perpetrated in Orange County and beyond, by Tien, Giap and their associates...but there was simply nothing they could do at the moment. Perhaps next month, next year.

Lao Fan had wasted nearly two months in pursuit of phantoms, and he realized that he'd placed himself in jeopardy along the way. His face and name were now known to every major law-enforcement agency in Orange and L.A. counties, his evidence and charges filed away for future reference. And he knew the risks involved with personal exposure. If Tien and Giap had operated, undisturbed, for this long, there was every reason to believe their syndicate had lawmen on the payroll, eyes inside the various departments

Lao Fan had visited in search of help. He realized, belatedly, that by attempting to assist his neighbors in their plight, he might have marked himself for sudden death.

Was he becoming paranoid, or had he gained an extra shadow in the past few days? Were footprints in the flower bed beneath his bedroom window left there by the meter man, or an assassin checking out the floor plan?

When the phone call came, he was taken completely by surprise. The caller introduced himself as Leonard Justice, and he spoke in a mellow voice that overrode the telltale whisper of long distance. He was based in Washington, D.C., coordinating certain racketeering strike force efforts, and Lao Fan had come to his attention through a mutual acquaintance in L.A. Names were beside the point, but Justice understood Lao Fan had been collecting evidence against a certain Ngo Tien? A simple yes or no would do, and they wouldn't discuss the details on the telephone. There was a possibility that Justice could assist him with his problem, but some background information would be needed for the files before he could proceed.

Lao Fan had nothing to conceal, and he responded freely to the stranger's questions, touching on his military service, immigration to the States, employment since arrival and his motives for the personal attack on Tien. It crossed Lao's mind that Tien might use a ruse to find out more about his enemy, but he dismissed the thought and laid his cards on the table. If the Asian drug lord knew so little of what happened in his own backyard, it would be worth the risk to let him know that he was dealing with a grim, determined adversary.

Leonard Justice had been noncommittal, and the conversation wound down. There were some minor points about Lao's story he would have to run through channels, bits and pieces of the evidence that would require corroboration. If it all checked out he would be back in touch, and contact with an operative in the field would be arranged. Lao Fan had thanked the stranger for his time and cradled the receiver, certain that he wouldn't hear from Washington again.

But he was wrong.

The second call from Leonard Justice came through two days later, and the federal agent had apologized for the delay. Lao's background information and his story had been double-checked for errors or omissions—no offense intended—and his record came back clean. More to the point, it seemed that Lao had barely scratched the surface in his scrutiny of Ngo Tien. Would he consent to meet an undercover agent, with an eye toward helping bring the warlord down?

Lao had required perhaps a heartbeat to respond, and so the meeting was arranged for Long Beach, two days hence. He would have much to tell the agent when they met, for in addition to his notes and photographs, Lao Fan had recently received a string of urgent calls from members of the refugee community, recounting grievous wrongs they had suffered at the hands of Tien's enforcers or the Thunder Dragons. None of them would have the nerve to testify in court, but if Lao could find some other way to help them, to relieve their suffering and punish those who victimized them through extortion, robbery, and rape . . .

Perhaps.

There still might be a way, and hope had been enough to make him keep the rendezvous in Long Beach. He had taken pains to guarantee that no one followed him beyond the borders of the Asian neighborhood where he maintained a small apartment for himself. If Tien had traced him here, Lao Fan would give the jackal credit for invisibility, along with all his other proved skills.

"Hello, Lao Fan."

The voice, so close behind him, made him jump. He swiveled, half expecting Giap or one of his gorillas, and was startled by the tall, dark stranger. The face was new to him, beyond all doubt, but there was something hauntingly familiar about the graveyard eyes.

"It's been a while," Mack Bolan said.

CHAPTER FOUR

Lao Fan was having trouble with the face; that much was obvious. He recognized the voice—or thought he did—but he was looking for a person who, for all intents and purposes, was dead and buried. Bolan finally decided it was time to help him out.

"So, how's the leg?"

A smile broke over Lao Fan's features, and he had it now.

"I did not recognize the face."

"The old one got too heavy for me. Actually I've been through a couple of them since Na Trang."

"I thought I recognized the eyes. How are you, Sergeant?"

"No more sergeant, no more Bolan."

"Ah, of course. The name would be as heavy as the face. What are you called?"

"Mike Blanski, this time." Bolan scanned the bustling pedestrians, in search of anyone who might have stayed too close, too long. "Let's take a walk."

"When I arrived in the United States, I learned about your difficulties with the law," Lao said. "I also heard that you were dead, and then..."

"Let's say the news was premature. How long have you been stateside?"

"It will be ten years next month. When Saigon fell, I spent some time with the resistance in the mountains. After that there was Bangkok, Malaysia, Singapore."

"You still have hopes of going back?"

Lao shrugged. "How many Taiwanese still cherish dreams of 'going back to China,' when they've never been there in the first place? Some of them are middle-aged, and they have seen their homeland only as a shadow on the far horizon. I've forgotten how to hope."

"It's funny," Bolan said. "For a second back there I thought I recognized you."

"You are right. I've changed. Perhaps too much…or not enough. Who knows?"

"I don't remember any second thoughts in Nam."

Lao merely shrugged, and for a moment he wouldn't meet Bolan's gaze. "It's a different world," he said at last. "A different war."

The Executioner had met Lao Fan by accident—or fate—on his withdrawal from a two-man penetration mission into Laos. He had tagged an NVA commander and a pair of Pathet Lao collaborators, but the strike had put an enemy pursuit team on his track, and they had nailed his backup—Sloan, a corporal from Ohio—on the first leg of a grueling four-day chase. The Executioner had been wounded, losing it, when he crossed the path of Montagnard guerrillas on patrol. They had been tracking Charlie, spoiling for a fight, and the arrival of a solitary, wounded Yankee in their midst had been an unexpected turn. Their medic saw to Bolan's wounds, and they were ready for the NVA when Hanoi's finest walked into the ambush. Watching from the sidelines, Bolan had observed what fighting men can do against unlikely odds, when homes and families were riding on the line.

When it was over, Lao Fan volunteered to see the tall American delivered safely to his base of operations. On the homeward trek, two men of widely different cultures had begun to know each other, one to one, and they had come away from the experience as friends. A few months later, when the Montagnards joined hands with Bolan's Penetra-

tion Team Able for a sweep along the DMZ, they met again.
Outside Na Trang, the ambush had been on the other foot,
and Lao had caught a piece of shrapnel in his thigh, which
had damaged the femoral artery. A tourniquet and Bolan's
swift decision to abort the mission, carrying Lao Fan himself through miles of reeking jungle, saved the gutsy Asian's
leg and life. The vestige of a limp was visible when Lao was
worried or exhausted, and the Executioner had noticed he
was limping now.

"I take it from your presence here," Lao said, "the calls
I have received, that you have solved your problems with the
government."

"It's like you said—times change. Our interests sometimes coincide. I'm interested in what you have to say."

"There is a man called Ngo Tien."

"I know the name."

Lao Fan regarded Bolan with surprise and new respect.
He had no way of knowing that the Executioner had been
in San Francisco just the day before, completing preparation for a strike against the Asian syndicate, which had been
growing lately in the shadow of the Golden Gate. A week
had been consumed in charting territories, picking out the
drops, casinos, powder factories that earned the mob an
estimated $67 million yearly, tax free. He had identified a
pair of would-be warlords, lately feinting for position, eye-
ing each other's throats, and Bolan thought it was a situation he could exploit to good advantage, given time. The call
from Leo Turrin had distracted him from his objective, but
the little man in Washington had done his homework, and
at mention of Lao Fan, the Executioner had put his northern war on hold. Orange County and an old friend needed
his attention; all the rest of it would have to wait.

"Tien and his associate, Anh Giap, are tyrants in the refugee community. They pose as men of generosity and kind-
ness, known for many gifts to charity and their support for

new arrivals, but they steal back ten times what they give. If you know Tien, you know he is involved with gambling and drugs, pornography and prostitution, terrorism and corruption of the very people he pretends to serve. He owns the leaders of a street gang called the Thunder Dragons, who extort protection money from the Asian merchants and assassinate the few who dare resist. The Dragons, on their own or with Tien's help, have been responsible for seven murders that I know of. No one even tries to keep track of the rapes, the robberies and other crimes they perpetrate against our people.''

It was a familiar story for the Executioner. Historically each group of immigrants to the United States had been composed of men and women who were mostly poor and frequently the victims of political or ethnic persecution in their homeland, searching for a new beginning in a land where tolerance and equal opportunity were written into law. Inevitably, being human, some among the new arrivals had been wily predators, the sort who had survived through ruthless cunning in their former lives, and now reverted easily to type as rich, new fields were laid before them. In the latter nineteenth century, Italian and Sicilian immigrants had brought the Black Hand, the Camorra and the Mafia along like so much excess baggage, and they were the first to suffer from the jackals who had preyed upon them earlier, at home. A flood of Eastern European immigration on the eve of World War I had borne its share of anarchists and radicals along, like flotsam on the tide, and in the early 1980s, refugees expelled from Cuba by Fidel had been deliberately selected to include the residue of prisons and asylums, as a parting ''gift'' to the United States. Mack Bolan didn't fault the Cubans, Asians or Italians as a whole, but he was dedicated to annihilation of the predators at any cost, regardless of their race or the religion they pretended to observe.

A lifetime of experience on foreign and domestic battle-grounds had taught the Executioner one thing above all else: there was a similarity about his enemies that no coincidence of racial traits or ideology could finally disguise. They came in every shade of white, black, brown and yellow; they were left-wing radicals or ultraright reactionaries, ethnic militants or Klansmen, godless Communists or the fanatical devotees of a god who called for bloody sacrifice. Above all else, they worshiped *power*, subjugation of their fellow human beings, and their native tongue would always be the language of brute force. In Vietnam, and later in his one-man war against the Mafia, Mack Bolan had grown fluent in the language of his enemies. He spoke it like a native, and the savages had learned to listen when he called their names.

"On the phone you mentioned some logistic details."

"I've collected names and photographs," Lao Fan replied. "I have the address of a loft where heroin is processed, several gambling clubs, a house of prostitution and a studio where pornographic films are made, sometimes with children. Also, I have names and addresses of merchants who pay tribute to the Thunder Dragons on a weekly basis."

"And you've taken this to the police?"

Lao made a sour face. "Police, the sheriff's office, FBI and Drug Enforcement—they are all the same. Some say they do not have the jurisdiction, others need more evidence. The merchants will not testify for fear of seeing their families slaughtered, so police claim there is nothing they can do."

"And you don't buy it."

"The majority of officers, I think, are honorable men who fear for their careers if they attack a man of power, or if they initiate investigations they might not finish with success. Some are afraid to move against Tien and Giap because it might appear that they are persecuting Asians, as a race." He paused. "I also think that Ngo Tien has many friends, and some of them wear badges. Perhaps others wear judges' robes, or hold elected office."

"Off the record," Bolan told him, "Washington has similar concerns. I'd like to bypass normal channels, if I can."

"It should not be a problem. I can help you, and I have made several friends in the community who feel as I do."

"Whoa, let's take it one step at a time." The soldier let a note of warning creep into his voice. "I'm not recruiting any backup here. Until I'm certain what I'm up against, I'll want to check it out alone."

"There are too many jackals, even for the bravest tiger."

Bolan smiled. "You might be right, but I don't plan to meet them all at once. Why don't you fill me in about that movie studio you mentioned?"

"Mmm." Lao Fan made a disgusted face. "It is a place of shame, where women prostitute themselves and children are defiled. Tien has been raided twice, at other studios, but always his employees pay the fines or spend the ninety days in jail. So far, Tien is lucky: films of children have not been discovered, and his underlings refuse to name their master."

"Are you sure about the kiddie porn?"

Lao nodded. "I have spoken to the mother of a seven-year-old girl, whose daughter was the 'star' in one of Tien's productions. I have also managed to obtain a videocassette, but there is nothing on the tape that points directly to Tien. This child was lured from her apartment by a member of the Thunder Dragons. Later, when Tien was finished with her, she was taken home, together with a warning from the gang. Her parents know what *might* have happened to their daughter, and they know what *still* might happen if they talk to the authorities. They have seen others who were not so fortunate."

"Okay. If the police are out, then maybe Tien could use a movie critic. Someone who can help him with a little editing, and set him up for Oscar time."

"You know of such a critic?"

Bolan matched the Asian smile. "I might. We'll need an address on that studio, as well as a floor plan, if you've got it."

Lao rattled off an Irvine address, roughly equidistant from the local university and Orange County's John Wayne Airport. Bolan didn't know the street, offhand, but he would find it when the time arrived.

"Regrettably I have not been inside," the little Montagnard informed him. "You will recognize it as an older house, and large, the sort that has been turned into apartments for the students. This one, though, is owned by Ngo Tien, through dummy corporations. I am told that different rooms are used for making several films at once."

"I hate these greedy types. They always go for quantity, instead of quality. I guess our critic ought to set Tien straight on that score while he's in the neighborhood."

Lao Fan couldn't suppress a chuckle. "I believe I might enjoy this after all."

"Don't put your party hat on yet. If Tien and Giap have half as much to lose as I suspect, they won't be letting go of it without a fight. It could get ugly in a hurry."

"We have been in ugly fights before, my friend."

"That's true enough, but I was thinking of your neighbors sitting home afraid to testify."

"There are a few, especially among the younger men, who feel as I do. They believe that something must be done."

Mack Bolan sighed. It always came down to the younger men. "It's premature to think about a general campaign," he said. "I don't want innocent civilians getting in the way."

"You're right, but I—"

"Will man the phone, in case I have to make a quick connection," Bolan finished for him. "If I need a backup, Lao, you'll be the first to hear about it. Guaranteed."

"You should not take this risk alone," the Montagnard replied.

"It's how I play the game." He hesitated. "When you mentioned other men just now, how many did you have in mind? What kind of hardware do they have?"

"I have discussed the matter with perhaps a dozen. Six or eight of those are ready to defend themselves, their families, against the Thunder Dragons if it should be necessary. They have pistols, shotguns. One or two have hunting rifles."

Bolan stored the information in his mental data bank for future reference. "I'll be in touch this evening," he promised. "In the meantime, get your people ready for the storm. We don't know how Tien will take the interference, but I'd bet it won't be lying down. He might hit back at anyone in sight."

"It shall be done."

"And watch yourself."

"I really think—"

"Not this time." Bolan shook his head in an emphatic negative. "Later, maybe."

"As you say. Take care, Mike Blanski."

"Always."

Bolan watched the slender figure disappear, ingested by the jostling crowd of tourists and vacationers intent on living up the final weekend of the summer. Monday morning it was back to work or school for most of those who moved around him smiling. None of them would ever know that war had been declared within arm's reach, while they pursued a single-minded search for sun and junk food, sex or simple relaxation.

And the soldier had no doubt that war was coming. Ngo Tien and his associates were not the sort of men to fold their tents and slip away, intimidated by a show of armed resistance. Anyone who had survived three decades in the Saigon underworld, competing with the Tongs and Triads for his daily bread, was made of sterner stuff. The shift of operations to America, including coexistence—up to this point—with the old-line Mafia, bespoke a man of ingenuity and daring, one who was accustomed to success at any cost.

It angered Bolan that the Asian refugee community should be subjected to a reign of terrorism by the likes of Tien. It should have been enough that they had lost their homes—and families, in many cases—starting life from scratch in new surroundings that were strange and often hostile. They deserved much better than the millstone that Tien and his collected savages had come to represent.

Despite the circumstances of his being in Vietnam, Bolan had developed admiration and respect for the South Vietnamese. He had seen them strive and suffer, helped them when and where he could, and in the end, his best—the best of thousands like himself who gave their youth, their lives—hadn't been adequate to hold the predators at bay. Mack Bolan didn't linger over memories of Asia, torturing himself with should-have-dones and might-have-beens. As one man in the hellgrounds, he had done his utmost until private tragedy had intervened, but he didn't delude himself into believing that a different set of circumstances, his continued presence in the war-torn nation would have changed the final outcome. Vietnam had probably been lost from the beginning, the pursuit of victory derailed by national devotion to a mere "containment" of the enemy. America had entered Nam with a commitment to maintain the status quo, a situation that was already untenable and doomed to failure.

But vacillating policy and diplomatic blunders didn't touch the people where they lived. Abandoned by America, the South Vietnamese had gone on fighting for their homes and families, against the odds that would eventually overwhelm them, crush them to the earth. For their resistance thousands had been murdered, thousands more consigned to grim "reeducation camps," where they would learn to spout the party line or else. For those who got away, sometimes with nothing but the clothing on their backs, the contents of their pockets, the United States had been a shining beacon in the storm.

There was a stubborn, fighting spirit in these people that allowed them to survive, in spite of everything. But there was also fatalism, an acceptance of adversity that led them to submit at times when others might have risen in revolt. A generation of abuse and exploitation had elapsed before they took up arms against the French, and even then the impetus of global war had been required to light the spark. More generations might elapse before the refugees stood up to someone like Ngo Tien...unless another spark was struck to light their way.

But Bolan would proceed with caution, all the same. A single spark could touch off many different kinds of fire, and some, if uncontrolled, might do the refugee community more harm than good. In Vietnam, while smoke was clearing from the Tet offensive, journalists had asked a military spokesman for the rationale behind the leveling of Hue by massed artillery. With logic that civilians, safe at home, could never hope to understand, the officer responded "it was necessary to destroy the town, in order to save it." Bolan, as a frontline warrior, was familiar with scorched-earth salvation, and he had no wish to see it in Orange County. Rather, he preferred the surgeon's touch, a deft and clean removal of malignant tissue that would leave the body functional, intact and on the mend.

Ngo Tien had had his own way long enough. The worm was turning, slowly, and unless Mack Bolan missed his guess, it had already learned to bite. A nibble, first, for openers, and if it all worked out, the turning worm might swallow Tien alive.

CHAPTER FIVE

Bolan made a drive-by of the studio and circled once around the block to memorize approaches and escape routes, checking out security. The place was more or less as Lao Fan had described—big and old, surrounded by a dwindling number of its peers, the rest all gone to rooming houses and apartments. Of the pedestrians he saw that afternoon, an easy three-fourths had the look of students: faded jeans and Army-surplus jackets, new athletic jerseys, hair that seemed to find no middle ground between the options of a military buzz and sundry shoulder-sweeping styles. There were no books in evidence, as classes wouldn't meet before next week, but boys and girls alike seemed bent on studying one another.

Bolan left them to it, concentrating on his target. There was nothing in the way of physical security out front: no fence, no dogs, no lookouts. Any effort to secure the place against attack would certainly have raised some eyebrows—and some questions—in the neighborhood, and Ngo Tien was smart enough to realize his best, built-in security lay with the area itself. Nobody ground out porno films in Irvine, where you were an easy stone's throw from the university, and while your neighbors might be busted for possession on occasion, it was mostly misdemeanor action, laying in a little grass, some pep pills for the all-night study sessions. If the owner of the house had thrown up bars and fences, he would merely have succeeded in attracting more attention to himself; without the trimmings, he was virtually invisible.

An alley ran behind the big, old houses, granting access to the Dumpsters that had replaced the ancient, single-family trash cans of another generation. Small garages had been added to a number of the houses, but parking was a problem and the curb out front was jammed. No Parking signs assured that Bolan had the alley to himself, and he discovered that the studio's backyard had been converted to a paved parking lot, offering sufficient space for half a dozen cars. He marked a Cadillac, a van, two foreign compacts in the tiny lot, and saw the camera positioned to provide the occupants with visuals on new arrivals.

They would see him coming, possibly retain his likeness on a videocassette, if he approached his target from the rear. His plans didn't include a screen test, and he wrote off the alley, returning to the street and searching for a place to park. Chevettes, VWs and other bargain wheels were wall to wall, and on his second pass, the soldier gave it up. He double-parked outside the studio, and fished around beneath the rental's seat until he found a cardboard window sign that read: Police—On Duty. Bolan propped it on the dash, reflecting that it might have prompted some artistic vandalism in a different neighborhood, deciding that his wheels should be all right for the duration of his visit to the studio.

He pocketed the keys and left the car unlocked, against the possibility that he might have to make a hasty getaway.

Bolan wore a custom-tooled Beretta 93-R underneath his sport coat, in a shoulder rig that made the weapon easily accessible. He wasn't anticipating any fireworks, but the Executioner had seen plans go up in smoke before, and he wasn't about to brave the dragon's lair unarmed.

As he approached the front door, the peephole mounted on a level with his chest, he palmed a leather wallet from the outside pocket of his coat. The badge inside was genuine enough, though it hadn't been issued in Orange County, and he hoped that it would stand a cursory inspection, granting him the necessary time to launch his spiel. If he could get a foot inside that door, he thought, the rest should follow naturally.

And it was simple, right. Like falling into an open grave.

He punched the bell repeatedly and pounded on the door, trying to communicate urgency. It took a moment, even so, but then a muffled voice addressed him through the mail slot, questioning his business. Bolan flipped open the wallet, held it so that nothing else was visible to anyone behind the peephole, and declared himself.

"Police. You wanna open up?"

"We didn't call for the police."

"I know that, pal. I've got an urgent message for your boss. Of course, if he don't care about the raid..."

Assorted bolts were thrown, and Bolan pocketed his shield before the door swung open on a chain, a pasty face with wire-rimmed glasses thrust into the breach.

"What raid?"

"The one that's due to bust your ass in thirty minutes. Do I see your boss, or shall I meet you all downtown?"

"Okay, hang on a second, will you? Jeez!"

The door closed in the warrior's face and nervous fingers grappled with the chain before it finally surrendered. When the pale face reappeared, there was a greasy sheen of perspiration on the doorman's forehead. Bolan shouldered past the guy and went inside.

"We haven't got a lot of time," he growled. "Let's shake it up, all right?"

The doorman pulled himself up to the limits of a strapping five foot seven, putting on a solemn face. "I need to know what this is all about," he said, attempting to display authority. "What kind of raid is this we're talkin'? Who's behind it?"

Bolan shook his head in wonderment. "I thought you guys were connected. No? Well, it's a shitty time to find out that you don't know what the hell's been going on!"

"Why don't you fill me in?"

"You run this operation?" Bolan made no effort to disguise the skepticism in his tone.

"Nobody sees the man unless they go through me."

He thought that it wouldn't be difficult to go through this guy, but he played it by the numbers. "Fine, you wanna dick around and waste more time, you got it. Who are we expecting? Try the county vice boys, with a backup team from child welfare. Hey, you like the sound of that so far? I hear a rumble there could be a couple Feds along, to eyeball any inventory you smooth operators may have sitting on the shelf. They're building Mann Act cases, can you dig it? Anybody running chicken interstate these days, they're looking at a minimum of ten to twenty hard time in Atlanta."

"Holy shit!"

"You'll *think* shit, when they turn your skinny ass out on the mainline. Chicken hawks are in demand, I hear. They've got a couple thousand muscle-bound gorillas who'd just love you."

"You'd better talk to Mr. Diep."

"I guess I'd better, sunshine."

"Come with me."

"I wouldn't miss it for the world."

FEW MEN ARE FORTUNATE enough to be well paid for doing something they otherwise would gladly do free. Dan Diep was such a man, and every morning on his way to work, he thanked the several gods of his acquaintance for the favors they had bestowed upon him. Never a religious man, Diep still believed in hedging all his bets. It never hurt to be prepared.

Preparedness, in fact, was part of Dan Diep's job, including supervision of security inside the Irvine motion picture studio. He also handled distribution, inventory, the procurement of performers and supplies. A patron of the arts, he took extraordinary care in selection of his actresses, convinced that winning cinema required sincerity on screen. A man could make it on the strength of his physique, the size of his equipment, but a woman needed special handling, encouragement at every stage of the production. If a girl was wise enough to place her future in his hands, she would inevitably be rewarded with success.

This afternoon, as Diep sat in on filming of a crucial scene, he was able to congratulate himself on the selection of another rising star. The guy was nothing special, hung like Mr. Ed and less articulate, but no one would be watching him, in any case. The woman's moves were something special, and the way she rolled her eyes at just the perfect moment . . . well, she had been equally convincing in Diep's office during her audition for the part, and he suspected that she hadn't shown him all her tricks. Perhaps this evening, if the shooting schedule had not taken too much out of her . . .

He felt himself responding, knew that it was time to leave. The others would be waiting in his office, and they all had pressing business to attend to on the streets. He rose from the director's chair and excused himself.

They had a Wild West feature under way in Number 2, *Night Riders*, and the set of Number 1 was vacant for remodeling. Diep would have liked to spend a moment on the other working set, but he was late already and his guests would be impatient. They were troubled men, with jobs they didn't enjoy as Dan Diep loved his own, and he had kept them waiting long enough.

Today they would discuss a distribution problem, and as always, it would lead to angry words concerning the Italians. The Carlotti Family had maintained a stranglehold on pornographic film production until relatively recently. The shift toward independent operators, several of them backed by Ngo Tien, was cutting into Family profits, and a war of sorts was looming in the industry. Within the past six months, Carlotti's strong-arms had been touring theaters, inspecting inventory, confiscating or destroying films that didn't bear his trademark. Actors had been warned to stay away from crews and projects that weren't controlled by the Italians, and one actress—who had not only chosen to ignore the warnings but had boasted of her courage in the company of "friends"—had been abducted, beaten, slashed with razors by a pair of thugs who told her she could find her future work in horror films, minus makeup.

Through it all, Ngo Tien had stayed his hand, resisting the temptation to retaliate in kind. When films were stolen or destroyed, he hurried to replace them, tacking on a bonus for the owner of the theater, to cover any inconvenience. If actors were intimidated, Tien responded with a hefty increase in their salaries, assurances of confidentiality, armed escorts to and from their homes. Raw talent was recruited out of state, with special charter flights laid on to guarantee the safe arrival and departure of new faces from Las Vegas, Phoenix, Dallas. Thus far, other than the slashed woman, there had been no casualties, and Don Carlotti's profit margin had continued to decline.

Uneasy peace, however, didn't satisfy Tien's salesmen and distributors. They had been feeling heat from the Italians, walking on the razor's edge between détente and all-out war. The general consensus favored swift retaliation—one or two had spoken of assassinating Don Carlotti as the first step in a drive to decimate his Family—and Diep had been hard-pressed to keep the troops in line this long.

The problem lay with Ngo Tien and his reluctance to endanger recent gains by taking any major risks. A businessman at heart, despite his chosen stock-in-trade, Tien saw profit in tranquillity and shied away from violence when he could, accepting certain provocations as the price of competition. He wouldn't respond with force unless he recognized a threat of grave immediacy, or unless a relatively painless victory was guaranteed. Dan Diep was charged with keeping his distributors and troops in line until such time arrived and orders were received from Tien or Giap.

The others wouldn't like it, but it was Diep's job to make them understand, or failing that, to keep them in line by force. He would attempt to use sweet reason first, and if that failed, then he would let them feel the fist inside the velvet glove.

A dozen pairs of eyes snapped toward him as Diep closed the office door and took his seat. He had a respite of perhaps three seconds, then the hailstorm of complaints descended on him, fingers jabbing at his face, a dozen angry voices yammering at once. He knew what they were saying, though he couldn't decipher any of it. He allowed them half a minute to relieve themselves of pent-up tension, finally bringing down his open palm against the tabletop with a report like muffled gunfire.

"Silence!" No one was fool enough to argue with him. "We will conduct this meeting with the usual decorum. Everyone will have a chance to speak, though I suspect that I could tell each of you what you intend to say."

"With all respect—"

"I am not finished."

Daring anyone to interrupt, he let the silence stretch while he scanned their faces: Anglo, Asian, one Hispanic thrown in, as he liked to say, for flavor.

"You are angry with Carlotti," he continued, when he had their full attention. "You desire retaliation in the streets—destruction of his theaters perhaps, or something even more extreme. You would provoke a war that might prove costly to us all."

"Carlotti has provoked the war. Are you forgetting that?"

"I have forgotten nothing. Our employer wishes us to wait and take no action at the present time. He is negotiating with Carlotti, and there is a possibility that all your problems will be solved without resort to violence."

"We must negotiate from strength. The Mafia will not respect an adversary who submits to threats, and then expects to win concessions."

"Who among us has submitted?" Diep inquired. "Have we decreased production? Are we placing films in fewer theaters today than yesterday? Last week? Is Don Carlotti gaining back the income he has lost to us?"

"He threatens us. His men are on the street, and they are armed. If we are fired on—"

"You defend yourselves, of course. But you must not initiate the contact. Is that clearly understood?" He waited while they nodded, muttering reluctant acquiescence. "When some action is deemed necessary, you will be the first to know, and your instructions will be handed down by me."

They studied him with grudging resignation, slowly nodding in acknowledgment of his authority. Diep knew they feared him, but their real fear lay with Ngo Tien. As worried and as angry as they were, they dared not move against the man who paid their salaries. Not yet.

"I will discuss your various concerns with my superiors and let you know—"

A sudden uproar in the corridor derailed his train of thought. He heard a woman scream, and men were cursing, shouting, as they jostled one another in the hall. Diep slid back his chair, rising to his feet.

"A moment, please, while I investigate the cause of this disturbance."

"Could it be Carlotti?"

"He wouldn't dare."

"You want to bet your life on that?"

"Be quiet! You are in no danger here."

But was that necessarily the truth? As Diep approached the office door, he wondered whether Don Carlotti might try to wipe out competition with a blow directed at its source. Disruption of the studio would be a setback in Tien's campaign to dominate pornography in Southern California, and while it wouldn't wipe him out, by any means, it just might be the final straw that pushed him toward retaliation for the insults they had all suffered recently.

Diep, however, had more immediate concerns. Like the preservation of his stock, equipment, personnel. Survival might become a problem if Carlotti's troops were trying to invade the studio, but he would deal with that concern when it was verified. Experience reminded Diep that he would probably discover several of his players bickering—or even brawling—over some imagined grievance. Actors seldom came equipped with even tempers, and the sort he had to deal with were, at best, erratic.

Putting on the stern face of a father forced to discipline unruly children, Dan Diep stepped into the corridor... and realized that, somehow, he had lost control.

"WHAT'S GOING ON in here?"

The guy followed Bolan's thumb in the direction of a door that had been numbered 2. The door was closed, but moaning sounds were audible from somewhere on the other side.

"We're shooting," Pasty Face replied.

"Oh, yeah? Is this the kiddie show?"

The doorman swallowed hard. "I wouldn't know. If you'll just step this way..."

"*You* step that way. I need to roust these numskulls out of here before they wind up with a starring role in *Mr. Mugshot Goes Downtown*."

"Hold on a second! You can't go—"

He went, ignoring further protests from the doorman, barging in on the production of another hard-core epic. Number 2 had been designed to simulate a stable, from the look of things, with bales of hay piled all around and bridles draped across a makeshift stall partition. In the stall itself two "cowboys" wearing fancy gun belts over birthday suits were going through their paces with a busty "farmer's daughter." Bolan's presence didn't seem to break their concentration, but he drew a nasty grimace from a pasty AC/DC-type who occupied a cheap director's chair.

"Oh, cut, for heaven's sake!" The Milquetoast's voice was heavy with exasperation. "This is still a closed set, darling."

"It just opened, sweetheart." Bolan brushed the bearded cameraman aside and moved to catch a better view of the performers, keeping everyone in sight. "The heat's arriving shortly, and I wouldn't want your people here to get caught with their pants down, if you catch my drift."

"The heat? Oh, shit, that's a wrap! Get dressed, my children! Get the hell out, *now*! I'll be in touch."

Before the stars could get themselves untangled, their director was a memory, the folding chair tucked underneath his arm. The cameraman was busy breaking down his gear, apparently accustomed to such interruptions.

"Shake it up," Bolan growled at no one in particular, already moving toward the door. "If the vice boys catch you here, you're on your own."

The female lead was on her feet, jiggling with righteous indignation, everything in motion simultaneously. "Hey," she bawled at his retreating back, "I've got my First Amendment rights!"

"So take them with you," Bolan snapped. "Throw in a quarter, and you can get yourself a cup of coffee."

Pasty Face was waiting for him in the hallway, shifting nervously from one foot to the other, worrying a ragged fingernail between his teeth. "I really ought to clear this up with Mr. Diep."

"So clear it, Alice." Bolan jabbed a finger toward the door of Number 3. "You got another party going on in here?"

"They're shooting, but you really shouldn't—"

"Bullshit! If I wait for you to bring your boss around, you'll all be blowing kisses to me from the back seat of a black-and-white."

The second set was more conventional, a bed at center stage and actors simulating passion, with the woman top-side, working, while her partner rolled his eyes and tried to match her rhythm.

"Break time!" Bolan shouted, grinning as the lady missed her mark and toppled sideways, cursing. The director was a wiry Hispanic, dressed in black from head to pointy, patent leather toes, and he was scowling as he moved to intercept the Executioner.

"Hey, what the fuck you think you're doing, man? You got a problem? You can't see we're busy here? I oughta kick your ass for messing up that take!"

Bolan broke the weasel's nose, the blow dislodging custom shades and dropping the indignant artist on his butt, blood streaming through his fingers as he clapped hands to his face.

"Heads up!" he told the others, as they gaped at him in wonder. "We're expecting critics from the vice squad shortly. If you're not prepared to argue ratings with them, I suggest you grab your socks and tell your story walking."

In an instant, they were scrambling past him, the performers struggling into jeans and T-shirts on the way. Bolan saw that no one cared enough to bring the film's director with them. In the corridor he looked around for Pasty Face but couldn't find him, wondered if his guide had finally gone in search of the elusive Mr. Diep.

He tried the door on Number 1, revealing a vacant room that had been stripped of furnishings in preparation for another film to come. He moved along the hall to Number 4 and poked his head inside, immediately riveted by chintzy curtains, the diminutive bed, scattered toys on the floor.

Bolan's stomach was churning as he retreated and closed the door softly behind him. Peripheral movement alerted him, brought him around, and he saw Pasty Face drawing near with an Asian in tow.

"Here he is, Mr. Diep."

The Vietnamese wore the face of grim death. "May I ask who you are?" he inquired. "And your reason for being here?"

"Sure," Bolan told him. "I came here to shut your ass down."

CHAPTER SIX

Dan Diep didn't flinch, but he froze for an instant, face deadpan, before the sneer surfaced. "I see."

"I don't think so."

"You showed my assistant a badge, I believe. I have not seen a search warrant."

"Ah, my mistake."

The Beretta was warm in his hand as he leveled the sights on Diep's forehead. "Think this'll do?"

Diep appeared on the verge of a comeback, but common sense beat out bravado. He settled for silence, and shot hateful glances at Pasty Face, laying the blame for his present embarrassment squarely upon his assistant.

"No children today?" Bolan asked. "What's the story? You break for the back-to-school sales?"

"I don't know what you're talking about," Diep responded, his jaws clenched in anger.

"You don't? Well, let's clear that up, shall we? A mogul like you ought to know what's been happening in his own studio."

Bolan grabbed Diep's lapel, jerked him off balance and put enough spin on the move to propel him past Number 2, on toward the children's room. Pasty Face followed without his assistance, convinced by the 93-R and the prospect of swift, sudden death.

"Go in," Bolan urged. "It's not locked."

When his hostage was slow to respond, Bolan cocked the Beretta and picked out a target a few inches south of Diep's belt buckle.

"No, wait!" Diep stepped into the child's room, his aide-de-camp trailing, with Bolan the plug in the bottleneck.

"What do you smell?"

"Disinfectant."

"Wrong answer. That's misery, pal, and you're the cause. I'm in charge of the cleanup, and I've got my own disinfectant, right here."

"Were you sent by Carlotti?"

"Don Giro? Now why would he send me to hassle a sweet guy like you?"

"I believe you know why."

"Maybe so." Bolan fished in a pocket, came out with a compact incendiary device the size of a ballpoint pen. "Either way, you've been served with your notice. This place is a memory."

"Wait!"

Bolan pitched the device over Diep's upraised hands, saw it bounce on the small bed, the coverlet catching at once. "Hang around, if you like," he told Pasty Face. "Who knows? It might help your tan."

Moving back down the corridor, Bolan looked in on the set of the Western and dropped off a fire stick amid bales of hay, left the door standing wide to encourage the flames. Diep was shouting a general alarm, and the warrior left him to it, retreating toward wide, curving stairs. Bolan made it, was on his way down, when a voice answered Diep from below, and another, then several at once. Angry voices, a few of them frightened, all male.

Bolan froze on the stairs, leaning over the banister, watching a dozen or so men mill around in the lobby. A couple had pistols in hand, and others were digging for hardware when one of them picked out the man on the staircase.

"Up there!"

Bolan squeezed off a 3-round burst, saw one man stagger and fall as the others scattered for cover. Return fire was spotty, a few rounds impacting on ceiling and walls, but he couldn't descend while they waited below him. A stun grenade would have been useful, but Bolan was traveling light, and his option—retreat—left him only the rear of the house, and he would be cut off from his wheels.

The warrior backpedaled, dodging a new burst of fire, and retreated the way he had come through the billowing smoke. He could hear gunners mounting the stairs, shouting questions and calling to Diep. They were careless, but still out of range. He tossed off a warning burst, pinning them down while he looked for an exit.

He passed by the Western set, holding his breath, eyelids narrowed to slits in the thick, acrid smoke. On the far side, he saw Diep and Pasty Face standing together, alerted by the gunfire that echoed and barked on the stairs. Clouds of smoke from the children's set sealed off the end of the corridor, masking Bolan's view of the windows and doorways beyond. Diep was holding a small fire extinguisher, foam and soot streaking his clothing, bitter hatred reflected behind gimlet eyes.

"I will see you again," the producer declared.

"In your nightmares."

He ducked into Number 3, skirted the bed with its rumpled sheets, ripped the cheap curtains from the double-hung window. He slid the pane open and kicked off the screen, using one precious moment to lean out across the sill, gauging the drop. It was fifteen feet, give or take, placing his touchdown in flowers and mulch, but he'd run out of options. Outside in the corridor several voices had answered Diep's hail, and the gunners would be on him in moments.

He holstered his side arm and slid one leg over the sill, holding on to the sash with one hand as the second leg followed. Behind him a silhouette burst through the doorway as Bolan pushed off into free-fall, the earth rushing up to receive him. He landed feet foremost and folded, allowing momentum to carry him out of the shrubs in a tight shoulder roll. By the time head and shoulders were thrust through the window above him, he was sprinting for safety, wild rounds gouging turf at his heels.

The Executioner hit the fence running and scrambled over, scourging his palms in the process and snagging his slacks on a nail. Fabric tore, blood was drawn, but he cleared the top after a heartbeat's delay, landing in the alley.

Behind him and muffled by distance, he could hear Diep urging his troops to keep up the chase. Bolan had moments to decide on his next move, and he knew none of the choices was good. He could strike off on foot, or he could attempt to regain his own vehicle, risking a dead-end collision with enemy guns in the process.

Before he could make up his mind, a sleek sports car roared into the alley and screeched to a halt on the gravel beside him. The drop top was lowered and Bolan had palmed the Beretta, was lined up to take out the wheelman when something restrained him. The driver, a lovely young woman with dark, flowing hair, snapped a glance at the pistol and shouted, "Get in!"

It was Bolan's best offer thus far. He scrambled around to the passenger's side, barely settled on tuck-and-roll leather before she reversed, rubber smoking, and shot backward into the street. Pure, dumb luck gave her two empty lanes, and she ran through the gears, tortured tires finding traction and squealing in protest.

Bolan checked the lady out, discovered she was Asian, probably Vietnamese. "I've got a car out on the street," he told her.

"Fair enough."

They reached the corner, took it on two wheels and hurtled toward his rental three doors down. Across the street a group of student types were just unloading from an ancient station wagon, milling on the curb outside an apartment house. They swiveled toward the sportster, a couple of them pointing as the driver locked her brakes.

"I owe you one," the warrior told her.

"Nonsense, Mr. Bolan."

One foot on the pavement, Bolan froze. "I beg your pardon?"

"I don't think you have the time." She flashed a winning smile. "But if you'd care to follow me . . ."

"Where to?"

"A safe place. Guaranteed."

Behind him warning shouts were audible from the direction of Tien's studio. He caught a glimpse of movement in the doorway, made up his mind as a pair of gunners burst onto the porch.

"You lead," he said.

"You're on."

She waited while he slid behind the rental's steering wheel and fired the engine, pulling out ahead of Bolan as he dropped the four-door into gear. No less than half a dozen men were pouring down the walkway now, a couple of them veering off across the lawn to intercept him. But they couldn't afford to use their guns in front of witnesses. Bolan offered them a jaunty wave as he pulled away, accelerating in the sports car's wake.

He had no fear of being followed at the moment. From appearances the gunners would be parked behind the studio and, by the time they reached their cars, he would be out of sight. They might have seen his license plate, though, and he made a mental note to ditch the car, make contact with another rental agency as soon as possible.

Before that, however, there was still the problem of the woman and her appearance on the scene in Bolan's hour of need. Coincidence was one thing, Good Samaritans another, but she knew his *name* and that set off alarm bells inside the soldier's skull.

A trap?

There seemed to be no other explanation, but a trap arranged by whom? And to what purpose? No one should have known that he was in the area, and if his enemies were somehow made aware of his arrival, he couldn't imagine any reason for the strange, oblique approach. If Ngo Tien had known about his plans to hit the studio, for instance, wouldn't the Asian have laid on extra guns instead of helping Bolan to escape?

He wondered if the woman's ethnic stock might hold the key to a solution, but without more clues to work from, Bolan had to give up playing Sherlock. He'd been investigating Asian gangs in San Francisco when the call from Leo Turrin came, and he was facing them again in Orange County. More coincidence? Had Bolan's adversaries to the north somehow alerted Tien? And if they had, against all odds, where did the woman come in?

The obvious solution to his problem was a simple one: he merely had to keep the red convertible in sight and follow where she led, taking special care to watch for any signs of ambush. When the woman told her story he would know if she deserved his thanks.

Another fifteen minutes saw them safely out of Irvine, running north and west on Highway 405 through Costa Mesa, Fountain Valley, into Westminster. The sportster caught an off ramp, cruising north along Beach Boulevard, and Bolan followed her to Buena Park, another thirty minutes as the traffic crawls. His guide led Bolan through a winding maze of residential streets, the soldier focusing on landmarks all the way, until she pulled into the parking lot of an apartment complex facing toward the Santa Ana Freeway. The Executioner followed her around back and watched her park beneath a metal awning. When she waved him toward the empty space beside her own, he shrugged and backed his vehicle in, allowing for a rapid getaway if necessary.

"Won't your neighbor need his parking space?"

"They moved last week. I don't believe in waste. Do you?"

"That all depends."

"On what?"

"On who gets wasted."

Bolan followed her across a narrow strip of dying lawn and up a flight of stairs to her apartment. Silence met them as they entered, but he spent a moment checking out the four small rooms, one hand on the Beretta in its rigging. She was waiting, watching him as he rejoined her in the living room.

"You strike me as a careful man."

"I try to be."

"So, how'd you blow it with Dan Diep?"

He countered with a question of his own. "You know the guy?"

"I know a lot of people."

"One too many, possibly."

Her laughter had the ring of tinkling crystal. "I don't think so, Mr. Bolan. Can I call you Mack?"

"I don't know what to call you yet."

"My name is Lisa Ky. A drink? I'm having wine."

"No, thanks."

He took a seat at one end of the sofa, which permitted him to watch the door without exposing himself to any hostile eyes outside the sliding windows of her balcony. Despite the fact that they were on the second floor, with no tall buildings close at hand, he wasn't taking chances. Lisa poured herself a glass of wine and joined him on the couch.

"Let's start at the beginning, shall we? I'm a journalism major—or, I *was*—at Cal State, Long Beach. Anyway, I'm taking a semester off to get the feel of working in the business, handling the news, you follow?"

"So far, but I don't see where we're going."

"Patience. I've been working up a series on the Asian Mafia, whatever experts might be calling it this week. My special interest lies with Ngo Tien, Anh Giap, and their apparent stranglehold on the Vietnamese community. That's how I know about Dan Diep, their nasty little studio, assorted other goodies on the side."

"Okay, that's half an answer."

Lisa sipped her wine and smiled. "You're curious about how I know *you*."

He nodded, waiting.

"As I told you, Mack, I'm into journalism. *Everybody* knows Mack Bolan."

"Everybody doesn't know where they can pick him up at half past four on Friday afternoon."

"Oh, that."

"Yeah. That."

"I must confess, my interest isn't limited to Tien and his associates. I guess you could say I've been a fan of yours since high school. I've collected stories, built a dossier of sorts. The past few months I've had some thoughts about a book."

"Forget it, Lisa, it's been done."

"I know. I thought the treatise out of Princeton was a lot of crap."

He couldn't hold back the smile. "I had a similar opinion, but they say the subject of analysis can't always analyze himself objectively."

"More crap. But you were right about the book. I'd need a special angle if I ever hoped to make a sale."

"An angle like 'The Day I Saved the Executioner'?"

"It's catchy, but I honestly had something else in mind."

"Which brings us back to how and why."

"The how's no problem. I've got contacts in the media, remember? I'm a working girl with access to the wires. I knew you were in San Francisco even though the networks haven't put it all together yet. Go on and call it intuition, if you like. I *knew* and, from the other news up north, I had a fair idea of why."

"That doesn't answer how."

"My local contacts are as much within the refugee community as with the press. I know about Lao Fan—does that surprise you?—and I'm aware that he's been agitating every law-enforcement agency within a hundred miles to make a move on Tien. So far he's come up empty and the syndicate is laughing at him, but he has a hard corps of believers, followers, in the community. It stood to reason that if one means didn't work, he'd try another."

"I'm still waiting for the how."

"Perhaps I should have mentioned that I know about your previous connection with Lao Fan from Vietnam."

The soldier felt the short hairs of his neck stirring, and knew he wasn't sitting in a draft. This woman was barely old enough for recollections of the war itself, forget about specifics of assorted covert operations in the DMZ. Her source was dangerously well-informed, but where in hell had she obtained such ancient data?

"You've been talking to Lao Fan?"

"We've never met, although I've seen him several times."

"I'm curious about your sources."

"Yes, I thought you might be. But I haven't finished answering your question as to how I knew that you were here."

"I'm listening."

"The plain truth is, I started following Lao Fan. I knew he'd meet with someone, even if he had to try recruiting gunmen of his own. He's tricky, but I tailed him out to Long Beach, and I recognized you on the spot."

"Your contacts in the media again?"

She nodded. "Texas jailers take a lousy photograph, in terms of art and composition, but they serve quite well for cinching an ID."

"And when we split, you followed me to Irvine?"

"Bingo. Once you hit the general neighborhood, I knew Dan Diep must be the target. Did you kill him?"

"No."

"Why not?"

The Executioner ignored her question, turning it around. "You've answered how you found me. I'm still waiting for the why."

"Could be I think your method is the only hope for rooting out Tien's parasites."

"Could be... but I don't buy it."

"You're a clever man. I guess I shouldn't dance around the subject any longer."

"I've been getting tired just watching you."

She forced a laugh, but she clearly wasn't feeling jovial. "All right. I have a special interest, shall we say. And no one in the local refugee community informed me of your wartime contacts with Lao Fan."

"Go on."

"This isn't easy for me, Mack. I'm sorry." Lisa hesitated, and he could have sworn that she was blushing. "I can't call you that. It doesn't work, okay?"

"Okay." He waited while she pulled herself together, putting jumbled thoughts in order.

"I know something of your business with Lao Fan, because I heard the story from my mother when we lived in Vietnam."

"Your mother?"

Lisa nodded. "She was called Luan Ky."

Bolan felt as if a solid right had landed in his solar plexus, paralyzing lungs and heart, everything at once, preventing him from drawing breath.

"You recognize the name," she pressed. "I see it in your eyes."

"I recognize the name."

"I'm told that I resemble her...I mean, when she was my age."

"Yes." He saw it now and wondered how he could have failed to see it instantly.

"She's dead, you know."

"I didn't, but I'm sorry."

"My survival is her legacy...and yours."

He waited for the other shoe to drop, a silent scream unwinding in the vacuum of his soul.

"I couldn't watch and let them kill you," Lisa whispered. "Could I, Father?"

CHAPTER SEVEN

Saigon, South Vietnam

Eric Crane couldn't stop staring at the woman from across the crowded barroom. She caught his eye despite the haze of smoke and general confusion of the place, her beauty rendering the journalist as close as he would ever come to being speechless.

"There's a classic."

Sergeant Mack Bolan sipped his beer and spent a moment studying the room. He picked out the woman at once, and he didn't have to ask the correspondent whom he had in mind. "She works here," Bolan told him. "Waitress."

"She's a classic, all the same."

A short day back from covert action in the north, the Executioner was not inclined to disagree. The waitress seemed to hold herself aloof from her surroundings, smiling when she had to, dodging eager hands. Mack Bolan had been in the bar before, although he generally sought a less frenetic atmosphere, and he remembered idly watching as she worked the room.

The room was *all* she worked, according to prevailing scuttlebutt, and while some cocktail waitresses found ways to supplement their income on their backs, this one had earned a reputation as "the Ice Maiden," one who drew the line at taking GIs home. If Bolan ever knew her name, he had forgotten it.

"So give," the journalist was prodding him. "I know you had to be on something hot. You must have *something* for the folks back home."

"'Fraid not. You'll have to go through channels if you want a scoop on this one."

"Channels!" Crane made no attempt to hide his scorn. "With all respect, your 'channels' make me feel a little like a mushroom."

"I don't follow."

"Everybody keeps me in the dark and feeds me bullshit."

Bolan chuckled, drained his beer and flagged the nearest waitress for another round. "You might have heard, we're in the middle of a war here, Eric. Some operations just don't fall within the category of the public's sacred 'right to know.'"

"I'll buy that, Sergeant. Hell, I know about security and classified material and all the other goodies. I'm all for it, but I've got a problem. What the hell am I supposed to do for *stories*?"

Bolan grinned. "Why don't you make them up like everybody else?"

"Low blow, my friend." At least a portion of the journalist's offense was alcohol-induced, another measure of it feigned. "A few of us are trying to report the truth about this war, and I regret to say that we're not getting much cooperation from the brass."

From anybody else it might have sounded phony and contrived, but Bolan knew Eric Crane and recognized sincerity behind the beery bluster. Within the past few weeks he had acquired a sneaking admiration for the journalist, but they hadn't started off as friends.

Upon arrival in Saigon Crane had been the classic liberal reporter, with a large left-handed ax to grind. Committed to the concept of a war immoral in itself, he'd been quick to criticize American involvement in an Asian "civil war" and was adept at sniffing out reports of military negligence, brutality, corruption. Crane had never tampered with the facts, the Executioner would give him that, although his

editorial opinions frequently appeared to have no contact
with reality. Some journalists in Nam were more adept at
manufacturing the news than just reporting it, with empha-
sis on American-South Vietnamese "atrocities." When
Crane laid down a story, it was straight enough, and Bolan
differed from the newsman only in the long view, his assessment of how isolated incidents compared to the importance of the conflict as a whole.

Mack Bolan cherished no illusions that the South Vietnamese regime or its American supporters were a band of
squeaky-clean philanthropists. Corruption was endemic in
the area of Asian politics, on both sides of the Bamboo
Curtain, and no army mustered in the course of human history had ever been without its share of misfits, fast-buck
artists, psychopaths who saw their duty posting as a license
to go hunting humans. In his time the Executioner had been
obliged to drop the net on several of his fellow soldiers—
three of them were facing charges in the death of a civilian—but he also knew the stakes in Vietnam, the dangers
that arose from standing back and watching while the savages consumed another nation, unopposed.

Eric Crane had failed to see the soldier's logic, looking at
the war through eyes conditioned by a New York desk job
and the pseudoliberal cocktail party circuit. He couldn't
adapt his viewpoint to include "the other side"... at least
he hadn't managed prior to joining Bolan in the field one
night eight weeks before.

"I understand you've got yourself a monicker," he'd said
when they were introduced.

"Which one?"

"The Executioner."

"It fits, sometimes."

"You have—what is it?—eighty kills?"

"I don't keep score."

"Somebody does."

"I'm here to do a job. I don't play numbers games."

"I'd like to watch you do your job."

"Why's that?"

The journalist had shrugged. "Let's say I need to get another angle on what happens in the field."

"I've read your stories, Mr. Crane. I'd say you have your angle down already."

"Hey, let's make it Eric, okay? And I can call you—"

"Sergeant."

"Sure." His grin had nearly slipped but Crane retrieved it with an effort. "Is there any reason why I shouldn't tag along with you sometime? I mean, *all* your work can't be classified."

"I'd have to clear it up through channels," Bolan told him. "And I couldn't guarantee your safety."

"No one asked you to."

"We don't run routine missions, Crane. No three klicks out and find a shady place to sit and wait for Charlie. We're a penetration team. You slow us down, we leave you for the regulars."

"Don't worry, Sergeant. I've been out with SEALs and Special Forces in the past few months. I'm still around."

"Are *they*?"

"Your confidence is overwhelming."

"Face it, guy, before this afternoon you were a byline, nothing more. This little chat does not—repeat, does not—mean that we know each other. Are you reading me?"

"You're loud and clear."

"All right. We've got a project coming up that might be suitable. I can't go into details with you now, but it's the kind of thing you might find interesting."

"Try me."

Clearance had been swift, and Bolan later learned that Crane had called some markers in to get himself a ride with Pen-Team Able. They were airborne, out of Tan Son Nhut, before the Executioner had briefed him on their mission and their destination.

"Some call it the Steel Circle," Bolan advised, "but you won't find a fortress, per se. There are tunnels and bunkers, staging areas, occupied villages. Charlie's run free in the district for so long the peasants are getting fed up with it. Some of them want to relocate, but that doesn't fit the VC propaganda plan. Lately the mayors and headmen have been catching hell. We have word that a column of sappers are planning to 'punish' a village tomorrow at dawn."

"And you've got a surprise party cooking?"

"You guessed it. With luck we can head off a massacre, maybe trace Charlie back home to his base camp and kick his ass there."

"You're ambitious."

"Just hopeful."

Their LZ was four kilometers away from the village, allowing for touchdown and dustoff without major risk of alerting the lookouts whom Charlie was certain to post in advance of a raid. It was dusk when the choppers set down, and full dark in the forest as Bolan led out seven hand-picked commandos and Crane trailing behind him in single file.

They were a full kilometer away from their target when Bolan knew something was wrong. The report of small-arms fire, reduced by the distance between them until it was scarcely an echo, and then Bolan picked up the first transient odor of smoke on the breeze. They were too late; he knew it as well as he knew his own name. Charlie's schedule had shifted, for reasons they might never know, and the village was under attack even now as they slogged through the forest.

Too late and still they had a job to finish. Bolan passed a warning down the line and tried to pick up his pace, hampered by the need to check the trail for booby traps and signs of ambush. It was still slow going, and the sounds of automatic fire had died away before they covered half a kilometer, the scent of burning stronger now, pervasive as the night wind blew a draft of smoke in their direction.

Much too late the Executioner had realized as they approached the village from the south, each member of the team alert with M-16 or Nikon camera as they broke the tree line, moving through ashes of the village they had come to save. There had been thirty hootches, give or take, but it was difficult to count them now that they had all been razed. The Vietcong had used scorched-earth strategy and they'd been effective.

The streets of the disaster area were littered with dead livestock, which had been reamed by automatic weapons fire. For a moment Bolan thought the raiders might have been content with leveling the village, slaughtering its stock, without annihilating human residents. That pipe dream dissipated when they finished their preliminary sweep and found the ditch.

From all appearances the village occupants had been compelled to dig their own mass grave. The ditch was nearly thirty feet in length, ten wide and nearly six deep. It must have taken hours to dig, and Bolan tried to put himself inside the minds of the intended victims, searching for a vestige of the horror they must have felt as they prepared themselves for death.

Beside him Crane was studying the twisted bodies with a sick expression on his face. The grim eyes lingered over women, children, old men, arms and legs entwined, blood mingling as it soaked into the thirsty earth.

"Why aren't you taking pictures?"

"What? Oh . . . yeah."

The Nikon's flash was like a burst of summer lightning, leeching color from the huddled corpses even as it captured them on film. The newsman shot a full roll on the grave then used another on the village proper, snapping ashes, shattered crockery, the flaccid shapes of dogs and chickens, goats and buffalo. He had the final shot lined up when Private Loudelk checked in from a sweep of the perimeter.

"Due north," he told the Executioner. "Just like you thought. We knock on it, I'd say we have a decent chance to fry their asses."

"Crane! We're going in pursuit. I think you ought to sit it out."

"No way. I mean...I want to see what kind of men could do this."

"Fair enough, but if you fall behind—"

"I'm on my own. No problem, Sergeant. This is one I can't afford to miss."

They followed Loudelk's lead and found that Charlie had been daring, even reckless, in his passage through the jungle. Sated with their recent victory against an unarmed adversary, the guerrillas didn't booby-trap the trail or set out flankers to protect their rear. If anything, they seemed intent on advertising their responsibility for the annihilation of a peaceful village, certain that the massacre would serve as an example to their other shaky allies in the region.

After half an hour Bolan knew where they were headed, and the men of Pen-Team Able picked up speed. If Crane was losing it he gave no sign, and Bolan nursed a sneaking admiration for the journalist, in spite of the opinions that divided them. There was a man behind the propaganda smoke screen, and the Executioner believed the reporter might be worth knowing if he got the chance. And there weren't many journalists the big man cared to know.

The bunkers moved from time to time, but these had been picked out by aerial reconnaissance ten days before, a target marked for demolition at some future time. Inside the Steel Circle Charlie acted like a rich man in his castle, moving where and when he pleased, but that mobility, the grand illusion of security, was purchased with the sweat and blood of peasants who were forced to help in digging tunnels, fortifying bunkers, storing arms and ammo against a future rainy day. For every willing volunteer there was a slave compelled to work at gunpoint, who was well aware that human life and suffering meant nothing to the Vietcong.

The leader of the VC raiding party had been wise enough to post a pair of sentries at the base camp. Corporal Zitka took one down without a whimper; Loudelk iced the other, creeping up on him like silent Death and cutting off his wind with hands like iron claws. The other brave VC were busy patting one another on the back, reliving all the glory of their recent conquest.

Silently the Executioner deployed his troops for battle, keeping Crane beside him where the journalist could be, for the moment, relatively safe. There would be no safe havens once the fight was joined, and Bolan had been gratified to note that few of their opponents had retired to sleeping quarters in the bunkers. Doors had been left open, beckoning, and with a little luck, the critical advantage of surprise, they might achieve a swift, clean sweep.

Eight weapons roared in concert, tumblers slashing through the flesh of their human targets. Pen-Team Able gave no warning, sought no quarter, took no prisoners. The skirmish was a vengeance mission, pure and simple, with the vestige of a lesson thrown in for those terrorists who cared to see. A dozen Communists went down before the first barrage, their startled comrades scrambling for the safety of the bunkers or the forest, only to discover grim Death waiting for them there, as well. Grenades lit white-hot thermite conflagrations in the bunkers, human torches lurching through the exits into tight converging streams of automatic fire. In eighty seconds it was finished, eerie silence settling across a killing ground, which stank of roasting flesh.

More photographs as Crane moved out among the dead. When he returned to Bolan's side his eyes were hollow, haunted. "Welcome to the *real* war," Bolan said.

The journalist had tried to force a smile, failed miserably, gave it up. "I think I understand."

And in his later columns Crane had demonstrated understanding of the larger issues that apparently surprised the man himself on some occasions. He could still sniff out a PX scandal with the best of them, and he was known to scourge the brass for their inflated body counts, but there was greater balance in his writing now, an effort to acquaint the public with a war that had two sides.

There had been other missions, other forays into darkness, and a bond had formed between the hunter and the news hawk. They might still agree to disagree on certain points of policy, but they were in accord concerning the necessity of standing fast against the savages. Whatever else the jungles taught Eric Crane, he knew now that survival was at stake.

"She's perfect." Crane's words brought the warrior back to the here and now.

"No one's perfect," Bolan answered, working on another beer. But she was close, he had to give the scribbler that.

A trio of Marines were getting grabby, but the waitress managed to avoid their hands as she had managed to elude so many others in the past. She kept her smile in place when they got ugly, snarling at her, calling for a different waitress. Bolan washed the incident away and spent a moment studying the faces that surrounded him. Approximately half were servicemen, the rest Vietnamese who made their living out of catering to men in uniform. He picked out prostitutes and pushers, con men on the make, the denizens of a nocturnal world that consuls and ambassadors would never see.

The soldier took it in, digested it and let it go. He hadn't been assigned to monitor the morals of the natives or the life-styles of his own compatriots. He was a fighting man, and as such Bolan recognized the need for relaxation in between the battles, a compulsion to unwind that took as many different forms as there were men in combat. Some retreated into books, some into bottles; others found relief in target practice, calisthenics, drugs or sex. A few appeared to hold their edge around the clock, and Bolan knew that they were walking time bombs, ticking toward a detonation that, with any luck at all, he wouldn't be around to witness.

Closing time and Bolan realized that it was nearly dawn. The night had been a blur, and while he wasn't drunk, he felt the pressure of a few too many beers behind his eyes. Emerging from the smoky bar was like a small rebirth, his nostrils instantly responding to the different scents of cooking food and recent rain.

"I'm wasted," Crane informed him, frowning like a freshman who has lost his homework. "Hell, I should have knocked off hours ago."

"There's nothing wrong with you that a couple quarts of coffee wouldn't fix."

"It's coming up, I promise you."

"Some bacon?" Bolan prodded him. "They fix it nice and greasy at the mess hall."

"Damn you!"

As they passed an alley they were distracted from their banter by a shrill, abbreviated scream. The sound of slapping blows immediately followed, with a coarse male voice demanding silence, ordering compliance.

"What the hell?"

Before the soldier could respond, Eric Crane was off the sidewalk disappearing into darkness. Bolan followed him, the beery haze retreating as he put his mind in combat mode.

It was the Vietnamese waitress cornered near a garbage bin by the three Marines she had rejected in the bar. One of them had her arms pinned, while the others pressed around her, pulling at her clothing, sliding brutal hands beneath.

"What's going on here?" Crane demanded, reaching out to rest his left hand on the shoulder of one would-be rapist.

The Marine didn't respond in words. Instead, he pivoted and drove an angry fist into the newsman's solar plexus. In the circumstances it wasn't the best approach, which he discovered when a stream of vomit splattered in his face.

"God*damn* it!"

Crane was down and gagging when the Executioner stepped in. He gave the soggy leatherneck an elbow shot that broke his nose on impact, snapping off his top incisors at the gum line. Whirling to face his second adversary, writing off the guy who had his hands full, Bolan dodged a looping right and bored in underneath the swing. His knuckles beat a fast tattoo against the other's ribs, his victim folding, primed and ready for the knee that rose to meet his face with stunning impact.

Number three had tried to push the girl away, but it wasn't that easy. She had turned upon him, cursing, clawing at his face, and the Marine was ducking, dodging, trying to protect himself from nails that had gouged long furrows in his cheek. At last, in drunken rage, he hit the lady with a straight-arm shot that rocked her on her heels and nearly took her down. The bully was prepared to follow through when Bolan clapped big hands against the Marine's ears and watched the snarling lips fall open in a silent scream. The roundhouse kick was frequently a lethal move, but Bolan pulled it at the final instant, satisfied to break the big man's jaw and leave him groaning in the litter of the alleyway.

The woman didn't speak as Bolan turned to Crane and helped him to his feet. She followed them in the direction of the alley's mouth but hesitated as they reached the street.

"You cannot take him back to base like that," she said, surprising Bolan with her deft command of English, her avoidance of singsong chant and vulgar slang that often passed for conversation in Cholon.

"It's fine. He's just a writer."

Crane responded with a feeble growl of indignation. "Just a writer! What the hell is that supposed to mean?"

"It is not far to where I live," the lady continued. "Your friend could rest and get his strength back."

"I could use some strength here, Sergeant."

Bolan finally agreed and trailed the woman down a narrow side street, two blocks farther to a two-room, walk-up flat. She brewed a pot of aromatic tea, and Crane was badgered into downing half a dozen cups before he started to regain his old vitality.

"I guess we showed those bastards, didn't we?"

"You showed them," she agreed. "I wish to thank you both."

"Forget it," Bolan said.

The woman shook her head in an emphatic negative. "I cannot. You have saved my honor, and perhaps my life. Such things are not forgotten."

"Fine. I'll settle for another cup of tea."

She called herself Luan Ky, and when she smiled the Executioner believed that Crane was right. This one was perfect.

Bolan had returned to the bar the next evening on his own. Recuperating from his rest and relaxation, looking forward to an outing with the Rangers, Crane had begged off with a show of mock indignation. "There you go," he had complained. "You guys in uniform are always stealing girls from me. If I was smart, I'd sell this frigging camera and sign up for basic training."

Bolan walked Luan home that evening, and the next. The first time she asked him in, he had declined, refusing to take advantage of her momentary gratitude. The next time Bolan had agreed, but he made no aggressive forays as they sat together on the swaybacked sofa, drinking tea and sharing thoughts about the war. Luan had lost a brother in the Tet offensive, and neither of her parents long survived the death of their firstborn. On the third night Bolan walked her home; when he reached for her she went into his arms with all the ardor of a drowning person who finds a life preserver suddenly within reach.

For thirteen nights they were inseparable. Bolan had seen Crane but briefly in that time and when the newsman wished him well with Luan he thought the words had been sincere. A summons to the north with Pen-Team Able called a temporary halt to their affair, and on returning from the DMZ the Executioner had found a cable waiting for him. Bolan's parents and his sister had been killed at home in Pittsfield. His brother, Johnny, was in serious condition, but the doctors thought that he would live.

There would be memories of Luan Ky in the weeks and months to come, but Bolan's war had veered away from mainstream, following a different, solitary course. He could no more recapture thirteen days in Saigon than he could breathe life into the dead; his past was buried, and his future had been tinted crimson, daubed with blood. There had been nothing to suggest that Luan Ky carried life within her.

Nothing, until Lisa Ky had stepped into his life—no, *saved* his life—and named him as the father she had never seen.

CHAPTER EIGHT

"I never realized."

It sounded lame, but it was all that he could think of at the time.

"My mother didn't realize herself until you had been called away." Was there a hint of condemnation in her voice? And could he blame her if there was? "She learned of your departure from a friend of yours. A newsman, I believe."

Eric Crane? It fit, all right. Crane had briefly spoken to Bolan after the warrior received the telegram from Pittsfield. There'd been no time for detailed explanations, but the newsman knew that Bolan had been called home on a personal emergency. From what had followed in the headlines, Crane had learned the nature of the incident and Bolan's personal response. But in the meantime there had been ample opportunity for him to pass the word along. He could have seen Luan Ky, might even have gone looking for her with the news.

And had the correspondent known that she was pregnant? It was doubtful, given Luan Ky's almost bashful personality, that she would have revealed her secret, even to a friend. In time, of course, disclosure would have been inevitable, but he had no reason to believe that Crane had stayed in touch. Three months after Bolan's own departure, Eric was working on a major daily stateside handling the crime beat.

"How did your mother die?" The words caught in his throat and, when he finally got them out, they left him feeling hollow.

"She became involved with a resistance movement after Saigon fell. It was her job to find out certain information from police and military officers, about deployment of their men, that sort of thing. Most of the information was received in bed."

A frosty edge had crept into her voice and Bolan wondered if she blamed him, after all, for what had happened to her mother. Had he known that Luan was pregnant, would the fact have altered anything that he had done in Pittsfield or beyond? The soldier had no easy answer, and he saw no point in playing games with hypotheticals. He hadn't known, until this day, and there was nothing either one of them could do to change the past.

"The Communists began suspecting her when several of her 'clients' turned up dead or missing. As I understand it, use of prostitutes to gather information or arrange assassinations was an old, familiar tactic in Hanoi. She was arrested and interrogated, finally condemned. I saw her for the last time on the afternoon before her execution."

Lisa Ky had plainly used up all her tears, and she discussed her mother's death in much the way she might have summarized the news of famine in Ethiopia. She remained detached, almost aloof, and Bolan wondered whether screaming anger might not have been preferable in the circumstances. Anger, even hatred, he could cope with; cool indifference to the murder of a woman he had cared for, one who had imparted life to Lisa Ky, was something else again.

"You find me cold," she said, as if his thoughts had been spelled out in ten-point type across his forehead. "So I am, in some ways. As a child in Saigon I discovered that detachment was the best defense against life's pain and disappointment. By the time my mother died, I had already seen it coming. Can you understand?"

"I think so," he responded, wondering if it was true. With all that he had seen—and done—could Bolan comprehend the way a child becomes a woman under fire?

"How old were you when she was...when it happened?"

"Twelve. A few of mother's 'customers' were getting interested, but all that changed when she was brought to trial. You have to understand, no single person is convicted of sedition in the new 'republic.' If a man or woman is condemned for crimes against the state their family loses everything. I had no home, no friends that I could trust. I might have been arrested on some trumped-up charge, despite my age...and so I ran."

"Ran where?"

"The streets at first. Then Bangkok. You're familiar with the boat people, I think."

He nodded.

"Refugees were fleeing Vietnam before Saigon was captured by the Communists. The apparatus for escape was already in place, well tested, by the time I got around to using it. There were some doubts, at first, that we would be allowed to enter the United States, but here I am.

"As a child my mother told me stories of my father—in the war and afterward. Your various campaigns against the underworld were not unknown in Vietnam, and after Saigon fell the Communists enjoyed broadcasting news of crime in the United States. You know the kind of story, 'Crazy veteran of a losing war in Asia goes berserk at home,' that kind of thing.

"My mother warned me often not to speak about my father. As a small child, I believed she was ashamed, but later it was obvious the danger that we might have faced if anyone had known I was the daughter of the Executioner."

"I'm sorry."

"Don't be. It was really quite exciting, once I learned the knack of keeping secrets. All around me, there were children who had nothing to conceal, like little robots, learning how to love the state. I had a mystery wrapped up inside me, and the longer I kept it to myself, the stronger I became. Does that sound foolish?"

"No."

"An Asian family took me in when I arrived in the United States. They live in San Francisco, and I treat them as my parents, but they give me freedom to decide what I must do. They know my mother was a victim of the Communists, but that is all."

A hundred questions crowded Bolan's mind. He picked out one and let it go. "How did you find me, Lisa?"

"Everything I told you was the truth...well, more or less. I *am* a journalism major, and I *am* involved with members of the local refugee community attempting to collect hard information on Tien, Giap and the Thunder Dragons." Lisa hesitated. "But I know that isn't what you meant.

"A short time after I arrived in the United States, I learned that you were dead. Believed dead, I should say. Some kind of shoot-out in New York. It was old news before I heard about it, and I checked out papers in the library, on microfilm, to get the details. Somehow I felt worse than when my mother died. I'd lost my secret...I don't know. Whatever, I was in my freshman year of college when the news broke that you weren't dead after all. I still don't know how you pulled that one off, but I've been keeping track of you through news reports and any other way I could since then. I almost flew to Texas when I heard you were in jail down there, but you were gone before I raised the money for an airline ticket."

"Just as well," he said. "You don't want to associate your name with mine."

"Why not?"

He frowned. "If you've been following my press the way you claim, the answer should be obvious."

"I'm not afraid of dying, Father."

Bolan felt a chunk of ice begin its slow descent along his spine. "Okay. That doesn't mean you have to rush it, either. Everybody gets there in their own good time."

"I want to help you here in Orange County."

"Lisa—"

"Hear me out. I know Tien's operation, places you should visit. I can point them out to you, so there'll be no mistakes."

"You mentioned you've been following Lao Fan. If you've got all this information at your fingertips, why haven't you thrown in with him?"

"He doesn't know me, and he can't afford to trust a stranger now. For all he knows I might be sent by Ngo Tien to waste his time, or even get him killed. Besides, I had a private interest, and I knew he'd get in touch with you somehow."

"In fact, he didn't," Bolan told her. "It's a classic case of pure coincidence."

"So I got lucky," she responded, smiling. "I was overdue."

"What can you tell me that I don't already know about Tien's operation?"

"I've been cultivating one of Tien's best couriers. He wants me, and he thinks he can impress me into bed by telling me about his business. Does that shock you, Father?"

"No."

If she was disappointed by his answer, Lisa hid it well. "He took me on his rounds last week and showed me all his stops. I have a list of twenty-seven places where Tien receives his payoffs, stores illegal gambling machinery, you name it."

Bolan shook his head. "No sale. I've got more targets than I'll have the time to use already."

"Do you have the time and address for a major heroin delivery tomorrow? Did you get that from Lao Fan?"

The soldier frowned. "I'm listening."

"I thought you might be, but the information isn't free."

"Still listening."

"I meant it when I said I want to help the refugee community. Tien is like a millstone tied around their necks."

"I'm waiting for the 'but.'"

"Okay. The 'but' is this—I want the story when you're finished. An exclusive. Something that will put me on the map with local outlets, maybe networks."

"I don't have a public information office, Lisa."

"You could use one, but I'll settle for the possible. *This* story, tight and tidy, wrapped up in the bag before somebody turns it into *The Untouchables*."

"Sometimes these things don't work out tight and tidy. You sound like you've got the ending written in advance."

"Let's say that I've got confidence."

"It comes in handy," Bolan told her, "but too much of it can get you killed."

"I know my limitations."

"That's a start. I'll need that time and address."

Lisa blushed. "I don't exactly have it, at the moment."

"Oh? I guess we're wasting time."

"No, wait. I couldn't get the details out of Lee without...well, anyway, I thought that was supposed to be *your* specialty."

"His name is Lee?"

"Lee Kuan."

"And he's got all the information?"

"Absolutely."

"Well, I guess I ought to have a chat with Mr. Kuan."

"You mean we ought to have a chat."

"Forget it, Lisa. There's an outside chance I might not have to ~~kill~~ him for the information that I need. One look at you, and any chance he has—however slim—goes out the window."

"So? I mean, you came to kill these people, didn't you? It's what you do."

"And you're prepared to live with that?"

"I am."

"Okay, let's try this on for size, and you can take it as my final word. I will not have you in the way. Too many things could blow up in my face, and if that happens, I'll have all that I can handle looking after number one. You might be killed, or you might slow me down and get *me* killed."

"I'm sorry," Lisa said, "I didn't think it through. You'll still need someone though, to point him out."

"You have his address?"

She was frowning. "Yes, I do."

"Apartment number?"

"Yes."

"That's plenty. I can look him up tonight, or in the morning. Either way, there won't be any need to mount a harebrained cowboy operation on the street with innocent civilians in the line of fire."

"I see."

Was that a hint of disappointment in her tone? He wrote it off to failing hopes that she would play an active role in his campaign against Tien's operations in Orange County. Bolan hadn't grown accustomed to the notion of a daughter yet, and he wasn't about to risk her life in the pursuit of savages.

"About this story you intend to write," he said, "I'm interested in your hook, the angle you might use."

"Don't worry," Lisa answered, "I'm aware of all the risks that come with show-and-tell. It's not a father-daughter piece."

"I think that's wise."

She frowned. "I know that's wise. I've read your clips, remember? I'm into what you do, but I don't want to live it every day, with gangsters breathing down my neck and using me to draw you out."

"The way it stands, then, no one knows about...I mean, that we're...?"

"Related?" Lisa finished for him, smiling as she shook her head. "Nobody."

Bolan nodded, blotting out the mental images of others who had joined his personal crusade along the way and lost their lives as a result, the people who had been mistaken by his enemies for keys to bringing down the Executioner. He didn't need another burden on his soul. Not here. Not now. Above all, not his daughter.

He was having trouble with the concept, even after all that she had told him. It didn't seem possible that such a secret could endure through the years, without some clue, some flash of insight tipping him to the existence of a child. Somehow he had imagined that the fact of parenthood would be intuitively inescapable, the same way twins had been reported to communicate their joy and pain across long distances without a formal contact. He didn't believe in ESP, but he had experienced enough of life to understand that there were hidden bonds between the members of a family, unbreakable except, perhaps, in death. There had been times when Bolan had awakened from a troubled sleep, obsessed with the immediacy of an urge to call his brother, and on one or two occasions, Johnny had been grappling with a case where sage advice had come in handy. It wasn't telepathy, of course, but then again...

He thought about the child he'd never known. She was a woman now, and he had missed the precious growing years completely, caught up in a one-man holy war against the world at large. He wondered if she ever hated him for leaving her behind, abandoning her mother to a seedy life and early death. The mental image of Luan Ky in hostile hands made Bolan's skin crawl, and he pushed it out of mind. So long ago, and he was only learning now that she had given up her life in an attempt to halt the savages. Her death was an extension of his war, and there was nothing on God's earth that he could do to make it right.

"I wish—" *Wish what?* "Lisa, if I'd only known..."

"And what could you have done?" she asked. "Would you have brought my mother to America? Perhaps she could have joined you, and you could have settled down." There was a note of irony—or was it mockery?—in Lisa's voice. "I could have gone to public school in Pittsfield, or wherever. Right?"

He felt her eyes upon him, met her level gaze and simply answered, "No."

"All right, then, what's the difference?" There seemed to be no bitterness behind her words. "You took the only course available considering your personality, the circumstances. Others might have folded, looked for someplace safe to hide. You turned your loss around and made it count for something."

Lisa moved to sit beside him, took his hand in both of hers. "I had my father, in a way," she told him softly. "With the life I led in Vietnam it helped to have a secret all my own, that no one else could touch. And I was proud of you. I used to fantasize that someday... Well, it doesn't matter, does it?"

Bolan tried to clear his throat without phenomenal success. "It does to me. I should have been there for you, Lisa."

"Give yourself a break," she said. "You couldn't possibly have known. I don't hold anything against you, and it doesn't make much sense for you to lay a guilt trip on yourself."

"I can't do anything about your mother," Bolan told her, "but you have to understand, I won't allow you to become involved in what's about to happen here. I will not risk your safety—not for an exclusive story, or for any other reason."

Lisa thought about it for a moment, finally nodded. "I'd be foolish if I tried to tell you how to run your business. But I want that story, understand?"

His smile was wary. "I don't read tea leaves, but I wouldn't be surprised if certain inside information came your way in the next few days."

"That's all I ask."

"No promises," he cautioned. "Once an action's joined, it could go either way. Your scoop might wind up being an obituary."

Something close to panic flared in Lisa's eyes. "Don't say that!"

"A reporter should be braced for any possible conclusion to a story."

"I don't want to think about that now."

He smiled. "Me, neither." Bolan's stomach growled, as if to punctuate his comment. "What I'd like to think about right now, is dinner."

Lisa flashed a dazzling smile, rebounding from the morbid moment. "Hey, I'd ask you over, but you're here already. I can cook, you know?"

"I might have guessed."

"You like spaghetti?"

"Always have."

"The sauce may take a while, but it should give us time to get acquainted."

"Fine."

He watched her as she moved off toward the kitchen, separated from the parlor by a breakfast bar, and Bolan marveled at the life he had created with Luan Ky. Could she repay the universe, in some small measure, for the count-less lives he had taken? Was the very fact of her existence Bolan's reason for survival in the Asian hellgrounds? Did he finally, at long last, have a legacy to leave behind?

Another legacy, he thought. Before the child that he had never seen there was his war against the savages. That struggle justified itself, and Bolan sometimes thought it might be taking on a sort of independent life, that it might manage to survive him when he fell.

Two legacies. Dual gifts of life and death. How many men could look back on their own existence and declare as much? Just when he was convinced that life held no more rude surprises, he was proved wrong.

The soldier watched his daughter working in the kitchen. He listened to her chatter, responding automatically, his thoughts unfocused. When he closed his eyes, he saw Luan Ky.

CHAPTER NINE

Lisa Ky had given him the Anaheim address, and he had driven twice around the block, examining the high rise from all angles, noting that the owners billed it as "the perfect compromise between security and luxury." He wasn't interested in the luxury this evening, but security was something else.

He knew from experience that many large apartment houses these days had been transformed into scenic fortresses that required keys or special plastic cards to gain admittance. There were ways around such systems, but he didn't have the time or the equipment for clandestine entry if the building had sophisticated barriers in place. If necessary, he could always take his quarry on the street, but in the meantime he would take a closer look at Lee Kuan's home.

The parking lot was underground, and while an apartment key was needed to raise the wooden arm that blocked the entrance, there was nothing to prevent a man from slipping underneath or stepping easily across. Inside the place was lit by incandescent bulbs in tiny cages, spotted fifty feet apart in four long rows. The lighting granted Bolan ample shadow for concealment, and he wondered how the tenants ever bought their landlord's line about security. An army could have hidden in the underground garage, but getting there was only half the battle. He was still outside the complex proper, and he had to get inside to reach his prey.

Aside from its "secure" entry ramp, the dungeon had two exits, via elevator or a flight of stairs. The elevator could be summoned with a key to any one of several hundred flats, but that left Bolan out, and he could not afford to wait around for other tenants to leave. No witnesses meant no reprisals, and he counted on invisibility—the mystery it generated—to provide him with some combat stretch in Orange County.

Bending to the lock that kept the stairway door secure, he tried two different picks before he got it right. Before he closed the door again he tried the knob, made certain that he could release the inside latch whenever necessary. The security was a joke.

The number Lisa gave him indicated Kuan's apartment would be six floors up, and Bolan took his time, conserving energy, examining each floor in turn through tiny mirrors set into the numbered metal doors. On gaining access to the stairwell, Bolan found that he could disembark on any floor he chose without encountering another lock.

Strike three for "tight security."

On six he cracked the door and listened carefully for any sound of movement in the corridor beyond. It was approaching midnight—early by L.A. standards—and he didn't care to stumble over anyone returning from a dinner party. Silence greeted him, and after counting off two minutes Bolan stepped into the hallway and closed the stairwell door behind him.

In a complex organized with real security in mind, the planners might have mounted cameras in the halls. He tossed a glance in each direction, spotted nothing that resembled video equipment and proceeded on his way. Odd numbers on his left, the even on his right.

He found Kuan's door and, from this point, it could go two ways. If Bolan's mark was home, the Executioner would drop in for a chat and leave the final outcome to his startled host's discretion. If Lee Kuan was absent, Bolan was prepared to wait a reasonable length of time, and they could have that talk when Lee came home.

He punched the bargain-basement doorbell that was mounted underneath a peephole in the center of the door. When that brought no response, he knocked insistently.

Still no answer.

If his pigeon was at home the guy was either deaf or drugged, and neither fit the profile Lisa Ky had given him. She had described Kuan as "a party animal," but one who stuck with liquor, women, the conventional accoutrements of free-and-easy bachelor life.

He picked the lock in something under thirty seconds, marveling at a "security" apartment that wasn't equipped with dead bolts on its door. He left the lights off, waiting several moments for his eyes to adjust to the darkness. When he knew that he could navigate the flat without caroming off the furniture, he checked it thoroughly—the combination living room and kitchen, two small bedrooms, single bath.

Strike three for "luxury."

The four-room apartment would rent for six or seven hundred dollars per month and, for his money, Kuan could tell his friends that he had found "the perfect compromise between security and luxury." In fact he had a sixth-floor cracker box with stucco walls, an inexpensive carpet on the floor and vinyl in the bathroom that made little cracking noises under Bolan's weight.

The tub-and-shower unit was a fiberglass contraption that didn't match the colored tile on countertop and walls. No matter; he was looking for a hideout, not high fashion. Bolan stepped inside, drew the mismatched curtain shut behind him and settled down to wait.

It might be hours before Kuan returned, but the Executioner was patient, long accustomed to the waiting that preceded a kill. He hadn't come with death in mind, but neither would he flinch from closing Lee Kuan's books if it became apparent that the punk was jerking him around. Before he left her, Lisa Ky had made it clear, in almost callous terms, that she had no abiding interest in the runner's state of health.

It troubled him, such coldness in a woman who was little more than child herself, but he ascribed it to her background in Saigon, in transit to the States. She had already seen more death than most and growing up alone, beneath the stigma of her mother's execution by the Communists, was bound to leave some scars. All things considered, ~~she~~ had turned out well, a daughter to be proud of.

It was still a concept the Executioner was having trouble comprehending. Children were supposed to come with marriage, part and parcel of the home-and-family domestic scene he had given up forever back in Pittsfield. It was difficult to comprehend that part of him had taken root and grown *outside* himself, without his knowledge, to become another walking, talking, thinking human being. Bolan understood the biological mechanics of the act, but he was having trouble with the ethical, emotional and spiritual sides.

Above all else, he wondered why he still felt empty. In the circumstances, he imagined that he should have been delighted or depressed, oppressed by guilt or swept away by joy, but he felt none of those responses. There was a certain warmth, of course, but mostly he was numb, unable to react appropriately without faking it. He wondered if the years of nearly constant violence had, at last, burned something basic from his soul. Was he somehow less human—less *humane*—than he had been in Vietnam, in Pittsfield, at a hundred other stops along the hellfire trail?

His train of thought was interrupted by the fumbling rattle of a key, the opening and closing of a door. He strained to catch the sound of voices, finally decided that his quarry was alone, and very likely drunk. A flare of lamplight from the living room, and Bolan listened as his prey drew back the sliding windows leading to his balcony, admitting night sounds and a draft of smoggy air.

He drew the Beretta, which had been fitted with its custom silencer for the occasion. If he had to ice Lee Kuan he hoped it could be done without alerting every neighbor on the floor. With any luck at all, the presence of a weapon would be adequate persuasion to ensure a quiet, peaceful chat.

He waited, thought he heard Kuan muttering to himself as he approached the bedroom. Bolan heard his quarry stumble as a chair reached out to trip him, heard him curse underneath his breath. The creaky vinyl signaled his arrival in the bathroom, and the night-light on the wall cast long, distorted shadows on the shower curtain.

Training his Beretta on the shadow, Bolan heard Lee Kuan release his zipper, drop his slacks, the buckle of his belt producing a metallic sound on impact with the floor.

Bolan nudged the plastic curtain aside, emerging from the shower as his quarry spun around to face him, mouth gaping in stunned surprise.

The Asian staggered backward, buttocks flattening against the sink. He almost stumbled, hobbled as he was by slacks and briefs, but caught himself before he fell.

"Who are you?" he demanded.

"Pull your pants up," Bolan countered. "I'm not here for show-and-tell."

A wave of color hit the Asian's cheeks as Bolan snapped the bathroom lights on, but he fumbled with his clothing, finally made himself presentable.

"Who are you?"

"Don't repeat yourself, Lee. People think you're goofy when you do that."

"What do you want?"

"Information."

"Information?"

"There you go again."

"I don't know anything."

"I'll bet you do."

"I swear—"

"Don't bother, Lee, I'm not your priest." He held the muzzle of his weapon level with the young man's face. "I want to talk about the heroin."

He watched a measure of color fade from Lee Kuan's cheeks. "I don't know what you mean."

Bolan thumbed the automatic's hammer back, the weapon sliding out to full arm's length as he took aim on Lee Kuan's nose. "Wrong answer."

"Wait a minute! Heroin, you said?"

"Five seconds."

"Christ, I don't know—"

"Four."

"I don't know what you—"

"Three."

"I don't know what you mean!"

"And two."

"I'd tell you if I knew."

"Goodbye, Lee."

"Wait!" The runner threw his hands up, as if open palms could stop a parabellum mangler from smashing into his face. "I'll tell you what you want to know."

"I'm listening."

"Tomorrow. One o'clock. We're picking up the shipment at a warehouse out in Newport Beach."

"Who's 'we'?"

"The boys, you know? The guys I work with."

"Give me numbers."

"Jeez, you think they clear all that with me? They tell me where to go, and I show up on time. That's it."

"Is this a special shipment?"

"Special? Yeah, I guess. It's big, I know that much. The grapevine has it part of what we get is being sold to the Italians."

Bolan's smile was as cold as death. "That's good to know. I'll need the address."

Lee Kuan rattled off the numbers and repeated them identically upon command. "Hey listen, man, that's everything. I swear."

"You said that."

"Huh? Oh, yeah."

"I wouldn't like to think that you were holding out."

"You kidding? Shit, you think I get a piece of what they're bringing in tomorrow? I'll be old and gray before I see a dime. I'd like to live that long, you follow?"

Bolan frowned. "That leaves me with a problem, Lee. If I just let you walk, you'll drop a dime and blow the meeting. I can't have that."

"I won't, I swear to God."

"I ought to trust you, then?"

"Why not?" Before the words were out, Kuan recognized how hollow they must sound. "I mean—"

He bolted, lunging through the open doorway toward the darkened bedroom. Bolan squeezed off a hasty round, splintering the doorframe, moving after Lee Kuan made his break. The guy was framed against the bedroom door in silhouette. The Beretta coughed again and Bolan was rewarded as the running figure lurched, began to stagger.

Kuan was at the breakfast bar when Bolan cleared the bedroom. Blood was streaming from a ragged shoulder wound, he was digging for a weapon in a drawer. Swinging up a snub-nosed .38, Kuan stroked off two in rapid fire, and Bolan went to ground behind an armchair, craning out in time to see his target disappearing through the sliding doors onto the balcony.

The guy had nowhere left to go, and Bolan hit him with a double punch, chest high, that swept him off his feet. The railing caught Kuan behind his knees, and with a strangled, dying scream he disappeared.

The warrior didn't have to check the kill. His rounds had been on target, and the six-floor drop would snuff out any sign of life the slugs had missed. His work was finished here, but if Kuan had been straight with him, he had another job to do. In Newport Beach.

CHAPTER TEN

Pham Liao Bach was at his best when under pressure. As he watched Ngo Tien, he imagined that the older man was showing signs of strain.

"What happened?" Tien demanded.

"Someone entered Lee's apartment. He was shot while standing on his balcony. He fell. Beyond this point..." He left the statement dangling as he spread his open hands and shrugged.

"Was this an act of war?"

"I am investigating every possibility. An answer should be in our hands before the day is out."

"Should be?" Anh Giap regarded Bach with thinly veiled contempt. "You cannot say?"

"These things take time."

"I need no time. I *know* who killed Lee Kuan."

"Then by all means enlighten us."

"It was Carlotti. The Italians."

Pham Bach smiled indulgently and shook his head, dismissing Giap as he addressed himself to Ngo Tien. "I fear that I must disagree. Carlotti's people have no reason to attack us at this time. They have agreed, in principle, to an alliance for the distribution of our Bangkok merchandise, and any late disruption of the shipment would impede their current operations worse than it would harm our own. In any case, if Don Carlotti was preparing to initiate hostilities, I doubt he would select a target like Lee Kuan. I knew the boy, of course, but in objective terms his death means nothing to our business."

"It means that we have been attacked!" Giap put in. "Insulted! There is loss of face to be considered."

Bach ignored him, concentrating on Tien. "It would be rash to move against Carlotti when we have no evidence of his involvement in the crime. Permit me to continue my investigation. When the merchandise is safely in our hands, and we have all the facts about Lee Kuan, there will be ample time to think about revenge."

Tien pushed his food away untouched and cleared his throat. "I also question whether Don Carlotti would attack us now, in such a way." Giap was ready to protest, but Tien held up a hand for silence. "If the Mafia intended to attack us, they might come for me, for you, Anh—they might even come for Bach. But what could they achieve by murdering Lee Kuan? He was an errand boy. It makes no sense at all."

Anh Giap was frowning. "All right," he said, "who killed him then? Who else has any reason to attack us in this way?"

Bach drew a baleful glare from Giap as he replied on Tien's behalf. "I am investigating Lee Kuan's personal affairs. There is a possibility his death has no connection whatsoever with business." Seeing Anh Giap's skepticism, Pham Bach forged ahead. "Lee was a womanizer, boastful of his conquests. It is possible that he incurred the anger of a jealous lover."

"Nonsense!"

"There is yet another possibility, which I am hesitant to mention at this time, without corroborating evidence."

"Go on," Tien quietly commanded.

"There are rumors—unsubstantiated, as I say—of recent animosity between the Thunder Dragons and some other groups, specifically the Cubans and Colombians, who may regard our competition in the powder trade as cause for some alarm. Lee Kuan was friendly with the Dragons, and their enemies may have selected him to serve as an example."

Giap was scowling. "You expect us to believe this?"

"I expect no more than time to gather facts. If I am proved wrong, I will be pleased to act upon the evidence that we possess."

"I need no evidence," Giap growled. "I *know* Carlotti is behind this insult to our family."

Tien shook his head. "I will not launch a war and jeopardize our operation on the basis of a feeling. If Carlotti murdered Lee, I want the proof."

Anh Giap made a sour face and slapped the table with his open palm, but he didn't attempt to change his partner's mind. They knew each other far too well for that.

"I trust that your investigation will not jeopardize the Bangkok shipment?"

"I have made the necessary preparations."

"Very well. I will not keep you from your duties any longer."

It was a relief to feel the sunshine on his face. Bach took his time to reach the waiting car, informed the driver of his destination as he slid in back. It was a victory of sorts, manipulating Tien until he backed Pham Bach against that old neanderthal Anh Giap, but years of practice made the action almost automatic, stripped it of its visceral excitement. There had never really been a contest, after all.

Bach had been serving Tien—and Giap, to some extent—since 1970, when he had found employment with the drug lord as a runner making small deliveries on the streets of Saigon, bringing home the cash and messages from customers. Lee Kuan had occupied a similar position, but the boy was dead now, valuable only as a catalyst, the spark for an impending conflict. Bach was not concerned about Lee's death, because he knew precisely who had pulled the trigger, why and what the killer must have learned from Kuan before the deed was done.

He wouldn't share that knowledge with Tien—not yet, at any rate. It would be premature to play his hole card, when the stakes hadn't been raised to their potential maximum. It meant deceiving Ngo Tien, but Bach was an accomplished master when it came to selling lies as truth. In more than sixteen years of service to the drug lord, he had harbored many secrets from Tien and Giap, and they were none the wiser.

Neither knew, for instance, that his meeting with Tien in Saigon all those years ago had been precisely orchestrated, prearranged by planners in Hanoi. It served the purposes of Bach's superiors to plant an agent in Tien's syndicate, and Bach had been a perfect choice. Indoctrinated by the KGB's Department 6, with overall responsibility for gathering intelligence in China, Vietnam and North Korea, Bach had graduated to a covert actions post with North Vietnam's secret police. A fresh face on the scene, he was selected by his masters to infiltrate Tien's operation, rising through the ranks to stand beside the gangster as his strong left hand, reporting back meanwhile to his Hanoi control.

When Saigon fell and Tien prepared to flee, it was decided that Pham Bach should join his superior in exile. Problems of communication were resolved in time, and Pham Bach had been instrumental in establishing the syndicate on foreign soil. The refugee community in Orange County was a fertile breeding ground for new recruits. Many young men already disillusioned by their poor reception in America were intent on making fortunes for themselves while paying back the Anglos for their insolence, their natural assumption of superiority. The Thunder Dragons were a fledgling social club when Bach had taken them in hand, providing them with guidance, motivation, arms and cash.

In time the gang was self-supporting, and returned a tidy profit to its secret sponsor on the side.

Narcotics was the stock-in-trade of Ngo Tien, and Bach had used his Communist connections to ensure that loads of potent China White arrived on schedule, free of interference at the pipeline's eastern terminus. In the United States it was a relatively simple matter to corrupt or hoodwink various officials who were used to dealing with established syndicates. For some the payoff had become a way of life; the others, honest to a fault, had been conditioned to believe that drugs were smuggled by Italians, with a smattering of blacks or Hispanics sprinkled in the pot for local color. Asians were regarded—and correctly, for the most part—as an honest breed who kept their noses clean and steered away from crime at any cost. It took a bold man to suggest that refugees from Asia were involved in smuggling heroin, and the DEA was short of agents at the best of times.

Pham Bach cared nothing for the profits earned from drugs. He was a soldier of the People's Revolution, totally committed to the ultimate destruction of America and heroin, from all appearances, was an effective weapon in his war. Aside from the demoralizing aspects of an ever-growing addict population, the narcotics traffic bred assorted other social ills: political corruption, street crime, urban paranoia and a general decline of social order. Drugs alone would never win the war, Bach knew, but anything that sapped the strength and will of his opponents was an avenue to be explored, pursued to its conclusion.

Any social or political disruption of the Asian refugee community would be a bonus, frosting on the cake. Pham Bach despised the cowards, whining lackeys who had fled their homeland rather than remain to participate in people's revolution at the grass-roots level. Some of them were fascist gangsters like Tien, the rest of them were fools, and

Bach regarded all of them with fine contempt. It was now within his power to make them sorry they had ever sided with the running-dog imperial regime and, in a few more hours, Bach would taste the fruits of victory, a lifetime dedicated to the revolutionary struggle.

He had arranged to bring the people's revolution home to Ngo Tien directly. The drug lord was primed to play a leading role in Pham Bach's drama, with a sacrifice of flesh and blood. The sweetest irony of all concerned the agent who would put the grinding wheels in motion. Bach had opted for a hero the Americans could recognize at once, a veteran of the oppressive war in Vietnam who had provided leaders of the revolution with a deluge of delightful propaganda in the past.

No matter that the agent was his mortal enemy. If all turned out according to Bach's plan, the human catalyst would never even know that he was being used. Until, perhaps, it was too late.

Bach smiled, already looking forward to his next encounter with the enemy.

"WE HAVEN'T GOT much time. Let's run it down once more."

A shoe box occupied the center of Lao Fan's dining table, representing the Alameda Merchandise warehouse in Newport Beach. Felt pens had sketched in the windows and doors, as well as a ladder in back and skylights on top. Bolan's midmorning recon had filled in the details, except for the clincher.

He still had no way of predicting what might be inside, and he didn't like going in blind.

Seven men ringed the table, Bolan and Lao Fan included. The others were former refugees, friends of Lao Fan who had voiced the desire to stand up and be counted against Tien and Giap. Two were veterans of combat in

Vietnam, while the other three—younger, but no less determined—had practiced shooting their guns on their own, using tips from Lao Fan to increase their proficiency. All were prepared, so they said, for a fight to the death.

Bolan hated enlisting civilians, but Lao was his handle, his reason for being in town in the first place. He knew that the Montagnard scrapper could carry his weight in a fight, and if Lao said the others could hold up their end, it wasn't Bolan's place to refuse. In the end, whether Tien stood or fell, they would have to take charge of defending themselves against predators, wolves in the night. There were high risks involved, but they all knew the odds going in— Bolan had made sure of that—and they stuck to their guns.

Bolan ran through the drill one more time. He was taking the roof, on his own, while Lao Fan saw the ground troops in place and made sure that they covered their posts as assigned. There were three doors at ground level, not counting bays where a semi had been parked that morning while unloading its cargo. Two men on the front door, with one on each side, and two more on the loading docks. Even if Tien had an army inside, the strategically located gunners should keep them pinned down while he entered from topside and finished his work.

Each man knew his assignment when Bolan was finished, and Lao Fan would see them in place without needless delay or commotion. In casual dress, with their weapons concealed, they should draw no particular notice from lookouts or roving police, but the soldier left nothing to chance.

"If the bluecoats turn up while we're working, break off, every man for himself. We can rendezvous later and pick up the pieces, but no one—I repeat *no one*—draws down on a cop. Understood?"

Lao Fan spoke for the others. "We know who our enemies are."

Bolan nodded. "Okay, then. If something goes wrong while you're still getting into position, abort on the spot. If we can't do this right, we don't do it at all."

"Understood."

"Right. Let's check out the hardware."

Three shotguns, two with folding stocks, one with its barrel cut back to the legal minimum of eighteen inches. One Ruger carbine in .44 Magnum. An M-1 carbine and an Army-surplus M-14, converted into semiauto for civilian sale. A number of the new recruits had side arms—.38s and .45s—with extra magazines and loose rounds weighing down their pockets. Lao assured him all of them could tag their chosen targets, but he knew that plinking silhouettes would never be a substitute for hard experience. If shots were fired this afternoon, the targets would be shooting back.

"I don't want any fancy plays," he told them. "Take your lead from Lao and keep your weapons under cover. If you have to use them, shoot to kill."

"This day has been a long time coming," Lao Fan interjected, glancing at the others. "We would like to thank you for your help."

"So far, I haven't done a thing. If I were you, I'd save the thanks until we get results."

"I have no fear."

"You should. We're going up against an army of professionals—if not this afternoon then tomorrow or the next day. Tien and Giap won't take this kind of interference lying down."

"We are prepared to die, if necessary," one of Lao's companions told him.

"Dying is the easy part. To help your friends, your families, you have to stay alive as long as possible. Dead heroes get a fancy send-off, but they don't have any value to the living."

"Tien and Giap have drawn the line."

"And we're about to cross it. You should all be ready for a shake-up on the other side."

"Each of us has suffered at the hands of Ngo Tien, or from his cronies in the Thunder Dragons. Money taken from our pockets, food and comfort stolen from our families. It is enough. We are prepared to stand no more.

"Whatever happens," Lao Fan told him, "we are ready."

"Fair enough."

But were they? With the possible exception of the combat veterans among them, were the Asians caught up in playing Minuteman? Were they responding to the frontier image of America that still cropped up from time to time on television, in the movies?

Bolan knew as well as anyone that one man, standing firm against the savages, could make a difference. On the flip side of the coin, he also realized that untrained vigilantes, acting out of fear or anger, posed a greater danger to themselves than to their enemies. He hoped Lao Fan had chosen wisely in selecting his recruits, but it was too damned late for any substitutions now.

Three hours. It was all they had, and after that they would be in the soup together, playing every move by ear, responding to the enemy's reactions and attempting to survive against the odds. A shipment of the sort described by Lisa Ky would rate a fair security detachment, and if rumors of a split with the Italians were correct, Lao Fan's militia might be faced with unexpected opposition in the form of hardmen from the Mafia.

It would be interesting, to say the least, and Bolan hoped his troops were up to coping with the challenge. If resolve could take the place of battlefield experience, they might just have a chance.

So many things could still go wrong; he didn't want to think about the possibilities, but they barged in on Bolan's thoughts. If a stray patrolman noticed Asians in the neighborhood and got too curious, decided to investigate, the operation would be scuttled instantly before he had a chance to look inside the warehouse. If Tien or Giap had lookouts posted—which was probable—and they should recognize Lao Fan or one of his commandos, there would almost certainly be hell to pay. If Bolan found himself outnumbered in the warehouse, while Lao's gunners kept the hostiles penned inside . . .

But these thoughts led nowhere. Too much concern was worse sometimes than overconfidence. A soldier could allow for every possibility of failure, hedge himself around with reasons to delay a strike until he froze and found himself immobile, easy pickings for the enemy. Timidity in combat was a fatal weakness, but thus far it hadn't been a problem for the Executioner.

Whatever might be waiting for his little troop in Newport Beach, he only knew one way to check it out. No soft probe this time. With a major load of China White at issue, it was blood and thunder all the way. His thunder and, with any luck at all, the blood of enemies to grease the war machine.

With any luck.

Except that Bolan knew a warrior made his own luck in battle. A warrior, or an armed civilian playing soldier in a righteous cause.

Unfortunately righteousness and victory were not habitual companions. Evil had been known to triumph, while defenders of the right were trampled into dust.

CHAPTER ELEVEN

Lao Fan checked out the dashboard clock, compared it to his wristwatch and scowled as he shifted restlessly behind the steering wheel. Five minutes remained, and Lao felt he'd been in place too long already. Someone would be sure to notice him, despite the fact that he had parked his car in shadow, close against the rear wall of a warehouse that hadn't been occupied for months.

From his position, Lao Fan could observe their target thirty yards away, and he could also cover three of his recruits in case of trouble prior to zero hour. The weapon on the seat beside him was a Chinese replica of the Kalashnikov, imported to the States for sportsmen under terms of recent trade agreements with Beijing. It had been tooled for semiautomatic fire, but Lao had done some tinkering of his own when he acquired the rifle, using parts and tools available from local paramilitary outlets, and the piece would spit six hundred rounds per minute now. Spare magazines were tucked inside the glove compartment and in the pockets of the raincoat he wore despite predictions of warm weather and sunny skies.

It was the kind of weapon he had used most frequently in Vietnam, though he had also killed with knives, with strangling wires, his own bare hands. Sometimes, when Lao Fan held the rifle, he could almost smell the forests of his homeland, feel the wind against his face and hear the night birds calling to their mates. Sometimes, for just an instant, he recaptured the suspense of lying in ambush on a jungle trail, waiting for the Communists to show themselves and die.

These days he scarcely thought of Vietnam, but it was in his dreams, emerging from the shadows of his deep subconscious when his personal defenses were relaxed. In dreams he fought the Vietcong, the northern regulars, and spilled their blood as they had spilled the blood of his compatriots, his kinsmen. In his dreams Lao Fan repaid the Communists for their treachery, the suffering they had heaped upon his homeland. And he woke up with the tears still wet on his face.

In waking hours Lao knew his enemies were not a clique of godless men ten thousand miles away. His enemies were here, and they were neither Communists nor strangers. Predators they were, but they were men of Lao's own race and background, preying on the very people whom they should have acted to defend.

Today, with Bolan's help, Lao would strike a blow against his enemies and hurt them where it mattered most: their bank accounts. He knew the going price for drugs, was able to extrapolate the costs involved in importation of a major shipment. Summary destruction of that poison cargo would inform Tien and Giap that they were dealing with a man—a group of men—who had endured enough of tyranny.

He was concerned about the men who had agreed to join him in the struggle. All of them were brave enough, and he had supervised their weapons training personally. One of them—Cao Diem—was a veteran of combat in the war for Vietnam; the other four—Mike Li, Lam Duc, Lin Phuong and Charlie Phu—were younger, but determined to defend their homes and businesses, their families. Lao worried all the same, because he didn't want their blood to stain his hands, and he could see no way of battling a giant like Tien without incurring friendly casualties along the way.

He raised a pair of opera glasses, studying the warehouse owned by Alameda Merchandise. No sentries were in evidence, but several cars were parked outside and as he watched, another dark sedan pulled up to take its place beside the rest. Three men in business suits and shades got out—all Anglos—moving toward the warehouse entrance while their driver stayed behind the wheel.

That made an even dozen men inside that Lao knew about. There might have been another dozen waiting prior to his arrival, and there would be no way of determining the enemy's defensive strength until such time as penetration was achieved.

He scanned the area for Bolan, found him on the second sweep and locked his glasses on the figure dressed in black. The skin suit would provide him no concealment in the light of day, but Lao knew the outfit also played a role in gaining Bolan the advantage of surprise. The Green Berets had called it psy-war, weakening an enemy through fear, surprise, the unexpected. In his nightsuit, face streaked with war paint, and hung with weapons, Bolan was a vision of grim Death incarnate. If his enemies were moved to hesitate for so much as a heartbeat when he showed himself, it just might be the slim survival edge he required to beat the odds.

Lao watched as Bolan scaled the loading dock, approached a metal ladder bolted to the warehouse wall. He saw the soldier check his flank, then scramble upward like a circus acrobat. As Bolan made the roof Lao relaxed, allowed himself to breathe again.

Too soon.

A slender Oriental was emerging from the warehouse through a side door facing Lao's position. Mike Li had him covered, crouched between two garbage Dumpsters with a shotgun in his lap, but Lao was uneasy, thrown off balance by the enemy's appearance.

Was the heroin delivery in progress? Were the hostiles getting nervous as they waited? Had they smelled a trap?

Lao tracked the gunner as he drifted toward the loading dock and paused beneath the metal ladder, waiting. From the far end of the dock a second lookout came into view, approaching number one with measured strides.

Lao tucked the rifle underneath his raincoat as he left the car. His keys were still in the ignition, and he left them there, the better for a swift departure. Anyone who tried to steal his car this afternoon would not survive to recognize his grave mistake.

And he was needed on the firing line before his troops grew nervous, tipped their hand. The Executioner would need him when he dropped in on a dozen gunmen and attempted to relieve them of their million-dollar stash.

With one hand on the rifle, clutching it against his side, Lao tried to set a normal pace across the blacktop toward Mike Li's position. Thirty yards, now twenty, and the sentries gave no sign of having seen him. He willed himself to strike the posture of a casual pedestrian—and knew he didn't have a hope in hell of fooling anyone, not while wearing a raincoat when the temperature was already rising toward the eighties.

If they saw him, tried to stop him, he would have to open fire, and Bolan might be forced to move before he was prepared. Lao cursed himself for not remaining in the car, but it was much too late for him to backtrack. He'd be equally suspicious in retreat, and he had almost reached the trash bins. Just ten more yards.

He was staring at the sentries when they spotted him, both men reaching underneath their jackets at the same time, digging for their guns.

A ROW OF SEVEN SKYLIGHTS marched down the center of the flat warehouse roof, each one eight feet long by six feet wide. Through any given window Bolan had a dusky view of crates and boxes piled on top of one another, reaching halfway to the roof in places. The floor below was concrete, painted gray.

It was his second visit to the roof. His first, conducted in the predawn hours after Lee Kuan's swan dive, had revealed the stout Yale padlocks that secured each skylight. Bolan was surprised that they were able to open in the first place, but he knew that there was no accounting for the various peculiarities of architectural design. As the locks were advertised as pick-proof, he had obtained a pair of bolt cutters, and he used them now to snap the padlock on the middle skylight.

Bolan's choice had been deliberate. The crates beneath his chosen point of entry were stacked higher than the rest, providing the warrior with a shorter drop. Additionally he would gain a little extra time by putting space between himself and gunners who would likely be deployed around the exits. If they marked his entry, he'd still have time to get his balance back, prepare himself before the firestorm broke.

He was going in prepared for violent action. Bolan wore an Uzi submachine gun slung across one shoulder, the Beretta 93-R in its sling beneath his arm. On his hip he wore a brand-new Desert Eagle .44, the heavy autoloader manufactured by Israeli Military Industries. The Eagle's overall capacity was greater than his usual .44, the AutoMag, with eight rounds in the magazine and one more in the chamber. It fed on .44 revolver loads, eliminating difficulties with the custom-tailored cartridges required to make the AutoMag perform on cue. The average 240-grain projectile would leave the Eagle's muzzle at a crushing rate of almost 1,400 feet per second, holding speeds of better than 1,000 feet per second at a hundred yards. In practiced hands, it could secure consistent kills at twice that range.

Spare magazines for each of Bolan's weapons filled the canvas pouches at his waist, and he was carrying grenades—both fragmentation and incendiary—as a backup punch, in case he found himself too heavily outnumbered in the crunch. There would be nothing soft about his probe—not with a million dollars' worth of China White at stake—and Bolan meant to walk away with his troops intact, even if it meant leveling the warehouse. Which, he thought, might be precisely what was called for.

Kneeling, Bolan laid down his cutters and the severed lock. He raised the skylight's pane, twice pausing when the rusty hinges squealed in protest, frozen in his place until he realized that no one was responding to the sound. Long metal struts were folded flat against the sill and Bolan hoisted each in turn, their forked tips fitting notches in the eight-foot windowpane and holding it aloft. There would be room for him to squeeze through, feetfirst, but once he made the move he was committed. There would be no turning back.

The soldier checked his watch. Two minutes. Time enough for him to make a rapid scan of the interior and try to place his enemies before he made the drop. If he could spot them in advance, he'd be points ahead when it came time for him to take them down.

After a sweep along the central aisle directly underneath his lookout post, Bolan reassured himself that no gunners would be waiting to receive him at ground zero. Muffled voices to his left, from the direction of the foreman's office, told him where the meet was being held and where the cargo would most probably be found. From a scuffling of footsteps somewhere to his right, Bolan marked the presence of what he anticipated to be sentries on the other exits, covering all angles of approach.

He hoped Lao's people were alert and in position. When the hit came down, there would be no time left for reconsidering their fields of fire—only time to do or die, and nothing more.

The soldier held his breath, slipped both feet into empty space, slid backward, downward, until he was hanging by his fingertips above the row of crates. Exhaled. Drew in another breath and held it locked behind his teeth as he let go.

VINCENZO MORO LIT a cigarette, thought better of it, ground it out beneath his heel. Already tired of waiting, he was anxious to get on with the transaction, take delivery and get the hell away from there as quickly as he could.

It was unusual for Moro to be present at a major smack delivery, but the Don had insisted, and a man didn't argue with the capo if he wanted to maintain the style of life to which he had become accustomed. If the Don thought dealing with the zipperheads was special, Vinnie thought so, too—at least in public.

Still, it made him nervous, standing in such close proximity to so much heroin. The California laws were lax on matters of possession, true, but there were limits, and you had to be an idiot to think that forty keys of uncut China White would pass as anything but trafficking. That was heavy time, and while it would have been his first offense—for drugs, at least—Carlotti's second in command wasn't in a hurry for a tour of the courts and penal system. He would leave that to the meatheads who broke bones and peddled numbers for a living.

Moro drew his only consolation from the knowledge that his uncle had a scheme in mind to screw the Orientals. He would deal with them a while, use all his contacts to determine their suppliers, finally approach the Eastern dealers with an offer they couldn't refuse. Once he had undercut Tien and Giap, deprived them of their pipeline, mopping up would be an afterthought.

It never crossed his mind that Tien or Giap might have a double cross in mind, that he might walk into an ambush at the warehouse. Zipperheads were devious, he had to give them that, but Ngo Tien wasn't an idiot. He had to know that any move against Don Girolamo's nephew on a business deal would bring the wrath of God down on his pointy head. If Tien was ready for that kind of action, they would have been fighting now, instead of making deals in restaurants and hanging out on piers.

Instead it was the waiting that disturbed Vincenzo Moro. Bad enough that he should have to carry heroin himself, to set the stage for future deals. A show of faith, Don Girolamo called it, but he couldn't shake the image of a traffic cop, some oinker on a Harley noticing a busted taillight or whatever, going off the deep end as he asked to look inside the trunk.

Vince knew enough of California law to realize that normal driving would deprive the cops of any valid motives for a search . . . but what if Tien was dirty? What if the DEA or someone else was staking out the joint right now? The very fact of Moro's presence in the warehouse might provide the narcs with probable cause, and if they had a valid warrant when they popped the trunk on Vinnie's Cadillac, he would be up shit creek.

He wondered, briefly, if the slopes might be setting up a bust on purpose. They could feed him to the DEA, provide the federals with a major Mafia arrest, and maybe buy immunity besides. It was the kind of deal that Moro might negotiate himself, if he was feeling drastic heat; a chance to clear the slate with Uncle Sam while scuttling your major competition.

With a double cross in mind, he had prepared himself for trouble. He was riding in a Caddy borrowed from a member of his staff, and one of his technicians had cooked up a small explosive charge, attached beneath the gas tank. It was radio controlled, but he had made damn sure that it was tuned to one specific frequency. He didn't want a taxi radio or any two-bit children's toy to blow his ass sky-high, but he had confidence in his mechanics. On the side he also had a gunner standing by to waste the little bastard's family if anything went wrong. A roust by the DEA, whatever, Moro simply had to step aside and key the trigger in his pocket. *Whammo!* And of course he had no inkling who might wish to kill his friend and employee. The car was borrowed, after all. Thank God someone had pulled him over in the nick of time.

If anybody had an urge to sift the ashes for a trace of heroin, they would be welcome to it. He would hire a dozen chemists to dispute their findings, if it came to that, but how could anyone blame Vinnie Moro when the Caddy wasn't even his? It was incredible that one of his employees might be using drugs. He would consider mandatory urine testing as a new condition of employment with his totally legitimate construction firm.

Step one was cutting up the shipment, paying off Tien's go-between and getting out before some nosy beat cop got suspicious of the flashy cars outside and dropped in for a look-see. Moro's shooters were prepared to deal with any opposition, uniformed or otherwise, but killing cops was bad for business all around, and Vinnie hoped they would just get on with it, hand off and let him break for lunch before his stomach started growling.

Tien's negotiator was a chunky zipperhead with horn-rimmed glasses, hair slicked back like Rudolph Valentino. Moro had already given up on trying to pronounce his name, content to smile and nod each time the bastard tossed a glance in his direction. But the guy was moving toward him now, and Vinnie hoped they were finally getting down to business.

"You are ready to inspect the merchandise?"

Relaxing, Moro nodded. "I been ready since we got here, pal."

"Sincere apologies for the delay. There was a matter of some small importance to discuss with my superiors."

Vince let it pass. If they were calling out, alerting someone to prepare an ambush once his Caddy rolled away, he'd be ready for it. Gooks or narcs, it would be snowing in July before they suckered Vinnie Moro with a play that simple.

"I believe you have some cash? Four hundred thousand dollars?"

"Yeah, I've got the bread. I haven't seen your powder, though."

"Of course. This way."

The Vietnamese was moving out, with Moro on his heels, when something fell behind them with a crash. Somebody barked a warning, cutting loose with pistol fire that echoed through the warehouse. Vinnie's muscle had their guns in hand before the echoes died away.

"Hey, what the hell is this?"

Tien's go-between was snapping orders to his men, deploying troops, and if it was a staged reaction, Moro would have voted him an Oscar on the spot.

"It seems that an intruder has been sighted."

As he spoke a crackling burst of automatic fire erupted, somewhere on the other side of crates and boxes that obscured Moro's view. More pistol shots, another burst of autofire, and then all kinds of hardware opened up at once.

"Fuck this!" Moro shouted. "You blew it, pal. We're out of here."

His hardmen fell in step, two leading, another pair covering his flank, while Tien's negotiator tried to call him back. Ignoring him, Vincenzo Moro concentrated on the exit, just ahead, the borrowed Caddy and a short ride back to safety.

It was crazy, dealing one to one with monkeys like Tien and Giap. No way would his uncle forget this shit. No way at all.

His point man had already reached the door, had one hand on the push bar, when the world blew up in Moro's face and sent him spinning into darkness.

BOLAN LANDED on the crate off center, felt it shift beneath his weight and leaped again before it fell. He had blown it all to hell, as far as silent entry was concerned. He heard a warning shout behind him, running footsteps, and he ducked a pistol shot that pierced a cardboard carton, twanging metal just inside. Another round burned past his ear, and Bolan swung the Uzi into action, squeezing off a burst that caught his adversary unprepared and slammed him on his back.

The warrior broke in the direction of the warehouse office. When he was halfway there, a sentry stepped in front of him, completely unprepared to meet his death. Bolan zapped him with a 3-round burst that sent him spinning out of frame and out of mind. A shotgun roared, but it was somewhere to his left and maybe two aisles over, nervous gunners squeezing off at shadows when they couldn't find a human target.

Bolan reached the near end of his aisle and skidded to a halt before he was revealed to gunners clustering around the glassed-in office. Hazarding a glance he saw five men, all Anglos, making for the nearest exit while an Asian ran along behind them, trying to persuade them to stay. The other faces Bolan saw were all Vietnamese, and all of them belonged to men with guns.

He glanced along his backtrack, spotted no immediate pursuit and palmed a fragmentation grenade. He yanked the pin, released the spoon and lobbed the bomb overhead in the direction of the exit, counting down the seconds until the detonation split the air with sudden thunder. Choosing an incendiary can, he let it fly before the shaken gunners could regain their equilibrium, retreating under cover as the white-hot thermite coals rained down around him.

Gunners on his flank unloaded .45s in rapid fire, and Bolan went to ground, the Uzi an extension of his arm as it dispatched a stream of stingers to greet his opposition. Downrange, they were jerking, twisting, finally collapsing as he released the trigger. When a third man ran up on their heels, the last four rounds in Bolan's weapon were all it took to drop him in his tracks.

He fed the Uzi a new magazine, switched it to his left hand, hefted the heavy Desert Eagle in his right. They might be waiting for him when he showed himself, but some of the men were wounded, all of them were shaken, and they would be battling the flames attempting to preserve their million-dollar cargo while they still had half a chance.

He meant to take that half a chance away from them.

The soldier counted down from three and came out shooting.

PINNED DOWN behind the Dumpster, Lao Fan risked a glance in the direction of the warehouse, ducking back as shotgun pellets rattled the metal inches from his face. A burst of automatic fire gouged holes in the asphalt, and he scuttled to his right, popped up to return fire without the luxury of aiming, saw his rounds strike sparks against the warehouse as he dodged back out of sight.

Mike Li was dead. A single bullet through the forehead had dropped him seconds after Lao took the sentries on the loading dock. Almost before he squeezed the trigger, gunners had come charging from the warehouse, rushing out like children on a fire drill. There had been no time to count them, but he dropped two more before they pinned him down.

With Li dead, he was on his own. The others would be fighting for their lives on the perimeter, and Lao could neither help them nor expect help in return. He only wished that he could be inside with Bolan, helping to destroy the heroin, instead of battling for a few square feet of parking lot.

There had been more guns on the scene than Lao had counted, and he knew, too late, that Tien had called out an army to guard his poison cargo. If the drugs were lost to him, it would be worth their lives. But Lao wasn't prepared to let his go without a fight. Not yet. Not when he had a chance of breaking out, returning to the struggle on another day.

Explosions echoed inside the warehouse, like fireworks in a kettledrum, and Lao knew that Bolan had arrived with thunder in the midst of their assailants. If he lived, he'd be blasting out in moments. Lao was supposed to have the car revved and waiting, Mike Li riding shotgun, when the Executioner emerged. He couldn't raise the dead, but he could still provide the wheels—or he could die in the attempt.

As gunfire reached a hammering crescendo in the warehouse, pickets on the grounds outside began to waver, casting furtive glances toward the exits, edging back as if to join the battle that was raging inside. Lao took advantage of their hesitation, dodging out of cover, tagging one and then another as they tried to stop him, running flat out for the car with angry hornets stinging at his heels.

He made the Chevy, slid behind the wheel and twisted the ignition key, unwinding slightly as the engine came to life. He primed the rifle with another magazine and put the car in gear, accelerating toward the warehouse. At forty yards he saw the Lincolns bearing down on him from left and right, a pincer movement, and he wondered where they'd been hidden all this time.

It was a trap, and they were closing it with grim precision, gunners in the vehicles sniping at him as the drivers held a hard collision course. Lao braced his rifle on the windowsill and raked a burst across the windshield of his adversaries on the left, rewarded by a screech of brakes and swift deceleration as the driver froze, hands rising to his shattered face.

The second Continental nailed him, but it was a glancing blow that merely ripped his bumper off. He was running clear before the driver could recover, swing his tank around. The warehouse loomed in front of Lao, with gunners scattering for cover. Stray rounds cracked his windshield, drilled the off-side fender, clipped his radio antenna, but he held the pedal down and thrust his rifle through the window, squeezing off short bursts to keep them hopping.

Twenty yards from impact Lao Fan hit the brakes and cranked the steering wheel around, his Chevy sliding broadside toward the rank of cars outside the warehouse. He was ready when the Anglo driver scrambled clear, a .38 in hand and squeezing off before he had a decent target. Lao responded with a burst that swept him off his feet and left the man draped across the grille of a Mercedes.

Bolan suddenly erupted from the nearest exit in a blast of gunfire, pivoting and pausing long enough to feed his enemies a short burst from his Uzi. Spotting Lao Fan he headed for the car—and froze as he observed the Lincoln tank approaching, limping on a twisted wheel.

The warrior struck a duelist's stance, a heavy autoloader sliding out to full arm's length as he sighted down the barrel and squeezed off in rapid fire. A line of fist-size holes marched across the Lincoln's windshield, and the tank began to drift, shuddering on impact with the Dumpster where Mike Li had made his last stand.

Before survivors had a chance to scramble clear, the Executioner had found his place beside Lao Fan and they were off, accelerating toward the street and safety. In his rear-view mirror, Lao could see smoke curling from the doors and windows of the warehouse, gunners running forward then lurching back as tongues of flame reached out to sear them. With one eye on the road, he tried to spot the others, but his friends were nowhere to be seen.

"It was a trap," he said, aware that Bolan must have known as much by now.

"I'd say."

"Your source?"

"Deserves a closer look," the Executioner responded. And it had to be the recent brush with death, Lao thought, that made his voice as cold as graveyard marble.

CHAPTER TWELVE

During the drive from Newport Beach to Buena Park, Mack Bolan grappled with a nagging apprehension, verging on a sense of loss. He hadn't yet accepted the fact that he had a child; it was too soon for him to think of her betrayal, view her as an enemy. But Bolan had no choice.

The plain fact was that Ngo Tien had set them up in Newport Beach. His gunners had been waiting for the Executioner—for *someone*—and the only problem with their game plan lay in their underestimating the opposing force. If the warrior had been on his own, if Lao hadn't been waiting with the car, he would be lying in a cold drawer at the county morgue right now. The play had been that close.

And costly. Two of Lao Fan's men had been killed, and while the heat was on their families couldn't afford to claim the bodies for a proper burial. The men had gone in minus any hard ID, at Lao's insistence, and it would require some time for the police to trace them. Before investigators started calling, Lao would have the families of all concerned securely stashed away, beyond the reach of law enforcement or the hunters Tien was bound to set on their trail.

As for the Executioner, his problem lay considerably closer to the heart. He'd been suckered, nearly taken out, in Newport Beach and he could think of only two possible explanations for the ambush. Either Tien had doubled his security with Lee Kuan's death in mind, or someone with foreknowledge of the shipment had betrayed him.

Lao Fan was exempt from his suspicions. He'd known the gutsy Montagnard too long, had risked and shared too much with the man to doubt him now. The other refugees were new to Bolan, but he trusted Lao's judgment, and it seemed illogical that any man would risk his life in open combat to preserve his cover on a double cross. Lao's recruits were not professional dissemblers; they were merchants, family men compelled by circumstance to take up arms. One of them might have fooled a stranger, even Bolan, but he doubted that a phony could have passed Lao's scrutiny without alarm bells going off.

And dammit, that left Lisa Ky.

She hadn't known about the raid specifically, but she had been responsible for Bolan targeting Lee Kuan, and she had known about the heroin delivery, at least in general terms. It was entirely possible that Kuan had passed along specifics in an effort to impress her, building up his reputation as a man with hot connections in the underworld. And if she knew the time of the delivery, the place...it would have been so easy. All she had to do was drop a coin and pass the message on, no questions asked.

But why?

He didn't like the new direction of his thoughts, but try as he might, there seemed to be no viable alternatives. If Lisa hadn't tipped the opposition, then that meant the trap had been a pure coincidence, entirely unrelated to the fact of Bolan's presence in Orange County.

No. It wouldn't play.

Security around a drop was one thing: sentries, snipers, even armed patrols on wheels. But Newport Beach had been a suck, with hidden gunners, hidden cars, all primed in expectation of a hostile strike. The gunners Bolan met outside the warehouse hadn't been standing guard. They had been hunting human prey.

There was an outside chance that someone near Lao Fan had spoken to a relative or friend, that word had traveled through the grapevine back to Tien and Giap, but the warrior didn't believe in chance. Not when the odds were shaved so close he could feel the razor at his throat. Coincidence was one thing, and betrayal was another. Each phenomenon possessed its own distinctive feel, unique from any other.

Bolan knew that he had been betrayed, somehow, by someone. At the moment, all the indicators pointed straight at Lisa Ky. His daughter.

The soldier ticked off motives for a possible betrayal. Lisa might be harboring a grudge, well tended through the years, against a father she had never seen. The father who had left her mother with a child to raise, abandoning them both as if he didn't care. Left to feed upon themselves, those feelings of abandonment, rejection, would be fertile soil for anger and resentment, even hatred. Men—and women—had committed murder in the name of lesser grievances, and Lisa might have wished him dead in punishment for leaving her alone in Vietnam.

She might, and then again...

He ran their one and only meeting on the viewing screen of memory, alert for clues that might provide him with an answer to the riddle. Lisa had seemed confident and well adjusted, certain of her own identity and Bolan's. She had been content, from all appearances, to touch his life in passing, see him on his way once she declared herself. He had assessed her as a born survivor, toughened by the life she had led, yet soft enough to love.

And soft enough, perhaps, to hurt?

He knew that children killed their parents, and vice versa, with depressing regularity. The trigger grievance might be trivial—an argument about the family car, unfinished homework, curfews—but the violence sprang from deep and dark emotions held too long inside. It was entirely possible, he realized, that Lisa Ky might want him dead *because* he was her father. She might feel she owed it to her mother, to herself, a sacrifice to break the chains of childhood spent in loneliness and anguish, forcibly deprived of love and family.

His eyes were burning, and he knew the smog wasn't to blame. He made his mind a blank, deliberately shunning thoughts of Lisa or her mother, gaining distance from the new emotions that might hamper his reaction time in an emergency.

If Lisa was his enemy, he had to be prepared for any hostile move she might attempt. He couldn't think of killing her, wouldn't allow himself to frame the image in his mind, but neither was the Executioner prepared to sacrifice himself. If it came down to killing . . .

Bolan found the entryway for her apartment complex, put his rental through the twists and turns that brought him to her door. At first his mind refused to register the black-and-white patrol cars, daylight stealing something from the drama of their flashing colored lights. An ambulance was waiting with the rest, its driver and attendant marking time beside their vehicle, a sign that they'd come too late.

He found a parking space and palmed the wallet that contained his phony FBI credentials. It should be enough to get him through the door, and once inside the soldier would be playing it by ear.

A uniformed patrolman stopped him on the sidewalk, mumbled an apology and waved him on when Bolan flashed his tin. Another bluff and he was past the burly sergeant on the stairs, instructed to liaise with a Lieutenant Carmody inside. He spent a moment on the threshold, studying the too familiar scene as plainclothes officers and lab technicians went about their business, snapping photographs, retrieving evidence and dusting everything in sight for fingerprints.

A group of men were clustered near the sofa, and he drifted over, joined them unobtrusively. To his relief, the body sprawled behind the couch was male, a stranger. Asian, thirtyish, he might have died from either of the bullets that had drilled his forehead, half an inch apart.

"Who is he?"

"Who are *you*?" the eldest of the plainclothes officers responded, frowning.

Bolan held the wallet open long enough for all of them to catch a glimpse of his ID. "Mike Blanski, with the Bureau. I've been working Asian gangs."

"That so? I thought I knew my way around your duty roster pretty well."

"I just got in last night. The New York office sent me out to check reports about a gang war cooking. Looks like we were right."

"You think so?"

Bolan's smile was noncommittal. "I was told to ask for a Lieutenant Carmody."

"You found him. Blanski, was it?"

"Right."

The homicide investigator took a silent eyeball poll among his men. "This thing about a war is news to us. How solid is your line?"

"I wasn't sure of that myself, until I rolled on this." He nodded toward the corpse. "I'd say it's pretty solid, wouldn't you?"

"Might be. We've got another solid stiff in there." The gruff lieutenant shot a glance in the direction of the bedroom. "Want to check him out?"

He shrugged. "Why not?"

The second man had died on Lisa's bed, vermilion blotches on the quilt and blankets where his life had drained away through wounds in forehead, throat and chest.

"Somebody's thorough," Bolan quipped. "This all?"

"Were you expecting someone else?"

He forced a smile. "I'm not expecting anything, Lieutenant. I just figured, two guys dead in their apartment, maybe they got lucky with the shooters."

"We don't know if it's their apartment," Carmody responded. "I've got people running down the manager. We ought to have the tenant's name before too long."

"No ID on the meat?"

"You kidding me? We found some car keys on the guy out there. I've got a uniform comparing them to everything outside, but I'd lay odds they fit a car reported stolen sometime in the past two days."

"Professionals?"

"You got it."

"Armed?"

"For bear."

The soldier frowned. "So, how'd they blow it?"

Carmody was studying his face as if he ought to recognize the Executioner. "I wouldn't know. We got here after."

"Right. But still, it's funny, don't you think?"

"Two stiffs? Hell, yes, it breaks me up."

He forged ahead. "Two pros, both packing, and it looks like neither of them had time to use his piece. If they were living here, that's one thing, but—" he waved a hand to indicate the feminine decor "—this doesn't strike me as a place where hardmen go to crash."

"Okay. So what?"

"So, if these pros were hunting, where's the pigeon? Who dropped in to chill the iceman?"

"You're just full of questions, aren't you?"

"Always."

"Any answers I could try for size?"

"Not yet. I'll let your office know if I come up with anything."

"Oh, would you?" Carmody could not disguise the acid in his voice. "We'd all appreciate it *so* much."

"Anytime."

"I'm sure."

Bolan let himself out of the charnel house, swept past reporters who were gathering outside, unlimbering their microphones and minicams. Until he reached the street and merged with traffic, he wouldn't allow himself to think about what he'd seen in Lisa's flat.

It was a possibility that he hadn't considered—members of the syndicate abducting Lisa, forcing her to tell them everything. But from the evidence still leaking on her carpet, in her bed, the snatch hadn't come off as planned. Had there been other gunmen who succeeded in subduing Lisa? Had she killed the shooters on her own, or was a wild card now involved? And if Tien didn't have Lisa Ky, where was she?

Bolan knew that he'd have to answer all those questions for himself, and quickly. Lisa had become the key to his campaign against Tien and Giap. If she was still alive, he had to find her, learn if she was friend or foe.

His knuckles whitened as he clenched the steering wheel. If she was dead, there would be hell to pay.

GIROLAMO CARLOTTI WAS ANGRY. The news that his nephew Vince was lying up in Hoag Memorial, attached to life-support machinery, had shaken him. It brought an honest tear to Giro's eye, but grief was an emotion better left to women. They were trained from nursery school to weep and let their feelings out, while men were forced to cope with grief in silence. Anger was a fitting substitute, and Don Carlotti was adept at using it to crush his enemies.

He didn't have an explanation for the shooting yet, since none of Vince's gunners had survived. From all appearances it was a massacre, with twenty dead for starters and reports still coming in. His people in the sheriff's homicide department told him there were more dead gooks around the warehouse than his own *amici* could account for, and the element of doubt was all that stopped Carlotti from declaring war on Ngo Tien before the sun went down.

The handoff was supposed to be a milk run, swapping cash for smack and thereby honoring the first phase of his "bargain" with the Asian syndicate. He had dispatched Vincenzo as a gesture of respect, and also to make certain that the slopes lived up to their end of the deal. Carlotti didn't trust Tien or Giap as far as he could throw his armor-plated limousine, but he'd given them a chance.

And it had gone to hell, in spades.

Now he had Vincent lying up in ICU, a vegetable that couldn't breathe without machines. He had five gunners dead, a car impounded by the sheriff's office and close to half a million dollars up in smoke. All that, and he had never even *seen* the heroin.

Carlotti knew that it was possible to stage an ambush, make it look like someone else had blown a meet, while you were really pulling all the strings. He'd used the trick a few times in the past himself, but never on a scale like this. It boggled Girolamo's mind to think that Tien and Giap would sacrifice a couple of dozen men for show, but Orientals had a different view of life and all. Those Japs, the Yakuza, hacked off their little fingers when they wanted to apologize for something and with minds like that, you never knew exactly what was going on.

If any single thing was keeping Ngo Tien alive, it had to be the sheriff's lab report that said the heroin—or most of it, at any rate—had gone up in the warehouse fire with what appeared to be a suitcase full of cash. It made no sense at all for Tien to torch the money and the smack, and while it might have been an accident, Carlotti could afford to wait and see. His men were watching Tien and Giap, with stand-

ing orders to reach out and touch someone if either of the
pointy-headed bastards tried to pull a disappearing act.

Don Girolamo, meanwhile, had assorted funerals to arrange, insurance policies to honor for the families of his
dead. Carlotti took care of his own, as in the old days with
DiGeorge, and he was pleased to think his people stuck
around as much from love as from the proved standbys,
greed and fear. He would be visiting the widows personally,
in the next few days, with envelopes of cash and promises
of further help when times got hard. One of the gunners had
a foxy little mistress stashed in Hollywood, and Girolamo
thought a special invitation might be necessary to assuage
her grief. A bit part in a movie he was backing, possibly—
providing she came through in her audition . . .

Carlotti felt a stirring in his loins and spent a moment
concentrating on the dead, to let it fade. There would be
time enough for Hollywood when he discovered what the
hell had happened out in Newport Beach. If Tien and Giap
were pulling off a fast one, it would be their swan song. If
they believed the brotherhood was dying on its feet, so much
the better; it would come as a surprise when the capo
brought them down and ground them underneath his heel.

Carlotti kept abreast of all the headlines, and he knew
about the troubles in New York, Cleveland, Detroit and
Kansas City. Men of power and respect were being carted off
to jail like peasants, sentenced to a hundred years or more
for violating laws that hadn't even been around when he was
coming up. The Feds were breathing down Carlotti's neck,
as well, but he was too damned clever to conduct his business on the telephone, or with a dozen witnesses around to
parrot every word he spoke. There had been efforts to plant
moles inside his Family, but he had pioneered the use of
polygraphs to weed out infiltrators, feeding any liars to the
fish off Santa Catalina. Girolamo knew the lie detector
wasn't perfect, but he was a practical administrator, a sur-

vivor. If he snuffed an innocent or two along the way, it was a damn sight better than allowing Feds to burrow in his Family like maggots in a side of beef.

And the reports of Don Carlotti's imminent demise were very much exaggerated. He was hanging in until the undertaker carried him away, and it would take a better man than Ngo Tien to put him down.

The major problem would arise if he was wrong about Tien and Giap. If they were innocent of pulling off the ambush, that meant he was dealing with an unknown quantity. A wild card. Scowling as he lit a fresh cigar, Carlotti scanned his list of enemies in search of any who possessed the troops and expertise to stage a major skirmish in his own backyard.

He could eliminate the San Francisco crowd immediately. Gianotti's crew was relatively small, and what they lacked in numbers definitely was not made up in ferocity. If anyone had asked Carlotti, he might have suggested that the Gianotti Family had been rubbing shoulders—or whatever—with the local gay community. The way things went these days, you never knew.

There were a couple of guys in Vegas who might try a squeeze in Southern California: Spina, from Chicago, and Gambretti, from New Orleans. Both of them were tough, impetuous, with cash and muscle back of any move they chose to make. Just now, however, both of them were also looking at indictments—skimming, racketeering and extortion—that ought to occupy their minds and leisure time for something like the next two years.

So much for Vegas.

Any farther east, and you ran into Families that were still recovering from recent trials, still squabbling among themselves about who ought to fill the several empty thrones. New York was going apeshit, people dying in the streets like it was 1929 or something, and Miami was recovering from the demise of Don Ernesto Julianno. Funny that the old man would collapse that way, while he was scoring seconds on his Cuban mistress, but Carlotti knew that there were more unpleasant ways to die.

The Cubans and Colombians were nuts enough to stage a major daylight raid, but the capo couldn't see them pulling off a hit without depositing a few stiffs of their own. From all appearances, the dead were strictly Asians and *amici*—all of which brought Don Carlotti back to Tien and Giap.

There was an outside chance some other gang of zipper-heads had crashed the party, jockeying to bump Tien from the driver's seat. The Yakuza was out, but there were rumbles from the Chinese Triads lately over Vietnamese intrusion on the smack trade. Gooks were all the same to Don Carlotti, but he didn't want to kill the *wrong* gooks if he had a choice. It would be bad for business, make Carlotti look as if he didn't know what he was doing.

And you had to watch the Triads, after all. It wasn't like they were the new kids on the block; they had been running opium in China, settling their feuds in blood, before the brotherhood took ship from Sicily to colonize America. They had more soldiers than a beach had grains of sand, and if they had to lose a couple of dozen men to tag their target, they would do precisely that.

Carlotti didn't fear the Triads, but he wasn't suicidal, either. If he had to take on the Chinese, he wanted to be certain in advance and make damned sure his first punch was a knockout.

One group Girolamo didn't have to fret about in all of this confusion was the Feds. He had heard the rumors, all about a secret strike force primed to go outside the law if necessary to destroy the brotherhood, but in his mind it all boiled down to bullshit. No one he had ever talked to had a shred of proof, and it was crazy when you thought about it. Years ago, when one of Hoover's boys had blown his cork and started planting bombs in Tucson, trying to provoke a war between Bonanno and the Licavolis, it had all come out in headlines and the FBI had been a laughingstock. Carlotti couldn't see them trying any shit like that again, not with the Congress prying into everything they did and counting every dime they spent these days.

The capo shook his head. It had to be the Chinese, or else a double cross by Tien and Giap. Whichever, he would know before the day was out, and then he could begin to lay his plans for sweet revenge. If Vinnie ever came around, he would be proud of how his Uncle Giro handled things. And if he didn't . . . well, Carlotti had another nephew in Manhattan Beach who had the makings of a capo, once you cut through all the college crap and got him squared away.

Whichever way it all shook out, the Family would endure. Don Girolamo felt it in his bones. His enemies were dust already, they were just too frigging dumb to know it.

CHAPTER THIRTEEN

"I wish to know what happened."

Ngo Tien made certain his voice didn't betray the anger welling up inside him. Even with a trusted aide like Pham Bach, he would allow himself no visible display of negative emotion. Anger was a weakness his enemies might turn against him in their own good time, and he didn't intend to offer them the weapons of his own destruction.

Bach, for his part, had the stone face down to absolute perfection. Watching his assistant, Tien would not have guessed that anything was wrong. He certainly would never have suspected that a multimillion-dollar drug consignment had gone up in smoke that afternoon, as well as nine good men who had been soldiers in his private army.

Tien didn't consider the Italians as he made his mental body count. The fate of Vincent Moro and his men made little difference to Tien, beyond the fact that it reduced his list of suspects. If the raid had been conceived by Don Carlotti, it had been extremely careless of the mobster to include his nephew in the list of victims. There had also been the matter of Carlotti's cash, destroyed along with the consignment they had planned to share.

The single greatest argument against Carlotti as the mastermind behind the raid, however, was the fact that several of the hostile gunmen were Vietnamese. It might be possible, of course, for Don Carlotti to seduce a young adventurer or two with money, dreams of power, but the two attackers killed by members of his staff were men respected in the refugee community. Cao Diem had fought against the

Communists in Vietnam and suffered greatly for the cause. Tien didn't know Mike Li, except by reputation, and the street talk told him Li was holding down two jobs, was engaged to marry in the fall.

But they weren't alone. Survivors had reported contact with another man, an Anglo, dressed in black and armed for war.

"What happened?" This time he allowed the barest trace of anger to be heard.

"Our warehouse was attacked by persons interested in disrupting the narcotics shipment."

"Obviously." He pinned Pham Bach to his chair with eyes like cold steel blades.

"I mean to say that actual disruption was apparently their goal. They made no effort to collect the money or the heroin, though both were readily accessible. Instead a fire destroyed both, along with several hundred thousand dollars' worth of merchandise inside the warehouse."

"They were Asian," Tien reminded him.

"The two we killed were Asian," Bach corrected. "We cannot surmise the nationality of those who managed to escape. If you recall the statements of our two survivors, which describe a man in black—"

"Of course."

Tien felt his anger building toward the point of detonation. Was Bach consciously attempting to insult him, treating him as if he were a senile fool? If so, the man would find that he could be replaced, despite their years together and the service he had rendered in the past. There was no room for insolence in Tien's command.

"I know him," Bach said quietly.

"Know who?"

"The man in black. At least, I *think* I know his name."

"Who is he?" Anxious now, the smell of sweet revenge already taunting Ngo Tien, he leaned forward in his chair.

He caught himself, sank back and made a steeple of his fingers as he waited for an explanation from his aide.

"The men we killed this afternoon are cronies of Lao Fan," Bach said.

It was unnecessary to identify the latter. He'd been a thorn in Tien's side now for months, approaching the police and sheriff's office with demands for an investigation, even running to the FBI with information he shouldn't, by rights, have had in his possession. The American obsession with due process had protected Tien from any serious annoyance up to now, and he had taken no reactionary steps against Lao Fan, content to let the peasant brood and mutter to himself, a living testimony to the fact that Tien and his associates were still above the law.

But now, if Bach was right, Lao Fan had stepped across the line. Perhaps embittered by the stern rejections he received from law-enforcement agencies, perhaps reverting to his wartime character, the son of muskrats dared to take up arms against Tien. Worse yet, he had enlisted "soldiers" in his cause, and they were primed to die on his behalf.

Of course he was indulging in the rankest form of speculation. They couldn't be sure of anything until Lao Fan was taken for interrogation. Tien would have his answers then, and if it proved that he was wrong, he would release the peasant with sincere apologies. Assuming Lao survived.

A question nagged him. "And the man in black?"

Bach's smile was narrow, cold. "A friend of Lao Fan's from the war, if I am not mistaken. You may recognize the name. Mack Bolan."

There was something...for an instant, Tien believed he had it, but the image slipped away and it was lost. So long ago, the war. So much had happened since. "I do not know the name," he said at last.

"In Vietnam, he was referred to as the Executioner."

Of course. The memories came rushing back at Tien, complete with all the sounds and smells of teeming Saigon streets. He hadn't known the tall American who was renowned for sniping Communists, but word of Bolan's deeds in combat made the rounds of bars as did so many other stories from the killing fields. Years later, Tien recalled, the man had run amok at home, assassinating mafiosi for a time. There were reports that he was killed in New York City, followed by a quiet time until he was arrested in some Southern state. He'd been held for trial, had once again escaped.

"Why Bolan?"

"The description," Bach replied, "plus his connections with Lao Fan. The two of them were friends in Vietnam, and now they share a common interest in suppression of...free enterprise."

"Do we have reason to believe that Bolan is in California?"

"Aside from the descriptions offered by our own survivors?" Pham Bach nodded. "I have spoken with our friends in San Francisco. Earlier this week, they suffered losses in a raid on one of their casinos. Bolan was identified by three of their cashiers."

"And you believe that he came here from San Francisco?"

"Obviously. Lao Fan got in touch with him, somehow— or maybe they have been in contact all along. It does not matter, now. We have identified the enemy, and we must see to his destruction before he harms us any further."

Tien was silent for a moment, studying the problem. When he spoke, his voice was soft but deadly. "Find Lao Fan. I wish to hear his explanation in this matter."

"And if he resists?"

"The choice is his."

Bach left him, smiling as he closed the office door, and Tien remained behind his desk, immobile. He was rooted to the spot, surprised and mortified to realize that he was frightened by the specter of a man whom he had never even seen.

The Executioner. A name well earned, he understood, in Vietnam and afterward. A man of infinite capacity for dealing death.

But still a man.

And while the beating of a heart caused blood to circulate through Bolan's veins, a bullet or a knife could stop that heart, arrest that flow. He was a man, and nothing more.

He could be killed.

He *would* be killed, if he attempted to destroy the empire Ngo Tien had spent a lifetime building.

PHAM BACH WAS PLEASED with Ngo Tien. The seed was planted now, in fertile soil, and all he had to do was tend it carefully, sit back and watch it grow.

He had anticipated Tien's reaction to the news of Bolan's presence in Orange County, was prepared to overcome his skepticism with a phone call from their allies to the north, if necessary. As it was, the Executioner had played into Bach's hands, allowing various survivors from the warehouse raid to see him in the flesh. There could be little doubt about his interest in the family business now, and if some doubt remained, it would be swept away once Lao Fan had been introduced to Giap's interrogators.

Tien wouldn't have been amused if he'd known about Bach's role in bringing Bolan to the area, of course. Such zeal extended well beyond the call of duty; some might even call it treason, but they didn't share Bach's foresight or his dedication to a higher cause. They wouldn't understand that calling Bolan in, just now, ensured a major propaganda triumph for the people's revolution. They would never grasp the subtlety of Bach's design.

With Bolan on the scene, intent on slaughtering the syndicate, Tien's mask of staid respectability was bound to shatter, leaving him exposed as the unmitigated fascist gangster that he truly was. If Tien wasn't eliminated by the Executioner, he would be ruined in the public eye, along with countless other lackeys in the refugee community who had betrayed the revolution. Cowards that they were, the revelation of their decadence would ruin many, might drive some to suicide. The rest would stand revealed as traitors to their homeland and their race.

It was a golden opportunity, made sweeter by the fact that it would also climax in destruction for the Executioner.

In Vietnam the man had been a scourge of freedom fighters, working both sides of the DMZ, occasionally striking into Laos, Cambodia. His record boasted ninety-seven murders, heroes of the revolution slain from ambush by a Green Beret assassin, and there had certainly been others, killed but never counted in the jungle skirmishes, the border raids and night patrols. There had been a price on Bolan's head when he was summoned home from Vietnam, and the American withdrawal had done nothing to erase the memory of brothers martyred in a holy cause, their killer still at large.

There was no price on Bolan's head today, but honors would be heaped upon the man who brought him down. In Vietnam Bach's name would be revered, his service to the people's revolution honored by the men in charge.

And if he didn't live to hear their praise...well, he was ready to accept the martyr's fate that other heroes of the struggle had been forced to bear before him. Bach wasn't afraid of death, as long as he could take a number of the enemy along.

It had been difficult, throughout the years, to smile at Tien and Giap, to make believe that he was one of them, a brother underneath the skin. They had accepted his expression of desire for wealth and power, confident that other men were simply mirror images of their venality, their decadence. They had believed because they *needed* to believe, and it would kill them in the end.

If Bolan didn't kill them first.

The girl had been his shining triumph. Bach allowed himself a touch of pardonable pride as he considered the precise and final execution of his masterstroke. Lao Fan had been his lure, but the girl had been his hook, and Bolan had been quick to swallow both. The soldier might not know it yet, but he was trapped, as surely as a tiger in a pit. There would be no escape.

The girl would hold him, Bach was sure of that. For all his reputation in the field, the Executioner was soft inside, another peasant vulnerable to emotions, feelings. If the girl was wounded, he would bleed. And he wouldn't desert her, not while some hope of saving her remained.

Bach chuckled to himself, delighted with the scheme that had, so far, worked out precisely in accordance with his plans. His "master," Ngo Tien, would certainly have killed Bach outright had he known the details, but in time the scheme would be revealed. In time the drug lord would be made to see that he had been a pawn, manipulated by a hero of the people's revolution in a cause he could never hope to understand.

The girl would drive that lesson home, and Bach intended to be facing Tien when all was revealed. He wanted to enjoy the look of bafflement and pain, the shock that would destroy Tien's well-rehearsed facade.

But not just yet.

Bach's driver held the door and saw him settled in his seat before he slid behind the wheel. The big man waited patiently for his instructions.

"Home."

The Lincoln merged with traffic, nosing toward the freeway. Bach relaxed, secure in the knowledge that a miracle would be required to save his enemies. As a devoted Communist, he knew there was no God, and he didn't believe in miracles. Belief had been destroyed in childhood by the French and by Americans in adolescence. Trust and love had followed, slaughtered by the enemy and rapidly forgotten by a young man who had known no life outside of war.

An idiot hung on to faith while life caved in around him. Men of vision took their destinies in hand and shaped the world to suit their needs. When opposition was encountered, it was ruthlessly destroyed. The people's revolution was a logical extension of a young boy's quest for sanctuary, for revenge.

For all his prowess, all his journeys through the fire, the Executioner would prove to be a weakling in the end. Bach knew it, as he knew his own sure destiny: to live—or die—a hero of the revolution, and to have his name remembered when the names of Bolan, Tien and Giap had turned to dust.

LAO FAN FELL IN behind the Lincoln Continental, hanging back two car lengths, staying close enough to keep his prey in sight. They would be heading for the freeway on ramp, heading home, but he would follow just in case.

He had selected Bach deliberately for himself, uncertain how he might react at the sight of Tien and Giap. The deaths of Mike Li and Cao Diem had pushed him to the edge, and nothing would have pleased him more than to kill Ngo Tien before the sun went down. If doing so required that he sacrifice himself, Lao was prepared for that, as well. His life would be a pittance in the universal scheme of things, if he could only purge the dark malignancy embodied in his enemies.

It had been Bolan's choice to wait. He counseled patience, caution, while they sought more hard intelligence about the ambush. Someone had betrayed them, and Lao Fan had been betting on the girl, until he heard that she was missing, and that the dead men in her flat had turned out to be a pair of guns in Tien's employ.

The game was getting complicated. First the girl alerted Bolan to a shipment of narcotics, then his ambush was betrayed. Before Bolan could interrogate the girl, Tien had gone after her with soldiers, and his hit team had itself been hit.

By whom? And why?

Until the girl was found, there would be nagging questions left unanswered, lethal threats perhaps unrecognized. If she wasn't the key to a solution of the puzzle, she remained a vital piece toward its completion. Lao Fan hoped Bolan would recover her before the night was out. Lao had already waited long enough to wreak his vengeance on the leeches who would drain his people dry.

They caught the ramp at Anaheim Boulevard, rolling north toward Bach's condominium in Buena Park. If Bach had any calls to make, he might feel safer making them from home. Lao wished he could follow Bach inside, remind him of the fact that there was no safe haven in guerrilla warfare, no place he could hide.

In time, but not just now.

The war had taught Lao Fan to hide his feelings, live with pain that might have broken lesser men. He knew the price of weakness, had seen others pay for it with their lives. He wouldn't give his enemies the satisfaction of provoking him to hasty action now, when there was still so much at stake. So much to lose.

The traffic thinned as the Lincoln approached Bach's neighborhood, and Lao fell back, allowing two more cars to slip between him and his quarry. Knowing the address by heart, he had no fear of losing Bach before they reached their final destination. He would give the fox his lead and find a lookout post from which he could observe the condominium in safety.

If the timing of his face-to-face with Tien was any indicator, Bach would be engaged in calling up the troops. Anh Giap was technically the war chief of the syndicate, but Bach had the responsibility of gathering intelligence, communicating with Tien on matters of importance that might vary from the price of opium in Bangkok to the strength of rival forces on the streets of Hollywood. In effect he ran Tien's personal gestapo, and from that position he had gathered private troops around himself, a sort of palace guard who answered first to Bach.

Lao had been curious when he first learned of the arrangement, startled that Tien and Giap would countenance formation of a private army in their own backyard. In fact, Anh Giap apparently had tried to block the move, according to the word from various informants on the fringes of the outfit, but his arguments were overruled by Tien on the theory that two security forces were better than one.

Bolan's interest in Lisa Ky intrigued Lao Fan. It was enough, of course, that she had saved his life and led him to the warehouse where the ambush had occurred. If she had played a traitor's role, there would be questions, and the matter of a fitting punishment. If she had not betrayed them, if her life was now in jeopardy because of her involvement with the Executioner, Lao knew that Bolan wouldn't rest until he brought her safely home... or made her killers pay.

But there was something else behind the soldier's eyes when Lisa Ky was mentioned. Something he hadn't chosen to discuss with Lao as yet. They weren't lovers; there had simply been no time. If they had met before, cooperated in some other struggle, Bolan wouldn't doubt her now. And why should his acquaintance with her be kept secret?

Questions and Lao Fan had no idea where he should look to find the answers. Soon, if Bolan found the girl, his doubts and apprehensions might be swept away.

Until that time there was Pham Bach, and Lao would follow him to hell itself if necessary. When Tien's gestapo leader finished with his calls and ventured out to meet his troops, Lao Fan would travel with him like a shadow, clinging to his heels. He would be there when Bach slipped up, made one mistake too many, and he would be ready to collect the fee in blood.

But not just yet.

His job this evening, as twilight daubed the sky with soft pastels, was simply to sit back and watch. Perhaps, if Bach was very sensitive, he might already know that he was being followed. He might even send a team of his enforcers to scour the neighborhood, make certain that he was secure.

Lao Fan was smiling as he slipped a hand beneath the trench coat folded on the seat beside him. Fingers grazed the pistol grip of his Kalashnikov, made out the curve of its banana clip, the cool steel of its muzzle.

Let them come. Lao Fan was ready, and he would welcome them with open arms.

CHAPTER FOURTEEN

The dark had always been a comfort, but it frightened Lisa now. She sat on the floor beside the window, a pistol in her lap, and wished that she could turn on the lights. Even one would be a help, but she couldn't afford to take the chance.

Her weapon was a Colt Detective's Special. It was cool now, to her touch—not like before, when she had tucked it in the waistband of her slacks and burned herself. The snubby barrel nestled in her palm, so inoffensive, hardly threatening at all. When Lisa raised a hand to brush the hair back from her face, her fingers smelled of oil and gun smoke.

She was frightened, and with reason. She had killed two men that evening, and the police would be out looking for her, along with any other gunmen Bach might choose to send. Her choices narrowed down to jail or death, and she didn't deceive herself by thinking she would be safe in custody. If Bach had turned against her—and he evidently had—she knew he wouldn't rest until he saw her dead.

He must be acting on his own authority. She saw that now, too late, and realized that he had used her, played her for a fool. For all the talk about allowing her to prove herself, bring honor to her family, he had intended from the start that she should die.

Angered, her finger tightened on the trigger, and she brought herself back from the edge by slow degrees.

The shooters had been slick, she gave them that much. Dapper, neatly groomed, they had presented her with Pham Bach's compliments for work well done, inviting her to join them for a celebration of their victory. Mack Bolan and the leaders of the local Mafia destroyed in one fell swoop. She was delighted to oblige.

They had slipped up while she was in the bedroom, changing clothes and shifting contents from one handbag to another. Speaking in Vietnamese, too confident to whisper, one of them had casually asked the other if he had remembered to bring shovels. Number two had cursed, apologized and named a store where they could pick some up before their drive into the desert.

Lisa didn't have to ask them what they planned to dig for, what was going in the hole. Her life didn't precisely flash before her eyes, but she was conscious of the fact that stucco and a partly open door were all that separated her from sudden death.

The Colt revolver had been purchased on a whim two years before, when a girl in Lisa's dorm had been attacked and raped. Free lessons came with every purchase, and she had become proficient with the weapon, though she seldom practiced anymore. Its presence in a bedside drawer was reassuring, and while Lisa had rehearsed the situations where she might be called upon to shoot a man, she never actually believed that time would come.

Until it finally arrived.

The Colt had seemed heavier, somehow, and Lisa knew that it was an illusion. Swinging out the cylinder to check its load, she drew the hammer back and braced the weapon in a firm, two-handed grip. It was the way she'd been taught to fire at paper silhouettes, and it would have to serve her now, with human targets.

Her pulse was racing, pounding in her ears as she called for one of the men to help her; there was something on a closet shelf she couldn't reach. She heard them snicker, knew that one had made a crude remark, and told herself again that these men meant to kill her.

Lisa let her target step across the threshold, saw the flicker of his dying smile before she pulled the trigger. Dead on target at a range of twenty feet, the impact of the .38 slug drove him backward, clumsily rebounding from collision with the doorframe, sprawling on the carpet.

She reached the doorway as her second would-be killer slipped a hand inside his jacket, clawing for the weapon that could save his life. When Lisa shot him twice, from fifteen feet away, his face had frozen in a look of overwhelming shock. He was dead before he hit the floor.

There had been no time then to think about what she had done. Afraid there might be others waiting for her, she had fled immediately, driving straight to the apartment of a girlfriend who was on vacation. Lisa knew where she could find the extra key, and she was reasonably certain that Bach's gunners couldn't trace her there. But she was still afraid.

Betrayal was a relatively new experience for Lisa. She had grown up trusting in her family and friends, secure in the knowledge that they wouldn't let her down, wouldn't deliberately do her harm. Pham Bach had been her friend, or so she had believed, and his duplicity had been as shocking as her brush with death itself.

Too late, she realized that Bach had been deceiving her from the beginning. Ngo Tien knew nothing of their scheme, although his name had been invoked to give the operation credence. Angry and embarrassed, Lisa was surprised to find humiliation edging out her fear. When she remembered Pham Bach's promises, their conversations, pouring out her secret thoughts, her stomach churned with nausea. Immediately thankful that she hadn't eaten lunch or dinner, Lisa took a long, deep breath to calm herself and concentrated on the window.

Peering through a narrow aperture between the draperies, she had a view of sidewalk, scruffy lawn, a slice of parking lot. The flat had no back door, and anyone who came for her would have to enter by the front, through door or windows. She would kill them if they tried—a few of them, at least—but she had no illusions of her own ability to stop an army in its tracks.

Bach would have learned of her escape by now, and he would have his gunners on the street. With the confusion of the warehouse shooting earlier that afternoon, Tien would have no curiosity about the fact that Bach was mobilizing troops. If she attempted to communicate with Tien by telephone, it would be Bach or one of his associates who took the call, and Lisa dared not show herself. Not while the hunters were abroad, with orders that included shooting her on sight.

She thought of Bolan, knew that he could help her, knew as well that he would be suspicious of her, at best. The warehouse ambush had been staged for Bolan's benefit, and he was sharp enough to realize that Lisa must have had a hand in it. For her part, Lisa knew the trap had failed; a "special bulletin" on television had related the events, complete with body count, and there'd been no mention of the Executioner. The death of Mack Bolan would certainly have earned some comment, and the station's seeming ignorance of Bolan's presence in the area told Lisa all she had to know.

He had escaped. In spite of everything, the odds and numbers ranged against him, Bolan had survived and was still at large. Lisa wondered if he would be searching for her, if he might discover what had happened back at her apartment. It was certain he would want to question her, determine whether she had known about the ambush. After he was finished with his questions . . .

Would he kill her? Had he learned to think of her as family by now? Would righteous anger let him sever the illusory connection that had bound them for a day?

No matter. He was still her only chance, however slim, and Lisa had to get in touch with him somehow, at any cost. The telephone was out; she didn't have a number for him, and she knew that he wouldn't be wasting time in his rented room in any case. He would be on the street and hunting, like the others. Hunting Lisa. Hunting Ngo Tien.

The small apartment suddenly felt claustrophobic, like a prison cell. She knew it might be death to step outside, but sitting in the dark and waiting could be infinitely worse. If she was bound to throw her life away, at least she had the option of deciding where and when the sacrifice would happen. She could still decide that much and, in the process, she might teach a few more of Bach's soldiers that she was a woman to be reckoned with.

Two down. How many dozens left to go?

She had reloaded the revolver, and she checked her bag, counting her extra cartridges. Thirteen. Two loads, plus one, and Lisa smiled as she remembered all the cowboy movies she had seen in childhood, wagon trains and troops cavalry surrounded by Indians, preparing for the end. Invariably someone made the point of holding out an extra bullet for himself, in case of capture by the savages.

Her smile turned bitter. She wasn't about to help the bastards do their job. If Pham Bach wanted her, alive or dead, he would be forced to work for it, and she would take as many of his soldiers with her as she could. It was her father's way, and it was good enough for Lisa.

But she was still afraid, and killing two of Bach's assassins hadn't eased her fears. If anything, the proximity of death had heightened Lisa's apprehension, made her realize that this wasn't some abstract game. Her life was on the line, and if she meant to save herself, she would be forced to learn the rules as she proceeded, working through the maze.

She might not last an hour, but Lisa was doomed for certain if she failed to take *some* action on her own behalf.

Without a coach to walk her through the moves, she had to improvise and take each situation as it came.

She locked the door behind her, put the key back in its hiding place and kept the .38 in hand as she set off to meet the darkness.

HIS INTERVIEW WITH THE POLICE had taken Bolan nowhere. It was time to try the other side, and he decided to eliminate the middleman by starting at the top. Don Girolamo might not be expecting company, but he would speak with Bolan, one way or another.

The Carlotti mansion had become a fortress in a few short hours. Quiet, rolling grounds were now patrolled by men with riot guns and automatic weapons, walkie-talkies on their belts. Two Caddys were positioned near the wrought-iron gates, prepared to block the entrance if a kamikaze driver tried to force his way inside. The men behind the wheels were stone-faced, wearing shades despite the fact that it was now full dark.

The Executioner had changed into an expensive suit, securing his hardware with the sole exception of the Desert Eagle .44, which rode beneath his arm in custom rigging. They would find it if they looked, of course, but he was counting on his edge to see him through. Carlotti's war tonight would be with the Vietnamese, and he wouldn't anticipate attacks from other quarters.

As Bolan braked his rental to a stop, the gates were opened far enough for one of Don Carlotti's men to step outside. The gunner's hands were empty, but a glint of iron was showing at his waist, and his companion had a 12-gauge leveled at the car's windshield, covering the action from a decent vantage point. He might not score a killing shot the first time, but the odds were definitely running with the house.

"You got some business here?" the yardman asked.

"I need to speak with Don Carlotti."

"Yeah? Says who?"

"The name's Omega."

"Wouldn't matter if your name was Rolex. Don Carlotti isn't seeing any visitors tonight."

"That's firm?"

"It's carved in stone."

"Okay." He shrugged and palmed a business card, relayed it to the gunner with a flourish. "Give him this, with my regards, and tell him New York sends their best."

The gunner's mouth fell open and he did a double take, from Bolan to the ace of spades and back again. It was the death card, carried only by initiated members of the Mafia's elite gestapo, men with the authority to hit a capo on their own initiative, provided they could later prove a case of dire necessity for La Commissióne. The Bolan wars had wrought some drastic changes in the Black Ace network, but a few of them were still around, and Bolan had occasionally profited from trading on their fearsome reputation.

"Just hold on a minute, sir, okay?" The gunner's tone had changed from cocky self-assuredness to humble pie. "I want to check this with the house."

"Of course."

The gate men held a hasty confab, and the soldier with the riot gun retreated, wrestling a walkie-talkie off his belt and calling for instructions. Half a minute passed before the word came back, and Bolan's playmates rolled the heavy gates aside.

The mouthpiece handed back his ace of spades, and Bolan saw him brush his fingertips against his trousers, like a man who had been forced to handle something strange and possibly contagious.

"They'll be waiting for you at the house, sir. Hundred yards or so along the drive, there. You can't miss it."

"Thanks."

"No problem, sir."

All things considered, Don Carlotti had a smaller home than Bolan had expected. Twenty rooms at most, but he had paid a fortune for the wooded acreage on which it sat, imported trees and shrubbery meticulously tended by a troop of gardeners who kept the foliage green and healthy in defiance of the moods displayed by Mother Nature. Giro had exquisite taste in real estate, you had to give him that. But he was still a savage, and the very fact of his existence was offensive to the Executioner.

It would have been a treat to take Carlotti out, but at the moment, Bolan needed him alive. It wouldn't serve his purposes to smoke the capo, risk a free-for-all with members of the palace guard, when he had other goals in mind. Before he started closing down the game, he wanted one more face-to-face with Lisa Ky. And failing that, he had to know her role in all that had transpired since his arrival in Orange County.

It was no small order, and he had no reason to believe that Don Carlotti was responsible for Lisa's disappearance. Touching base with the opposing sides was simply common sense, a necessary step in narrowing his field of suspects down to manageable numbers.

They were waiting for him at the house, as promised, Don Carlotti's houseman and a pair of flankers, armed with Ingram machine pistols. Bolan let the honcho see his ace and hit the shooters with an arctic smile.

"You have to understand we weren't expecting any visitors," the houseman said.

"Of course."

"I'm sorry, but I have to ask you for your piece."

"You *have* to?"

"Don Carlotti's orders, sir."

"I see." He passed over the Desert Eagle, watching as the gunners checked it out. "You don't mind if I keep my pants on, do you?"

"No, sir. Sorry. This way."

He trailed his escort through the open doors, along a corridor that could have doubled as a target range. Halfway along, the houseman stopped in front of a door and knocked.

"Come in."

The voice was softer, more refined than Bolan had expected. He already knew Don Giro on the basis of his reputation as a hitter under Julian DiGeorge. Carlotti had come up the hard way, but his eyes were keen, invested with intelligence, and there was culture in the way he held himself, awaiting introductions.

"Don Carlotti, this is Omega."

"Leave us, Benny."

"Yessir."

"Call me Giro." There was tempered steel in Don Carlotti's grip, and Bolan gave him back the same. It wasn't quite a test, but it was close enough. "What brings you to my home on such a night as this?"

"New York instructed me to send you their regards. They know about your problem here, and I was told to check it out."

"My problem? I'm afraid I don't know what you mean."

"You lost four soldiers and a suitcase full of cash this afternoon. You've got a nephew tucked away in ICU who needs machines to help him breathe. Does any of this ring a bell?"

"I guess it's true about how bad news travels fast."

"Believe it. The commission is afraid you're sitting on a war out here, and it's about to hatch."

"Whatever happens, I can handle it myself."

"That's not the problem, Giro."

Play "Action Poker"
to see if you can get

- ◆ 4 hard-hitting, action-packed Gold Eagle novels just like the one you're reading — FREE
- ◆ PLUS a useful pocket knife — FREE

Peel off the card on the front of this brochure and stick it in the hand opposite. Find out how many gifts you can receive ABSOLUTELY FREE. They're yours to keep even if you never buy another Gold Eagle novel.

Then deal yourself in for more gut-chilling action at deep subscriber savings

Once you have read your free books, we're willing to bet you'll want more of those page-crackling, razor-edge stories. So we'll send you six brand new Gold Eagle books every other month to preview. (Two Mack Bolans and one each of Able Team, Phoenix Force, Vietnam: Ground Zero and SOBs.)

- ◆ Hot-off-the-press novels with the kind of no-holds — barred action you crave.
- ◆ Delivered right to your home.
- ◆ Months before they're available in stores.
- ◆ At hefty savings off the retail price.
- ◆ Always with the right to cancel and owe nothing.

You will pay only $2.49 for each book — 11% less than the retail price — plus 95¢ postage and handling per shipment.

Enjoy special subscriber privileges

- ◆ With every shipment you will receive AUTOMAG, our exciting newsletter FREE.
- ◆ Plus special books to preview free and buy at rock bottom discount.

Gold Eagle No Bluff, No Risk Guarantee

● You're not required to buy a single book—ever!
● Even as a subscriber, you must be completely satisfied or you may return a shipment of books and cancel at any time.
● The free books and gift you receive from this ACTION POKER offer remain yours to keep — in any case.

"Oh? Maybe you should tell me what the problem *is*."

"Bad timing," Bolan told him, "and your choice of enemies."

"My enemies chose me," Carlotti growled. "You want to tell me what's behind all this concern?"

"Why not? It shouldn't come as any great surprise to you that Asians have been moving in on Family businesses across the board. New York, New Orleans, San Francisco. Hell, they're buying up casinos in Las Vegas like the goddamned place was going out of style. They've got us maybe five to one on soldiers, nationwide, and if you want to handle China White these days, you'll have to feed the dragon."

"Tell me something new."

"Okay. New York is in the process of negotiating an alliance, like the old days. Territories, prices, cease-fires—all that shit. They're close to ironing out a deal between the Chinese Triads, some of the Vietnamese and the commission. Later, when they get the bugs worked out, they'll try it out with Tokyo."

"I'm happy for them," Don Carlotti grumbled. "What's that got to do with me?"

"You're making certain people nervous, Giro. You start whacking zipperheads tonight, tomorrow, and the settlement goes up in smoke before it's even ratified. New York can't take the chance. There's too much riding on the line."

Carlotti's face was twisted by a scowl. "*New York* can't take the chance? Since when am I a button for the Families? I don't see any of their people on the line."

"You're seeing me."

"They've got you running errands like a fucking gofer. If New York's so interested in what goes on out here, why don't they send some troops and help me clear this up?"

"The troops are waiting, Giro."

"Yeah? So tell me why I get the feeling I'm their target?"

"Like I said before, it's timing. Everybody knows you're getting shit on here, and there's a payback coming, but you've got to take it easy for a while. When the commission gets its act together, there'll be plenty time for kicking ass."

"You know about my nephew. What am I supposed to tell his mother? Sorry, Sis, I can't play hardball with the gooks right now, New York's got business with the bastards who put your boy on ice?"

"Three weeks, a month at most, and you can give her a bouquet of yellow ears. An early Christmas, eh? But if you jump the gun and screw things up, you stand alone."

"I've been alone before."

"Against the whole commission?"

"Goddamn it, this is wrong! We're blood, here. What makes all these gooks so damned important?"

"Think about the old days, Giro. The brotherhood had to deal with Irish, Jews and Germans, Polacks—every color of the rainbow. Deals were made, and sometimes we were on the short end of the stick but where are all those other guys today?"

Carlotti frowned. "It's all a setup, then?"

"The brotherhood's not giving anything away. Sometimes you go along to get along, but when the other bastard turns his back..."

"A month, you said?"

"The max."

"I've got some people who gonna think I've lost my balls."

"They give you any flak, refer them to me."

"No, I can handle it. I just don't want to keep them on the string too long."

"Four weeks, at the outside. You've got my word."

"Okay."

"There's just one other thing..."

"I'm listening."

"A girl, Vietnamese, named Lisa something. Way I hear it, she was tight with one of Ngo Tien's leg breakers. He got wasted yesterday, and now the girl's gone missing."

"So?"

"Some think you chopped the boyfriend. They've been wondering if you know where she is."

"I don't know where she is, or who she is," Carlotti grumbled. "She can go fall off the earth, for all I care."

"You'd know if any of your boys had picked her up?"

"Hell, yes, I'd know. We run on discipline out here, not like the Families back east, where every cowboy in the world starts shooting up the countryside. I find out one of my boys made a move without my say-so, it's the last move that he ever makes."

"I'll take your word on that."

"I guess you'll have to."

"Right. It's been a pleasure, Giro."

"Hmm."

"I'll be in touch."

"Four weeks, Omega. We know how to count out here, remember that."

"I have a perfect memory."

The houseman walked him to his car in silence, handed back his weapon, standing with his flankers as the rental pulled away. The mouthpiece on the gate had nerve enough to raise a hand, and Bolan flashed him a salute that left the weasel smiling as he hit the pavement, taillights winking out of sight.

Carlotti was a long shot, and he hadn't paid. Whatever had become of Lisa Ky, the Mafia was not involved so far. That left the soldier with a limited array of options, and he swept them all away in favor of the blunt, direct approach.

If Lisa was with Tien, he meant to find out for himself. Tonight.

CHAPTER FIFTEEN

Ngo Tien conducted business from a suite of penthouse offices in downtown Anaheim. His building was a fourteen-story high rise, but the structures flanking it on east and west were taller. Bolan chose the eastern neighbor, with a two-floor drop and more than thirty feet between the buildings.

He wasn't prepared to seek Tien at his home. Before he made that last, irrevocable move he wanted to know more about the man, acquire a stronger feeling for his enemy. A briefing on the line to Washington had given him bones, but it was time to add some flesh and see his target as a living, breathing man.

As a simple drop, it would have been no more than forty feet, but he would also have to span the strip of open space that lay between his target and his lookout post. One slip, the smallest of miscalculations, and the sanitation people would be hosing his remains off the sidewalk.

Accomplishing his first objective had been relatively easy. Cleaning crews ran through the high-rise towers after dark like bees in a hive, anonymous and faceless. Bolan had donned regulation coveralls, and no one questioned his presence. No one expressed the slightest curiosity about the duffel bag he carried. There appeared to be no system in the way the janitors attacked their work, and Bolan doubted anyone would miss him.

It took him forty seconds to complete assembly of the crossbow, fifteen more to draw and arm the weapon. Forged of tempered steel, the bolt was thirteen inches long and resembled a needle with its sharpened tip, the narrow eye through which a slender nylon line was strung. Designed for penetration at a range of thirty yards, Bolan knew the piton should provide him with a solid anchor on the other side.

He chose a target well back from the knee-high parapet, took aim, squeezed off. The lifeline whispered in its flight, described an arc, went slack on impact. Bolan caught it, gave a solid tug and tried it with his weight. When he was confident that it would hold, he ran the coil around a forced-air unit mounted on the roof and tied it off.

The Executioner was dressed to kill. He wore the night-suit underneath his coveralls, the Beretta 93-R readily accessible in shoulder rigging. A stiletto and garrote completed the ensemble, with a pair of leather gloves to spare his palms on the descent. He wore no safety harness, conscious of the fact that it would make no difference if the rope gave way 150 feet above the pavement.

Bolan straddled the parapet, swung his leg over and sat with his back to the roof, his feet dangling in space. Both hands tight on the rope, one leg over. Bolan caught a glimpse of the streetlights beneath him, then rolled, winding up with his face to the sky.

He slid down the rope like a fireman descending a pole, using sneakers and gloves for a brake as he hurtled toward touchdown. They would find the rope later, but he intended to be long gone by then. He wouldn't be returning the way he had come.

Bolan tried out the access door, found it securely bolted from inside, a hedge against prowlers and thieves in the night. He had counted on being locked out, and the barrier didn't discourage him. Circling the roof on a recon, he picked out the air-conditioning unit that serviced Tien's suite, labeled Penthouse in red letters that were starting to fade. Close at hand, the exhaust vent was covered by sheet metal cowling, secured to the roof by a half dozen screws.

Bolan picked out a screwdriver, loosened the cowling and set it aside. The exhaust vent was three feet by two, wide enough in a pinch, but with no room to spare. The warrior's pencil flash showed him a right-angle turn at the bottom, eight feet below. He would have to go in feetfirst and hope for the best.

It was cool in the shaft, but he knew that the feeling would fade as he worked his way farther inside. He wasn't claustrophobic, but it would be tight all the same. Once inside, past the elbow, retreat was ruled out as an option. If Tien had the shaft covered, somehow, the game would be over before it began.

At the base of the shaft, Bolan turned with his back toward the lateral passage and knelt, pushing off with his hands, twisting sideways and sliding until he lay flat on his back, head and shoulders remaining outside. At the top of the shaft, he imagined a glitter of starlight, impossibly out of his reach. Bolan wondered if this was the way an iron lung might feel: tight and constricting, the weight of the world on his chest.

Pushing off with his hands, digging in with his heels where he could, Bolan watched the illusory starlight wink out. Midnight darkness enveloped him, smooth metal inches away from his face, yet invisible. Wormlike, he covered a distance of twenty-odd yards before faint light constricted his pupils.

The vent was set high in one wall, with another twenty feet farther along. The shaft branched away beyond that point, serving other rooms, sketching a maze.

Bolan rolled on his side and probed through the slots in the vent cover with his pencil flash, scanning the office. The source of dim light was a digital clock, its numerals greenish pale in the darkness. His flash picked out file cabinets, sofa and chairs, a long table with magazines neatly arranged on its surface.

A waiting room, Bolan decided. The desk would be occupied by a receptionist, nine to five, Monday through Friday, but no one was here to receive him tonight. The warrior checked out the exit, the door to Tien's own private office, and came up with nothing to indicate he was expected. If there was a trap waiting for him, the hunters were skillfully hidden.

Bolan brought up his forearm and hammered the vent cover sharply. It tumbled away, struck a chair and rebounded to land on the carpet. He froze, the Beretta in hand, knowing this was the time for an ambush if one was prepared. They could take him now, springing from cover, guns blazing.

Nothing stirred in the office below him; no sound issued from Tien's sanctum. Bolan gave it a ten count, then eased through the opening.

The receptionist's office would hold no surprises, and Bolan brushed past her desk, trying Tien's door. He wasn't surprised to discover it was locked. On his knees, with the flash in his teeth, he extracted the picks from a pocket and got down to work on the tumblers.

Two minutes later he had it. Tien's desk was easily ten feet across, his swivel chair reminding Bolan of a throne done up in leather. Dark, expensive paneling was polished to a shine and decorated with the assorted scrolls and plaques that Tien had received for service to the refugee community. A bank of filing cabinets occupied the far wall, tucked away behind the desk, securely locked.

It would take moments to defeat the locks, long hours to peruse the contents of the cabinets. Bolan didn't have the time for anything approaching thorough scrutiny, but having come this far, he couldn't turn away without at least a casual look. There might be something—notes, a ledger— that would supply him with a handle on Tien's game.

And, in the process, he would search for any clues that might provide him with the whereabouts of Lisa Ky.

He spied the photograph by accident, a fleeting image on the tight periphery of vision, there and gone almost before it had a chance to register. On impulse, Bolan left the filing cabinet and moved to stand behind the massive desk, imagining himself in Tien's position. There was something odd about the photograph. He played the pencil flash across its glossy surface, picked it up.

And froze.

LON THIEU WAS TIRED, and he was angry—at himself, for being low man on the totem pole; at Ngo Tien, for choosing him to stand the graveyard watch outside his office. Most of all, Lon Thieu was angry at the bastards who had tried to grab Tien's Bangkok shipment, kicking off his problems in the first place.

There were uniformed patrolmen in the building, and Tien had always trusted them before, but with a war approaching he had grown more cautious. An attack upon his office, the destruction of his files, might throw the family's business into chaos, wasting time while precious contacts were restored, financial ledgers reconstructed from information filed with Tien's accountants. Thus the order had come down from Tien and Giap: a sentry must stand watch outside the office, day and night.

Tonight, Lon Thieu had been selected for the "honor," and he had endured the teasing of his friends who had more interesting missions to perform. In truth, he hadn't wanted any job at all this evening. He'd been prepared to make his move on an Anglo waitress in a cocktail lounge controlled by Tien, and after three long weeks of laying groundwork, Thieu was confident of swift success.

But that was finished now, at least until tomorrow. He was stuck on sentry duty. If he hadn't feared Giap the way some men fear God, he might have told his captain what to do with the assignment. But he *did* fear Giap, had witnessed the dismantling of a family soldier charged with insubordination, and he knew no Anglo waitress could be worth his life.

At least he was alone, a circumstance that Lon Thieu recognized correctly as a tribute to the nature of his job. If there had been a major risk of hostile action, several gunners would have been assigned, and he would have been forced to listen as they lied about their sex lives, their cool elimination of imaginary enemies. As long as he had to waste his evening, Thieu preferred to be alone, with time to think about the Anglo waitress and the things that he could teach her, given half a chance.

But it was boring. After several hours on a folding chair outside the office, he was nodding and his butt was sore. With no one to observe or criticize him, he saw nothing wrong with ducking out to find the uniformed security patrolmen at their station, scoring coffee and some conversation to relieve the tedium of waiting endlessly for nothing. When they had to make their rounds, he trudged back up the stairs alone—the elevators having been shut down at six o'clock—and settled in his chair once more, to watch the empty corridor. With any luck, the building's janitors would reach his level soon, and he could watch them buff the floors for sport.

He nearly missed the noise, and would have, if the building hadn't been so deathly quiet. Indefinable, a muffled sound that he subconsciously associated with the office, though he could not have described it to preserve his soul. A sound...

Which was repeated, unmistakably emerging from behind the very door he was assigned to guard.

Lon Thieu stood up, approached the door cautiously and stepped back. He slid a hand inside his jacket, drawing courage from the automatic pistol hidden there.

A prowler? He'd never been around the office after closing, and was therefore unfamiliar with the normal night sounds of the building. Was he letting his imagination run away from him, creating enemies where none existed?

No. The sound was real, and Thieu knew that he had to check it out. A simple matter, with the passkey he was given for emergencies. A look inside, to prove his own fears groundless, and he could relax, forget about the sounds of steel and mortar settling.

And if there *was* a prowler? Thieu gave his gun another reassuring pat and forced a smile. He'd been chosen for the job, entrusted with the safety of the family's financial records. He would kill, if necessary, to preserve that trust and carry out his duty. It should make no difference that he hadn't killed before, had never fired a shot in anger at another human being. He had practiced regularly with the pistol, and could cut a decent pattern in a silhouette at fifty feet or better. It was easy.

But Thieu wondered if he ought to call the watchmen. They were paid to chase intruders, after all, and with assistance there would be less chance that he would have to kill.

Or die.

He took a few steps toward the stairs, and stopped abruptly. Assuming that there was a prowler, he—or they— would almost certainly be scouring the files for information that could be used to damage Ngo Tien. If uniformed security assisted him in capturing the prowler, they would call the police, and somewhere down the line Tien's secrets would be spread out on a stranger's desk as evidence, subjected to the kind of scrutiny Tien and Giap were seeking to avoid. Lon Thieu would be responsible, and he didn't think he would be rewarded for involving the authorities.

Alone, then. Glowering, he drew the automatic, flicked off the safety and thumbed the hammer back. The SIG-Sauer P-226 held fifteen rounds, and if he couldn't do the job with that, Thieu thought he might as well go home.

The outer door was locked, but that proved nothing. In his absence, an intruder could have picked the lock, slipped in and locked the door behind him. Thieu would have to go inside and check out the suite, one room at a time.

He palmed the passkey, fumbled for a moment with the lock before he got it right. The tumblers made a tiny snicking sound, and the sentry jumped as if a gunshot had exploded in the corridor. The prowler might have heard it, might be waiting for him just beyond the door, and Thieu would never know until it was too late.

All right. When it became a question of survival, dignity was insignificant. He would approach the office as he might a war zone, treating every shadow as an enemy in need of killing. If his fears proved groundless, he could shrug it off, secure in the knowledge that his antics had gone unobserved.

The office door was standing open about half an inch. He took a short step backward, raised his foot and slammed his heel against the heavy paneling, already moving as the door swung back and slammed against the wall. He wallowed through a clumsy shoulder roll, designed to spoil the aim of anyone inside, and came up on his knees, the automatic trembling in a double-handed grip, eyes wide and scouring the shadows.

Nothing. Lon Thieu wobbled to his feet and rushed around the desk, prepared to fire on anyone who might be crouching there, but he was all alone in the reception room. That left Tien's office proper, and the sentry held his breath as he advanced across the deep pile carpeting, his pistol leveled at the silent door.

Would it be locked? And if it was, would his passkey give him access? He had already proved himself; there was no need to be fanatical about a simple watchman's job.

A glint of metal, glimpsed peripherally, stopped him in his tracks. He swiveled to the right, confused at first, until he recognized the squarish object lying on the carpet at his feet. A swift glance upward, at the wall above his head, confirmed that someone had dislodged the air vent's grille. The screws had been torn free; there were no scuff marks on the wall. An entry, then. Intruders dropping in, instead of climbing out.

The short hairs on his neck were shifting, rising to attention as he doubled back to stand before Tien's office door. Thieu knew he ought to sit down at the secretary's desk and keep the damned door covered while he called Anh Giap for reinforcements. It would be a reasonable thing to do, but he was on the hook already. If he had remained on station, he would certainly have heard the prowler crashing through the air vent, could have stopped him cold before he penetrated farther. As it was, he would be punished for neglect of duty; he couldn't afford a charge of cowardice on top of all the rest.

The door, then. If his key didn't work, he would be forced to shoot the lock, kill everyone inside the private office. No survivors meant an opportunity to rewrite history, explain away his negligence and spare himself some pain.

He tried the knob and found the door unlocked. After a moment's hesitation, Thieu knew that he was out of time. It must be now or never.

Through the door and crouching, with the pistol braced in both hands, the sentry was startled to behold his target in the flesh. He tried to shout a warning, strangled on the words and found he couldn't breathe.

And then, the world blew up in Lon Thieu's face.

MACK BOLAN HEARD the outer door crash open, knew that he had somehow been discovered. He didn't concern himself with what had tipped the sentry; it was too late, now, to put things right. Another moment, while the hunter made a cursory examination of the outer office, and he would be forced to kill or die.

He laid the glossy photograph facedown on Tien's desk and drew the Beretta from its shoulder rigging. It was fitted with the custom silencer this time, but he couldn't expect his adversaries to be comparably equipped. A firefight in the penthouse could alert security below, and Bolan heard the doomsday numbers falling as he waited, conscious of the fact that he was running out of time.

Beyond the tall door, someone's cautious footsteps were being muffled by the carpeting. It sounded like a single man, but he couldn't be sure. With seconds left to spare, he found the desk lamp with his free hand, twisted it around to face the doorway, pausing with his fingers on the switch. Bolan was prepared to pin whoever crossed the threshold in the spotlight, dead at center stage.

He waited, listening to nervous fingers as they fumbled with the doorknob, finally got it right. The sentry came through in a rush, as if he had rehearsed the movement in his mind and failed to practice in the flesh. His crouch was awkward, wobbling until it dumped him on his knees.

Their eyes locked for a heartbeat, in the semidarkness, then the warrior switched on the desk lamp and watched his enemy go blind. Before the guy could fire, a parabellum double-punch had drilled him through the forehead, toppling him backward in a sprawl no living form could ever imitate. The first dark rush of blood was leaking into the expensive carpeting as Bolan stood above his fallen enemy and saw that he was dead.

He holstered the Beretta, backtracked to the desk and raised the photograph again. Its composition was pedestrian—two figures, smiling at the birdy, saying "cheese," arms tight around each other in a gesture of affection. Bolan recognized the face of Ngo Tien from mug shots he had seen. He also recognized the face of Lisa Ky, despite the time that had elapsed since she had posed for what could only be a family portrait.

Dizzy, heedless of the risk, he sat down for a moment in Tien's chair. There could be no mistake concerning her identity, the sports car standing just behind her with a giant birthday bow taped to the center of the windshield.

If the girl was Tien's, how had she known about Luan Ky? How had she known that Bolan would be visiting Orange County, where he could be found? If he possessed such details, why should Ngo Tien have risked his daughter, running games with Bolan, when a sniper could have done the job in record time? If Lisa *did* belong to Tien, who sent the gunners to her flat? And who had punched their tickets on the spot, before their work was done? Where was she now?

Too many questions.

And Bolan knew that he would have to answer all of them, before he could proceed. It was enough that he had found and lost a daughter in a single day. The sudden emptiness inside him would take time to fade, but it wasn't a mortal wound. The danger lay in flying blind, against an enemy who seemed to know his every move before the moves were made.

It was a defect he intended to correct without delay.

He set the photograph back in its place, left two drawers on the nearest filing cabinet open, giving the appearance of a prowler who had been disturbed and put to fight. The sentry would be further confirmation . . . and a small down payment on the debt he owed to Ngo Tien.

He killed the desk lamp, zipped up his coveralls and left the outer office, welcoming the cool air of the corridor. As far as the security patrolmen knew, he was another member of the cleaning crew, about to take his lunch break, suddenly remembering that he had left his lunch pail in the car. The sentry's body might not be discovered until morning, but in any case, he would be miles away before then.

In search of answers to the many questions preying on his mind.

In search of Ngo Tien and "Lisa Ky," the father-daughter team that held an answer to the riddle he must solve.

The Executioner was hunting. God help anyone who tried to interfere.

CHAPTER SIXTEEN

A knock on the door startled Ngo Tien out of his private reverie. "Come in."

Anh Giap was frowning as he entered, closed the study door behind him, settled in his favorite chair without invitation.

"So?"

"We missed him," Giap replied.

"I see."

A team of gunmen had been sent to fetch Lao Fan from his home, and they had failed. The coroner's ID on two of the attackers from the warehouse raid had pointed clearly to the Montagnard. The dead men were—had been—his friends, and they were known among their neighbors as proponents of the notion that community resistance could destroy Tien's stranglehold. It was a shock to find them bearing weapons in broad daylight, laying down their lives in such a hopeless cause, but Tien was pleased to have the riddle solved, his enemies supplied with faces, names.

"Perhaps he has already run away?"

Giap shrugged. "His clothes were in the closet. I believe that he is still close by."

"Then we shall have him. I would know what caused this sewer rat to turn against us, leading others to their deaths."

"My people have been told to bring him in alive, if possible. There is a possibility he may resist."

"Do what you must. Alive or dead, Lao Fan will serve as an example to our would-be enemies. His fate will teach them what must surely happen to the peasants who oppose us."

Anh Giap's frown was deepening. "I have bad news."

Tien felt his stomach tightening, as if in preparation for a blow. "Go on."

"I have reports of an intruder at your office. It appears he entered through the air ducts and was interrupted while examining your files. He killed the guard on duty, and we have no witnesses."

"Lao Fan?"

"Perhaps. I cannot say."

"Was anything removed?"

"A number of the files were opened, as I said. My men are under orders not to touch them. Only you can say if any documents are missing."

"The police?"

"Have not been called," Anh Giap assured him. "The discovery was made by one of my lieutenants, stopping in to make sure that the sentry was awake. He summoned reinforcements, and the office is secure."

"You will accompany me?"

"Of course."

"I do not understand these people. What offends them so that they will throw away their lives to cause me minor inconvenience?"

"I think they must be jealous," Giap replied. "They envy your position, your achievements. They are jackals, snapping at the tiger's heels."

"Then we must deal with them as jackals."

"As you say."

"They have insulted me and caused me to lose face with the Carlotti Family. We may have difficulties with the Italians, if they think that our own people turn against us."

"I will crush Carlotti, if you only give the word."

"Not yet. Before we take on other enemies, our own house must be put in order."

"I am ready."

"Better that the work should be performed by So Minh and the Thunder Dragons."

"They are children." Anh Giap's voice was filled with scorn.

"They are expendable. I want your seasoned troops to be available in case of further difficulties."

"When we find Lao Fan—"

"He may not be our only enemy," Tien interrupted.

Giap scowled. "His friends will wish they had been still-born when I finish with them."

"I was thinking of another."

"Who?"

"Pham Bach believes that Lao Fan may have called upon an Anglo friend for aid. You recognize the name Mack Bolan?"

Giap looked confused. "I don't believe—"

"The media insist on calling him the Executioner."

"From Vietnam? The man who fights the Mafia?"

"His interests are apparently not limited to the Italians."

Dark suspicion grew in Giap's eyes. "Bach told you this? How does he know?"

"It is suspicion, nothing more. Our friends in San Francisco have encountered Bolan there, and Bach believes he may have traveled south. Lao Fan apparently befriended Bolan in the war, and there is reason to believe they may be working hand in hand."

"What reason?"

"The attack upon our warehouse was professional, well planned. Lao Fan would be hard-pressed to do as much with only merchants for an army."

"But the two we killed—"

"Were certainly Lao Fan's accomplices," Tien said. "But they were not the minds behind an operation of such magnitude. We must prepare ourselves to deal with Bolan, on the chance that Bach may be correct."

"A single man? I will be pleased to crush him like an ant."

"Do not forget his war with the Italians. They have tried to crush this ant for years, without success."

Giap snorted. "Further proof that it is useless to make bargains with the Mafia. They have no spirit. We should crush them now, before they have an opportunity to summon reinforcements."

"Our enemies are numerous enough already. There is still a chance Carlotti may attack us if he thinks us guilty of the damage to his nephew and the others."

"He is thinking of the money."

"As am I. In wartime, business suffers. We are businessmen."

"When threatened, every man becomes a warrior."

"Let us first identify the threat. If Bolan has indeed decided to assist Lao Fan, I think he may respond to an attack on the man's associates. The Thunder Dragons are a perfect lure."

Anh Giap smiled for the first time since entering the study. "And when Bolan shows himself, we crush the dragon slayer."

"Don Carlotti should be suitably impressed."

"Perhaps there is a way to deal all our enemies at once."

Tien eyed his old friend closely. "I am listening."

"As this Bolan has a reputation for attacking the Italians, it would not be out of character for him to kill Carlotti."

Startled by the simple brilliance of the plan, Tien cracked a slow, appreciative smile. "And if he fails—"

"We could assist him."

"You have turned into a strategist."

"I always was."

"Have I been underestimating you, old friend?"

"Perhaps."

"An error I shall not repeat." Tien's frown was thoughtful. "We must learn if there is anything that makes a killing by the Executioner unique, some trait the police would call a signature."

"It should be simple to discover."

"When you have the information, we will speak of ways to bring Carlotti out of hiding."

"That will not be easy."

"Easy tasks are seldom worth the tiny effort they require."

"Agreed."

"Provide Pham Bach with names of Lao Fan's associates. The Dragons should begin their work as soon as possible."

"It shall be done."

Alone once more, Tien poured himself a whiskey, raised his shot glass in salute to Fate. The liquor burned his throat and swept away the final traces of his prior apprehension. If the so-called Executioner was stalking him, he meant to turn the tables, let the hunter know precisely how it felt to be the hunted. He would kill them both, Lao Fan and Bolan, for their impudence in challenging his rule.

And if Pham Bach was wrong, if Lao had never summoned Bolan...well, the soldier still might play a role in Tien's design. He just might topple Don Carlotti, scattering the old Italian's troops and leaving Ngo Tien alone upon the field.

There would be repercussions from a strike against Carlotti, but if Bolan was identified as the assailant, the capo's brother mafiosi wouldn't spare a second glance for Tien or Giap. They would be concentrating on a predetermined enemy, immediately recognized, who had eluded them for years. When Tien delivered Bolan's head, the fools would be prepared to grant him anything he might request...including, he suspected, virtual autonomy in Southern California. Who would dare to face the man who had destroyed the Executioner?

His outlook brighter than it had been for a period of days, the Asian poured himself a second drink to celebrate. Congratulations were in order. All he had to do was wait, and everything that he had dreamed of since his flight from Vietnam would be delivered to him on a silver platter.

It was time.

In fact, Tien thought, delivery was overdue.

PALE DAWN FOUND Lisa parked outside an Asian restaurant in Garden Grove. The restaurant was closed, but lights still burned inside, and Lisa knew the odds were good that she would find Anh Giap or one of his lieutenants on the premises. It would be easier than driving to her father's house, where she might have to face Pham Bach, or bluff her way past handpicked members of his staff. Anh Giap would listen to her story, and he would protect her. Bach, for all his cunning, wouldn't dare to challenge Giap or his troops in open combat.

Lisa was building up her nerve to cross the street and try the door, when she was surprised to see a line of cars approaching, rolling through the early-morning mist with lights extinguished, silhouettes of several men already visible inside each car. She didn't recognize the vehicles, but waited as they parked outside the restaurant, one man emerging from the lead car, entering the restaurant while his companions waited on the street.

The woman recognized the leader of the Thunder Dragons, So Hoo Minh, by sight. The others would be members of his gang, arriving to receive their orders for a strike. She

counted seven cars—with four or five men each—and knew
that something major must be under way. It would relate to
Bolan and the warehouse raid, of that much she was certain. Nothing else would lead Anh Giap to bring the shock
troops out in force at such an hour, primed for war and
anxious for an opportunity to flex their muscles.

Lisa froze.

The Dragons answered first to Bach, and while Anh Giap
was his superior, Bach often acted as a law unto himself. For
just a moment, Lisa wondered who was handing out the
orders here. If Bach was going against Anh Giap and Ngo
Tien, her warning would be even more important. Critical,
perhaps.

She gripped the steering wheel, her knuckles white, debating whether she should follow Minh inside, risk everything to see Anh Giap, or simply bide her time and wait. The
choice was taken from her as the front door of the restaurant swung open and So Minh appeared, with two men on
his heels. She recognized Pham Bach at once and was startled by the sight of Anh Giap bringing up the rear. The older
men looked solemn, but Minh was smiling as he shook
Bach's hand, returning to his car. Another moment and the
caravan moved out, while Bach and Giap went back inside
the restaurant.

She waited for the surge of panic to subside. Anh Giap
wouldn't betray her father; Lisa knew that much with crystal certainty. The man whom she called her uncle had mis-
trusted Bach for years. They might have gone to war when
she was still a child, but Tien stood firm between them, using each to benefit the family business, drawing on his
friendship with Anh Giap to keep the bear in line while
picking Pham Bach's nimble mind for innovations, strate-
gies. She knew Giap would believe her story, trusted him to
keep her father safe from harm, but she couldn't approach
him with Bach so close at hand.

It wasn't her goal to touch off war within the family, but if that war was coming on its own, she had to help her father gain the upper hand. From adolescence, Lisa had aspired to an executive position in the empire his hands and brain had fashioned out of nothing, gleaning gold from simple earth and sand. She knew the sources of his income, understood the family business as her mother never had, but nothing she had learned repelled her in the slightest. She was proud of Ngo Tien, immensely proud to be his daughter. Pride had driven her into the corner where she huddled now, alone, afraid.

For Ngo Tien was a believer in tradition. Women were the bedrock of the home, the family, and men were chosen by their genes to face the world outside. Deprived of sons, her father was content to raise his only daughter well and see her happy in the new world that was their adopted home. He realized that in America, a woman could become a doctor, an attorney—anything at all—and he was willing to accept the possibility that Lisa might decide to build a personal career. The one thing Tien could not—*would* not—accept was Lisa's personal involvement in the business. Where the participation of a son would have been welcomed, taken for granted, the involvement of a daughter was taboo. When she had broached the subject with her father, he had slapped her face and packed her off to college.

Pham Bach's scheme to snare the Executioner had seemed the perfect way to show her father he was wrong. If Lisa could perform such daring feats, she must be fit to stand beside him in administration of the family empire. There would be no question of her courage, her tenacity, her cunning.

But the plan had generated a sour taste almost from the beginning. Lisa wondered how Pham Bach had known so much about the woman named Luan Ky, a patriot who had been murdered by the Communists in Vietnam. Bach had her file—no mean accomplishment, considering that it belonged to the Vietnamese security police—and Lisa grimaced at the memory of the tortures Luan Ky had suffered, finally giving up the names of ancient lovers, friends, acquaintances.

Mack Bolan had been one of those, and the coincidence of timing, linked with Lisa's age, had been the inspiration for Bach's scheme. He had approached her surreptitiously, his knowledge of her eagerness to serve her father telling him precisely what to say, and Lisa's own misgivings had been swiftly overcome by the desire to make her father proud.

In retrospect she wondered whether Bach had hatched the plot alone, or if some other guiding hand had steered him onto a collision course with Bolan. Lisa thought of Luan Ky's file again, the details it contained, and wondered how the document had fallen into Pham Bach's hands. It didn't seem the sort of document that friendly agents would have taken time to steal, much less to pass along.

Her mind refused to take the final step. She knew that Bach was dangerous, deceitful, but she balked at branding him a traitor to his people. He had served her family for years, in Vietnam and the United States, accepting exile as his due when Tien and Giap were driven from their native land. Not once, in Lisa's presence, had he uttered any word of sympathy for the apparent victors in a struggle that hadn't been settled yet, by any means.

It was preposterous, and yet . . .

She felt a sudden urge to chase the Thunder Dragons' caravan. Their destination would be trouble; their agenda, violence. Lisa had no inkling of their targets, but she sensed that Bolan would be on their list. Pham Bach would see to that.

And if the Executioner was still in Orange County, if the warehouse ambush hadn't wounded him or frightened him away, he would be hunting, too. The Dragons, rolling in formation, might provide him with a target that was too seductive to ignore. If he could catch them all together, he could strike a telling blow against his enemies.

And Lisa meant to be there when he struck that blow.

She was aware the soldier might suspect her of betraying him. By now, there was a chance—however slight—that he might even know her true identity. If so, she could expect the Executioner to cut her down on sight. But while a chance remained for her to speak with Bolan, let him know about Pham Bach, the treachery Bach had worked against them all, she had to take the chance.

It wouldn't matter to the soldier that Pham Bach was bent on bringing down her father. But he *would* be interested, she thought, in Luan Ky's fate, and Bach's apparent link to those who had dispatched his onetime lover. If he cared enough about the woman and her memory, he might be satisfied with Bach, So Minh, the Thunder Dragons. He might let her father go in peace.

Lisa put her car in motion, falling in three blocks behind the Dragons' caravan. She would stay close enough to keep them in her sight, without alerting Minh or his companions to the fact they had acquired a tail. Somewhere, somehow, their path would cross the Executioner's, and Lisa would be ready.

She was betting everything she had on her ability to make the man listen. Failing that, she was prepared to kill him, even if it meant her own life in the bargain.

Turning up the radio to drown her thoughts of death, she drove into the rising sun, pursuing dragons toward the killing fields.

THE LIST OF TARGETS Bolan had received from Lao Fan wasn't comprehensive, but it would suffice. If anything, he had too many choices; he'd have to pick and choose before his blitz began, selecting pressure points that would create the maximum discomfort for his enemy. He'd be running short of time when he began to move, and every blow against Tien's forces had to be precisely calculated for its ultimate effect.

His thoughts returned to Lisa—Tien, not Ky—and Bolan felt a cold knot forming in his chest. It had been foolish to accept her story, even with the details she had offered in the way of confirmation. It was obvious that she had used him—*tried* to use him—but the nagging questions still remained.

If Ngo Tien had been forewarned of Bolan's presence in the area, if he was sharp enough to track the soldier down, why should he risk the girl and rescue Bolan from his own crack troops? The answer might lie in Tien's dealings with the Mafia, but Bolan didn't have enough hard data in his hands to sort it out.

It seemed improbable that Tien had spared his life in order to arrange the warehouse incident. If so, the scheme had backfired, with the Asian losing more than his Italian counterparts and Bolan slipping through the net unscathed. It was a careless, harebrained plan, and it didn't impress the Executioner as something Tien would dream up on his own.

A hidden motive, then, still indecipherable with the evidence in hand. For reasons of his own, the Asian drug lord had decided Bolan was more valuable alive than dead. Or had he?

Bolan's thoughts returned to Lisa, her description of Luan Ky's arrest and execution by the Communists. He wondered which portions of her story were correct, and if Luan Ky was dead, as Lisa had described, how could the girl obtain such details of the case?

The soldier shook his head and concentrated on the war he'd set in motion. Targets. Bolan had a powder factory in Long Beach, gambling spots in Anaheim and Santa Ana, porno studios in La Mirada and a chicken ranch in Buena Park, a "house of joy" in downtown Garden Grove. He wouldn't have the time to hit them all, nor should a total sweep be necessary. After Bolan knocked off two or three of Tien's top money-making operations, his target should be ready for a quick vacation. Once he had the bastard checking underneath his bed for enemies, it would be time to play a little one-on-one.

He hoped to leave Lao Fan and his associates out of the upcoming action. They had paid a hefty price already, and Mack Bolan had no desire to see another innocent cut down on his behalf. Lao might have set the war machine in motion with his call to Leo Turrin, but the Executioner was driving now, and extra passengers were just so much deadweight.

If any help was needed, Bolan had another source in mind. With proper handling, he thought that Don Carlotti might be moved to take a stand and occupy Tien's shock troops while the Asian kept his personal appointment with death.

And afterward—if he was still alive—would there be time to search for Lisa? She possessed the answers to a dozen questions that tormented Bolan, but he knew that if they met again, he might be forced to kill her. She was with the opposition now, beyond the shadow of a doubt, and he could spare no mercy for the woman who had tricked him, tried to take his life.

If they could only talk . . .

There was a hollow place inside him where, for several hours, he had cherished the illusion of a family, some life outside the narrow confines of his everlasting war. The sense of loss wasn't acute, as if a lifelong friend had died. Instead of pain, he felt a creeping numbness in his soul and realized that he had never truly let himself believe. It had been pleasant, for a time, to think in terms of futures, a continuation of the family name, but it had been a fantasy. The Executioner had voted with his trigger finger back in Pittsfield, and his fate had long ago been sealed. The hour and the means of his destruction might be mysteries, but Bolan knew he wouldn't end his days with family and friends, a Norman Rockwell painting in the flesh.

The war was waiting for him. Always waiting. Bolan flipped a mental coin and chose the chicken ranch in Buena Park. It was as good a starting point as any, and the Executioner had nothing left to lose.

CHAPTER SEVENTEEN

The hardest part of waging war, Pham Bach decided, was the waiting that preceded final victory. Within the past few hours, all his plans—save one—had fallen into place as if by magic. Since his politics forbade him a belief in God, Bach was at liberty to claim the credit for himself.

It had been Ngo Tien's idea to mobilize the Thunder Dragons, sparing Bach the task of putting wheels in motion on his own initiative and trying to explain it later, when the game went sour. As it was, the fascist dinosaur would have to shoulder blame for anything that happened as a result of his command. Pham Bach didn't believe in fortunate coincidence, and so he had amended the instructions he gave So Minh, expanding the selected range of targets, making certain that the raids would send a shock wave through the refugee community.

By the time this day was over, Ngo Tien would be a hunted man among his people, sought by the police and angry refugees alike. The shame that marked him—and others of his kind—would not soon be forgotten. In defeat he would be useful to the people's revolution as a symbol of the old, despotic ways. His wasted life would be instructive, through example.

Lisa Tien appeared to be the only problem, and his men had failed to track her down. She would be terrified, of course, and looking for a place to hide. There was a chance she might have left town, but he was banking on her sense of duty to her family, the man whom she was literally dying to impress.

It was unusual, Bach thought, for such a modern woman to revert and place her faith in family, in tradition. Granted, she would turn tradition on its head if given half a chance, presuming to replace the son whom Ngo Tien had never sired, but there was still a trace of old-world flavor in her eagerness to please. It was her weakness, and Pham Bach had used it to his own advantage in the past. Perhaps he could again.

She knew the game with Bolan had gone wrong, that Bach was taking steps to cut his losses. Her disposal of the first two gunners had surprised him. A single target, man or woman, was inevitably vulnerable to manipulation and elimination by a larger force. If Lisa could be found, her flight could be directed, programmed, with her final destination chosen by Pham Bach. She could be guided like a lamb to slaughter... but they had to find her first.

He had some thoughts on that, as well, but the success or failure of his plan depended on coordination of his enemies, as well as allies. He delighted in the notion that Mack Bolan might be used to the advantage of the people's revolution. After all his crimes in Vietnam, the years he had spent obstructing social justice, it was fitting that the Executioner should make a contribution to the cause.

Above all else, it pleased Pham Bach to think of Ngo Tien's reaction when he learned that Lisa had been used against her family, to bring the empire down. It was a message Bach intended to deliver personally, in due time, but premature exposure of his plans would be as lethal as a bullet through the heart.

Bach intended to survive the coming holocaust. His mission in America wasn't completed yet, by any means. With Tien and Giap deposed, the refugee community in turmoil, his bewildered people would require a leader, someone who could help them bring new order out of chaos. Pham Bach would be available for such a worthy task—and in the process, he would also keep the pipeline open for a steady flow of Asian heroin to the United States. Narcotics had their uses, and the addict population of America was comparable to a Trojan horse. Each ragged junkie was required to steal or sell his scabrous body to support the killing habit, crime rates and disease expanding geometrically as each new addict joined the zombie ranks.

It was a tactic Bach might have viewed with apprehension in the early days, but long experience with the realities of life had taught him practicality. In war a soldier used the weapons that were readily available, with preference for those that did the greatest damage to his enemy. If heroin could damage the United States while turning in a profit for the revolution, why, so much the better. It was gratifying for the enemy to fund his own destruction.

Pham Bach's mind snapped back to here and now, the danger posed by Lisa Tien. There was a chance that she could still undo his plans, if he permitted her to reach her father with the word of his duplicity. Bach knew he must prevent that message being passed, at any cost.

He keyed the buzzer on his desk and waited for Lian Trang to close the door behind him. When his first lieutenant was seated, Bach asked, "What progress on the girl?"

"She has eluded us so far, but we will find her," Trang replied with quiet confidence.

"Our time is growing short. Her treachery to Ngo Tien must be avenged before she can poison his mind and turn him against us."

"I have soldiers searching for her now."

"We need a new approach," Bach said. "A lure the vixen cannot possible ignore."

"The Executioner?"

Bach nodded. "She may still attempt to reach him, use him on her own behalf. If we can draw him out of hiding..."

"Sacrifices may be necessary."

"We have sacrificed before."

"Yes, sir."

"I have a plan."

And for the next ten minutes, Pham Bach spelled out the scheme that would complete his triumph, dooming Lisa, crushing Bolan, toppling the empire Ngo Tien had spent a lifetime to construct. His plan wasn't explained in just those terms, but he conveyed the bare essentials to his strong right arm and swore Trang to secrecy.

Alone, Bach leaned back in his swivel chair and smiled.

The day held promise. In a few more hours, he would be a hero to the party, to his people. Pham Liao Bach might not believe in God, but he retained a certain faith in destiny. His sacrifices for the cause would not go unrewarded.

He would be a great man, yet . . . or he would be a dead man.

Either way, he would be gambling everything he had.

THE CHICKEN RANCH in Buena Park was an expensive-looking home, just off the Santa Ana Freeway. Bolan had obtained the address from Lao Fan, the fruit of Lao's surveillance, but he wanted confirmation prior to crashing in on what might prove to be an average, upper-income family. He got it from the television cameras mounted at the entrance to the drive, the draperies closed tight against a lovely Southern California morning. Entry to the "home" would be permitted by appointment only, and he doubted that the draperies were ever opened. If they had been, nosy neighbors might have caught a glimpse of hell on earth.

In gangland parlance, "chicken" was a synonym for boy-flesh, readily available for sale or rental by the hour to the sort of men—and women—who preferred their lovers on the early side of puberty. It was a seller's market, with demand outstripping the available supply of runaways and outcasts, victims of abduction by professionals who plied their trade from coast to coast. The toll of missing children mounted daily in America; their faces decorated billboards, posters, dairy cartons, television screens. A number of the lost wound up in Buena Park each month, and there were countless other "ranches" across the country catering to wealthy sports.

Bolan couldn't close them all, but he could put *this* rancher out of business. It would be the beginning of the end for Ngo Tien.

The different angles of approach would all be covered, and he saw no point in trying to be subtle. The direct approach had served him well thus far. Without a second thought, he wheeled his rental past the early-warning cameras, following the narrow drive and parking out in front. A Cadillac and sporty Porsche were tucked away on one side of the building, hidden from the street.

He caught a flicker of movement near the draperies as he approached the double doors. A giant with a pockmarked face, hardware slung beneath his arm, was waiting for him when he got there, scowling down at Bolan.

"We ain't expecting anyone," he growled.

"That's your mistake."

The hulk looked momentarily confused. "You got your ticket?"

"Sure, right here."

The guy was tall, but Bolan had no trouble with a forearm smash across the larynx, driving his opponent back against the doorjamb. The maneuver left his gun hand free, and he had palmed the Beretta, squeezing off two rounds at skin-touch range before Goliath could recover from his initial surprise. The doorman trailed a smear of viscous crimson as he settled to the floor.

So far, so good. No general alarm inside the house, no rush of footsteps to announce reinforcements closing in. The

Executioner relieved his late adversary of a standard-issue .45 and quickly checked the automatic's load.

He padded along a corridor with walls displaying samples of "erotic" art, each portrait featuring children in different stages of undress, with "caring" adults hovering nearby.

The scenes grew more explicit as he proceeded, symbolically initiating new arrivals to the pleasures of the flesh.

He tried the kitchen, came up empty. Ditto in the dining room. The third door opened onto a smallish office where a hardguy in expensive threads was kicked back in a swivel chair, his feet cocked on the desk.

"Hey, who the fuck are—"

Bolan shot him in the face with the Beretta, choosing silence at this juncture of his penetration. He could hear the numbers falling in his head, but there was time, yet. Precious time.

Upstairs. He tried the first room on his right, recoiling from what he saw. The boy was spread-eagled on the bed, secured at wrists and ankles. He was gagged to muffle any outcry, but his eyes told Bolan everything the soldier had to hear.

A naked man was scrambling to his feet, a towel strategically employed to shield his shriveled pride. His eyes were riveted on Bolan's face, the guns in Bolan's hands.

The .45 thundered in the confines of the room, reaching out to slap the aging rapist backward, towel and modesty forgotten in the last extremity. His flaccid shape collided with a folding table, and they went down together.

Bolan heard reactions to the gunshot in the corridor outside, but he took time to free the boy, release his gag and see him swaddled in a sheet. "Police will be here soon," he said, as if that knowledge could erase the nightmares that would haunt this victim to his dying day.

There was a muffled clatter on the stairs, and Bolan arrived in time to see a heavy man in boxer shorts and T-shirt running for his life with suit and shoes clutched in his arms. It was an easy, offhand shot, and Bolan put one square between the runner's shoulder blades, the impact driving him against the banister, over the rail and out of sight.

A naked woman with a wig in one hand and a dildo in the other nearly trampled Bolan as he stepped into the hall. Another customer. He clubbed her with the .45 and dropped her in her tracks. She could explain her presence in this hellhole to the uniforms when they arrived.

He started checking bedrooms, found a young girl hiding here, another small boy huddled there. In number four, the customer had nearly finished dressing. He was halfway out the window, frozen in his confrontation with a twelve-foot drop, and Bolan helped him with a swift kick from the liberated .45. The red-haired twins, for whom the jumper had paid extra, joined his other charges in the corridor.

The last door on the left provided access to a walk-in storage closet. Linens had been shelved on one side, cardboard boxes filled with reels of film and glossy still shots on the other. Bolan didn't have to study the material to know what it contained. He flicked his Bic and traced a line of fire along the shelves of linen, backing out as sheets and towels erupted into flame.

The children had already seen enough nightmares for a lifetime. There would be no repetition of their torment in the show-and-tell department, with the films and photographs displayed for vice detectives, prosecutors and defenders, jurists and the press. The Executioner was entertaining no illusions that his blitz would lead to prosecution of the animals responsible, and evidence was thus superfluous. He didn't plan to take any prisoners.

Incredibly the five children were waiting for him on the stairs. He herded them along and out of there, onto the neatly manicured lawn. Returning to the foyer, Bolan found a telephone and raised the operator, spelling out the address with a curt demand for fire trucks, black-and-whites, an ambulance. He left the instrument off the hook and put the place behind him, pausing long enough to reassure the children that help was on the way.

A clutch of worried-looking neighbors had collected on the sidewalk, drawn by the reports of gunfire. Bolan wheeled the rental past them, slowing as a balding man leaned in to shout a question.

"Wait up a second. What went on in there?"

"You missed the party," Bolan told him. "Go home."

"Don't speak to me that way! I have a right to know what's happened!"

Bolan killed the engine and was on him in a rush. "You've got it, guy," he snarled, collecting a handful of the smaller man's lapel and hauling him across the sidewalk, through the ranks of his astounded friends. Bolan dragged his struggling catch along the driveway, until they reached a point some twenty yards from where the children stood.

When Bolan let him go, the little man collapsed on hands and knees, eyes coming into focus on the children, with his mind uncomprehending. "What...I don't...this isn't..."

"Sure it is," he snapped, determined that the man should know precisely what he had ignored for years on end. "This is *exactly* what it looks like, neighbor." Fingers tangled in the thinning fringe of hair to wrench the head back, wide eyes swimming with disgust. "You've been content to live with this, now take a good, close look!"

"How could I know?"

"You didn't *want* to know!" Revolted suddenly by contact with the man, Bolan stepped away. "Go home," he repeated.

Sirens wailed in the distance as the warrior slid behind the rental's steering wheel and put the car in motion. One stop down, and he had scarcely made a dent in Ngo Tien's illicit operations. When the smoke cleared, Bolan had no doubt the house would be in someone else's name, the Asian mobster safely insulated from responsibility for his atrocious crimes.

No problem.

Tien could insulate himself until hell froze over, but he wouldn't find a sanctuary from the righteous anger of the Executioner.

"UPSTAIRS," Minh reminded his companions. "On the left."

"This Charlie Phu's a friend of Lao?"

"An ex-friend."

"Hey, that's good."

They spent another moment in the Lincoln, double-checking weapons, finishing a joint that Minh had passed around to build their courage. Daylight raids were nothing special to the Thunder Dragons, but their specialty had always been extortion from the merchants of the refugee community. Mass murder in a residential area entailed more risk of meeting the police and being caught red-handed.

Never mind. If the police arrived, Minh thought, he wouldn't hesitate to cut them down. The neighbors wouldn't be a problem; there'd be no witnesses recording license numbers, testifying for the prosecution. Only men in uniform could stop them now, and in his present mood, So Minh was confident he could overcome those odds, as well.

He felt omnipotent, a general riding at the spearhead of his army, trampling the opposition underfoot. A part of that sensation was the weed, he realized, but most of it was natural, the rush that he derived from violence, the confidence he gained from being trusted by Pham Bach to carry out a major operation.

Minh was big time now, and when he finished mopping up the peasants who had angered Bach, he would be in a prime position to request—*demand*—a higher place within the syndicate. It had been pleasant, ruling as the warlord of the Thunder Dragons, but his future in that role was limited, his followers increasingly recruited from the ranks of ignorant and disaffected youth with no potential. He could grill them on the basics until he was old and gray, and they would still be children playing soldier, getting off on all the guns and girls.

Minh wanted more from life. *More* guns. *More* girls. Above all else, he wanted more respect, more power. Fear was one thing, but respect was something else entirely. If he stuck with Bach and did his duty, Minh decided, he could have it all.

He didn't know why Charlie Phu and the members of his family were marked for death. There might be some connection with the recent warehouse raid, he thought, but Minh wasn't paid to think. Pham Bach had picked the targets, in his wisdom, and it was Minh's job to carry out the dirty work. It helped that he enjoyed the violence, craved it like a junkie needs his fix, but that was something he would have to work on, too.

When he had risen to the top, So Minh would have to stand apart from the mechanics of disposal operations, delegating the responsibility to others in the rank and file. It bothered him to think that he would miss the action, but advancement had its price, and bosses simply did not soil their hands with wet work. As a man of independent means, he would find other games to occupy his time, new sports to tap the wellspring of his energy. And sometimes, if he chose his quarry carefully, he might find ways to organize a hunt. It would be like the old days, with a trace of bittersweet nostalgia added for effect.

"Let's do it," someone muttered from the rear, the voice rousing Minh from his reverie. He slipped the Browning automatic back into his shoulder holster, buttoning his jacket as he climbed out of the car. The driver waited, one eye on the rearview mirror, ready with a signal on the horn if anything suspicious happened, any squad cars suddenly appeared. If they were cornered, it was every man for himself, and Minh didn't expect the wheelman to remain.

"Come on," he growled. "It's party time."

They crossed the lawn in single file and climbed the stairs to Phu's apartment on the second floor. Minh punched the bell and listened to the tinny chimes within, amazed that anyone with any self-respect could live in such a mediocre, run-down building. He was doing Phu a favor, he decided, sparing him a lifetime of such torment.

"Yes?"

The cautious voice spoke from behind the door, no sound of a chain or dead bolt being opened. Minh imagined sharp, suspicious eyes behind the tiny peephole.

"Lao Fan sent me," he explained. From behind the mirrored shades, he shot a sidelong glance at his companions, waiting on the stairs. "I've got a message for you."

"Go ahead, I'm listening."

He feigned exasperation. "Hey, I can't just stand out here and shout it through the door, you know?"

"Okay, then, write a note and slip it under."

Minh felt something snap inside his brain, a tangible sensation as he dropped the useless pose. "I've got your note," he said, "right here."

He palmed the Browning, thumbed the hammer back and fired a round point-blank into the dead bolt, kicking twice beside the doorknob with all his strength. Twilight shrouded the room beyond the threshold, curtains drawn and lamps turned down, but he could make out Charlie Phu retreating toward the bedroom.

Minh squeezed off a shot that staggered Phu, blood spattering the stucco wall behind his victim. Moving in, he fired again, and Phu went down, his body twitching, arms outstretched.

The gang lord was past him in an instant, homing on the sound of water running in the bathroom. Someone in the shower, startled by the gunfire, turned off the water as he approached.

Phu's wife was stepping from the shower as he entered, reaching for a towel to cover herself. Minh crossed the room in two long strides and snatched the towel away, a straight-arm thrust propelling her against the tile, the muzzle of his automatic wedged beneath her chin.

"All right!"

Minh glanced across his shoulder; saw the Dragons crowded in the doorway, studying the naked woman. He could read the sudden hunger in their eyes, the fear in hers.

"You like her?" he inquired of no one in particular. "You want her?"

"Sure!"

"Why not?"

"I like her fine!"

Minh shook his head in mock regret. "Too bad. We haven't got the time."

He stepped back, sighting down the automatic's slide and pulled the trigger. One of the casings landed in the sink and spun there, like a roulette ball, before it settled in the drain. He watched the woman's body sag, her rubber legs refusing to support deadweight until she finally toppled sideways, landing facedown in the bathtub.

"What a waste," one of his soldiers grumbled.

"Yeah, we should have taken her along!"

"Forget her. We've got work to do."

Minh felt the old familiar tonic coursing through his veins, adrenals pumping now that he was in the thick of combat. They had work to do, and he was looking forward to it, knowing it might be the last *real* job he did before he started scrambling up the ladder.

He would miss the violence, but it wasn't over yet. And while it lasted, So Minh would make the most of it.

GIROLAMO CARLOTTI SAT BACK in the leather chair, his cigar puffing storm clouds that hung near the ceiling. "Go on," he commanded.

In front of the desk, his new *caporegime* looked uncomfortable, shifting his weight from one foot to the other and swallowing hard. He hadn't been invited to sit. If he carried bad news, he could damn well deliver it standing.

"They're dead, sir." His voice was so soft that Carlotti could barely make out what he said.

"Dead? Dead *how*?"

"One slug each, through the back of the head."

"Goddamn!"

Carlotti was steaming. The loss of two runners was no major tragedy, granted, but these had been carrying better than twenty-five grand in receipts from Carlotti's command post in Watts, representing one-fourth of his afternoon's take from the numbers. Worse yet, the "coincidence" of their demise and the loss of the cash—coming hot on the heels of the warehouse disaster with Vinnie—told the Don that Tien and his zipperhead cronies were forging ahead with their plans at full speed. What the hell had Omega been playing at, begging Carlotti to sit back and take it for three or four *weeks*? He'd be ruined by that time, his soldiers wiped out and his bank account as flat as a squirrel on the freeway.

"There's more, sir."

Carlotti didn't have to feign a disgusted reaction. "Go on, spit it out."

"We found this with the stiffs."

The object on his desk was square, metallic, silver. Carlotti poked it with his finger, turned it over, finally picked it up and brought it closer for inspection. He could feel his breakfast shifting, threatening to reappear.

A marksman's medal.

Christ, how many years since he'd seen one? How long since the nightmares about Deej and all the rest of it had faded? Too damned long.

"You found *this* on the bodies?"

"Yes, sir."

"Nothing else?"

"That's it, sir."

"Shit."

"How's that."

Carlotti eyed the youngster coldly, judging him the way he might select a strip of beef for dinner. "Get your people on the street," he grated. "Anything they hear about Mack Bolan or a stranger asking any questions, phone it in, no matter what the hour. Understand?"

"Mack Bolan, sir?"

"You heard me, damn it! Get your ass in gear!"

"Yes, sir!"

Carlotti cursed beneath his breath. They made the soldiers so damned young these days, most of them had been killing time in juvey when the Executioner had toppled Deej and damned near put the Southern California Family out of business.

One man couldn't wipe out the entire Family, no way. What he *could* do was slaughter the capo, his closest advisers and take down an army of soldiers before he was finished.

No good. They would have to do better than that. Don Carlotti was not in the mood to lie down and play dead for some smartass who should have been dog food by now. He would deal with the problem when Bolan presented himself, and to hell with Omega's request that he sit on his hands for a month while the gooks gobbled up his concessions and raked off the cream for themselves.

If it came to that, the Don would call La Commissióne himself, and explain what was happening. Carlotti didn't plan to hide in the shadows while Bolan, the Asians or anyone else tore his empire apart.

Could it be a coincidence, Bolan arriving in town just as trouble was brewing with Tien and his troops? The suggestion of linkage between the events was disturbing. It smacked of a larger conspiracy, Bolan and Tien hand in hand for the purpose of crushing Carlotti. Perhaps he was paranoid, losing his grip, but the Don was covering all his bets, leaving nothing to chance.

It was war, either way, and the mafioso was ready. If some cocky bastard believed he could steal what Carlotti had worked for through half of his life, let him try. He was in for a damned rude awakening.

Smiling, the capo leaned back in the chair and began laying plans for his war.

CHAPTER EIGHTEEN

Lao Fan pulled up in front of Charlie Phu's apartment complex, found a parking space behind the latest squad car to arrive, and killed the engine of his car. An hour earlier, when he had tried to get in touch with Charlie to arrange a meeting, the police had answered, questioning his reason for the call. They wouldn't give him any details of the crime, but Lao had learned that Phu and his wife were dead. Their son, an eight-year-old, had spent the night with friends and thus was spared.

Lao didn't have to search for guilty parties. He had shadowed Pham Bach to the Oriental Gardens restaurant and waited, two blocks down the silent street, while So Minh and his Thunder Dragons got their orders. He hadn't been conscious of their targets, but the shield of ignorance wouldn't protect him from the guilt he bore. If he'd made some move to stop them, anything at all . . .

A uniformed patrolman intercepted Lao, then stood aside at mention of the captain's name :o found his contact in the living room, surveying blood smears on the wall. He was a slender man, with hair gone white and sunken eyes that had observed the worst life had to offer.

"Captain Tucker?"

"Who are you?"

Lao introduced himself, and the slim detective's hostile attitude immediately melted into one of dark suspicion.

"You were friends with the deceased?"

"I was."

"You see him often?"

"Once or twice a week. I saw him yesterday."

"What time was that?"

"We met for lunch."

"What did you talk about?"

"I'm looking for a job. He told me he might know of someone—"

"Who?"

"He didn't say."

"You didn't ask?"

"Of course. He didn't want to get my hopes up, until he had checked it out himself."

"Uh-huh." The captain's frown was wary, set in place from years of scowling at an ugly world. "Your friend have any enemies?"

Lao thought of Ngo Tien and held his tongue. "None that I know of."

"Nobody who wants him dead?"

"He never mentioned anything like that."

"Seem nervous lately? Off his feed? Like he had problems on his mind?"

Lao Fan pretended to consider it, responding with a shrug. "I didn't notice anything."

"It figures," Tucker sneered. "No one around here noticed anything this morning, either. Funny, don't you think? They didn't notice six shots, minimum, or any of the other noise there must've been. They didn't notice three or four guys trooping up the stairs and shooting off the lock, committing double murder here, and marching back the way they came. Sound sleepers, eh?"

"What happened?"

"I just told you. Someone shot the dead bolt off, and then they dropped your buddy in his underwear, before he had a chance to reach the shotgun in the bedroom. Did you know he kept a weapon?"

"No."

"They caught his missus in the shower. Someone blew her brains out. Hell, if any of our shooters knew the neighbors, they might still have been here when we got the call."

"You said that no one noticed anything."

"Old lady in the next block over called it in. She said the noise was keeping her awake."

"But no one saw the killers?"

"Nobody *admits* they saw a thing. That doesn't mean they're blind, you get my drift? Just careful."

Lao Fan understood and knew he would accomplish nothing sparring with the homicide detective. He was well aware of who had murdered Charlie Phu, and why the crime had been committed. In a pinch, Lao thought he could have named the killers, starting with So Minh, but he had nothing the police could use to build a case.

And in the last analysis, he wasn't interested in seeing the Thunder Dragons sent to jail. He wanted the Thunder Dragons dead, along with Minh, their leader, and Pham Bach, the man who sent them out to prey upon the refugee community. He wanted Ngo Tien and Anh Giap to share the mortal terror of their victims in the moments left before they died.

Outside he let the crisp, cool morning air caress his face. The smell of chronic air pollution would be welcome, after spending time inside the charnel house, where everything had reeked of blood and death.

Charlie Phu had been murdered in retaliation for the warehouse raid, his wife as a potential witness and a message to the rest of the community. Lao recognized Bach's handiwork as if the double murder were a painting, with the artist's signature available for all to see. Deprived of inside knowledge, the police were handicapped in their pursuit of the killers, but he thought that Tucker might suspect the Thunder Dragons. Members of the gang had been frequently arrested in recent months, and while the number of convictions hovered near the zero mark, their faces were familiar in the station house. The system couldn't cope with them, but the police continued to go through the motions, trying to perform their duty in the face of overwhelming odds.

Most of the Dragons were juveniles, given kid-glove handling by the state's judicial system. When they came of age, their records would be sealed against the scrutiny of prosecutors and arresting officers, providing each boy with another chance, a "fresh start" in the game of life and death.

But some of them would never see that day, if Lao had anything to say about it. Some of them—the killers of his friend, at least—would pay a higher penalty than two or three months "on the county," killing time and watching television in the juvey lockup. Some of them were killers now, and they were looking at a private penalty that fit their crimes.

Lao Fan had to find the Thunder Dragons and destroy as many of them as he could, before they had a chance to claim more lives. He owed that much at least to Charlie Phu. And to himself.

THE CARAVAN of Thunder Dragons had divided into smaller units half a mile beyond the restaurant, and Lisa Tien hadn't been able to pursue the lead car bearing So Minh for fear she would reveal herself. Instead she'd been forced to trail the last two cars, occasionally dropping out of sight so they wouldn't notice the tail.

There seemed to be no basis for her fear on that score. The Dragons were enjoying their "work," apparently dismissing the idea that anyone would try to interfere. Lisa wondered if police patrols had been deliberately lured away from target areas, but she had no way of finding out. She couldn't stop to call for help herself, risk losing contact with her quarry in the maze of streets and alleyways. Her range of choices had been narrowed down to one, and she would stick until she found a way to stop them in their tracks.

She thought about the pistol in her purse and nearly laughed. The image of herself attempting to disarm ten thugs was ludicrous. She would be dead in seconds, one more grim statistic added to the morning's score.

The flower shop was target number three, preceded by a corner grocery and a pharmacy, which specialized in Asian remedies and aphrodisiacs. The Thunder Dragons parked out front as they had done the last two times, the drivers staying with their cars and keeping watch while everybody else unloaded in a rush and swept inside. It took a moment for the noise to reach her ears, but then she recognized the screaming, overridden by sadistic laughter and the sound of breaking glass.

A potted plant exploded through the plate-glass window, showering the sidewalk with a rain of soil and shattered crockery. Another followed, and another, fresh-cut flowers close behind the houseplants, adding color to the wreckage. Moments dragged, and Lisa thought that surely someone in the neighborhood would have the nerve to summon the police. If only someone...

They were leaving, kicking at the broken pots and scattered flowers as they trooped back to the car. The last two out were carrying a man, perhaps of middle age, whose shirt and pants were speckled with fresh dark bloodstains. His scalp was torn and bleeding, wire-rimmed glasses dangling twisted, from one ear.

The florist's escorts dropped him in the rubble that had been his inventory, rattling off angry words that Lisa couldn't hear. By way of punctuation, one of the attackers took a short step backward, grinning all the while, and kicked his victim squarely in the face. The punter's buddy landed two more in the florist's rib cage, and the two finally retreated to the cars.

Lisa knew she could have stopped those two, at least. But after all she had been through, after killing two men on her own, she lacked the courage it would take to intervene. Experience and intuition told her that the neighborhood would come alive in moments, once the Thunder Dragons had retreated, and the florist would receive the best of care. Small consolation for his pain, the shambles of his business, but it was the best that Lisa Tien could offer as she put her car in gear and trailed the Dragons toward their next hit.

They were punishing the neighborhood, it seemed, conducting raids against the refugee community at large. She didn't know the individuals selected as the targets, but she could imagine their "offenses": balking at the payment of inflated tribute; threatening to notify police if they were squeezed beyond their means; expressing anger or contempt for hoodlums in some guarded comment to a "friend." Pham Bach would have his ways of finding out, and he wouldn't forget.

With Bach in mind, it never once occurred to Lisa that her father might be issuing the orders, picking out the targets for reprisal. In her own mind, Ngo Tien remained exalted, separated from the dirty work that kept his empire stable, kept it moving forward. Uncle Giap had always been the soldier, acting on her father's part, and when the two of them were forced to fight, the contest was conducted in an almost regal atmosphere, with chivalry and style.

Or so she thought.

Pham Bach had altered everything by emphasizing drugs above the more traditional pursuits of gambling and money-lending, squeezing tribute from the people on accelerated schedules, robbing them instead of merely reaping "taxes" for the benefit of Tien's protection. Bach, she knew, had engineered the warehouse raid in hopes of sparking war with the Italian syndicate, and it infuriated Lisa that she couldn't reach her father, tell him everything she knew.

And would he have believed her? On the off chance that a friendly voice had answered on the telephone, relayed her call to her father directly, would he take her word against Pham Bach's? Would he accept the fact that Lisa knew the family business inside out, had studied it against his wishes, and was well aware of who did what to whom?

Frustration soured her stomach, made her eyes burn, but she wouldn't yield to tears. She was a woman, but the fact of biological construction didn't make her weak; if anything, she thought, it made her stronger, more determined to succeed.

Her father must be warned about Pham Bach, but first the traitor's private army must be neutralized. For that she needed help, and not from the police.

She needed Bolan.

Somewhere in the urban sprawl of Orange and L.A. counties, if he was not dead already, Bolan would be searching for her, tracking her the way he tracked his enemies. She only prayed that he would find her soon, and that there would be time to speak with him before he tried to kill her.

THE POWDER FACTORY in Long Beach had been set up in a warehouse on the waterfront. Logistically the layout had advantages, including ready access to the water—handy for deliveries, evacuation in emergencies or dumping contraband in the event police came calling unannounced. On record, the establishment belonged to the Argyle Corporation, one more paper company controlled from a strategic distance by Anh Giap and Ngo Tien.

Lao Fan had scouted the operation, watched deliveries and pickups. There was no mistake, and Bolan knew that taking down the plant would hit his enemies precisely where they lived: in the vicinity of their collective bankroll.

He was looking forward to it.

There was no point in trying a ruse. Tien's staff was Vietnamese to a man, and Bolan knew that he would never pass. That left him the direct approach, and as he left the rental in a nearby alley, closing on his target, he was armed for war. An Uzi, his Beretta and the Desert Eagle made a killing combination, with some frag grenades and an incendiary can thrown in for added punch. Whatever went down, it would be loud.

He counted seven cars in the parking lot and doubled that to make allowances for workers who might pool to save on gas. Inside that plant no one was innocent. They earned their daily bread processing poison for the veins of children, men and women who were hopelessly addicted, thousands of them hanging on to life from one fix to the next, their every conscious thought devoted to the task of "getting well." Only savages were inside the powder factory, and Bolan didn't give a damn that one or two might hold a graduate degree in chemistry. An educated ghoul was still a ghoul, and Bolan's diagnosis was that the condition was invariably terminal.

Up the loading ramp, across the dock. He tried the access door, wasn't surprised to find it locked. The business of this plant was best conducted with a maximum of privacy. He circled, trying other doors against the possibility of negligence, discovered only that the troops were on their toes. He'd completed more than half the circuit when he found his entry point.

Aside from illegality, the major problem with a powder factory is ventilation. Noxious chemicals are used to process opium and morphine, to refine the finished product, and their fumes accumulate inside the plant. Additionally there is a persistent risk from particles of heroin suspended in the air, and careless lab technicians have become addicted—even overdosed—simply by breathing while they work. It was essential, therefore, that the staff wear masks and filters while the plant was ventilated to reduce their risk.

The brains at Argyle took the easy, inexpensive route, with loading bays cranked open three feet off the deck, and fans installed to suck the fumes and dust outside. The soldier caught a whiff of doom before he saw the setup, slipping on the gas mask that would cover him against ingestion of the product or debilitating vapors. Edging toward the open bays, the Executioner was prone and wriggling before he reached the entry. After straining for a glimpse around the corner, pulling back at sight of two armed guards, he finally had a chance to check out the operation.

His estimated head count had been close—twelve targets visible, with ten of those decked out in laboratory white, the other two in business suits and packing riot guns. The shooters had divided their responsibility, one stationed on the far side of the room to watch the street doors, his companion covering the open loading bays, prepared to meet an intruder with a charge of deadly buckshot. Bolan knew he had to take that gunner down—or draw him off—before he had a chance of starting what he'd come to do.

He chose a frag grenade and yanked the pin, released the safety spoon and rolled the bomb through the open bay in the direction of the tables where the chemists did their work. A warning shout came too late, and he was counting down to doomsday when a thunderclap went off inside the warehouse, rattling the cargo doors and toppling the ventilation fans. A cloud of chalky dust mushroomed through the open doors, obscuring his view, and Bolan seized the moment, sliding belly down across the threshold with his Uzi primed for action.

A shotgun blast exploded on his right, too high, and the warrior answered with a probing burst, rewarded with a strangled cry of pain. The other sentry would be up and tracking, but a choking mist of powdered heroin and smoke from the explosion screened his movements, kept the Executioner from scoring early in the game.

As if on cue, strategically positioned floodlights came alive, their brilliance dazzling in the gloom. From his position near the entrance, Bolan had a view of silhouettes in motion, blind men groping through the wreckage for an exit. In an instant he had counted half a dozen, figuring that at least two or three had been disabled by the blast.

He swung up the Uzi and laced the survivors with measured bursts of almost surgical precision, dropping the shadow figures in their tracks. A sudden, booming answer erupted from his left, and shotgun pellets rang against the corrugated metal wall as Bolan sidestepped, dived to the floor.

He pinpointed the gunner, slid the Desert Eagle out of military leather, sighting down the slide. At twenty yards he stroked the trigger twice, the impact lifting the target off his feet, propelling him three paces backward.

It was over. The warrior closed his mind to pleading voices, racked with pain. The savages had made their own bed; they could die there and the world would feel no sense of loss. If any of the wounded sought release from suffering, they merely had to strip off their masks and draw a breath.

Sweet dreams.

Retreating Bolan dropped the thermite can behind him, minus safety pin, and was halfway down the ramp when it exploded, finishing his work with a strategic application of cleansing fire. If they were fast, the firemen might preserve Tien's warehouse for him—most of it, at any rate—but it would do the mobster little good.

Before the day was out, a warehouse and a load of smack would seem like small potatoes to the former warlord of the refugee community. The guy was dead. He simply didn't have the sense to realize it yet.

THE HOUSE OF JOY in Garden Grove had been in business for a year. Its clientele included businessmen—and businesswomen—local politicians and celebrities, with an occasional influential police official. Tien's managers had earned a reputation for precise fulfillment of erotic fantasies, and customers were known to get their money's worth.

Mack Bolan had no special grudge against the brothel's customers, except where they were derelict in public duties by attending, and he held no grudge at all against the working girls who plied their trade inside. His anger focused on the management, the owners and the games they played with human lives while selling pleasure on a time clock.

Customers at Ngo Tien's establishment were welcomed by appointment only, each new patron on referral from established clients. All were screened, subjected to a thorough background check before they got the nod, and Tien's investigators seldom missed a trick. If this or that prospective customer had contacts in the world of finance, politics or law enforcement, "special" pleasures were available. The rates weren't precisely wholesale, but the client got an extra bonus in the form of videocassette recordings that immortalized the golden moments, shot by hidden cameras installed in every bedroom. Some were flattered by the outcome of their screen tests; most were mortified, afraid of scandal, glad to pay the price Tien demanded for the preservation of their spotless reputations. Money seldom entered into the arrangement. Tien had cash to spare, but he could always use a friend and ally in the courts or the police force, on the city council, in the state assembly. Friends took care of friends, and Tien had been well served by patrons of his pleasure palace.

Bolan couldn't cancel out the harm that had already been done, but he could bring the operation to a halt, and in the process he could also deal another blow to his enemy's pocket. The loss of income from a major brothel plus destruction of the building, furnishings and video equipment would be painful, at the very least. No mortal blow perhaps, but in conjunction with the other raids against his empire, it should help to get the mobster's full attention.

Bolan wore a business suit and carried a valise containing flares, incendiary sticks and smoke grenades. There would be average security, but he was confident the Desert Eagle and Beretta would be equal to the challenge he might face inside the house of joy.

A liveried butler answered Bolan's ring, his eyebrows rising in pursuit of a receding hairline as he faced the uninvited visitor.

"Yes, sir?"

"I'm here to check the books."

"I beg your pardon?"

"Books, you read me? The accounts? Head office sent me out to do a spot check."

"I believe there must be some mistake. We weren't expecting—"

"That's the point, guy." Bolan shouldered past him, pausing in a sumptuously furnished entry hall.

"I'm sorry, sir, you can't—"

"I did. You want to show me where the books are kept, or do I have to make some calls?"

"You really must discuss this with the manager."

"Yeah, right. So get him out here, will you? I don't have all day."

The butler scuttled off, and Bolan drifted on his own, ducking into a seldom used library, scanning the tall shelves of books that had probably never been read. He was turning to go when the butler returned, with a heavy-set Asian in tow.

"Mr. Tran, I'm afraid that I don't know this gentleman's name. He insists—"

"I insist on a look at the books. Any problem with that?"

Tran seemed puzzled. "This is rather unusual. If I may see your credentials..."

"Sure thing."

Bolan slipped a hand into his jacket, came out with the .44 Magnum and watched Tran go pale. Twenty feet lay between them, point-blank for the Eagle, and Bolan squeezed off a round without thinking about it, saw Tran on his way to the floor as the thunder exploded around him. The butler was gaping at Death in the flesh, bits and pieces of his former boss decorating his tux, as the soldier regarded him coolly.

"There's two ways to go," Bolan told him. "Be smart, and get out while you can, or be tough and go down with the ship."

"I'll be leaving now, sir."

"Thought you might. If you've got an alarm system, trip it before you take off, okay? I smell something burning."

"Yes, sir."

Bolan lit up a flare, wedged it into the seat of an overstuffed chair and moved on. He was mounting the stairs when the fire bell went off, loud and strident, alerting the girls who hadn't been roused by the gunshot. Too early for johns, and the "staff" hit the deck in their nighties, abandoning ship by the numbers in moves that had probably been well rehearsed. Bolan greeted them all with a smile, trailing fire sticks behind him in vacated bedrooms. The flames were producing thick smoke by the time he returned to the head of the stairs, but he still had a clear view of trouble below: a big guy, unusually tall for an Asian, with pistol in hand. Bolan's Magnum was screened from the enemy's view by the briefcase he carried.

"You're dead, man."

"That right?"

"Bet your ass."

"Prove it."

Dropping into a crouch and bringing his gun to bear, the Asian was slow for a man starting out with an edge. Too damned slow to survive, and he knew it the moment he saw Bolan's weapon, the muzzle as big as a cannon and winking flame before he could get off a shot. Heavy slugs opened vents in his chest, took the top of his head off, and then he was nothing but a wet pile of clothes at the foot of the stairs.

Bolan's briefcase was empty, and he dropped it on top of the body as he moved toward the exit. He wasn't done with Ngo Tien. There were still moves to make in the game before checkmate allowed him to pick off the king.

CHAPTER NINETEEN

It wasn't difficult for Lao Fan to find the Thunder Dragons. They were leaving giant tracks, and street talk followed them around the refugee community, anticipating targets, speculating on the motivation for the sudden raids. It was agreed that someone, somehow, had succeeded in provoking So Hoo Minh to the extreme, but no one offered an explanation for his rage.

Lao Fan, who held the answers, wasted no time trading information with his street informants. He'd seen the ruined shops, knew Minh and company weren't adhering to a faithful list of Lao's accomplices in the attack against Tien's warehouse. After Charlie Phu, the other targets had been nodding friends or casual acquaintances of Lao's, suggesting that Pham Bach didn't possess a comprehensive roster of his closest allies. Understanding brought a ray of hope, immediately followed by a stab of fear. There was a chance his other comrades would survive the first assault, regroup and help him plan a counterstroke. There was an even better chance that innocent acquaintances would suffer because of chance association with a hunted man.

He wouldn't find the Thunder Dragons all together, Lao knew that much from the start. The number of their raids and the locations, told him that the hoodlums had divided forces, striking off in teams to "punish" their selected victims. Later they would certainly convene to boast and share their tales of battle, but he didn't have the time to waste on waiting.

At the moment any group of Dragons would suffice, and knowledge of the streets suggested a solution to his quest.

The latest target that he knew of was a restaurant on Warner Avenue, in Santa Ana. Six blocks north, the Thunder Dragons had a favorite hangout, catering to teens and young adults, where they were prone to congregate on idle evenings. Playing out the hunch, Lao Fan decided that it might be worth a drive-by, on the theory that his quarry would be feeling a compulsion to describe their deeds for an appreciative audience.

He found three cars outside the club. The vintage Chevy was a treasure, doted on by the proprietor; the other wheels—an aging Caddy and a hearse—were marked with Thunder Dragon lightning-bolt insignia and instantly identifiable. Lao parked beside the hearse, got out and opened his trunk to choose his weapons.

It was early yet—the club had barely opened—but he had to make allowances for students cutting school, who might be on the premises. No alcohol was served inside, at least in theory, but the jukebox offered all the latest heavy-metal favorites, and the proximity of two competing high schools left the owner of the club with all the business he could handle, seven days a week.

Allowing for the innocent, Lao ruled out hand grenades. He didn't give a damn about the club, but he didn't intend to murder children. Glancing casually along the street, he double-checked the AK-47, slipped it underneath his coat and stuffed his pockets with extra magazines. Considering the cars, the damage they had caused so far, there might be anywhere from eight to fifteen Dragons in the club. They would be armed, at least a few of them with guns, and Lao knew it was foolhardy to take them on without adequate firepower.

The door instructed him to Pull, the order punctuated by a smiling yellow face. Inside the club was dark and warm, in contrast to the morning sun, which offered light but thus far had failed to raise the temperature appreciably. He spent a moment on the threshold, feeling terribly conspicuous and waiting for his eyes to make the change. Discordant music battered at his ears, too loud for normal conversation to survive.

The Thunder Dragons had a table in the back where they were holding court for half a dozen teenage hangers-on. Lao counted nine of them before he reached the bar and ordered a Cherry Coke and fries. He didn't plan to eat, but it was cover and he needed time to organize his move.

It was essential that he separate the Dragons from their innocent admirers. Lao considered posing as a truant officer, a cop, a messenger from Bach, rejecting each idea in turn. Official postures might provoke a situation with the innocents in jeopardy, and several of the Dragons had already noticed him, without apparent interest, as he waited for his order. None of Pham Bach's runners would take time to order food before delivering a message, and Lao cursed himself for sluggish thinking in a pinch.

No options, then. He swiveled on his stool, pulled back his raincoat and raised the AK-47, muzzle angled toward the ceiling. Squeezing off a burst that ripped through the acoustic tiles, he watched his targets scatter, several of them digging after their weapons as their high-school cronies ran for cover, screaming. Lao slid off the stool and stood his ground, waiting for his field of fire to clear.

One of the Dragons had been quick to overturn the table, but it was a futile gesture. Lao Fan stitched a line of holes horizontally across its center, rewarded by a strangled gurgling on the other side. Another member of the gang exploded into view, a shiny automatic pistol flashing in his fist. Lao was waiting for him with a burst that swept him off his feet and dumped his body into an adjacent booth.

The Thunder Dragons were recovering, and Lao Fan ducked as pistols opened fire from different angles, flattening himself against the bar. Behind him the proprietor was wounded as he tried to reach the telephone and went down, thrashing, on the floor. Lao raked a probing burst across the far end of the room, withdrew the rifle's empty magazine and slipped it in his pocket, feeding in a fresh clip on the move.

A couple of the Dragons saw him coming, but their shots were hasty, poorly aimed. Lao caught one of them with a disemboweling burst that dropped him in his tracks; the other was retreating when an automatic triple-punch smashed into his face.

Four men down with five remaining, and he wondered if the merchants in adjoining shops were conscious of the shooting yet. His ears had grown accustomed to the heavy-metal backbeat, razor voices screaming at the world about destruction and the charms of darkness. Lao had no idea how long the music would continue, or if it would adequately cover sounds of gunfire from the street, but he was bent on finishing his work before police arrived.

The Dragons finally made it easy. Lao could hear them whispering among themselves before they made their rush, and he was waiting, gauging their positions by the sounds of scuffling feet and sliding furniture. He dropped the first two as they rose from cover, tracking on to nail a third before the youth could use his nickel-plated .45. The two survivors came up firing, peppering the bar with bullets as they charged. Lao cut their legs from under them and sprayed them with the AK-47 as they fell, their bodies twitching with the impact as he emptied the magazine.

Reloading as he rose, Lao glanced behind the bar and found the wounded owner staring at him, teeth clenched in a snarl of pain. As he retreated toward the door, Lao switched his rifle onto semiautomatic, pumping two rounds through the jukebox and immediately silencing the voice of Mötley Crüe. Sobs and whispers behind him testified that the truants were emerging from their holes and picking over the remains.

Outside he tarried by the hearse, removed its gas cap and produced a handkerchief. One dip to wet the end with gasoline, and Lao reversed it, tucked the dry end deep into the spout. A wooden match burst into flame, and he was halfway to his car before the hearse exploded, showering the street with liquid fire. The Caddy would be next, and it was just too damned bad about the vintage Chevrolet.

Lao Fan was far from satisfied, but it would do for starters. There were other Thunder Dragons on the street, still preying on his friends. He mightn't find them all, but he could try, and when the pawns had been eliminated he would look for Bach.

The Thunder Dragons were an appetizer. Bach would be the entrée. If he played his cards right, Lao suspected Ngo Tien might be dessert.

SINCE THE EARLY nineteenth century, the central source of income for the Asian underworld has been narcotics. Long before the British merchants taught the Chinese the joys of opium, however, there was gambling, and it remains a staple feature of the Oriental crime scene, catering to rich and poor alike with varied games of chance that have survived the centuries with relatively little alteration.

As with prostitution, Bolan had conflicting views on gambling. If a man or woman had the nerve to risk their income, their life savings, on a bet, the Executioner didn't presume to interfere. His war was with the men behind the scenes who raked in millions from the tables, slot machines and floating games, investing that money in the narcotics traffic, murder contracts, child pornography, a hundred other filthy avenues of commerce on the dark side. If destruction of a neighborhood casino hurt his enemies and threw them off their stride, the joint was gone. Case closed.

The gambling hall in Anaheim was tucked away in rooms behind a family restaurant. It operated from the stroke of noon to midnight, if Lao's observations were correct, but Bolan didn't need an audience. His target this time was the facility itself, along with any cash on hand.

It wasn't lunchtime yet, but there were several customers inside the restaurant: two couples occupying booths, an old man at the counter nursing coffee. To the rear, a weary-looking shooter lounged beside a door marked Private, trying hard to stay awake by thumbing through a month-old girlie magazine. Before he could appreciate the foldout, Bolan's shadow fell across the page.

"You lost, man?"

Bolan slid into the booth across from Mr. Cool. "They tell me I can find some action here."

"Who's 'they'?"

"Word gets around."

The shooter checked Bolan's suit, his eyes. "You're early."

"That's a shame. I really don't have time to wait."

"What can I tell you?"

Bolan let him see the silencer-equipped Beretta. "You can tell me that we're walking through that door, or you can kiss your butt goodbye."

"You got it, man. Be cool, awright?"

Bolan smiled and thumbed the automatic's hammer back. "I'm cool."

"I see that, now."

The door was locked, but Bolan's front man knew the code and rapped it out with knuckles that were white from tension. Moments passed before the door was opened by the Asian pit boss, looking dapper in his tux. Before he had the chance to formulate a challenge, Bolan pushed the shooter past him, following the lead of his Beretta, reaching out to close the door behind himself.

It happened in a heartbeat. Bolan's hostage staggered, then dug for his iron before he had his balance back, attempting to conceal the move with artificial clumsiness. A single parabellum round punched through the shooter's temple at a range of ten feet and knocked him sprawling, while the pit boss turned a sickly shade of green.

"No need for you to join him," Bolan told the older man sincerely. "You can walk away from this and have a story for the grandkids if you play your cards right."

"I have no weapon."

"Fine. You *do* have money, though. I want it."

"You are making a mistake."

"It wouldn't be the first time, guy. Just stack it up and skip the warnings."

Bolan kept the pit boss covered while he packed the bankroll in a large valise. He didn't read the Asian as a hero type, but most casinos had some kind of weapons on the premises for cases such as this, and he wasn't prepared to let his guard down.

"How much?" he asked, when all the folding green had been bagged.

"Approximately eighty thousand dollars."

"Closc enough. Tell Ngo Tien it's a down payment on his tab. You got that?"

"On his tab. I have it."

"Good. Let's take a walk." Before they left the gambling hall, he holstered the Beretta, catching the obligatory flash of courage and relief behind his captive's eyes. "Don't think about it, guy," he cautioned. "Bankers generally make lousy soldiers, and they aren't much better in the corpse department."

"There is wisdom in your words."

They crossed the restaurant together. Bolan parked his hostage on the last stool by the door and dropped a five-spot on the counter. "He could use a cup of coffee," Bolan told the waitress. "Better make it nice and strong."

He made the short hike to his car and dropped the heavy satchel in the trunk with his accumulated hardware. He had planned initially to raze the building, but the cash withdrawal from Tien's black account would keep the mobster fuming, and he had more targets on his shrinking list waiting for his personal attention. If his luck and timing held, he would be ready for a one-on-one with Ngo Tien by early afternoon.

The Executioner was looking forward to it.

PHAM BACH HAD TRACKED the progress of the Thunder Dragons through reports of their attacks as morning melted into afternoon. The raiders were on schedule, doing well, but other troops were also on the street, and lately all the news was bad. From Buena Park and Long Beach, Garden Grove and Anaheim, reports rolled in of syndicate establishments attacked and looted, some of them in flames, employees slaughtered. At a club in Santa Ana, members of the Thunder Dragons had been hosed with automatic fire while killing time between their raids. Police were looking into rumors of a gang war, and his contacts in the sheriff's office had been on the phone with urgent warnings to desist from any further provocation.

Bach wasn't yet ready to comply. Before he caged the Dragons, he had business to complete, not least of which was the destruction of Mack Bolan. In his mind, Bach harbored little doubt that Bolan was responsible for the majority of losses suffered by the family. Lao Fan and his associates would be behind the rest, but they were being dealt with, and would soon be dead. The Executioner was Bach's primary target now.

Not that the Asian double agent disapproved of violence in the streets. Indeed, disruption of Tien's operation had been one of Pham Bach's goals from the beginning. But there was a difference between disruption and destruction. He didn't intend to see the syndicate demolished. Not before he entered into his inheritance.

The party still had uses for the network Tien had helped establish in America, and while the toppling of dinosaurs like Tien and Giap was an essential move, complete annihilation of their syndicate would rob the people's revolution of a potent weapon in the endless war against America.

The Executioner had served his purpose well, but it was time for him to die.

With that in mind, Pham Bach was still confronted with a world of problems. He didn't know Bolan's whereabouts, wouldn't have recognized him on the street, and he couldn't be certain if the Executioner was working actively with Lao Fan's men or on his own. Either way, the man would die before he saw another sunrise in Orange County.

When the telephone began to ring, Bach glared at it with unalloyed hostility. Bad news again, he thought with weary certainty. Of course, he might be wrong. Lao Fan might be dead. Or even Bolan.

Hoisting the receiver, Pham Bach recognized the reedy voice of an informant in the ranks of the Los Angeles Police Department. This one worked at Parker Center, and he kept an eye—or ear—on the internal workings of the city's organized crime task force. He was calling to report unusual activity on the Italian front, with the appearance of mobilization for all-out war. He professed ignorance of the causes, but under terse questioning he recalled that two of Don Carlotti's runners had been killed that morning, execution-style.

Bach thanked his contact for the tip and hung up. Carlotti seemed intent on satisfying the traditional Sicilian hunger for revenge. Dead runners in the Mafia meant nothing to Pham Bach, but he could see how the Italians might start jumping to conclusions. First the warehouse ambush had destroyed a shipment of narcotics, costing Don Carlotti half a million dollars on the spot. This new attack—whoever was responsible—would further fuel the fires of paranoia, and Carlotti might lash out at Ngo Tien before his enemies had been identified.

There was a chance, however slim, that the Italians might be ignorant of Bolan's presence in the area. If so, it was an oversight Pham Bach could easily correct.

He punched the number up from memory, identified himself and waited while the capo's houseman fetched his master. Don Carlotti's voice was taut with anger as he took the phone.

"You've got some fucking nerve to call me here."

Bach let it pass. "I have obtained some information I thought you might find interesting."

"I'll bet."

"I now have reason to believe Mack Bolan was responsible for the attack that left your nephew in his present, most unfortunate, condition."

"Yeah? Mack Bolan, huh?" He had expected more surprise. Carlotti's tone was thick with anger, but if he was startled, the Italian hid it well.

"You *know* this Bolan, I presume."

"Presume this, pal. I knew Mack Bolan when you zipperheads were squatting in your paddies, sucking rice. I saw him turn this city upside down and damn near put the Family out of business. Are you reading me?"

"There is no need—"

"My ass! You figure Bolan ran the warehouse action down, okay, let's say I buy it. Those were gooks your boys knocked off, in case you don't remember. Now, I've got more people wasted, and the bastard hung a goddamned marksman's medal on them. Are you with me so far, *Mr.* Bach?''

"I do not see—"

"Because you're fucking blind. That makes me wonder if this Bolan bastard might have cut a deal, you follow me? Let's say he signs a contract with some friends from Zipperland. He hates the L.A. Family, and his buddies have a world to gain from anybody dumping on the brotherhood. I hope you're getting this, because there's gonna be a quiz."

"You cannot believe—"

"Don't tell me what I can or cannot do, you piece of shit! I've been expecting someone from the sushi bar to call and tip me off on Bolan. It's the icing on the cake."

Bach swallowed rising anger, fought to keep his own voice calm. "By now, you must know that our own facilities have been the hardest hit. We think—"

"You ain't seen nothing, bright boy. If you think those love taps you've been getting are a *hit*, you'd better brace yourself, because the shit is coming down, and you're the drain."

"Rash words are frequently regretted."

"Hey, you want regret? How's this: you're dead, you fucking slope! You hear me? Dead!"

Bach grimaced as the link was broken, Don Carlotti slamming down his receiver. The double agent sat and listened to the dial tone for a moment, finally replacing the handset.

He had given thought to the provocation of a war, with Bolan as the catalyst, but things were slipping out of his control. Bach's plan had called for Ngo Tien to be exposed and prosecuted, even killed, with maximum publicity designed to shame the refugee community. A three-way war, with Asian troops against the Mafia, and Bolan playing both sides off against the middle, was a different proposition. From his safe position as covert manipulator of events,

Pham Bach had now become a target of Carlotti's violent rage, a man already marked for death.

But he wasn't prepared to die without a fight. A born survivor, Bach hadn't achieved his present status in the party or Tien's family by standing back and letting chance control his actions. He was a precipitator of events, a mover and a shaker. Tien was shaking now, and so was Don Carlotti, though the latter's rage prevented him from realizing he should be afraid.

In essence the Sicilian had deciphered Bach's original idea of using Bolan as a tool, a weapon. He would never know the plan had slipped away from Bach, assuming animation of its own. No one would ever know.

Pham Bach would have to get his house in order, swiftly, if he hoped to gain the edge that would ensure a stunning victory. He needed all his troops around him, armed and ready to proceed upon his order.

Smiling to himself, the momentary lapse behind him, Pham Bach started making calls.

"THAT GODDAMNED ZIPPERHEAD! Can you believe his freaking *nerve*?"

"He's got some balls, all right," the houseman grudgingly agreed.

"I'll tell you one thing. He should use them while he can, because I plan to cut them off and have them bronzed for cuff links. Goddamned foreigners have had their own way long enough."

On rare occasions when he thought about it, Don Carlotti saw himself as the ideal American. A son of immigrants, he had come up the hard way, dropping out of junior high school, checking into Hard Knocks University, where he obtained a Ph.D. in street survival. Having family in the Family didn't hurt, but when Carlotti studied his reflection in the mirror, he was looking at a self-made man. And he was proud of what he'd built.

One thing, for damned sure: no illegal immigrants or refugees from Bamboo Land were going to walk in and tell Carlotti that he had to stand aside while they moved in and gobbled up the family business. No damned way at all.

You didn't need diplomas on the wall to know when you were getting screwed, and Pham Bach's little phone call had been all the proof he needed. Half a dozen good men wasted, Vinnie breathing with assistance from machines, and now the frigging slope informs him Mack the Bastard was responsible.

Okay.

Carlotti hadn't studied Bolan's history in all the detail that some others had, but he remembered that the guy had been some kind of hotshot in the war. He killed a lot of gooks, but he was friendly with a lot of others, and the kind he got along with were the same damn kind who turned up on Carlotti's doorstep once the Reds had overrun Saigon. He understood, at least in principle, why they had come to the United States. For Christ's sake, his own papa had been running from police when he arrived at Ellis Island, more than fifty years ago. It was a great American tradition, hiding out.

But times had changed. When the old man had made his break with Sicily, the stateside underworld had been disorganized, with everybody whacking everybody else and warring over territory, Chinks and Jews and whatnot running down their ghetto games in their respective neighborhoods and kissing up to half-assed politicians on the side. Today, with things well orchestrated, in control, the last thing Carlotti needed was a crowd of zipperheads, Colombians and Cubans meddling in things they couldn't hope to understand.

The time had come for Tien, Pham Bach and all their buddies to be taught a lesson. They were going back to school, and this time Girolamo Carlotti would be planning the curriculum. It was a shame that none of them would live to spread the word of what they learned, but they could still be useful to the Family, serving as examples for the other outlaws who believed they could poach on Don Carlotti's territory. Anyone who thought the Don had grown soft with age had better think again. He was a rock, and enemies would smash themselves to pieces if they tried to break him down.

Carlotti didn't relish facing Mack the Bastard. It would take an idiot to welcome that, but he wasn't about to run away like some he could have mentioned. Let the wild card play his games with Tien and Bach, whoever. He was still a man, and men could die. *Would* die, if they had any thoughts of ripping off Carlotti's family.

Success had been a long time coming. There had been times when Carlotti thought he might not make it. Maybe he was too damned slow, not tough enough to make the grade. But in the end, his triumph had been won by sweat and blood. His sweat, the blood of those who tried to head him off, prevent him from achieving greatness. Those who tried to stand against him got themselves plowed under. They were history.

Like Ngo Tien and Mack the Bastard would be history before another day burned down in the Pacific haze.

The soldier was a misfit, out of style and out of sync in a society that turned its back on heroes. He was fighting on behalf of citizens who didn't give a damn. It was the new "me generation," and Carlotti knew precisely how to keep the yuppies and their children happy, catering to their desires, whatever those might be. No foreigner could do it half as well. No wild-assed warrior from the jungle could presume to stand against the might of Carlotti's war machine.

In retrospect, it almost seemed a shame that Bolan had to die. His passing would be like the ending of an era.

In payment, Bolan's death would pave the way for Carlotti's rise to even greater power in the brotherhood. A seat on the commission was assured to any man who bagged the Executioner, and he could almost smell the boardroom now, imagining the glances from his brother capos, dark with envy.

Too bad the bastard had to die.

Too bad he wasn't dead already.

CHAPTER TWENTY

The La Mirada funhouse was a split-level ranch-style, separated from its neighbors by some costly acreage. Its occupants ensured their privacy with fences, decorative hedges and strategically positioned trees. The house wasn't secure against attack, by any means—no fortress here—but Peeping Toms would be immediately obvious and could expect a rousing welcome from the tenant of the moment.

Strictly speaking, Ngo Tien's establishment was never "occupied." No living person claimed the address as a place of residence, though many had at one time or another passed a night within its walls. The property and house had been acquired with cash from one of Tien's elusive corporations, deeds and title registered in nonexistent names. The taxes were invariably paid on time, with checks drawn on the account of Michael Staniak, a name selected from the telephone directory by Tien and Giap, the latter scanning surnames while his partner searched for given names that pleased his ear. In the event the place was raided, the authorities would never nail down proof of ownership by any individual or corporate entity, and so would die their hopes of linking Tien to any criminal conspiracy.

It wasn't Bolan's task to build a court case or secure indictments. Lao Fan's recon of the house was all the evidence he needed, and he wore his warrant in a holster slung beneath his arm. If Bolan's enemies had any questions or complaints, they could be filed with the custodians of hell upon arrival.

Lao's surveillance and the whisper of the streets told Bolan that the La Mirada funhouse was a "party pad," which doubled as a studio for filming hard-core movies. Films or tapes were also made at parties, it was rumored, but without the knowledge or consent of those immortalized on screen. As with the brothel operation Bolan had busted earlier, Tien's customers and "friends" who came to pay for play were often forced to keep on paying, through the nose.

This afternoon the house was occupied, a van and several sports cars parked out front. The most expensive of them was a Maserati, white, with vanity tags that proclaimed it—or its owner—to be SLICK.

The soldier backed in his four-door rental, prepared for a hasty exit if the need arose, and eyed the van en route to his appointment with the doorbell. It would be ideal for hauling film or video equipment, but he knew that it could double as a bus for party girls, as well. Once Bolan was inside the funhouse, he'd have to play the game by ear, try to spare the relatively innocent—if any could be found within those walls.

A punker in a tie-dyed T-shirt answered Bolan's ring. The pattern of his shirt was apparently meant to complement his hair, which stood erect in multicolored spikes, affecting the appearance of a porcupine from outer space.

"What's happening?"

The punker didn't seem suspicious, and so Bolan played a hunch. "I've got a note for Slick," he said.

"I'll take it, man."

"Uh-uh. It's from the man. My orders call for personal delivery."

"That's cool. We're on a break now, anyway. Come on, we'll find him."

The funhouse had been furnished with minimal expense and something less than perfect taste. The VIPs who partied here weren't concerned with the decor in any case, and

Bolan noted that a number of the easy chairs apparently had been designed with easy sex in mind. He trailed his Technicolor guide through several rooms until they reached the soundstage proper.

From appearances, the crew was on a break. Two lissome ladies and their leading man were lounging on the bed and smoking something stronger than tobacco, none of them in a hurry to get dressed. The cameramen were huddled with a bearded, balding character who bore the earmarks of an aging flower child.

"Hey, Slick," the human rainbow called, "you got a visitor."

The flower child glanced up through wire-rimmed spectacles, eyes clouding over as he focused on an unfamiliar face. "Do tell. You letting people wander in here now, Jacoby?"

"What the hell, he's got a message for you, man. It's cool."

The soldier's smile was ice. "Well, not exactly."

"Huh?"

Slick's frown was etching wrinkles on his sallow skin. "You have a message from . . . ?"

"A message, right. It's short and sweet. You're out of business, Slick."

"I beg your pardon?"

Bolan showed him the Beretta, cocking it. The punker made an ill-considered lunge, and Bolan hit him with a left that broke his nose and left him on all fours, bright crimson challenging the T-shirt's soft pastels.

"I said you're out of business, guy."

"What is this?"

"It's your one and only chance to walk away," Bolan responded. "Any time I have to say things twice, I get a little itchy."

"You a cop, or what?"

"Or what." His eyes shifted to the cameraman, the "actors," back again to the director. "Leaving? Or does this become a snuffer in the final reel?"

"I'm out of here," Slick told him. Turning to the cast and crew, he grated, "That's a wrap. We're finished for today. Get dressed, get out."

The trio on the bed were slow to comprehend the message. Bolan helped them with a parabellum two-punch that destroyed the nearest camera and sent them scurrying for street clothes. Fishing the incendiary starters from his pocket, Bolan dropped one on the rumpled bed, another on the carpet, rolled a third beneath the hanging drapes. All three were burning brightly as he trailed the stragglers to their cars.

"You've got balls," Slick told him as he slid behind the Maserati's wheel. "Too bad you won't be keeping them."

"My worry," Bolan answered. "You'd be better off to watch your own."

He saw the film crew off, made sure the fire was spreading properly and took his leave. The blitz was getting old, and while he had a short list of targets left, he felt that it was time to raise his sights.

But first he would check in with Lao. The gutsy Montagnard should still be on the street, but he had left a number for the Executioner and it was manned around the clock, for the duration. Bolan wasn't looking for a backup, but he wanted to touch base and verify his targets prior to making any crucial moves.

Above all else, he sought word of Lisa, anything at all that would pinpoint her whereabouts. He wouldn't rest until he found the lady, got some answers to the questions that were haunting him. He had to know the truth about Luan Ky, the syndicate's involvement in her fate and the role that Lisa might have played.

With truth in hand, he could decide if Lisa Tien deserved to live or die. It was a choice the soldier didn't relish, but he was prepared to make it all the same.

THE MARKET in La Palma was the final stop, and So Minh would be glad when they were finished. He was looking forward to the celebration of their triumph, the release of pent-up energy that he'd find with one—or several—of the party girls the Thunder Dragons kept on call. The party would be awesome, all the more so as it marked his elevation to a higher rank and station in the syndicate.

Of course he couldn't hope for everything at once. A slugger would not be promoted to vice-president his first day on the job, but with a foot in the door Minh knew he would eventually have it all. His youth and stamina, his willingness to handle wet work, all combined to make him the superior of some who had been sitting in posh offices for years. The older management was losing touch with the realities of commerce on the street, and Minh would be delighted to refresh their memories. It would be educational for all concerned, and his approach would show them that he had brains as well as brawn, initiative as well as balls.

Minh concentrated on the storefronts as they drove the final block in silence, every member of his entourage alert for traps, the stray patrol car, anything at all that would signal danger. So far they were on a roll, and he hadn't touched base with central for an update on the other teams. If they were meeting opposition, they could sort it out themselves.

The market was a combination grocery and department store, with household goods and sundries, paperbacks and magazines, a little pharmacy in back. Though small by supermarket standards, it retained a dozen paid employees on the day shift, and its owner had begun to think about a condo in the canyon. More important, he'd been sluggish with protection payments lately, and the street talk had him cozy with Lao Fan. Minh was inclined to doubt the latter information—the proprietor was far too snobbish to associate with peasants—but Minh had his orders, and he didn't plan to second-guess Pham Bach. There was no future in it, and he had too much to lose.

His orders were to trash the store and leave the owner with a message: mend his ways, or pay a steeper price next time around. No killing had been ordered, but Minh knew it might be necessary with a dozen hostages on staff and shoppers wandering the aisles in unknown numbers. If it came to killing, he was ready, but he hoped they wouldn't have to slaughter everyone in sight.

So loud. So messy. And a massacre wouldn't look so good.

Jolted back to cold reality, Minh realized they had stopped. He hauled out the Browning automatic and checked its load, replacing the depleted magazine. There was no point in taking chances; if it came to murder, they would do the job efficiently, without remorse, and run like hell before the cops arrived. No witnesses, no case.

With eight men at his back, all armed, Minh sauntered through the double doors and scanned the market with a practiced eyed. Two clerks on registers in front, assorted box boys crouching in the aisles, adjusting prices, stocking shelves. He counted fifteen customers before he gave it up, deciding they would have to run a sweep, hold everyone in the back while they were working on the merchandise.

He brought up the automatic, sighted on an unattended register and slammed a bullet through the keyboard. Someone screamed in produce, but he had their full attention now, his soldiers fanning out to make sure no one found an exit, sounded an alarm.

"Listen up!" he ordered, feeling like a star and warming to the role. "We need to do some quick remodeling. If everyone will step back to the dairy section, in the rear, we'll have you on your way in no time."

Sullen glances from the tallest of the box boys, but he moved out with the others, picking up his pace when one of Minh's commandos stuck the barrel of a sawed-off shotgun in his face. Despite some muttering, the thirty-odd assembled captives offered no resistance. Minh hung back to cover them, the other seven raiders striking off to ransack shelves and generally reduce the store to chaos.

The proprietor surprised So Minh, emerging from a door behind the dairy cooler, eyes like saucers, sputtering with rage as vandals spilled his inventory on the floor and trod it underfoot. "You can't do this!" he blustered, clearly lacking the conviction of his words.

"I'll bet we can," Minh said and shot the man in the kneecap, dropping him before he had a chance to scream.

The shot disturbed his soldiers, briefly, but they hurried back to work as soon as they determined Minh had everything under control. They worked with hands and knives or swept the shelves with brooms secured in housewares, calling back and forth across the aisles to one another. Sugar, flour, cake mix rose in shifting dunes, while standing freezers vomited their contents on the floor. A shotgun blast in beverages, and it was raining Coca-Cola, 7-Up, a dozen different brands and flavors. Steaks, chops and chicken hurtled through the air like small organic UFOs.

Minh passed the time collecting driver's licenses from his assorted captives, warning each in turn they would be hunted down and killed if they provided accurate descriptions to police. The Asians knew his reputation well enough to be afraid, and if a couple of the Anglos broke their silence . . . well, his people all resembled one another to the Western eye. Arrests were possible. Indictments were unlikely. Any notion of convictions was a joke.

"Enough! Let's go!"

The market, spotless when they'd entered, now resembled something from a postapocalyptic horror film. Minh half expected zombies to come lurching through the wreckage, passing by the frozen foods in search of juicy shoppers they could snack on. It would take a while to clear the mess away, more time to get the market running smoothly. Meanwhile the proprietor could learn to walk with canes and use his rubber leg for something other than an anchor. Time and money down the drain.

They emptied out the registers in passing, splitting better than a thousand dollars between them. Minh was generous, surrendering his share, content with the reward Pham Bach had promised him. His mind was on the celebration of their sweeping victory and all that lay beyond.

He called his troops together on the sidewalk, lined them up to face the market's glass facade. "I think we ought to say goodbye in style," he said, the Browning sliding out to full arm's length before he finished speaking.

Minh was sighting down the slide and squeezing off in rapid-fire as his companions took their cue, unloading through the plate-glass windows with their side arms, shotguns, everything they had. The street reverberated with their thunder, and glass showered the pavement like some kind of frozen waterfall.

Minh didn't care if anybody took a hit inside the store. For now it was enough to hold the power in his hands and feel its recoil, smell the dragon smoke and listen to its roar until his ears were ringing, deaf to any other sound.

So caught up was he in the moment that Minh never heard Death coming for him in the street.

THE CALL TO LAO FAN'S contact had destroyed Mack Bolan's schedule, causing him to scrap his list of targets on the spot. He'd been unaware of the retaliation undertaken by the Thunder Dragons, and he meant to stop them if he could, before more innocents were drawn into his war.

The problem, simply stated, dealt with finding targets. From the vague report, he knew the Dragons had to be striking preselected victims, moving swiftly in between their raids, and he had no idea who might be on their hit list. If the punks had any brains at all, they would have split their forces into several strike teams, thereby covering more ground and making apprehension of the whole group virtually impossible.

No matter. Bolan had to try, and so he mentally erased the list of gambling clubs and numbers banks, intent on running down a member of the gang if possible and sweating him for information. Bolan wasted forty minutes cruising aimlessly around the refugee community before he struck the mother lode.

The vehicles were parked outside a modernistic grocery mart, and Bolan recognized the lightning-bolt insignia that Lao Fan had described. He made a drive-by, parked around the corner, doubled back on foot. If they were in the store, he would prefer to take them coming out on foot instead of playing cops and robbers with a running firefight through the heart of town. If there was killing to be done, he hoped to end it here.

He reached a point directly opposite the market, sun glare on the tinted windows blocking any view of what went on inside. It was likely that the market was another target on their list, a business to be trashed for some imaginary slight to Ngo Tien and his associates. The Executioner debated going in, dismissed the notion when he thought about civilians in a cross fire, trapped in narrow grocery aisles without a place to hide.

And so he waited. Moments passed before electric doors hissed open and the Dragons sauntered out, carrying their weapons openly. One of them—the leader, from appearances—said something to the others, swinging up an automatic pistol as he spoke and firing through the broad front windows of the market. In a heartbeat, his companions were laying down a withering barrage of fire.

No time for conversation, after all. Bolan braced the heavy Desert Eagle in a firm two-handed grip and started working up the line, from left to right. Three rounds, and he had dropped three of the Thunder Dragons in their tracks before the others knew that anything was wrong. Round four took out a gunner who was turning, searching for the source of unexpected weapon fire, and the others scattered, taking refuge in the shadow of their cars, one fading back in the direction of the store.

The warrior fired a round at that one, saw the runner stumble, scrabbling on all fours with blood like modern artwork on the wall behind him, then Bolan had to dive for cover as surviving Thunder Dragons brought him under fire. His choices were a station wagon and a Pinto. Bolan took the wagon, huddling against its fender while it took a storm of hits from pistol rounds and buckshot.

Too damned slow, he thought, and cursed his timing. He was cornered with a lethal no-man's-land between him and his wheels, the Dragons anxious for a chance to pot him when he showed himself. Obligingly he risked a glance around the wagon's tailgate, picking out an enemy in silhouette as one of them attempted to improve his field of fire. He nailed the guy and reduced the odds as he retreated.

Bolan wondered if the locals would attempt to call the police while rounds were flying, or if they would merely wait to see who won. He knew it might go either way, but he wasn't amused by the idea of a patrolman driving blindly into what had recently become a war zone. Bolan knew that the Thunder Dragons would have no reservations about firing on a cop.

Time to finish, then. But how? A rush was suicide, but it was damned near equally as dangerous to disengage. He made it fifteen yards to reach the corner, and another moment on the turn, where he would be exposed. Four guns against him, at least one of those a shotgun, and he knew it would require a miracle for him to make the dash unscathed.

He also knew that there was no alternative. He had to move, and soon, before his shaky post became untenable. He shifted to his left, popped up between the wagon and the Pinto, emptying the Magnum's magazine in rapid-fire to keep the hostile heads down. Feeding in a new clip as he scuttled toward the jumping-off point, Bolan drew the Beretta from its sheath and flicked the fire-selector switch to automatic, giving him the capability for 3-round bursts.

Within the next few seconds, the warrior knew he would be needing everything he had. He also knew that none of it might be enough. And if the Dragons stopped him here, then what?

Then nothing.

Lao, or someone else, would finish what had started in Orange County weeks before the Executioner arrived, and somehow, someday, they would see it finished. It was their fight, after all.

Five seconds. He counted backward, with the doomsday numbers ringing in his head like funeral bells.

Thinking fleetingly of things left unfinished, the warrior broke from cover and met the Thunder Dragons with a thunder of his own.

LISA HAD BEEN PARKED outside the club in Santa Ana, waiting for the Thunder Dragons to emerge, when Lao Fan arrived. She watched him enter, nearly panicked at the muffled sounds of gunfire from within, was about to cross the street when he emerged, apparently unhurt, and torched the Dragons' wheels. She considered going in despite the fire, but knew she would be wasting time. The boys she'd been following were dead, and she had to make another contact with the gang.

She cruised the streets without direction for the best part of an hour, stopping several times to ask if anyone had seen the Thunder Dragons. Posing as a girlfriend of So Minh, she drew blank stares and curt denials from the individuals she questioned, moving on each time in search of someone who wasn't afraid to answer with the truth. Discovering their cars outside the market owed more to chance than any skill on Lisa's part, and she pulled in uprange, a block away, to watch and wait.

Engrossed with private thoughts and concentrating on the store, she almost missed the Executioner's approach. At first he was a mere pedestrian, observed peripherally and dismissed, but there was something in his silhouette that drew her back, forced her to take a second glance. Her heart was leaping as she made the recognition, and she was prepared to join him, warn him off, when So Minh and his soldiers left the market.

Lisa froze, prepared for anything except what happened next. She had expected Minh and company to get back in their cars, and she was braced for Bolan's move to stop them. She was *not* prepared to see the Dragons line up, face the markct like a firing squad and unload their weapons through the plate-glass windows. Startled by the sudden thunder, Lisa glanced at Bolan, found him swinging into action with a weapon of his own, its echo melding with the clamor of the other guns. Two Dragons down, a third, a fourth, and then the others realized that they were under fire, dispersing, scuttling for cover and returning fire as best they could.

Time froze and Lisa seemed to take forever fumbling with her ignition key. The engine of her sportster finally growled to life and she released the brake, manipulating shift and wheel on instinct as her mind went momentarily blank.

She knew that Bolan must not die. Not here, like this. She also knew that he might kill her on sight, without a second thought, in payment for her treachery, but she would have to take that chance.

Accelerating toward the cross fire, Lisa lifted the revolver from her lap and held it ready. She could never hope to score a hit on moving targets, not the way her hands were trembling, but she might be able to distract the Dragons, keep their heads down for a moment.

She was standing on the brakes as Bolan burst from cover, firing on her right, his first rounds hammering across the street mere inches from her windshield. On her left, the Thunder Dragons were emerging from their hiding places, firing wildly, stray slugs peppering the storefronts opposite and etching spiderweb designs on windowpanes. Instinctively she chose a target, fired two shots, and was amazed to see the gunman stagger, clutching at his side.

"Get in!" she shouted, feeling Bolan hesitate, considering his options in the fraction of a heartbeat that remained. "Goddamn it, *hurry*!"

She felt him drop into the seat beside her. With sudden thunder in her ears, Lisa thought that she was dying, but then she saw the soldier's target spinning, toppling from his hiding place behind a squat VW.

"What are you waiting for?" the soldier asked, his voice cold steel before the stutter of a different weapon jarred her into action.

Lisa tromped on the accelerator, fought the shudder of the steering wheel as screaming tires found traction and gained momentum, tearing through the nearest intersection, echoes of erratic gunshots fading at their backs like distant fireworks.

She'd done it.
Bolan was alive, and he would have to listen now.
Unless he killed her first.

CHAPTER TWENTY-ONE

"You have a way of turning up at crucial moments," Bolan said.

"I've been out looking for you."

"Me? I never would have guessed." He made no effort to disguise the sharp, sarcastic tone.

She held the sportster to the posted limits, seeming to proceed without direction through the streets of Santa Ana, Costa Mesa, Fountain Valley. Bolan knew that she was killing time and working up the nerve to tell him something, but his tolerance for games was wearing thin.

"You set me up," he told her flatly, watching Lisa flinch as if the words had been accompanied by a blow. "At least three decent men are dead because of you."

"I know that. Don't you think I know?"

The soldier frowned. "I guess your father was a little disappointed, even so. I mean, those three were small-fry, right? And he shelled out a heavy price to bring them down."

The color had evaporated from her face. "You know about...my father?"

Bolan's smile was carved in stone. "I know it isn't me, for starters. And I've seen the birthday snapshot on his desk. I might be slow out of the gate, but I can still add two and two."

"What now?" There was uncertainty and fear in Lisa's voice. He liked the sound, and hated liking it.

"Some answers. Straight this time, without the con."

"I don't know where to start."

"Let's shoot for the beginning, and I don't mean Genesis."

"All right." She seemed about to speak, thought better of it, choking on the words. "It might be better if you asked me questions."

"Fine. How did your people know that I was coming?"

"Lucky guesswork, I suppose. The way I understand it, word came down to Bach from San Francisco. Do you know Pham Bach?"

"I haven't had the pleasure."

"He's my father's chief adviser, second in command behind Anh Giap. He heard from contacts on the Bay that you were working there, and I suppose he thought it would be wise to have a plan prepared in case you headed south."

"That brings us back to you."

"I guess it does." She hesitated, putting thoughts in order as she drove. "You have to understand that it was Bach's idea. I'm sure my father didn't—doesn't—know a thing about it. Bach approached me with a so-called foolproof plan to save my father from his enemies and prove myself to him at the same time. All I had to do was play a role and stand aside when things got heavy."

"Prove yourself?"

"My mother died when I was seven. I've been filling in for her in one way or another ever since. I love my father, can you understand that? For the past few years he's been excluding me from every aspect of the family business."

"He was doing you a favor, Lisa."

"So, who asked him to?" The sudden flash of anger in her tone surprised him. "He never had a son. I'm all he's got. Why can't I help him now, the way I always have?"

"You *want* a piece of this? The drugs? The prostitution? Murder?"

"I accept my father as a man who may have made mistakes in judgment, but you have to understand his background, the environment in Vietnam."

"I've been there," he reminded her. "The whores might sell it to survive, but it's all gravy to the pimps. You're smart enough to know that, Lisa, and I don't believe that you're about to tell me heroin is necessary for survival."

"Who opened up the traffic?" Lisa challenged him. "Your CIA and Air America. Go back through history. Who introduced the poppy in the first place? White men!"

"So, a few of you decided you could be just like the worst of us and turn a profit. That's a lame equation, Lisa. All you wind up with is scum times two. It won't hold water."

"I'm not interested in your opinion."

"Fine. Let's skip the history and bring it back to now time." Bolan's voice was cold. "You're quite an actress, but you didn't write the script. I want to hear about Luan Ky."

"She's dead. That much of it was true."

An old wound whispered open in his heart, and Bolan clenched his fists to keep from striking out. "Go on."

"Bach has a file. He let me read it. All about her life, the charges that were finally filed against her by the Communists... her execution."

"When and where?"

"Saigon. Nine years ago."

"This file... was it official?"

"I believe so. I have nothing to compare it with, but there were standard forms, reports from an informer, mug shots, things like that."

"Did your associate—"

"Pham Bach."

"Okay. Did he say where he got the file?"

"I didn't ask him, but it did seem odd. I've thought about it since, but I can't work it out. Nine years ago Pham Bach was *here.* If we assume the file's authentic, how could he receive it from the Communists?''

''Offhand, I'd say he's either got a mole with the security police back home—which seems unlikely—or he's one of them.''

The lady wore a stunned expression. It hadn't occurred to her, or if it had her conscious mind had pushed the thought away, refusing to acknowledge it. Forced to face the issue now, her heart and brain were racing into overdrive.

''There must be some mistake,'' she said at last, when she regained a measure of control.

He shrugged. ''It covers everything we know so far. It gives us motive.''

''How?''

''The Reds despise your father and his cronies even more than I do. They despise and fear the honest refugees, as well. What better propaganda weapon could they have? The righteous, patriotic refugees are dealing drugs and pimping, feeding off their own like leeches with protection payments, gambling, loan-shark rackets. It's a gold mine, instant headlines, maybe even TV movies. There's enough muck there to tarnish every decent Asian in the state.''

''And you?''

''I don't have many friends left in the Socialist Republic. Some of those in power might remember me. I wouldn't be surprised if one or two of them were tickled by the thought of getting me to help the cause.''

''I know that Bach was using me. He's tried to kill me once, already, but the rest of it . . .''

''Okay, *you* tell me where he got the file.''

She had no answer for him, and they covered several blocks in silence. When she found her voice again, it held an unexpected note of optimism. ''If you're right about all this, it means my father's innocent,'' she said. ''But if he didn't know—''

"He might not know about your friend's connection with the Reds," he interrupted. "So far, I have no proof either way. He's still a pimp, pornographer and pusher, not to mention smuggling, illegal arms transactions, bribery and murder. He controls the Thunder Dragons, Lisa. You must know that."

"Bach gives orders to the Dragons."

"And he gets *his* orders from your father, right?"

Again, no answer.

Bolan gave her new directions, to a safehouse Lao maintained near U.C. Irvine. It had strapped the little Asian's budget, but the war had schooled him in preparedness at any cost.

"I want you tucked away when this unravels. No more flying rescues. I'll be borrowing your car so I can fetch my own."

The lady bit her lower lip to keep from crying. "If you have to take it out on someone, punish me," she said. "I lied to you about Luan Ky. I set you up."

"Maybe later."

"Damn you!"

It was a damned peculiar world in which a daughter's love could only find expression through conspiracy and murder. Bolan was accustomed to logic of the streets, the sewers, but he obviously hadn't seen it all. Not yet.

The urban jungle still had things to teach him, and the Executioner might offer certain lessons in return.

FINDING LISA TIEN hadn't been easy for Lian Trang. He'd been forced to step inside her mind, run through her options and eliminate the impossibilities. She wasn't at home; the police had seen to that. A contact with her father would be risky, instantly reported to Pham Bach, and Trang believed that Lisa would consider that before she placed a call. Her options were extremely limited, and while she might

have fled the area, Lian Trang was banking on a more
unorthodox approach.

He thought the girl would try to reconcile herself with
Bolan.

On its face, the plan was madness, but audacity was
valuable in a crisis situation, sometimes reaping strange and
unexpected benefits. Assuming she suspected Bach of
treachery by now—and given her response to the collectors
he had sent to her apartment, that much was assured—she
might attempt to sell the Executioner on Pham Bach as vil-
lain, shifting heat away from Ngo Tien and working out a
way to save herself, besides.

Audacious, possibly insane...but it might work.

Lian Trang was proud of his ability to pick the brains of
others, crawl inside their thoughts and try them on for size.
His intuition, prescience, gave him an advantage in the hunt
for human prey. It made him lethal, and his special talents
had been recognized, rewarded, by Pham Bach. In time, if
all went well, Bach would replace his nominal superiors,
assuming domination of the family with Trang beside him.

But it was time to think of first things first. The girl could
ruin Bach's plans—and by extension, all of Trang's—if she
survived to reach her father or the Executioner with tales of
Bach's duplicity. The Anglo soldier might do everyone a
favor by cutting Lisa down on sight, but Trang couldn't afford to take that chance,

He found her, finally, through chance as much as skill.
Trang reasoned that his prey would try to get in touch with
Bolan, but she wouldn't have the means of making contact. Thus reduced to searching for her man, she would
adopt the strategy most likely to produce results: in short,
she would stake out a likely target, hoping that the Executioner would eventually come to her.

The choice of targets had confused him, with the recent
strikes against Tien's operations county-wide. Bewildered by

the glut of possibilities, Trang had decided that the girl wouldn't select a stationary site. Aware of Bolan's passion for mobility, his tendency to play the Good Samaritan with peasants, she would choose a moving target that the Executioner couldn't resist.

The Thunder Dragons.

That decision made, Trang's task had still been far from easy. Following the Dragons on their lightning rounds was difficult enough, but choosing which of their contingents Lisa might select defied all logic. In the end, he found her by a process of elimination, tracking down each squad of Dragons in its turn, aware that he might miss his quarry anywhere along the route and lose his opportunity forever.

She was trailing So Hoo Minh when Trang picked out her sports car half a block ahead. He followed at a cautious distance, reasonably certain she wouldn't be looking for a tail, still veering off from time to time and running parallel, returning to her track like any mongrel following a bitch in heat. He was a block behind her, idling against the curb, when So Minh's raiders took the market down and Bolan crashed their party on the street.

The Executioner's appearance changed Trang's game plan. Greater caution was required, and Trang had nearly stopped a bullet from the leader of the Dragons as he followed Lisa from the shooting scene. From there her track was nebulous, meandering through suburbs and commercial areas with no apparent destination firmly fixed in mind. She would be pitching Bolan, trying desperately to sell him on some plan or other that would save her life, her father's, and Trang thought there was an outside chance that she could make it work.

In Vietnam, according to Pham Bach, the Executioner had also been known as "Sergeant Mercy," after his attention to the needs of peasants and the wounded of both sides. Compassion was a fatal weakness in Trang's view of life. It marked the kind man as an easy touch, a target for the wretched of the earth who begged for food, first aid, a simple helping hand. Once any man began to think of others first, his days were numbered. Looking out for Number One was Trang's philosophy, his personal religion, and he gloated in the knowledge of his adversary's mortal flaw.

Possessed of no such weakness in himself, Lian Trang was confident that he could take the Executioner. He wouldn't risk an equal match, of course. The showdown was a relic of the Western cinema, consigned to history along with button shoes and wide-eyed innocence. Today, in movies and on television, even cowboys shot their adversaries in the back. It was a judgment call, entirely rational, and never mind those myths about the fastest gun in town.

Beside him on the seat, concealed beneath a copy of *The Wall Street Journal*, lay a customized Colt Python with a Tasco four-power scope mounted on its eight-inch barrel. Trang had loaded the .357 cartridges himself; the 180-grain semijacketed hollowpoint projectiles would achieve muzzle velocities of 1,600 feet per second. The lethal manglers would still be travelling at 1,400 feet per second at 100 yards, and Trang didn't intend to let his targets get that far away.

There was still a chance that Bolan might do part of Trang's work for him, but that hope was fading by the moment, by the mile. The longer Lisa Tien survived in Bolan's presence, the more likely she would be to sell the Executioner on her proposal. It was troublesome that Bolan hadn't killed her outright, but his chivalry was showing. This time, it would cost the man his life.

Trang kept his distance, following his prey through residential streets in Irvine, slowing down when the sportster's brake lights started winking from two blocks ahead. He drifted past a narrow driveway, saw them parked and cut a U-turn at the intersection, doubling back. He parked against the curb directly opposite, unmindful of the fact that he was on the wrong side of the street, and tossed the newspaper to the floor.

The Python felt delicious in his hand.

THEY STOOD beside the sports car, Bolan facing Lisa, jangling her car keys in his palm. "You should be safe here. Stay inside and off the phone. If anybody's looking for your car, they'll come to me."

"You're going to kill him, aren't you?"

Bolan didn't have to ask her whom she meant. With all that she'd been through, everything she'd seen and done, the lady still was frightened for her father.

"Probably." He lacked the interest and the energy to lie.

"You can't," she told him stubbornly. "I won't allow it."

"Lisa—"

"*No!*"

He recognized the gun she leveled at his chest. It was the snubby .38 that she had used outside the market, and he hoped his memory was clear.

"It's empty, Lisa," he informed her. "Six rounds to a customer. You spent yours on the Dragons, and I haven't seen you reload."

"Guess again. I'm betting I have one shot left."

She might, at that. The angle kept him from examining the chamber next in line for firing, and for all he knew, death might be waiting for him there. It scarcely mattered, either way. He couldn't let her stop him now.

"I'm going, Lisa. If you want to stop me, you can try."

"You don't believe I'm capable."

"I *know* you're capable. I've seen your work, remember? But I don't believe you're willing. Not like this."

"You're wrong."

"Okay."

Half turning, Bolan reached out for the door, ignition key in hand. He wondered if a roundhouse kick would do it from his present stance.

Lisa closed her eyes and pulled the trigger.

Bolan flinched at the report, immediately realized it hadn't issued from the gun in Lisa's hand. The aural shock wave reached his ears a heartbeat after the projectile struck her rib cage, boring in beneath her breast to mutilate one lung, its twisted, reaming path causing lethal damage to the liver, stomach, spleen. She was dead before her knees folded beneath her and the soldier lunged to catch her as she fell.

The movement saved his life, a second bullet scorching empty air as Bolan spoiled the sniper's aim. Trang's third round struck Lisa, but she never felt it. Riding Bolan to the ground, her corpse protected him until he wriggled clear and rolled behind the nearest tree for cover.

So far Bolan hadn't glimpsed the sniper, but he knew his adversary wasn't working from a stationary roost. Lao Fan had checked the neighborhood too carefully for that. Somehow, in his eagerness to pry the truth from Lisa, Bolan had missed a tail. They had been shadowed from the market—or perhaps the girl was under close surveillance all along. It scarcely mattered either way. Survival was the priority, with sweet revenge an eager candidate for second place.

He palmed the Desert Eagle, was about to make his move when three quick shots slammed into the trunk behind him. They were parting shots, he realized too late, and tires were screeching on the pavement as he scrambled to his feet.

With a hundred yards between them, Bolan didn't waste a round on the sedan, which quickly turned a corner and disappeared. He caught a glimpse of startled neighbors on adjacent doorsteps, peering over hedges as he moved back up the driveway.

Lisa Tien lay facedown in a spreading pool of blood. He turned her over, brushed a strand of hair back from her face and closed the startled eyes. So young, but she had seen it all.

Bolan slid behind the sportster's steering wheel, put the car in motion and the lady out of mind. The dead could take care of themselves. If nothing else, they were immune to pain, betrayal, loss. The dead were lucky, Bolan thought, and stopped that destructive morbid train of thought.

The living still demanded his attention, and before the day was out, a number of them would be joining Lisa Tien. He thought about her faceless killer, knew that he might never have a chance to bag the guy, and realized it didn't matter. Shooters were available on any corner if the price was right. His proper targets were the men behind the buttons, those who laid the plans and called the shots without endangering themselves.

You couldn't kill a snake by hacking at its tail, and Bolan knew he wouldn't break Tien's Asian syndicate by sniping two-bit soldiers on the street. He had to reach the leaders—Tien, Anh Giap, Pham Bach—and finish them before they had an opportunity to wreak more havoc.

Before he faced the serpent, though, he had to find Lao Fan. He would be needing some assistance on the final play, and while it pained him to enlist civilians in his cause, the Executioner had come too far to turn back now for want of help. Lao Fan had volunteered with his companions, and they might as well be treated to another slice of Bolan's everlasting war.

There was, he knew, enough to go around.

CHAPTER TWENTY-TWO

"I couldn't wait around," Lian Trang said earnestly. "The neighbors would have called the police, I swear."

Bach waved an open hand, dismissing the apology. "You're certain that the girl is dead?"

"No question. With a hit like that, they're out before they drop." Trang frowned. "I should have killed the man, as well, but I was concentrating on the girl."

"As you were told to do. The man is not important. He will come to us."

That much, at least, was certain. Bolan wouldn't let it rest, wouldn't retreat and leave the field to his opponents. Lisa had been with him long enough to tell her story, implicating Bach in the deception and attempts on Bolan's life. If she had spilled the truth before she died, the soldier would be seeking explanations, lusting for revenge. And if, against all odds and rules of logic, she had managed to maintain her pose as Bolan's daughter, he would still be coming, seeking vengeance for his murdered child.

No matter how it played, the Executioner would be along—tonight, tomorrow. Soon. He might be on his way already, even as they spoke.

"The troops are ready?"

"Everything has been prepared as you instructed."

"Excellent." He wiped the narrow smile away and donned a solemn face. "I must inform our leader of his loss."

Trang's smile had more in common with a grimace. "Ngo Tien will not be pleased."

"He must accept the obvious. His daughter was in league with Bolan. Why else would she spirit him away from confrontation with the Thunder Dragons?"

"It is obvious to *us*. We are not mourning for a child."

"He is a businessman. The empire must take precedence over personal difficulties."

"As you say."

Bach changed the subject. "I have just received a call from So Hoo Minh. He is distraught about the losses suffered by his men. I have agreed to meet with him this afternoon, but... he may not be rational."

"My men can pick him up."

"That won't be necessary. He is coming here, but I may need your help if he is not amenable to reason."

"You'll be covered."

"Very well. Our business of the moment is concluded, I believe."

Trang closed the office door behind him, leaving Bach alone. The double agent raised his hands, with fingers spread, and studied them, alert for any hint of trembling. There was none, and he relaxed, secure in the knowledge that he still had full control of both himself and his immediate surroundings.

It was inconvenient, certainly, that Bolan had escaped Trang's ambush, but he wouldn't be so fortunate when next they met. Bach recognized the soldier's style, his modus operandi, and he knew the scattered raids were generally followed by a full assault on Bolan's major target. Ngo Tien would fill that role in Orange County, and while Lisa might have mentioned Pham Bach's name to Bolan, Bach had confidence in his survivor's instinct. When the smoke cleared, Bolan would be dead and Bach would walk away. It was his destiny.

But first there was his meeting with the honorable Ngo Tien to be considered. Bach hadn't decided yet upon the proper means of telling Tien about his daughter's death. Should he accept responsibility and strike the pose of one who has the courage to destroy a high-placed traitor? Or should he adopt discretion, blaming the killing on Trang's outraged sense of duty to the master and the empire? Either way, Tien would be forced to see the wisdom in his daughter's liquidation. There could be no question of her innocence. Bach had the Executioner's first visit to her home on tape.

He slipped the VHS cassette into his briefcase, smiling as he closed the latches, set the combination. Shot without the girl's complicity or her consent, it showed a smiling Lisa Tien in Bolan's company, emerging from the sports car given to her by her loving father. Side by side, they climbed the steps to her apartment, disappeared inside. Devoid of sound, the tape might have depicted friends or lovers. It was obvious the man and woman were not enemies.

The tape would break Tien's spirit. Bach was confident of that, and he was counting on the old man's fumbling reaction to facilitate a Bolan strike. They would go down together, Ngo Tien and his relentless Executioner, with Bach remaining to inherit all they left behind. He might receive a medal for eliminating Bolan. At the very least, he would receive an empire.

He pushed the reverie away and rose to leave, the briefcase nearly weightless with its single piece of evidence inside. Bach rode the elevator down, rehearsing his reactions to whatever Tien might say or do. From screaming rage to abject grief, he would be ready with an answer, tailor-made to soothe or fortify.

In Vietnam, before he had accepted the assignment that became his life, one of his comrades had referred to Bach as a chameleon. He took it as a compliment, in reference to his skills as a survivor, the ability to be—or *seem* to be—whatever his immediate superiors demanded at a given moment.

He could be a sycophant, a bully or a stick of furniture, depending on the situation, and he offered no apologies for his ability to come out of the shit heap smelling like a rose.

Bach's flexibility was sometimes misinterpreted by casual acquaintances as lack of dedication to the cause. No one who truly knew him made the same mistake. Beneath the changing face, the ever-shifting attitude, Pham Bach's commitment to the people's revolution had been carved in granite. Those who knew him best might realize the granite was his heart.

The death of Lisa Tien meant no more to him than the passing of an insect. She had been a traitor to her people and her homeland, lusting after the illicit riches her father had amassed by preying on the common man. Her execution was a simple payment on the tab her father had accumulated through the years, blood debts in favor of his race, now ripe and ready for collection.

Starting now.

Pham Bach was the collector, and he loved his work.

FOUR MEN HAD GATHERED in the back room of a small Vietnamese café. There had been seven, once upon a time, but three were dead now, the survivors solemn, grim faced. If they shared a common bond of fear, it didn't show.

"I would not willingly delay another moment," Lao Fan told his three companions. "Ngo Tien and all his kind must be destroyed. They should have been wiped out in Vietnam, but it is our misfortune they survive. We have a chance to solve the problem now."

The Executioner spoke up. "Don't set your hopes too high. The problem never goes away. You've got a chance to shake the players up, revise their game plan, maybe scrub the team. You won't get rid of vice or drugs by killing Ngo Tien . . . but it's a start."

"A start," Lao Fan repeated, putting on a smile that would have terrified his enemies if they had seen it. "Let us begin."

"Before we start, I have to warn you," Bolan said, addressing the survivors Lam Duc and Lin Phuong. "You think the game's been rough so far. The fact is, we've just been warming up. If you're not ready for the main event, it's time to stand aside."

The men exchanged brief glances, Lam Duc answering for both. "Our lives are here now, in America. We have nowhere to run, no place to hide. If we allow these jackals to humiliate us in our shops, our homes, then we are less than men."

"The odds aren't good. I'd say you stand a sixty-forty chance of being killed within the next twelve hours."

"I am not a gambler. Place my enemies before me, and we'll see who is the better man."

"Not better, necessarily. They have more weapons. They for damn sure have more troops."

Lin Phuong was smiling as he spoke. "Is this what the Americans refer to as a pep talk?"

Bolan shook his head and grinned. "All right, you heroes. Have it your way."

They were dragon slayers, laying plans against a crafty reptile that had scorched or swallowed larger enemies on numerous occasions. Two of them had seen no combat prior to their assault upon Tien's warehouse, but determination welded them together as a fighting unit. Bolan had no doubt that Phuong and Duc would do their part when the time arrived. He only hoped the effort wouldn't cost their lives.

"Tien's family is like an octopus," he told them. "We've been hacking at the tentacles and causing some pain, but if you want to kill an octopus, you have to hit him right between the eyes. Cut off the tentacles, and they grow back in time. Destroy the brain, and you've got seafood on the table."

"Ngo Tien must die," Lao Fan declared. "Tonight, if possible."

"He won't be standing on the corner, waiting for a hit," the Executioner reminded them. "We'll have to go and get him. But we need some hard intelligence before we make the move."

"Intelligence?"

"The optimum would be a floor plan of his house, a layout of the grounds, the numbers on his staff and hardforce. As it is, we're mostly flying blind."

"A cousin of my wife was hired by Tien last summer to tend the gardens," Phuong informed the group. "We discussed the property on several occasions."

"Could you make a sketch?"

"Perhaps a rough one."

"Rough's a big improvement over none at all."

As Phuong got busy with a pen and paper, Bolan turned to Lao. "I need to know about Pham Bach," he said.

Lao shrugged. "A toady for Tien and Giap. In military structure, Ngo Tien would be the general, Giap his colonel, Bach perhaps a captain."

"Could be he's about to give himself a battlefield promotion."

Lao was visibly confused as Bolan launched into his story, sparing nothing. By the time he finished it, the Montagnard was frowning deeply, both hands resting on the table with their fingers interwoven.

"You believe Pham Bach may be a Communist?"

"He's obviously got connections somewhere," Bolan answered. "Lisa had the feeling Bach was running down his game without her father's knowledge. From the way it ended, I suspect that she was right. If so, our man may have a ringer on his team."

"An infiltrator?" Lao Fan thought about the prospect for a moment, finally shook his head. "This counts for nothing. Tien must die."

"I'm not excusing anything he's done," the Executioner replied. "He's going down, no matter what it takes, but I don't like surprises, either. If we're dealing with a double agent or a wild card here, I'd like to make provisions."

"You believe Bach may betray his master?"

"I believe he has. So far it's been a covert game, but when we turn the heat up, anything could happen. Lisa told me Bach controls the Thunder Dragons, and he has his own enforcement team."

"He has a group of bodyguards, approximately twenty-five," Lao said. "I do not know about the Dragons. Orders are dispatched, and they are carried out. I have assumed they came from Tien or Giap."

"No contradiction there. If Bach's been paying off the Thunder Dragon leadership, he wouldn't want to tip his hand. It would be SOP until he felt a pressing need, and then..."

"The dragon wakes?"

"Could be."

"Dissension in the ranks can be an excellent diversion."

Bolan smiled. "We'll use it if we can. Meanwhile, I'm thinking of another end run that should keep Tien occupied."

He sketched the plan for Lao and his associates, responding to their questions where he could. The scheme was risky, but it had potential. If he pulled it off, a major block of hostile troops would be effectively removed from play. And if he failed...well, they were still no worse off than they had been at the start.

Lin Phuong was finished with his sketch, and Bolan took the time to study it. Too modest, Phuong had underplayed his memory and skill. The finished product showed Tien's house, a curving driveway, trees and shrubbery, a man-made "lake," the whole estate surrounded by an eight-foot wall. The Asian mobster clearly liked his privacy, and he had paid a fortune to preserve it. The facade of Tien's accessibility to members of the refugee community wouldn't stand up to any kind of major scrutiny.

"I don't suppose your cousin told you anything about security arrangements?"

"There are men with guns, of course. And television cameras. There were no dogs then, but in the meantime, who can say?"

The Executioner wasn't concerned with dogs. He *was* concerned with guns, the troops that Tien would have collected while he waited for the final stroke to fall. An army might be waiting for them when they made their move, and they were only four.

He shrugged off the momentary pessimism. The odds meant nothing in themselves; the progress of his war had proved that point a hundred times. Survival on the killing field derived from skill and strategy, audacity and nerve, as much as from the simple numbers. Those who said God threw his weight behind the big battalions put their faith in raw statistics, overlooking human qualities like courage and intelligence. The numbers mattered, certainly, but they would never tell the whole story.

"All right," the soldier said, "here's what we do."

FOR THE FIRST TIME in his life, So Hoo Minh felt embarrassed as he stood before the Thunder Dragons, studying their faces as they waited for his words. On any normal day, the warlord would have seen respect—perhaps a trace of awe—upon the younger faces, simple deference on those that were his age or older. Now, this afternoon, he read suspicion in their eyes, some disappointment, here and there a vague suggestion of contempt.

He hadn't failed them—not precisely—but his leadership was balanced on a razor's edge, and it could still go either way. Minh knew that he must win them back at once, or lose it all. The promises Pham Bach had made were empty, useless if the Dragons turned against him now. If things went sour, he might not leave the room alive.

"You all know what went down this afternoon," he said, and watched the faces harden as he spoke. "Nine soldiers wasted at the Paradise, another four outside the market. Two men wounded. I'm not going to shit you, brothers— this has been the worst day of my life. I look at you and know exactly what you're thinking. Hell, if I was in your place, I'd feel the same. I wish it had been me instead of all those brothers wasted."

A ripple in the audience, and Minh immediately wondered if he might have gone too far. Among the forty-odd assembled members of his gang, there must be thirty guns, at least. What could he do if one of them decided to grant his wish?

"I wish it had been me," he repeated, his stomach knotting, muscles clenched against the impact of imaginary bullets, "but I can't bring any of those brothers back to life. We followed orders, did our job, and we got fucked. That's it."

He paused to scan the faces once more. So many eyes. He could have cut the tension in the clubhouse with a knife.

"I can tell you one thing, brothers—just because that's it, doesn't mean it's *over*. Someone has to pay for what went down this afternoon. They have to pay big-time, with everything they've got. But I'm not going to bother you with that."

Minh played his ace.

"I'd say the Thunder Dragons need another warlord. Someone who can pull the club together, make you all the winners you deserve to be. I'm stepping down and taking care of this unfinished business on my own."

The ripples spread, becoming audible.

"Hey, wait a second!"

"What'd he say?"

"You can't step down!"

"I'm sorry, brothers, but my mind's made up. I blew it, and it's up to me to put things right in any way I can. I've got a meeting set with Bach, and we'll be talking over reparations for our losses. Cash won't bring your brothers back, I know, but it's a start. Whatever Bach kicks in, the Dragons keep."

"We want the shooters," someone shouted from the back rows. "Give us names."

"I don't have names," he answered. "If I'm lucky, in a few days I can give you bodies. It'll be a parting gift."

"Where are you going, man?"

"You can't run out on us like this!"

"I let you down," Minh told them, hoping that he hadn't overdone the fake emotion in his voice. He didn't have to feign the apprehension. "You need someone else to turn this club around."

"We've got a warlord, man! Hang tough and do your job!"

He hesitated, every inch the actor. Christ, if he could pull this off they ought to let him have a special Oscar. "I don't know. How many of you feel that way?"

Most of them raised their hands, and some were on their feet, demanding that So Minh remain in office, taking care of business, punishing the bastards who had shamed the Thunder Dragons on their own damned turf. He marked the few who sat with both hands in their laps and filed their names for future reference, but at the moment he was riding high, the victor in a contest where he would have been well satisfied to score a draw.

He grinned and spread his hands, achieving an approximation of humility. "What can I say? You guys insist, I've got no choice. I'll stay and help you track the bastards down.''

Applause. It was the first time in his life that anyone had actually clapped for any word or action of So Minh's. He was impressed, as much with his own performance as with the gullibility of his audience. The idiots had swallowed every word and they had come back clamoring for more. Minh thought he could have sold them acreage on Venus, and they would have jostled one another to be first in line for corner lots.

He moved among them like a politician, shaking hands and thanking them for their support, his mind already miles away. He had a meeting with Pham Bach to think about, the reparations he was now obliged to seek for losses suffered by his men. How many of his vocal backers would desert him in an instant if he came back empty-handed?

Most of them.

The odds against Pham Bach delivering on any reparations were extreme, and Minh knew he would have to find another scam before the Thunder Dragons reconvened to hear the verdict. Something would be necessary to divert their anger, channel it against a common enemy.

But who?

He thought about it, pumping hands meanwhile, and no one seemed to notice when the warlord's smile grew broader, brighter. It was really simple, when you thought about it. Bach would pay the reparations Minh demanded or he would become the enemy. The mood his troops were in, it would be easy to convince them that the older man had set them up for reasons of his own. Perhaps Bach was afraid of Minh, his troops, convinced that they had grown too powerful too quickly. Maybe he was jealous, greedy for the share of tribute Ngo Tien allowed the gang to keep from weekly payoffs. Maybe Bach thought he could do without the Dragons, carry on the whole damned show himself.

It made no sense, but So Minh knew his troops weren't in any mood for logical debate. He would return with cash in hand, or he would call for war against Pham Bach. It was the only way for Minh to save himself.

And in the process he might just come out a winner.

GIROLAMO CARLOTTI WAS worried. The first Bolan strike had been small by the soldier's own standards, and so far there had been no follow-up. That was the troublesome part. When that bastard in black had a target picked out, there was no time to breathe; it was one hit right after another until his mark had nothing left and the soldier came in for the slaughter like some kind of bullfighter planting his sword.

And no way in the world did it figure for Bolan to knock off a couple of runners, then fade like a ghost. It was wrong, and the wrongness had the Don pacing his study, one eye on the telephone, waiting for news off the streets.

There was plenty of word, but it all dealt with Tien and his zipperheads getting their asses kicked up to their ears. Since the first crack of dawn the reports had been coming in steadily, tolling a death knell for Carlotti's competitors down in Orange County. A whorehouse, a chicken ranch, gambling, narcotics, the skin flicks. Someone was hammering Tien like a twopenny nail, and Carlotti would have been content to sit back and enjoy the show... except for Bolan.

He was out there, somewhere—watching, waiting. But for *what*? Carlotti's operations were exposed in several areas, his books and escort services especially vulnerable to attack, and yet his only casualties had been a pair of piss-ant numbers runners. It was spooky, and the capo didn't like it one damned bit.

Ironically he would have felt more confident if Bolan had been tearing up the town, attacking every business of Carlotti's he could find. It would have been disastrous, but it at least would be normal. Pacing back and forth beside the silent telephone and waiting for the Executioner to make another move was something else entirely.

As if in answer to his thoughts, the phone rang shrilly, making Don Carlotti jump. He got it on the second ring and growled into the mouthpiece.

"Yeah?"

"I'm calling for Carlotti."

The mafioso recognized the voice, although he'd heard it only once before. "You've got him."

"You've been following the morning news?" Omega asked.

"I keep in touch."

"If I were you, I wouldn't swallow everything that turned up on my plate."

Carlotti frowned. "You got a point to make?"

"Word is, your competition isn't suffering as bad as the reports make out."

"How's that?"

"Spring cleaning," the black ace replied. "They're cutting out deadwood and closing ranks. Could be they're spotting you to take the fall."

"Like hell. I haven't raised a hand against those bastards yet."

"Bad luck. It's simple, planting evidence to fit your suspect. You know all about that, don't you, Giro?"

He ignored the shooter's mocking tone. "I thought we had a fucking truce."

"There's been a breakdown. From the smell, I'd say we've got a rat on the commission, playing both ends off against the middle."

"Jesus Christ! You mean to say this whole time I've been sitting on my hands because some goddamn turncoat got a resolution passed?"

"We're checking into it. Right now, I'm authorized to tell you that the truce is off. Each Family is actively encouraged to defend itself as necessary."

Carlotti felt the first rush of adrenaline. "All right! Now you're talking. Let me have an hour, and I'll make those bastards wish they were back in Saigon sucking rice."

"About this Bolan thing..."

"Go on."

"I understand you took a minor hit."

"Two buttons. Nothing heavy yet."

"My information is, he's cut a deal with the Vietnamese."

"That bastard!"

"A word to the wise. Keep your eyes peeled and bag him if possible. You know the council has cash on his head. I'm inclined to believe they have other rewards lined up, too."

"You don't mean—"

"With a vacancy pending, why not? Who could fill the spot better than someone who saw through a traitor and brought down this wild card to boot?"

"Well, if you put it like that..."

"That's the way I would put it."

"You know, I been thinking I ought to branch out."

"Now's the time. All it takes is one head in the bag."

"I heard that. Well, hey, thanks for the tip. If you ever need anything..."

"I've got your number."

"Right."

The connection was broken, and Don Carlotti was briefly concerned by the thought of Omega at large, hanging on to his marker and biding his time on the payback. Of course, if Carlotti was on the commission...

If Bolan was in league with Ngo Tien, the morning's strange activities might just make sense. Suppose the Asian had it in his mind to thin the ranks but he couldn't afford to handle it himself. Too messy, when you thought about it, and the troops get hinky in a purge. Mack Bolan was the perfect tool, and never mind how Tien had made connections with the Executioner. Some bullshit from the war, for all Carlotti knew or cared.

It was a natural. The soldier whacked Tien's selected sacrificial lambs, eliminating deadwood up and down the line, providing evidence that seemed to point at Don Carlotti as the hitter. In the process, maybe Bolan couldn't resist a couple potshots at Carlotti, and he dropped a marksman's medal off to show he was still around and thinking of the Family. Carlotti thereby was presented with a choice: go hunting for Bolan, leaving his flanks exposed to Tien's assault, or take the war to his competitors, and run the risk of finding Bolan on their team, geared up for doomsday.

With the cards on the table, Carlotti realized he had no choice at all. It would be suicide to sit and wait while Tien gobbled up the territory he had worked and fought for through the years. A swift offensive was the surest guarantee that he would be around tomorrow, and he might get lucky in the process. If he played his cards right, he might bag that head Omega had referred to, grab himself the big brass ring and ride it to a seat on La Commissióne.

Ironically he didn't feel intimidated by the thought of Bolan teaming up with Tien and company. The soldier's strength had always been his solitude, the way he stood outside the system, raining fire on anyone who crossed his path. United with the zipperheads, he would be one more monkey in the middle of a Chinese fire drill, scrambling around with no idea of who was on his side and who was out to singe his ass.

The soldier's "brainstorm" just might get him killed, and Don Carlotti spent a moment smiling over that. It was poetic justice, like the climax of a classic opera.

Carlotti took a seat and reached out for the telephone. He couldn't wait to hear the fat lady sing.

CHAPTER TWENTY-THREE

Ngo Tien's home had been transformed into an armed fortress. Bach was ushered through the gates by cold-eyed troops equipped with shotguns and semiautomatic rifles.

Such a show of force was daunting, but Pham Bach refused to be afraid. His mission carried elements of danger, to be sure. Traditionally bad news often doomed the messenger, but Tien was civilized and he would understand despite his loss, his grief.

If Bach was wrong on that score, he was dead.

His driver found a space between two carbon-copy Continentals, got out to open Pham Bach's door. A member of the palace guard was standing by to usher Bach inside, his deference concealing stolid singleness of purpose. This man, like the others, was employed to plant himself between the ruler of the syndicate and any enemies. If he was ordered to destroy Pham Bach, the mask of courtesy would drop to reveal a hardened killer underneath.

So many guns, and Bach had come unarmed. His driver had a pistol underneath his coat, a submachine gun tucked beneath his seat, but he'd be outside when Bach sat down with Tien to spin his tale of Lisa's death. If things went badly, Bach would be long dead before the driver met his own fate in the yard.

Tien's home had been described as elegant and plush in various society reports. Palatial might be closer to the mark, but Pham Bach was familiar with the trappings and he didn't crave them for himself. If he was placed in Tien's position—*when* he took control of the established syndicate—he would assume the mantle of authority and wealth as one more aspect of the role he played in service to the people's revolution. He would live the life of royalty, but he wouldn't enjoy it.

Tien's study was located on the second floor, a pleasant room with French doors, overlooking gardens tended by a staff of Asian refugees, patrolled now by the troops whose job it was to keep Tien safe. Bach's escort knocked and waited for the soft command to enter, standing back to let Bach pass before he shut the door and took his post outside.

Bach waited on the threshold while Tien studied something in the yard below, eventually drifting back to take a seat behind his desk. He waved Bach to the sofa, leaning forward with his elbows on the desk top. Pham Bach noticed that the self-styled emperor had aged since last they met, hard years accumulating in his face, the restless movements of his hands.

"You have some information to report?"

"I come with grievous news," Bach said, trying to inject sadness in his attitude and tone. "I must apologize for darkening your day with such—"

Tien waved the rote formalities away. "The news, perhaps, *before* apologies?"

Bach cleared his throat, allowing nervousness to help him mimic grief. "Your daughter, Lisa, has been . . . killed."

The warlord slumped back in his chair, the color draining from his face. For just an instant, Bach thought Tien might have a heart attack, but he watched the older man recover slowly, fighting for control before he spoke.

"Killed how?"

"I understand that she was shot."

"By whom? Carlotti's people?"

"No, sir." It was now or never. "She was sighted by a member of my staff, Lian Trang, in the company of an

Anglo man Trang thought he recognized. Trang followed them—"

"This Lian Trang killed my daughter?"

"He followed them to a house where Lisa and the Anglo were apparently expected. As they stood outside, Trang recognized the white man as Mack Bolan. When he opened fire, obeying standing orders—"

"Bolan? Lisa with Mack Bolan?"

"Regrettably, yes, sir."

"She must have been abducted as a weapon to be used against me. Bring Lian Trang—"

"They rode in her car, sir, with Lisa at the wheel."

"A hostage, then. He forced her to cooperate at gunpoint."

"Trang observed no weapons. He was acting under orders."

"Who issued orders to assassinate my daughter?"

"*You* gave an order to eliminate the Executioner at any cost."

"And is he dead?"

Bach spread his hands, humility personified. "Unfortunately, no. Trang's first shot struck..." He hesitated, eyes downcast. "The enemy was swift, and Trang could not remain with witnesses on hand."

"A pity that my daughter was not *swift*." Tien's voice reminded Pham Bach of a deathbed rattle. He was suitably encouraged, and emboldened to proceed.

"In fairness to Lian Trang, I must point out that Lisa risked her own life, choosing one of your prime enemies as a companion."

"She did *not* choose Bolan. I will not believe—"

"The evidence—"

"Will be reviewed before I pass on Lian Trang's fate," the aging emperor decreed. "Until that time, he will be held secure against escape or any 'accidents.' "

Bach spun the combination tumblers on his briefcase, sprang the latches to extract the videocassette. "Before you punish Trang for following his orders, there is something you must see."

"Not now."

"It cannot be postponed."

"I said..." Tien faltered, finding something in Bach's face, his posture, that conveyed a note of urgency. He aimed an index finger toward the console television with its built-in VCR which occupied one corner of the study. "Show your *evidence*."

Bach set the channel, loaded the cassette and stood aside, his eyes on Tien. Bach had already seen the tape and he could easily have narrated the scene from memory. A long shot of the sports car, Lisa smiling at the wheel with Bolan riding shotgun, solemn, cautious. From the car, they moved along the sidewalk, climbing narrow stairs to her apartment on the second floor. The soldier hung back slightly, letting Lisa go ahead because she had the key. Another moment, and they disappeared inside.

Rewinding Bach ran through the tape again, then killed it as the door swung shut a second time. Ejecting the cassette, he left it on Tien's desk, returning to the couch.

"When was this made?"

"Two days ago," Bach said. "The afternoon before our Hong Kong shipment was destroyed in Long Beach."

"You believe my daughter was responsible?" It was a simple question now. There was no challenge in the warlord's voice.

Bach shrugged. "She knew Lee Kuan, the soldier who was killed mere hours after that was filmed. Kuan knew about the shipment, time, location."

"You have more to tell me."

"Sadly, yes. Last evening I sent men to bring your daughter home as a security precaution. I believed that she could answer certain questions and erase some doubts."

"What happened?"

"Both my men were killed, found shot to death in her apartment. She had fled without a trace . . . until this afternoon."

"And Bolan?"

"The search continues. I have reason to believe he may be coming here tonight, in an attempt upon your life."

"He will be welcome."

Bach knew it was time to disengage. "Once more, I hope you will accept my most sincere regrets."

"Of course."

He hesitated at the door. "About Lian Trang . . ."

The warlord waved his hand, a gesture of dismissal. "He will not be punished. This shame I must bear alone."

The houseman walked Bach through the building, back to his waiting car. Bach's driver had an edgy look about him, visibly relaxing when his master reappeared. When both of them were safe inside the car and rolling, Bach leaned forward, placing one hand on the driver's shoulder.

"Home," he said. "I am expecting company."

ALONE INSIDE HIS STUDY, Ngo Tien examined the destruction of his family, the ruin of his life. If trusted aides and cameras could be believed, his daughter had betrayed him, joining forces with a mortal enemy to bring down everything that Tien had worked for since he fled from Vietnam. Her death was but the least part of his pain.

He didn't speculate on Lisa's motives. There had always been a sort of distance between them since her mother's death. When Lisa was a child, she had been fiercely independent and he had admired her strength, but she had always kept her father at arm's length. In later years, when she evinced a fascination with the family business, it had been his turn to put her off, insisting that she scuttle any plans of working by his side, pursue her education and become a true child of America.

Tradition had been part of Tien's reaction to the notion of a daughter in the syndicate. He realized that in America, the female of the species was permitted—even actively encouraged—to succeed, excel in business, industry, a range of fields historically monopolized by men. At heart he had no argument with women's right to earn a living or become tycoons, but circumstance had placed him in a tenuous position. In the world of crime he was compelled to deal with old-world minds and mores, with men whose visions of the family and woman's place were carved in granite. Ngo Tien would have become a laughingstock if Lisa had been granted entry to the male preserve of gangland. Weakened in the eyes of his potential enemies, he would have been confronted with an endless string of challengers for dominance within the empire he had built from nothing.

There were other fears, as well. Historically the Asian crime lords—and, to some extent, their counterparts in the United States—were men of twisted chivalry. They might be pimps, pornographers, purveyors of narcotics that enslaved a whole new generation, but they still held family in high esteem. Unwritten codes of honor theoretically exempted wives and children from attack, reprisal, any of the bloody work that came along with profits in the world of syndicated crime. There were exceptions, vicious deviations from the norm, but Ngo Tien had always felt that Lisa would be safe while she maintained a distance from the family trade.

Might things have turned out differently if he had welcomed her into the syndicate with open arms? Tien placed no faith in fortune-tellers or in mystics, and he wasted no time now in second-guessing fate. He couldn't take back words and actions, any more than he could alter Lisa's choice and bring her back to life.

He was too late, perhaps, for all concerned.

But there was still an empire to be governed, enemies to be repelled before they ruined everything. If Tien had no heir, he still had a responsibility to his associates and his employees, men who looked to him for guidance and protection, shelter from the storm.

He wondered, briefly, how his daughter had encountered Bolan in the first place. On the face of it, the whole thing seemed preposterous, but he couldn't deny the photographic evidence Bach had laid before his eyes. And yet the odds...

If she was searching for revenge, it would be easier to think of Lisa working for the FBI or DEA. At least those agencies had offices and agents that were physically accessible. A college student in Orange County was more likely to be struck by lightning than to meet Mack Bolan on the street, and Tien was willing to dismiss the possibility of mere coincidence. For Lisa to associate herself with Bolan, there would have to be some conscious effort, some elaborate plan.

He balked at the idea of Lisa making the initial move. She had no means of recognizing Bolan, tracing the nomadic soldier's whereabouts or making contact with him if he could be found. It was insane to think a student could succeed in reaching Bolan where the best minds of a dozen syndicates had failed for years on end.

No, Bolan would have made the overture, undoubtedly selecting Lisa on the basis of her family ties, preferring an accomplice who had access to the throne. He might have played upon her vanity or the resentment she felt for her father. Perhaps he had deceived her somehow into thinking that her actions would be beneficial to the family.

No matter.

Lisa had betrayed him, whether consciously or otherwise, and that betrayal had resulted in her death. Tien wouldn't argue with the punishment decreed by fate. His mission now was to preserve what still remained and guarantee stability for those who followed after.

For the first time in his life, Tien felt the weight of years upon his shoulders, knew that he was growing old. The fact of aging was no stranger to him, certainly, but he had always met the challenge with vitality, a sense of inner strength that made a mockery of passing time. Today he felt as if he might have aged a decade in the past two hours.

Shaking off his torpor, Ngo Tien stood and moved to stand before the windows, studying the grounds outside, his sentries on their rounds. He was protected here, but safety didn't hold the same priority it might have on another day, before his world began to crumble.

He would face the Executioner, exerting every ounce of energy he still retained to win a victory against his mortal foe. If he should fall in combat, it would be no tragedy as long as Bolan was destroyed in time, the empire preserved.

Tien's smile, reflected in the glass, was like the grimace of a skull.

IT HAD TAKEN an hour to organize the troops for Don Carlotti's personal inspection, calling in reserves, but everything was ready now. A squad of thirty-seven men had been assembled on the lawn in front of the house, each soldier weighted down with hardware, extra ammunition, some of them made bulky by the Kevlar vests they wore beneath their suits.

With Don Carlotti and his housemen it would be an even forty. Not the total of his troops, by any means, but it should be enough to deal with Ngo Tien and his army of zipperheads. Carlotti scanned the ranks with confidence, secure in the belief that forty men like these were worth two hundred sawed-off Asians any day. If he couldn't sweep Tien and Giap aside with what he had, he might as well give it up.

Studying his troops, Carlotti wondered if Omega would approve of his approach. Defend yourself by any means available, the guy had said, and that was what the Don meant to do. The chips could fall anyway they liked. If the commissioners couldn't restrain their own from making secret bargains with the zipperheads, they were in no position to contest Carlotti's handling of local problems. He would tell them that, and more, when he had Bolan's head and Tien's on ice in matching burlap sacks.

Those pompous bastards back east had been dictating policy so long that some of them believed they were infallible, above the laws that governed brotherhood affairs. They had a lesson coming, all about reality and changing times, and Don Carlotti thought he just might be the man to put that lesson over. It was time Chicago and New York remembered that there was a big, bad world beyond the Mississippi, and the universe did not revolve around Manhattan or the Loop.

The Executioner was going to help him make that point. The bastard didn't know it yet, but he was Don Carlotti's hole card.

"Everybody double-check your pieces," he commanded, setting an example as he drew the stainless-steel .45 and snapped its slide back, chambering a round. The weapon was an old friend, comfortable in his hand, and Carlotti twirled it on his index finger before tucking it away.

"Five men per car," he ordered. "One man on the radio and keep those channels open. I don't want a single fuck-up, understand? We're bound to be outnumbered, but I figure one American is worth at least five zipperheads. We're kicking ass and taking names tonight. No prisoners. Is everybody clear on that?"

Some of his soldiers nudged each other, grinning, while a few seemed more concerned, but no one tried to weasel out of the assignment. They were hardmen, handpicked for a mission that would place the Family back on top where it belonged, and if they couldn't do the job, Don Girolamo was prepared to die in the attempt.

"I gotta tell you something else before we go." He had their full attention now. "Word is, our little yellow friends have taken on a wild card by the name of Bolan. He's the shit who tagged our guys this morning, and we can expect to see him when we make our hit tonight."

"*Mack* Bolan?" someone piped up from the ranks.

"You got it. Most of you should remember what he did to Bobby Benedetto, and I know damn well you've heard a hundred different stories all about how bad he is."

A few of them were muttering among themselves, and Carlotti nipped it in the bud.

"I'm not about to lie to you boys, okay? This bastard has some moves, he's had a lot of luck, but he's no superman. He bleeds like anybody else, and if you whack him, he stays whacked. Which brings me up to the reward . . ."

Expectant silence, thirty-seven hard-case gunners hanging on his every word, a smell of money in the air.

"I want this bastard's head. It means a lot to me, okay? For old times' sake, whatever. I'm prepared to put my money where my mouth is, and I'll tell you what I'll do. The man who brings me Bolan's head tonight is looking at a bonus of a hundred grand, together with a month's vacation, all expenses paid."

Applause, this time, and Don Carlotti spent a moment basking in the adulation of his men. Behind him he could feel his housemen getting antsy, and he finally raised his hands for silence.

"Time to roll," he ordered. "We'll be checking radios when everybody's squared away. You wheelmen take it nice and easy, in formation, till I give the word. We don't need any traffic hassles with the boys in blue.''

Carlotti slid into the back seat of his armored Lincoln, flanked by his selected housemen, with a soldier riding shotgun up in front. All radios were functional, and the Don sent one car ahead, his own falling in as the second in line, six other crew wagons forming a caravan behind them. An observer might mistake them for a funeral procession, and Carlotti smiled at the comparison.

It *was* a funeral, in fact—for Ngo Tien, Anh Giap. Carlotti counted on some casualties among his troops as well, but any victory worth claiming always had a price attached.

With any luck at all the funeral might include Mack Bolan, thereby settling an ancient score and simultaneously setting up Girolamo for bigger, better things.

Carlotti had already conquered Southern California. He was ready to expand.

So Minh was reaching for the bell when Bach's front door swung open to reveal Lian Trang. The warlord of the Thunder Dragons offered up a halting smile, which was returned with interest as Trang stepped back to let him enter.

"I'm early," Minh explained apologetically.

"No problem, he's expecting you. You packing?"

So Minh spread his jacket open, offered no resistance as Lian Trang removed the Browning automatic from his shoulder holster. It was a formality, and he was praying Trang didn't decide to pat him down, discovering the ankle holster that he wore as backup—just in case.

"That's it?"

"I didn't think I'd need a lot of hardware," Minh replied.

"No reason why you should. We're all friends here."

He followed Trang along the familiar corridor to Bach's study. The guards outside Bach's door were not familiar, but he made allowances for the events that had been rattling the family the past few days. Bach had good reason for imposing strict security, if Minh's experience that afternoon was any guide.

Trang didn't follow Minh into the study. Bach was waiting, seated at his desk, his face impassive as he waved Minh toward an empty chair. "I understand you had some difficulties with your work today," he said, before the gang lord had a chance to speak.

"We did our job, all right. It cost me fourteen men, but we hit every target on your list." He hesitated, waiting for some modest word of praise, his anger mounting in the face of silence until he couldn't contain himself. "You should have told me there were shooters on our case."

"I did not know myself."

It was a lie, of course, but Minh couldn't prove otherwise. Instead he tried a different tack. "The Dragons think you set them up. They were about to fry *my* ass, until I offered to resign."

"So, you are unemployed?"

"Hell no, I shined them on. Before I finished, they were begging me to stay." His smile was nervous and impossible to hold. "They're pissed, though, I can tell you that. They're talking reparations."

"Ah." Bach's frown was an approximation of concern, but Minh wasn't deceived. "And the amount?"

"Ten thou per man."

"Ridiculous."

Minh shrugged, all weary resignation. "Fine. But I should tell you they're prepared to cut you off. No more collections, no more muscle, no more legwork. Zip."

"A threat?"

"A promise."

"There are other groups available."

"Of course. But they are small, disorganized. Without the Thunder Dragons, you will face a major loss of revenue for months to come."

Bach's voice was tensile steel. "I raised the Thunder Dragons from a troop of ragged children, and I can destroy them if I choose."

"You might not find it easy."

"You forget yourself."

Minh stiffened, knew that he was walking on a razor's edge without a safety net. The wrong word now could finish everything, and he couldn't depend on the snubby .38 to see him free and clear. It was a last-ditch measure, nothing more. He had to play his hand with skill, finesse.

"I have forgotten nothing. Promises were made..."

"I promised nothing to the Thunder Dragons."

"Promises were made to *me*."

Bach frowned. "Do you believe that your performance merits a promotion? Fourteen of your people dead, so much adverse publicity. I fear we may have overestimated your potential."

Minh could feel his stomach twisting. The bastard meant to cheat him, sell him out.

"You promised—"

"To consider your achievements," Bach responded, interrupting him before Minh had an opportunity to finish. "I have done so. The results are not impressive."

"But—"

"I would suggest that you attempt to reason with your colleagues. Any thought of blackmail would be most unwise."

"I won't be cheated!"

"Oh?" It was the first time Bach had smiled since Minh's arrival. "Won't you? And precisely what do you intend to do about it?"

"Kill you, if I have to."

Fumbling at his cuff, he palmed the .38 and aimed it at Bach's face across the broad expanse of desk. Minh's hand was trembling, and he braced it with the other, rising to his feet and stepping closer to his target.

Bach was rigid in his high-backed chair, both hands beneath his desk. A weapon? Minh couldn't take any chances.

"Let me see your hands!" he snapped, relieved to find them empty as the older man complied. "All right, we're going to talk money now. Forget about the damned promotion. I want cash."

"Of course." Bach's tone was all sweet reason. "Anything you say."

"I'll use this if I have to."

"I believe you, Minh. It seems that I will have to speak with Trang about security precautions in the future."

"If you *have* a future."

"Don't be hasty. We have cash on hand, and I assume you will require safe passage?"

It had not occurred to Minh, but now he realized that he was trapped. If he was forced to shoot Pham Bach, there would be nothing to prevent the guards from killing him on sight.

"Safe passage, yes."

"A wise decision. Now about that money—"

Minh was giddy, flying on adrenaline and trying desperately to think three moves beyond his present impasse. So it was, when Trang slipped in behind him, that he missed the whisper of the study door on deep-pile carpeting.

His warning, when it came, was the metallic sound of Lian Trang's pistol being cocked. Minh knew that he was dead, surrendering to instinct as he turned to face his adversary, instantly regretting that he hadn't taken time to kill Pham Bach.

Trang shot him twice, the bullets flattening on impact, pitching So Minh backward with the brute force of a mule's kick to the chest. He lost his .38 somewhere along the way and came to rest against Bach's desk, blood spilling wet and warm into his lap. Above him, Lian Trang was a giant, leaning closer for the kill.

"You blew it, man," Trang said. "I told you we were all friends here."

Minh tried to answer, but blew a crimson bubble from his lips instead.

And died.

CHAPTER TWENTY-FOUR

The hardsite was a compound in the wilds of Santiago Canyon, twelve miles from the heart of downtown Santa Ana as the crow flies. Triple that by car, for starters, and allowing for the urban crawl of traffic, Bolan gave himself two hours to complete the easy drive, secure his vehicle and make his final recon of the target. Lao Fan and his people had their missions memorized, and they were on their own.

Once inside the compound it was going to be every soldier for himself, and anyone who couldn't pull his weight was flirting with disaster.

Bolan drove the last four miles of winding canyon road without his headlights, creeping on the curves and hoping that he wouldn't meet some cocky, coked-up swinger flying in the fast lane. Head-on, with a wall of rock on one side and a steep drop on the other, limited the options. You could die, or you could die.

It might still come to that this evening, but the soldier didn't plan to waste his life on any close encounters of the highway kind. His prey was waiting for him, others on the way, and he didn't intend to disappoint them.

Ngo Tien's evacuation of his house in town had been observed by one of Lao Fan's spotters, relayed via telephone. The news was good *and* bad. The target would be harder to approach, more difficult to crack, but they would be removed from innocent civilians, neighbors who might wander inadvertently into the cross fire. As a trade-off, Bolan thought it wasn't bad.

He found a narrow access road and stashed the rental, suiting up in darkness, covering the final quarter mile on foot. He wore his nightsuit, the Beretta and the Desert Eagle snug in place, an Uzi submachine gun slung across one shoulder. Frag and phosphorous grenades, two satchel charges and an adequate supply of extra magazines for all three guns completed the ensemble. Bolan's combat payload topped forty pounds in weight, but despite the burden and the rugged uphill grade, he held a decent pace.

It would be downhill coming back. If he survived.

The compound's eight-foot wall was topped with razor wire. Twenty yards downrange, an ancient oak stood close beside the wall, thick branches reaching out and teasing at restricted airspace, offering the Executioner both a lookout post and means of entry.

He scaled the trunk, bark rough against his palms, and found himself a vantage point from which to scan the killing ground. Tien's manor was ablaze with floodlights, basking in the warmth of artificial noon. The grounds, by contrast, had been left in darkness, shadows pooling underneath the trees. The roving sentries showed a light from time to time, but for the most part they patrolled by instinct, long familiar with the grounds. He saw no evidence of dogs.

A quick check on the time. Still thirty minutes, so he settled down to wait. Lao and the others might be ready, though he hadn't seen them on the road, but Bolan was not taking any chances. Zero hour was approaching, and he felt no urge to rush the game.

There would be time enough for dying when the troops were in place.

While Bolan waited, he began to memorize the movements of the sentries, charting patterns, seeing them repeated at predictable—if not precisely regular—intervals.

Compact binoculars let him scan the house in more detail, identifying gunners on the porch, the balcony, the roof.

A formidable target, all in all, with something like a hundred yards of hostile ground to cross before he reached the house and its defenders. Bolan tried to count the roving sentries, got to twenty-five before he gave it up as hopeless, realizing he had tagged the same guy twice. When it was time, he would rely on speed, audacity and steel to see him through the pickets, past the housemen, on to Tien, Pham Bach, the rest. If any of the lesser targets turned up missing, he could still bat cleanup in the morning.

Bolan settled back and closed his eyes. The face of Lisa Tien appeared, first smiling, then relaxed in death. He still couldn't be certain that her final words, the charges leveled at Pham Bach alone, were truthful, but the lady was beyond his reach. Whatever debts she might have owed the universe were canceled, paid in full.

Some others still had running tabs, and Bolan was prepared to take whatever payment he could get tonight. The repo man was coming for their wasted souls.

But there was time to kill before collection could begin in earnest. Squatting in the ancient tree, his shoulders pressed against rough bark, the Executioner allowed himself to think of childhood, other trees and sunshine, skies the color of a promise waiting to be realized. A meadow, children, and from Bolan's nest he recognized them all. The summer days stretched out forever, beckoning him home.

His eyes snapped open, banishing the vision in an instant. Darkness, the reality of his existence, pressed around him, challenged by the blaze of light around the manor house a hundred yards away. When Bolan checked his watch again, he found that it was time. Lao Fan and his associates would be in place.

Muscles stiffened by his crouch protested when the soldier moved. He crept along the branch, a high-wire artist playing tag with ruination, knowing that a premature descent might warn the sentries, ruin everything. He thought about the limb, so sturdy at its base, and wondered if the rot or insects had set in a little farther out. Would the next step be his last?

It held and Bolan slithered down, suspended by his fingertips until he had his final bearings, knew that he was ready. Letting go, he dropped into the maw of darkness.

THE VIETNAMESE HAD TRIED to fox Carlotti with their footwork, but they were not swift enough by half. A spotter had reported the evacuation of Tien's Anaheim estate, and it had been a simple matter to divert Carlotti's caravan to Santiago Canyon. Rolling through the darkness with his troops around him, the Don felt like General Patton or Napoléon, advancing on his enemies.

Tonight he would make history and teach a lesson to the other sorry bastards who were nibbling around the fringes of his empire. The Colombians and Haitians, all of them, could feast their eyes on Ngo Tien's example, learning fear and new respect for the established power of Carlotti's Family. Next time they entertained ideas of taking over the brotherhood's territory, they might decide to pass...or they might die.

For years the status quo had called for peace and quiet, live and let live, while the blacks and Hispanics, Asians, every other color of the human rainbow dug their trenches, strengthening their foothold, branching out to dip their greasy fingers in Carlotti's pie. And it was time for some of them to get their hands whacked off.

The shift of targets had unnerved Carlotti for a moment, made him wonder if his caravan might not be rolling toward an ambush, but he swiftly put his mind at ease. The enemy was running, looking for a hole to hide in, and Don Girolamo knew enough of war to realize that when you had your opposition on the ropes, you had to follow up on the advantage. Keep the bastards reeling, finish them while they were down, and you could turn your back when it was done, secure that no survivors would come creeping up behind you.

The winding canyon road was making Carlotti sleepy. It was crazy; here he was about to crash in on the hottest party since DiGeorge got toasted, and it was all he could do to keep his eyelids open. He shook himself and had his housemen crack their windows, letting in fresh air. It perked him up, that old familiar smell of smog and in another moment Girolamo had his concentration back.

It was a good sign, he supposed, relaxing on the eve of battle. Was he really that damned confident of victory, or was he getting old?

Whatever, he was young enough and hard enough to teach some zipperheads a lesson they would not forget. Intruding on Carlotti's turf had been a serious mistake. The tide was turning now, and status quo would mean squat when he was finished with bastards who had tried to take the bread out of his mouth.

A few of them might get away, but that was fair enough. He needed some survivors anyway to spread the word. Carlotti's modesty forbade him playing up his strength too much, blowing his own horn, but with a few survivors on the street, the word would get around. Among the zipperheads at first, but it would spread like wildfire, and his other enemies would have a chance to reconsider any hostile moves they might have in the works.

It was a simple rule of advertising. Shoddy products needed glitz and fancy ad campaigns to put them over with the target public. Goods of quality were heralded by word of mouth. Carlotti's lesson to his enemies would rattle some cages, start some ripples in the pond, and word would spread to every nook and cranny of the underworld. By noon tomorrow, every poacher south of Bakersfield would be on notice that his days were numbered and his options limited.

But first there were zipperheads to be disposed of.

One more curve, and now Carlotti saw the wrought-iron gates, the wall of brick and stone that completely surrounded Tien's estate. He wasn't fazed. They were going through the gates like honored guests, and the walls wouldn't mean a thing once they were on the inside, kicking ass. If anything, the stone perimeter would help to keep their targets in, where Girolamo's soldiers could pot the Viets in their own sweet time.

Girolamo didn't want to rush with Ngo Tien. Before he pushed a bullet through the Asian's guts, Carlotti wanted to see panic in his adversary's eyes. He wanted Tien to grovel, beg for his life, knowing that his prayers would not be answered. If revenge was sweet, Don Girolamo had his heart set on a double helping.

With his point car at the gate, he keyed the walkie-talkie. "Everyone get ready," he commanded. "Any second now."

Tien's people stayed behind the gate, one of them counting cars and heads, another drifting toward the speaker on an intercom that would undoubtedly connect him to the house. A call for reinforcements, putting everyone inside the fence on red alert.

A gunner had emerged from the Don's point car, arguing with someone at the gate, one hand gesticulating while he kept the other at his side. Carlotti did not have to see the Ingram tucked behind the soldier's leg. His eyes were on the gate men, watching as the nearest gave his message to the intercom, then drifted back to join his mates.

When the three of them were bunched together, Carlotti's gunner made his move, the Ingram spitting fire as he brought it up, the muzzle-flash reflected on their faces like a flash of summer lightning. Girolamo saw them fall, and then the driver of the point car put it through the gates, encountering resistance for a moment, bulling through with a horrendous shriek of grating steel.

Carlotti followed in the number-two car, ducking as a hail of small-arms fire descended on the caravan. His men had rolled the windows up, but the Don still felt vulnerable, putting only so much faith in armor plate and "bullet-proof" glass. He might be forced to ditch the cars when they were done, another cool half million down the crapper, but it would be worth it if the armor did its job.

So far, so good, and they were sweeping up the drive, returning fire from hidden gunports as they closed the distance to the house. On right and left, Carlotti saw his flank cars breaking ranks and roaring off across the lawn. One of them caught a sentry on the grille and plowed him under, spitting out a shattered bag of bones and growling on.

For reasons he couldn't explain, Carlotti thought about the Light Brigade, their fabled charge, and felt a surge of pardonable pride. He was a hero when you thought about it, turning back a threat to both the brotherhood and the United States. If foreigners were granted freedom to subvert established order, tamper with the scheme of things, who could predict where it might lead? Today some smack, some numbers, and tomorrow...

Carlotti palmed his .45 and grinned. There would be no tomorrow for his enemies. Tonight was all the time they had, and he was calling all the shots.

THE RUNNER REACHED Tien's study just as the first rounds of gunfire erupted at the gates. Tien was already on his feet and moving toward the windows when the houseman hammered on his door.

"Come in."

A young man lurched across the threshold, freezing when he saw the gun Tien held leveled on his chest. It took a heartbeat for the mobster to identify his junior aide, and then he tucked the gun into an inside pocket of his coat.

"Carlotti's men!" the runner blurted when he found his voice. "Outside."

"I see that." Ngo Tien had turned back toward the windows, just in time to watch the first of several cars smash through his wrought-iron gates, absorbing small-arms fire without apparent damage. "It would seem that they are now *inside*."

He rattled off a string of orders for his troops and forced the runner to repeat them, wasting precious time in an attempt to guarantee that nothing further would go wrong. Carlotti on the grounds was one thing but Carlotti's soldiers in the house would be another. Tien was certain that his men could hold the enemy at bay until police arrived, and he would hasten the arrival of authorities by calling them himself.

He lifted the receiver of his telephone and listened for a dial tone, drummed his fingers on the plungers in a futile bid for some response. The line was dead. His fortress had been cut off from the outside world.

If they were isolated, they would simply have to do the job themselves. Returning to the window, he saw four cars barreling along the drive, four others veering off across the lawn in flanking movements, ruining expensive turf and mowing down several of his gunners. Outside the house, they pulled up in a ragged semicircle, engines idling.

To proceed they would be forced to leave the obviously armored cars and rush the house on foot. Outnumbered and surrounded, they would be cut down as they emerged. It seemed to be a standoff, with Carlotti's only other option lying in an ignominious retreat.

Tien smiled. It would be fitting if the mafioso was destroyed by his own strategy. He wouldn't shame Carlotti's soldiers by accepting their surrender. It was better that they be allowed to die like men—and thereby guarantee that none of them would come back later as an enemy with a score to settle.

It would be too much to hope that Don Carlotti was among the sacrificial goats.

As Tien stood watching, one car edged a little closer to the house, its gunports spitting fire. Tien saw one of his soldiers topple from the porch, another, and before he knew precisely what was happening, Carlotti's men were spilling from the cars, unloading on the house and its defenders with a thunderclap of fire as they advanced.

And there, was that Carlotti? Tien had never met his adversary in the flesh, but he had studied Don Carlotti's likeness on the television, in the papers: portly, waves of iron-gray hair combed straight back from his squarish face, an automatic pistol in his hand.

This Don Carlotti started snapping orders to his troops, assisted by a backup with a compact radio. Tien felt a sudden urge to fling the window open and fire down upon his enemies, but he resisted. Better for him to command his men in person, setting an example for the newer guns to follow, showing them that he was not afraid.

The problem was that Ngo Tien was terrified.

He had already lost his daughter, and outside these walls his empire had been suffering from hammer blows inflicted by his enemies. At this point, Tien was moved to ask himself how much more he could lose.

And with the answer came a liberation from his paralyzing fear.

He could lose nothing more of any value to himself. The enemy had shamed him and contrived to steal his daughter's life. The worst that they could do now was kill him, and Tien decided death might be a blessing in disguise. With luck he might inspire his men to victory and see them crush their foe. In any case, he was prepared.

Not even emperors could live forever.

LAO FAN HAD BEEN CAUTIOUS when he cut the razor wire, first testing it to ascertain that it was not electrified. That done, he scrambled over, dropping to a crouch in darkness, finger on the trigger of his AK-47 as he scanned the shadows for potential enemies.

From all appearances his entry had gone unobserved. He hoped Lam Duc and Lin Phuong would be equally fortunate in their respective quadrants. It was too much to expect that all of them would walk away unscathed, but they were friends and comrades in the struggle. Lao would grieve for them if they were lost, as he knew they would grieve for him.

His target was the house, the shining centerpiece of Tien's estate. Between the target and his entry point, two hundred yards of rolling lawn were punctuated irregularly by shade trees and shrubs, providing minimal cover in transit. He would have to use the darkness, pray that he wouldn't meet any sentries and give up the small advantage of surprise.

It was the only edge they had against an enemy of greater numbers, more sophisticated weaponry. Without surprise Lao Fan and his companions would be little more than targets in a shooting gallery, surrounded and cut off from all escape.

It might yet come to that once battle had been joined, but Lao was counting on a shot at Ngo Tien before he died. One chance to take the jackal with him and he would be willing to accept his fate, whatever it might be. If he could rid the refugee community of Tien's malignant shadow, Lao thought he might face the consequence with satisfaction, even pride.

The Montagnard had covered something less than forty yards when his attention was distracted by a flash of headlights at the gate, downrange. A car had pulled up in the drive, and from the glare behind it, he decided there were several others waiting for admittance.

Reinforcements?

Frozen in the shadow of a weeping willow, Lao watched as a passenger alighted from the car, said something to the gate men and then sprayed them with a burst of automatic fire. The vehicle surged forward, crumpling the wrought-iron gate as if it had been made of tinfoil, plowing through with others close behind.

He counted eight in all, and knew that Bolan's call to Don Carlotti had paid off. The stratagem had been designed to occupy Tien's troops while multiplying casualties, and as Lao watched the limousines fan out, preparing for their charge across the lawn, he thought it should succeed in that at least.

A pair of sentries passed him in the darkness, racing for the gates, completely blind to Lao in the confusion of the moment. They were firing as they came in range, no less than fifty weapons rattling along a frail perimeter that wavered, falling back in the direction of the house. A storm of bullets rattled off the armored crew wagons, chipping ineffectually at triple-thick glass, smacking wetly into puncture-proof tires. The line of cars wouldn't be stopped until they reached their destination, and the gunners who stood fast before them were inevitably crushed or blown away.

Lao didn't wait around to see what Carlotti was up to. His mission lay inside the house, and while the Don was providing the diversion, Lao was bent on taking full advantage of the moment. He had reached the patio, was moving toward the kitchen entrance when the door flew open and a startled gunman barred his path.

The gunner had an adolescent's face, but age was totally irrelevant as he began to raise his nickel-plated automatic. Lao Fan stitched him with a burst across the chest and left his body sprawled beside a chaise longue, sweeping through the open doorway in a crouch.

Inside Lao found he had the kitchen to himself. His late opponent might have been attempting to escape or simply taking on some errand for the master of the house, but he was dead now and the way was clear. Lao passed the sinks and stove, refrigerators large enough for a commercial restaurant, and shouldered through the swing doors that opened on a formal dining room. Tien lived in style; Lao had to give him that.

Homing on the muffled sounds of automatic fire and shotgun blasts, Lao moved in the direction of the parlor. An empty hallway, doors on left and right. He glanced in each direction, made his move toward the front of the house and the sound of frightened voices, punctuated and overshadowed by gunfire. Despite their superior numbers, Tien's security force had been taken off guard by Carlotti's audacious move, and they were having trouble recovering from the initial shock. Lao thought their disorientation might work in his favor as he slipped past the open parlor door, ducking a stray round from outside and homing on the stairs.

He was halfway to the landing when a strident voice behind him ordered him to stop.

Lao threw himself into the turn, AK-47 blazing as he made the move.

MACK BOLAN'S TARGET was the lighted window on the second floor, set back behind a narrow balcony. It might not be Tien's study, as he had surmised, but it would put him well above the firefight that was riddling the rooms on the ground floor. If Ngo Tien was upstairs, fine. If not, he would be trapped between the Executioner and Don Carlotti's hunting party, stripped of any exit, any place to hide.

A trellis draped with ivy rose beside the balcony, and Bolan scrambled upward nimbly, dismissing thoughts of sentries passing by and glancing upward. They'd be distracted by Carlotti's strike. Another moment and he had one hand upon the railing, one leg up and over. Screened from prying eyes below, he raised the Uzi, pressed one ear against the glass.

No sound inside, so Bolan tried the handle, found the French doors open. Stepping through, he scanned the empty room and drew small consolation from the fact that he'd been correct about Tien's study. He had missed his quarry, possibly by seconds, but the timing made no difference now. If the warlord was still inside the house, he had a chance.

He crossed the room and risked a glance into the corridor outside. The sounds of combat echoed in a stairwell somewhere to his left: men shouting, cursing, firing weapons at their enemies who ringed the house with fire and steel. He wondered how Carlotti's men had lasted this long, finally deciding that Tien's hard force must include more greenhorns than he had originally calculated.

The soldier left Tien's study, moving out along the corridor. He had no special destination fixed in mind, but would be forced to track his prey from room to room, the doomsday numbers falling even as his options dwindled.

Lao Fan and his companions should be on the grounds by now, perhaps inside the house itself. Another reason to be careful, with the risk of drawing friendly fire or dropping one of Lao's associates before he recognized his error. For a moment, Bolan had the feeling of a hunter in a house of mirrors, hopelessly confused and operating on pure instinct, praying that it wouldn't fail him in the pinch.

But he wasn't completely lost. The war was just ahead of him, and down a curving flight of stairs. If Ngo Tien had gone to join his soldiers, then he must have passed this way. If he had run...well, there were probably four dozen rooms for him to hide in, exits the Executioner could never hope to pinpoint in the time available to him.

So he would play the odds this time, and hope they didn't get him killed before he had a chance to do his job.

Ahead of him and one flight down, the war was suddenly a great deal closer, automatic weapons battering at one another in the stairwell proper, stray rounds digging plaster from the walls.

Mack Bolan put his dread on hold and went to find the killing ground.

CHAPTER TWENTY-FIVE

Pham Bach was sitting down to dine alone when Lian Trang found him. Hesitant at first, Bach's first lieutenant made his move and stood across the table from his master, waiting while Bach sampled first the soup, and then a glass of wine.

"A thousand pardons."

"Yes? What is it?"

"We have just received a telephone call stating that Ngo Tien's estate will be raided tonight."

"The police?"

Trang shook his head. "Carlotti."

"And your source?"

"A man. He would not give his name."

"You did not recognize the voice."

Trang thought about it for a moment, finally shook his head in an emphatic negative. "No, sir."

"And have you passed the warning to our leader?"

"I have tried. There is no answer, and the operator tells me that the canyon lines are out of order."

"Ah."

"You think the raid may be in progress now?"

Bach shrugged and focused on his cooling soup. "If so, we can be of little help. Tien has a force of eighty men around him. By the time we can collect our troops and make the drive to Santiago Canyon, it should all be over anyway."

"But if Carlotti has declared a war..."

Trang didn't have to complete the sentence. Bach was with him all the way, the logic inescapable. If Don Carlotti was

attacking Ngo Tien specifically, there might be hope. If he
was waging war against the family on every front, Pham
Bach would also be a target, slated for assassination.

Suddenly deprived of appetite, Bach pushed the soup
away, paused long enough to drain the glass of wine. "We
must prepare ourselves," he snapped, already on his feet
and moving toward the door, "in case Carlotti's people plan
an unexpected visit here, as well."

"It shall be done."

"And send a man to Santiago Canyon. He is not to contact Ngo Tien or otherwise involve himself in anything he
may see. I want him to observe and make a swift report."

"Yes, sir."

Bach had a dozen men in-house, another twenty-five on
standby, waiting for a call. The force wasn't as large as
Tien's reserve, but Bach had picked each member of the
team himself, selecting on the basis of experience and nerve.
There were no timid greenhorns in the ranks, no children
who had trained with weapons but had never fired a shot in
anger.

If his troops were insufficient, Pham Bach mused, he
should be able to depend upon the Thunder Dragons. With
their brand-new warlord installed and token reparations
paid, the gang should be receptive to Bach's needs...
especially if the price was right. And for a decent shot at
Don Carlotti, he would pay a fortune.

Undercutting the Italian syndicate and gradually wiping
out its influence in Southern California was a part of Pham
Bach's master plan, but he had visualized the operation
taking years. Instead Carlotti seemed intent on bringing
matters to a head, and if he failed in his assault on Ngo
Tien, Tien's empire, the Italian would be finished. If he
didn't choose the path of honor, laying down his life in battle, he would be a gravely weakened adversary. One, Bach

thought, who might be easily manipulated when the time was right.

He left Lian Trang to supervise the preparation of their personal defenses, moving toward his study. Pham Bach's home was not as large as Tien's, but it held everything he needed for survival, plus a fair amount of luxury to bolster the facade. His wall safe, larger than the average, was concealed behind a decadent portrait of mounted cavalry pursuing Indians across a wasteland. It had been described to Pham Bach by the salesman as "a piece of genuine Americana," and his words had clinched the sale.

Tonight the piece of genuine Americana was removed and propped against Bach's desk, the mounted soldiers seeming small and insignificant once they were stripped of their position on the wall. Inside the safe, Bach kept an automatic pistol he had used on two occasions in the past eight years, his several passports and a sum of fifty thousand dollars, cash. His private files were too voluminous to fit in the safe, but Pham Bach had them under lock and key, prepared to be transported or destroyed in an emergency.

Bach wasn't prepared to classify his situation in that category yet. He could afford to wait for the report from Santiago Canyon, making up his mind when he established what was happening. If any of Carlotti's men arrived meanwhile, Bach's troops on hand were theoretically prepared to stop a force three times their size and hold the enemy at bay while Bach escaped. He doubted it would come to that, but it was always best to be prepared.

Bach wouldn't flee his home unless compelled to do so by impending danger. Not that he felt any great attachment to the house or furnishings; far from it. Rather, as an agent of the people's revolution, he still had a role to play, and it included standing by, pretending to assist Anh Giap and Ngo Tien in any struggle with their enemies. In fact he wouldn't lift a finger to protect them, but he must *appear* to do so, just in case the grinning jackals should emerge victorious from their engagement with Carlotti.

The Italian would be helpful to Bach's master plan, in any case. If Tien and Giap were killed by Don Carlotti's soldiers, nothing would prevent Bach from standing in their place and exercising ultimate control over the syndicate. If Ngo Tien survived, somehow—or even managed to eliminate Carlotti—he would still be vulnerable to arrest, indictment, possible assassination by "Carlotti loyalists" on Bach's private payroll.

Tien's position had become untenable. And when he fell, Bach would be waiting in the wings, prepared to use the corpses of his enemies as stepping-stones to victory. It was important that the framework of the syndicate, at least, should stay intact for future service to the people's revolution, but Pham Bach had no attachment to the troops recruited by Giap or Tien. The more of them who died or fled this night, the better he would like it. Afterward when he was firmly seated on the throne of power, he would staff the family with soldiers of his own.

Bach weighed the old, familiar pistol in his palm and checked the firing chamber. Satisfied, he slipped the weapon in a pocket of his coat and emptied out the safe, extracting cash and passports. The assorted paperwork and money filled a briefcase, which would be his only luggage if he was compelled to flee in haste.

Content that he had taken every possible precaution, Pham Bach took a seat behind his desk and settled back to wait for news of Ngo Tien's demise.

LAM DUC NEVER MADE IT to the house. A stranger to the ways of war before he met Lao Fan, the shopkeeper had never fired a shot in anger prior to the assault upon the Long Beach warehouse. He had killed three men that afternoon, but he didn't feel like a combat veteran as he crept across the darkened grounds of Tien's estate, convinced that guards would see him, kill him, at any moment.

Lam Duc was frightened, though he wouldn't have admitted it to Lao, Lin Phuong or the American. Especially to the American, who had already done so much and risked so much on their behalf. Duc had come this far, in spite of fear, and he would carry out his mission to the best of his ability.

But he was still afraid.

He had been fifty yards from his appointed goal and moving slowly when Carlotti's caravan arrived. He was expecting the Italians, of course—he knew that the American had called them on the telephone to set up a diversion—but their sudden entry, smashing through the gates and charging toward the house, had taken Lam Duc by surprise.

Despite his inexperience, Duc recognized his golden opportunity and made a beeline for the manor house. He was assigned to enter if he could, and failing that, to cover any exits on the south side of the mansion, cutting off the occupants from possible escape in that direction.

Simple.

In their planning sessions it had sounded easy, slinking through the darkness like a burglar, dodging sentries as if they were deaf and blind. A piece of cake, as the Americans would say...although Lam Duc had never truly understood the phrase.

In any case, reality was very different from theory. In the flesh, his enemies were highly mobile and apparently alert. They had Duc heavily outnumbered, and he knew that any careless move might mean his death. The mass confusion caused by Don Carlotti's troops was helpful, but it hadn't been enough. Duc was thirty yards from his appointed destination when he stepped out from behind a tree—and found himself confronted by two guards.

In retrospect Duc was certain that his heart had stopped. He *knew* his lungs had ceased to function for an instant, but his mind was racing, images of sudden death—his own—unreeling on the monitor inside his head. And when he made his move, perhaps a heartbeat after stepping into the encounter, Duc had been every bit as startled as his enemies.

The shotgun was a 12-gauge pump, its barrel trimmed back to the legal minimum of eighteen inches and the shoulder stock replaced with an efficient pistol grip. At close range it was murder, and no more than seven feet separated Lam Duc from his enemies.

His first blast killed the sentry with the automatic rifle, lifting him completely off his feet and tracing crimson streamers on the breeze. The dead man's partner was responding, bringing up a handgun, when Duc worked the slide and shot him in the face at point-blank range. The gunner's head evaporated, splattering Duc with blood and bits of brain, the corpse remaining upright for an instant, finally surrendering to gravity.

Before the shock could penetrate and rob him of his will to move, Duc was breaking for the house, his goal a set of sliding glass doors facing on the southern lawn.

He almost made it.

Halfway there Duc saw the draperies flutter and veered to his right as they were drawn aside. The gunner standing just inside those doors didn't bother taking time to slide them back; instead he fired directly through the glass, his submachine gun rounds deflected slightly in the first burst, dead on target with the second.

Lam Duc felt the impact, lost his footing, was startled as he fell that there was so little pain. He had imagined that a gunshot wound would be excruciating, and the numbness in his abdomen surprised him. He was even more surprised when it spread down into his legs.

Duc fired a blast in the direction of his adversary, saw a puff of plaster as his round went wild. It was enough to make the gunner hesitate, for all of that, and Duc slithered on his stomach, digging with his elbows as he sought the cover of some nearby shrubbery. The brush would not stop bullets, but it might just spoil the sniper's aim.

Another burst chewed up the lawn behind him. He felt a bullet strike his leg, and he was conscious of the fact that blood was soaking through his jeans, but there was still no major pain. He felt almost fortunate that dying cost so little in terms of concrete suffering.

And he was dying—Lam Duc entertained no doubts on that score. If his present wounds weren't enough to do the job, with loss of blood thrown in, the fact remained that he was pinned down, under hostile fire, deprived of mobility. He couldn't run or find adequate cover for himself, and other sentries would be coming any time to finish off the job.

Above all else, Lam Duc was bitter at the thought of having failed. His comrades were expecting him to do his part, and he had let them down. It didn't matter so much that his life was pooling in his lap, but he regretted that his friends were waiting for him, unaware of his predicament, perhaps in greater danger now because of his failure.

He could never make it up to them, but he could try to take a few more of Tien's jackals with him, cut down the odds. When they came for him, he would be ready.

Fishing in a pocket of his coat, he found more shells, slick with blood, and started squeezing them into the shotgun.

That done, the dying merchant-soldier settled back to wait.

CARLOTTI CHOSE a moving target, sighting on the runner with his .45 and squeezing off two rounds that dropped him in his tracks. It felt just like the old days, and he wondered if the button men weren't better off sometimes without the worries of an empire on their shoulders, free to move around and whack some people out to keep things honest.

Just now the other side was doing its fair share of whacking. From his place between two armored Continentals, Girolamo counted three men down and out, another wounded, and there had to be more he couldn't see. They had reduced the odds substantially, but they were under heavy fire, and if they didn't move out soon, they stood a decent chance of joining General Custer in the record books.

The house had been Carlotti's destination from the start. He had to get inside, somehow, or he would never get his hands around Tien's scrawny neck. He scanned the battlefield for possible solutions to his problem, finally hitting one he thought might have a chance.

The cars were shot. An idiot could see that at a glance. Carlotti knew that he would have to dump them—if he got the chance—but in the meantime, they might still be useful.

Shouting to his wheelman and a couple of the nearest gunners, he got his point across. The driver worked his way around the capo's Lincoln, ducking shotgun pellets as he slid behind the steering wheel. Carlotti crawled in back, one of the buttons with him, while another gunsel took the shotgun seat, up front. They got the doors closed, and the sound of small-arms fire impacting on the armored body was like hailstones drumming on the tin roof of a Quonset hut.

"All right," Don Girolamo snapped, "if you can get this bucket running, back up there and give yourself a running start."

"Okay, boss." There was apprehension in the driver's voice. "But this thing isn't exactly a four-wheel-drive, you know?"

"I couldn't care less if it was a fucking tricycle. If we don't get inside that house, we're dead. Now *do it!*"

Grimacing, the wheelman took three tries to start the engine, finally revving it before he put the Lincoln in reverse. Carlotti felt the rear wheels lurch across a prostrate body, wondering if it was one of his, deciding that it didn't matter either way. The dead were out of it, and he'd come too far to waste a moment worrying about their feelings.

Forward, and they hit the steps with everything the Lincoln had, jolting Don Carlotti from his seat and down onto the floorboards. For a heartbeat, it appeared they wouldn't make it, then the rear tires dug for traction and the Continental started climbing, rocking like an elephant on four prosthetic legs, but climbing nonetheless, toward the double doors.

Converging fire was peppering the Lincoln, ringing off the bodywork, turning the windows milky white, but so far they were safe inside.

"Shoot back, goddamn it!"

Suiting words to action, Girolamo found the nearest gunport, poked the muzzle of his automatic through and squeezed off half a magazine in rapid-fire. Around him, gun smoke and hellacious racket filled the car as his two soldiers opened up with submachine guns, cartridge casings rattling and rolling on the floor around their feet.

They were doing roughly seven miles per hour when they hit the doors. It wasn't much in terms of freeway speed, but with the Lincoln's weight thrown up against a relatively flimsy lock, it did the trick with room to spare. Around them dust and plaster settled in a roiling cloud.

Carlotti fed his automatic with a fresh clip, taking full advantage of the accidental smoke screen as he gave the Lincoln's door a shove and staggered clear. An Asian gunner moved to intercept him, wrestling with the firing mechanism on an automatic rifle. Carlotti shot him through the forehead, blowing him away.

His men were on their feet now, submachine guns spitting through the haze and dropping sentries where they stood. More of Carlotti's soldiers were already clustered on the porch, a few more scrambling around the Lincoln, climbing on the trunk and firing as they came. With concentrated fire, they swept the parlor clean, spilled out into the corridor that split the ground floor of the manor house in two.

They had a foothold. Girolamo's men might not have time to clear the house, but they had cracked the final obstacle and Ngo Tien was now within the Don's grasp. Carlotti merely had to find the Vietnamese warlord, drag him out of hiding and administer the coup de grace.

LAO FAN WAS HUDDLED on the stairs when Bolan reached him, aiming short bursts at enemies who milled about below him, on the ground floor of the house. Tien's soldiers were returning fire in heavy volumes, riddling the banister, the walls and ceiling, forcing Lao to hug the steps and keep his head down as he tried to stay alive.

The odds were out of line, and Bolan took it on himself to even them a bit. He took one of the heavy satchel charges, set the fuse for seven seconds, swung the bag around his head one time before he let it fly. Lao saw it coming, covering his head with folded arms as Bolan took a long step backward, dropping prone and wriggling against the wall.

Below him hell erupted with a roar that left a ringing in his ears, a cloud of smoke and dust ascending from the ground floor, rolling toward the ceiling, interspersed with tongues of fire. The falling shrapnel was composed of shattered masonry and bits of furniture, stray objects wet and red that Bolan doggedly refused to focus on.

The guns were silent as he rose and moved to stand against the railing, picking out Lao Fan despite the smoke. The Montagnard was scrambling to his feet and climbing, glancing back to scan the ruin of the foyer as he joined Bolan on the landing.

"Tien?" he asked.

"Not yet."

"Then we must hurry."

They were turning when a pair of gunners, late to join the fight, erupted from the doorway on their left. Both men were packing shotguns, but they never had an opportunity to use them. Bolan hit them with a rising burst of parabellum manglers, spinning them around in awkward, mincing steps before they fell together, arms and legs entangled, blind eyes open to the light.

More frightened voices from below were immediately followed by a crash as something heavy breached the entrance to the manor. Bolan recognized the revving of an engine, lost it as a brisk cacophony of gunfire sounded from the general direction of the parlor.

"This way," Bolan told Lao Fan. "We have to check as many of these bedrooms as we can."

"I'll take the left."

It was a long shot, but he had to play it out, despite a nagging hunch that the warlord had gone downstairs before the Executioner arrived. If so, Tien might be dead by now... or he might be outside, preparing to escape.

Bolan picked up his pace, kicking doors and hosing down the opposition where he found it, letting frag grenades prepare the way if he was met with hostile fire. He killed five men and saw Lao Fan drop seven others as they worked their way across the second floor. He spent the time required to scan each face, but none of them belonged to the warlord.

Defeat.

Above them, yet another floor; the killing field below. Whichever way his prey had gone, the Executioner was clearly running out of time.

He played the hunch.

"I'm going down."

"And that floor?" Lao Fan jabbed his AK-47 toward the ceiling.

"Take it, if you like. I have a feeling that our pigeon's on the wing."

"I cannot take that chance."

Their eyes locked for a moment frozen in eternity. No words were necessary as they moved back toward the stairs and parted, Lao Fan climbing, Bolan turning toward the smoke and leaping flames that marked the ground-floor battlefield.

It would be nice, he thought, if he could see Lao Fan again in better times.

The soldier closed his mind to absent friends and hit the stairs, descending into hell.

THE LATE REPORTS from Tien's estate in Santiago Canyon had Bach worried, nervous. Because of the gunfire and explosions, his observer was afraid to make another pass. Thus far no stragglers had emerged and no police were on the scene, but officers were bound to surface soon. The neighbors might be few and far between, renowned for civic apathy, but even they could not ignore a full-scale war.

Bach had decided he should leave, for safety's sake, and take a brief vacation while the heat died down. It would require some time for the authorities to sort out victims, make IDs, determine what had happened in the canyon. Bach would be available to help them, in a week or so, but meanwhile, he believed discretion was the better part of valor.

He was clearing out.

The sudden exodus would come as a surprise to his subordinates—especially Lian Trang—but Bach wouldn't require their company this time around. A private plane was waiting for him, fueled and ready for takeoff the moment he arrived. His beach house on the coast of Baja California was perpetually stocked with food and liquor, all the various comforts of home. Preparedness was second nature to Pham Bach, and it would save him now, in spite of everything his enemies could throw against him.

He would leave Lian Trang in charge, an honor in the circumstances, with the understanding that he would be gone a week—ten days at most. When he returned, they would be helpful to authorities and answer any questions that didn't immediately jeopardize surviving family interests. Ngo Tien and Don Carlotti were the villains of the piece, Pham Bach a simple businessman who had been grievously misled by his superiors and trusted friends. No evidence existed linking him with any crime, and while police would certainly suspect him of the worst, their chances of securing indictments were extremely poor.

A short vacation in the sun, away from smog and enemies who wanted Pham Bach dead. The Asian double agent half imagined he could feel the surf around his ankles, smell the spicy food prepared by peasant hands.

When they were finished in America, perhaps he could export the people's revolution southward into Mexico. It was a notion worth considering.

But first he had to break the news of his departure to Lian Trang. Bach hoped his second in command would take it well, without complaints.

In fact, the news appeared to stun Bach's chief assassin. Trang's eyes clouded over as he listened, gnawing at his lower lip. He didn't speak until Bach finished, hesitating even then before his thoughts took shape as words.

"What will become of me?" he asked, a childish question fraught with peril.

"As I just explained, you will administer the family business in my absence. When I have returned, and we are free to operate as usual, you will assume Anh Giap's position as the warlord of the clan."

"When you return."

"Exactly."

"And if you do not return?"

"Why should I not?"

"Why should you run away?" Trang countered, hands clenched into fists against his thighs.

"I must divorce myself from Ngo Tien and this affair with the Carlotti family. If I remain, police will try to prove I am involved."

"You *are* involved."

"Of course." Bach spoke as if he were explaining complex theorems to a young child. "But I must not *appear* to be involved. Indictments at this juncture, even if defeated at a trial, might harm the family beyond repair."

"Am I to be indicted then?"

Bach frowned. "There is no evidence connecting you with any crime, unless you have been careless in your duties."

"I have not been careless," Trang insisted.

"Then you should be safe."

"I would prefer to go with you."

"Impossible. Your presence would destroy the image of a simple holiday."

"I will not stay."

"I beg your pardon?"

"I will go with you, or I will find another place to go, alone."

"You would betray me in this fashion when I need you most?"

"You need a scapegoat. I refuse to play the part."

"Ungrateful dog!"

Lian Trang was digging for the pistol worn beneath his arm, but Pham Bach got there first, his weapon rising into view above the desktop, sliding into target acquisition as he squeezed off two quick rounds. Trang stumbled backward, missed an easy chair by inches, sprawling on the floor. He showed no sign of life, but Pham Bach put another round between his glassy eyes regardless.

There was never any point in taking needless risks.

Here was another mess to be disposed of, and he would be forced to choose Lian Trang's successor. With the example fresh in mind, Bach hoped his newfound second in command would be more pliable, less prone to thinking for himself.

He punched the intercom and called for help. Already running short of time, Bach didn't plan to miss his flight.

The Baja beach was looking better all the time.

CHAPTER TWENTY-SIX

"Hey, boss, the goddamn house is burning!"

"I can see that, stupid!"

Crouching in a corridor half-filled with smoke, Carlotti cursed his inability to pinpoint Tien and give the little bastard everything that he had coming. Now the frigging house was burning down around them, and he had no time to make a sweep from room to room and floor to floor as he had planned. There was a decent chance his enemy would slip away, escape completely, and the knowledge ate at the Don's insides like an angry ulcer.

Hacking, coughing, squeezing off a random burst when one of Tien's survivors showed himself, Carlotti's men were grouped around him, standing watch as best they could. The capo hadn't counted lately, but he guessed that ten or twelve were missing, stricken permanently from the payroll in that first mad rush to take the house. And now that they had it, there was nothing they could do. The goddamned place was burning down.

Carlotti made his choice. "We finish checking out this floor," he growled, "and then we split."

"Split how?" one of the soldiers asked.

"We still got cars outside."

"You seen them lately? Fucking gooks were hitting them with everything they had. I'll be surprised if any of them run."

"So, then we'll *borrow* some, all right? Forget about the frigging cars and do your job."

Contrition, and a trace of fear. "Sure, boss. I only meant—"

"Shut up!"

On the capo's order, two men took the point, the others trailing as they crept from room to room, examining a dining room, a library of sorts, a second living room for "special" guests and a gymnasium. There were stiffs in several of the rooms, a couple of them minus faces, but Carlotti didn't think that any of them looked like Tien.

"What's left?"

"Looks like the kitchen."

"Shit."

"You want to check it out?"

"Hell, yes, we'll check it out. We're here already."

The point men flanked the door, their weapons ready, waiting for the signal to proceed. Carlotti thought about it, growing more and more disgusted by the moment. Ten or twelve good soldiers gone, eight limos shot to hell, and all he had to show for his investment was a couple of dozen zipperheads. It was enough to gag a maggot, and Carlotti felt the anger building up inside him, getting ready to explode.

"Clear out of there," he snapped, and waved the point men back with jerky motions of his .45. "I'll check this out myself."

"Hey, boss—"

He brushed past two or three restraining hands, his automatic cocked and locked. Don Girolamo hit the door back with one hand, stepping through into a slaughterhouse.

THUS FAR, Anh Giap had done his duty. When the sons of jackals crashed the gate, he had been swift to rally soldiers in the house, preparing to defend it with the last drop of his blood. A number of his troops were relatively green, but

Giap had placed his faith in their performance, trusting in their courage.

Until two of them had let him down.

The cowards had made their break when Don Carlotti's limousine began its lurching, awkward climb to reach the house. Their nerves had snapped, and they had dropped their weapons, slipping out of line—unseen, they thought— and making for the kitchen, where they doubtless hoped to leave the house and find some way to flee the grounds.

Disheartened, furious, Anh Giap had followed, overtaking them before they had a chance to slip outside. A bullet in the head would not have been appropriate; it was a soldier's death, reserved for men who did their duty, kept their honor more or less intact. As Giap crept up behind his prey, he saw a butcher knife beside the sink and picked it up, unconsciously appraising it for heft and balance as he closed the distance.

"Are we lost?" he asked, amused to see them jump before they turned to face him. They were desperate, and he could read the panic in their faces as they attempted to create an explanation that would save their worthless lives.

"Carlotti's men," one of them blurted out. "I thought some of them might attempt to break in through the kitchen."

"Yes!" The other bought it gratefully, pathetically. "And I came back to help him."

"You are both courageous men." Anh Giap was smiling. He enjoyed this game. "So brave, to leave your weapons and confront the enemy unarmed."

Their faces sagged, but the quicker of them, thinking fast, recovered in an instant. "I was out of ammunition," he declared. "But I still have my pistol."

He was reaching for it when Anh Giap stepped forward, thrust with the ten-inch blade, twisting as it bit through gristle, savaging the coward's larynx. Jets of blood from the carotid artery splashed over Giap's sleeve, his cheek and shirtfront, as the dying traitor staggered backward, butting up against another counter, sagging at the knees. His lips were moving, but his open throat couldn't supply the necessary sounds.

Giap spun and caught the second coward with a backhand swing that flayed his cheek and sent him reeling toward the door. One hand was on the knob, the other pressed against his bloody face, when Giap stepped up behind him, tangling fingers in the young man's hair and hauling back his head to leave the throat exposed. The butcher knife bit deeply, swiftly, cutting off a scream before it had an opportunity to reach the dead man's lips.

Giap toyed with the idea of cutting off their heads as an example to the others who might think of breaking ranks, but he was needed elsewhere. Firing from the direction of the parlor was sporadic now, and he worried that the sudden change in volume might not signal Don Carlotti's death. If the Italians had a solid foothold in the house...

He stepped into the dining room, smelled smoke and heard the voices of his enemies approaching. Giap didn't recognize Carlotti's voice, but there were several men—perhaps a dozen, maybe more—and he was cut off from his soldiers. Trapped.

Retreating to the kitchen, Anh Giap drew his pistol, checked its load and pocketed the half-empty magazine. A fresh one took its place, the pistol in his left hand, while he kept the long knife in his right. Outnumbered he must force the enemy to fight on his terms, his ground, and the struggle might be hand to hand before he finished with them.

He could hear them at the door, debating whether they should check the kitchen, and he waited, silent, like a spider frozen in the center of its web. Whoever crossed the threshold was a dead man, but his backup would be tricky, difficult to handle.

It occurred to Giap that he might die here, in the kitchen, and he pushed the morbid thought away. He had faced death too many times to fear the Reaper now, when he was in the autumn of his years. Whatever the Italians did to him, it would be nothing worse than what he'd done to others in his time.

The door flew open, and Giap recognized Carlotti from his photographs. The mafioso held a pistol in his hand, but he would never have a chance to use it.

Giap hacked at the capo's wrist, heard his automatic clatter onto the floor. Before Carlotti could recover from initial shock, before the pain of severed tendons registered, the butcher knife slid home between his ribs, Giap throwing all his weight behind the thrust and driving his opponent back against the wall.

Carlotti screamed, a high-pitched, piglike squealing sound. Other gunmen crowded in the doorway, pushing through to help their dying leader. Giap squeezed off in rapid-fire, not bothering to aim, his eyes locked with Carlotti's as the room became a shooting gallery. He felt the lethal rounds strike him, saw others strike Carlotti as his legs gave way.

Anh Giap surrendered to the pull of gravity, his fingers frozen on the butcher knife with strength enough to snap the handle off, the blade remaining with Carlotti. Giap felt nothing as he focused on the rushing darkness, letting go.

LAO FAN WAS GROWING DIZZY from the smoke as he continued on his rounds, examining each bedroom, storage room and closet on the third floor of the manor house. He knew the ground floor must be burning furiously by now, but there were still four rooms to check, and he wouldn't turn back until he satisfied himself that his job was done, his effort wasted.

Bolan had been right. The bastard had gone *down*, to either join his troops or slink away while they were holding off the enemy. Lao Fan had recognized the perfect sense of Bolan's argument, but he couldn't permit himself to leave so many hiding places unattended, run the risk that Tien would make his getaway because Lao had been negligent.

He had been stubborn.

He had failed.

Thus far the upper floor had been a disappointment. Lao had dropped two gunners on the landing, caught a weasel-faced accountant-type emerging from a bathroom with expensive slacks around his knees, but otherwise his search had been a total waste of time. No sign of Ngo Tien, Anh Giap, Pham Bach. The men he wanted most to see were gone—if they had ever been there in the first place.

Bolan might be having better luck. Harsh sounds of mortal combat still reverberated through the house, but they were fading now, the gunfire trailing off as soldiers of both sides took flight to save themselves from hungry flames. Lao Fan would soon need to find an exit from the building.

Four rooms and he approached the nearest door with measured strides, his AK-47 up and tracking. There was still a chance of finding someone, anyone, behind this door, the next one or the next. While any chance remained, Lao would try.

He turned the knob, stepped back and swept the chamber with his rifle as the door swung slowly open. Furtive movement in a corner, near the open window, and his heart leaped in his chest. A target, huddled in the shadow of an easy chair. Preparing to escape, or...?

"Wait, don't shoot! It's me!"

Lin Phuong unfolded from his crouch, the color slowly creeping back into his face. He held the Ruger Mini-14 rifle at his side, and Lao could see that his hands were trembling.

"Dammit, Lin!"

"I had to climb the trellis. There was too much fighting at the doors in front, and still more in the kitchen. I could find no other way inside."

"And here you are."

Lin nodded, almost managing a grin.

"You are aware the house is burning?"

He lost the feeble grin at that. "I feared as much. This means that I will have to climb back down the trellis."

"Maybe not. Come with me."

The shaky merchant fell in step behind Lao Fan as Lao moved back into the corridor.

"Three rooms," Lao said. "I mean to check them all before I leave. With you, it will be that much quicker. We can try the stairs before we think about your trellis."

"As you say."

They split off, each man ducking through the doorway to another empty room, combining forces for the final effort. Nothing. They were retreating toward the smoky stairs when three of Tien's defenders suddenly materialized on the landing, moving briskly toward them through the haze. Lao thought they must have been detailed to look for stragglers, clearing out the house while time remained. One of them called out to Lao and Lin, warning them that they had to leave without delay.

It took a moment for the guard to realize his critical mistake. His mouth fell open as he recognized—or failed to recognize—the two armed strangers dressed in black who stood before him. He had a weapon dangling at his side, but he wasn't prepared to use it and his move, when finally it came, was telegraphed by anxious eyes and body language, giving Lao Fan all the time he needed.

He triggered a short burst and dropped the gunner where he stood. Several paces behind the dead man, his more suspicious friends were braced for trouble. They were firing as their leader hit the floor, and Lao Fan threw himself against the wall, allowing gravity to bring him down before a line of bullets ripped the plaster just above him.

Startled by the sudden confrontation, slower off the mark, Lin Phuong wasn't so fortunate. He broke in the direction of an open bedroom door, a burst from his rifle wild and wasted, but he never made it. Huddled on the floor, returning fire by instinct, Lao Fan saw his comrade stumble, twisting with the impact of rounds that splashed his life in crimson plumes across the stucco wall. Lin toppled, triggering a final burst that came no closer to his targets than the first.

Lao caught the nearest gunner with a rising burst that gutted the guy and flipped him over on his back, heels drumming briefly on the carpeting. The dead man's sole surviving ally made a break in the direction of the stairwell, seeking cover in the smoke and firing blindly as he ran. But it wasn't enough to save him. Lying prone, Lao Fan put three rounds in the bull's-eye at a range of thirty feet, the force of impact toppling his target facedown on the floor.

He kept the dead men covered—just in case—and wormed his way across the floor to reach Lin Phuong. He didn't have to check the wounds to know his friend was dying. Dark eyes swam in and out of focus, dark blood soaked through clothing, etching outlines of Lin's body on the carpet.

Lin struggled to speak, the words barely audible.

"We got them?"

"Yes."

"All three?"

"All three."

"Then we are safe?"

"Yes, safe."

Lao knelt beside him, cradling his friend's head in hands that trembled.

"And Ngo Tien?"

"He will be punished. Have no fear."

"I am not afraid. We are safe now."

"Yes. We are safe."

The life ran out of Lin Phuong's body like the final grains of sand escaping from an hourglass, and he was gone. Lao struggled to his feet, was turning toward the stairwell when a tongue of flame raced up the steps, igniting carpet in the hallway.

Cut off from retreat in that direction, he retraced his steps until he found the room where he had met Lin Phuong. He crossed to stand before the open window, leaned outside and scanned the ground below, the ivy-covered trellis that would either bear his weight or pitch him to the earth in seconds.

Either way the fall probably wouldn't be lethal—soft grass below, no sentries visible from where he stood. If he should fall and break his neck, if he was picked off by a sniper as he scrambled down the trellis, Lao was ready to accept his fate as he was ready—grudgingly—to recognize that Ngo Tien had wriggled through his fingers. There would be no sweet revenge tonight. He must be satisfied with soldiers slain and damage done to the estate.

Unless Mack Bolan had been more successful in his hunt.

Lao offered up a silent prayer to nameless gods and scrambled through the window, stretching for the trellis as he cleared the sill. In the darkness, with the stench of burning on his clothes and hatred in his heart, he started down.

THE CAR WAS WAITING for Tien, driver at the wheel, as he emerged into the night. Behind him his men were fighting—dying—to protect him, and he felt shame burning in his cheeks as he prepared to leave them, running like a coward in the darkness.

Still there seemed to be no other course of action he could take. The house was burning, and Carlotti's men had breached the doors somehow, annihilating those who stood before them. Anh Giap had been right, Tien realized, about the quality of "soldiers" they were hiring, the amount of training necessary to prepare green troops for battle. But the business of making money had preoccupied his mind, prevented him from taking necessary action while they still had time.

Too late. The enemy had breached his defenses and his men were going down like bullocks in a slaughterhouse. There wouldn't be a second chance at victory this night. His only hope lay in escaping before Carlotti's people found him.

Anh Giap would have to find his own way out. For years, they had been as close as brothers, but survival took priority, and Ngo Tien was somewhat startled to discover that he still placed value on his life. In spite of Lisa and the ruination of his empire, he was still intent on clinging to the remnants of his life. In time he could rebuild, repair the damage done by Don Carlotti's troops. If he survived, found refuge from his enemies, there would be time to plot revenge.

His driver slid out from behind the wheel, stepped back to hold the door for Tien—and froze. It took an instant for the Asian mobster to accept the evidence presented by his eyes, and then the wheelman's knees gave way, his eyes rolled back to contemplate the bloody keyhole in his forehead.

Spinning on his heels, Tien found himself confronted by a tall man dressed in black, his face and hands cosmetically disguised. The prowler held a silenced pistol in one hand, the muzzle aimed directly at Tien's chest.

"Your choice," the graveyard voice pronounced. "We take a ride together, or I take a ride alone."

"I seem to have no option."

"There are always options."

"I am in your hands."

"Let's see the iron."

Tien spread his coat, obeyed the man's order to remove the pistol from his belt and drop it on the ground. The other's weapon waggled toward the driver's open door. "Get in. Slide over."

As he slipped behind the wheel, Tien glanced at the ignition, saw the key and gave a passing thought to firing up the engine, standing hard on the accelerator. There was one chance in a million he could make it, but the image of a bullet smashing through his skull deterred him, and he followed orders, sliding over to the shotgun seat. His captor took the wheel and turned the engine over, following the drive in the direction of the ruined gates.

"Your life depends on how you play the game," Tien was informed. "If any of your people try to stop us, you'll have one chance to persuade them otherwise."

In fact the twisted gates were now unmanned, Tien's soldiers either dead or drawn to join the battle for the house. He glanced back at the mansion, saw flames licking from the upper windows, wondered if his insurance agent would consider Don Carlotti's raid an act of war. The notion almost made him laugh, but he remembered Grim Death at the wheel, and laughter died before it found release.

He didn't ask the tall man for his name. Tien's mind was clear enough to realize that he had found Mack Bolan, the American responsible for Lisa's death. For just a heartbeat, Tien regretted giving up his pistol, but he knew that he could never match the soldier's speed. He was a businessman, grown soft with time, and Bolan was a cold professional, an expert at killing.

"Here's the deal," his captor said. "I want Pham Bach. You show me where to find him, play it straight, and you can walk."

"Why Bach?"

The soldier told him, sparing nothing, spelling out the ruination of Tien's daughter in explicit terms. Tien had no reason to believe this stranger over Bach, no cause to doubt his trusted aid of many years...and yet, the soldier knew so much. When he was finished, Tien sat silently, consumed with burning rage.

"We have a deal?"

Despite the heat that tinged his cheeks and tingled in his hands, Tien's heart was ice.

"If I know Bach, he will be looking for a place to hide."

"I'm listening."

"There is a private airfield . . ."

FIFTEEN MINUTES from the ruins of a dream in Santiago Canyon, Bolan caught a narrow side track, veering off toward Cowan Heights and following the one-lane blacktop to its terminus. The airstrip was designed for crop dusters and other small craft. A half dozen Pipers and Cessnas were lined up on one side of the runway.

The gate had been padlocked, but Bolan saw movement inside and he held the wheel steady. Chain link burst open like fishnet on impact, the Cadillac scarcely aware of an obstacle thrown in its path. Near the hangar, he made out the shapes of three men—two in suits, one the pilot—preparing a two-engine Cessna for takeoff.

"Pham Bach!"

It was Tien's first remark since he had given out directions and lapsed into silence, eyes fixed on the dash. He had taken the news about Bach and his daughter like death on a plate...which the soldier supposed that it was, in a way. Tien must be dying inside, but he still had enough anger left to wish death on the man who had sold out their friendship, demolished his life.

Bolan braked to a halt twenty yards from the plane, going EVA instantly, palming the big Desert Eagle. Before he could line up a target, the pilot and one of the suits were already inside, Pham Bach's backup producing an Ingram machine pistol, crouching and scuttling for cover.

Tien burst from the passenger door of the Caddy, unarmed, shouting curses at Bach as he ran for the plane. It was hopeless, the engine was catching, but Tien, in his rage, seemed convinced he could hold the bird down with a sheer force of will, drag out his enemy and inflict his revenge.

Fifteen yards and the tail gunner let off a burst that caught Tien in midstride, cutting short any hope of a face-to-face meeting with Bach.

Bolan aimed at the muzzle-flash, squeezing off three rounds in rapid-fire, riding the recoil and holding his target in view as the gunner sat down on the tarmac, his Ingram forgotten, the life running out through the holes in his chest.

The pilot had contact now, taxiing onto the runway as Bolan stood up, his piece braced in both hands. He had six rounds left, and he used them all in a thundering burst that put two through the windshield and two rounds in each of the engines. The Cessna kept rolling, dead hands on the throttle, flames trailing behind, but it had no direction, doubling back on its course. Bolan shielded his face with one hand as the plane careened into a small Piper.

The explosion engulfed everything—Cessna and Piper, the next two planes in line. Bolan basked in the radiant heat waves and watched as the asphalt began to turn liquid, small fires from the spilled gasoline lighting beacons around the main funeral pyre, marking its boundaries. More work for the fire fighters, Bolan supposed. He would call them from town in another half hour or so.

In the meantime, Pham Bach and his schemes were consigned to the hot, cleansing fire. He might never know just what the savage had planned, who his ultimate sponsors had been, but it made no difference.

The dragon was slain, and if others should rise from the ashes, so be it. For now, it was triumph enough to stand back and take heart in the flames.

"For Lisa," Bolan said, and put the fire behind him, heading back for town.

EPILOGUE

"It isn't much, but it's a start."

The satchel, filled with eighty thousand dollars, sat on the kitchen table between Lao Fan and Bolan.

"So much death," Lao said. "Three widows, and the child. I will make certain it is evenly divided."

Bolan rose to leave. "I've overstayed my welcome, Lao. The meter's running."

"There is nothing I can say to adequately thank you for your help."

"There's nothing you should have to say."

"I wish..." Lao thought about it, shook his head and smiled. "No matter."

Bolan shook his old friend's hand and let the screen door softly close between them. "Watch yourself," he cautioned.

Lao Fan's smile became a hearty grin.

"There is no dragon to be frightened of, just now."

"There'll always be another dragon. You know that as well as I do."

"Yes, but in the meantime, we can live again. And when another shows his face, perhaps the people will not wait so long to rise up."

"You never know."

"But I can hope."

The soldier nodded, smiled. "Why not?"

There would be other dragons, other savages, as certainly as there would be a sunrise in the morning. But the people—some of them, at any rate—had learned to make a stand. And next time...

Next time?

Bolan shook his head. Tomorrow, he thought, would have to take care of itself.

TAKE 'EM NOW

FOLDING SUNGLASSES
FROM GOLD EAGLE

Mean up your act with these tough, street-smart shades. Practical, too, because they fold 3 times into a handy, zip-up polyurethane pouch that fits neatly into your pocket. Rugged metal frame. Scratch-resistant acrylic lenses. Best of all, they can be yours for only $6.99.

MAIL YOUR ORDER TODAY.

Send your name, address, and zip code, along with a check or money order for just $6.99 + .75¢ for postage and handling (for a total of $7.74) payable to Gold Eagle Reader Service. (New York and Iowa residents please add applicable sales tax.)

Remove from pouch...

unfold once...

unfold twice...

and they're ready to wear.

GOLD EAGLE
Gold Eagle Reader Service
901 Fuhrmann Blvd.
P.O. Box 1396
Buffalo, N.Y. 14240-1396

GES-1A

Offer not available in Canada.

You don't know what NONSTOP HIGH-VOLTAGE ACTION is until you've read your 4 FREE GOLD EAGLE NOVELS

LIMITED-TIME OFFER

Mail to **Gold Eagle Reader Service**®

In the U.S.
P.O. Box 1394
Buffalo, N.Y. 14240-1394

In Canada
P.O. Box 609
Fort Erie, Ont. L2A 5X3

YEAH! Rush me 4 free Gold Eagle novels and my free mystery bonus. Then send me 6 brand-new novels every other month as they come off the presses. Bill me at the low price of just $14.94— an 11% saving off the retail price - plus 95¢ postage and handling per shipment. There is no minimum number of books I must buy. I can always return a shipment and cancel at any time. Even if I never buy another book from Gold Eagle, the 4 free novels and the mystery bonus are mine to keep forever.   166 BPM BP8S

Name _____ (PLEASE PRINT)

Address _____ Apt. No. _____

City _____ State/Prov. _____ Zip/Postal Code _____

Signature (If under 18, parent or guardian must sign)

This offer is limited to one order per household and not valid to present subscribers. Price is subject to change.

MYSTERY BONUS GIFT

HVSUB-1CR